The Dust That Remains

John D. Conandes

For YOU who watch my every step.

FOREWORD

One of the most crucial stages in life happens during the years a young person begins to venture outside the safety of the home and family circle. *The Dust That Remains* captures the experiences of two young brothers who learn to work alongside their grandfather and realize that the promise of their livelihood is ever present but is also threatened by greed and abuse. With much to learn about the ways of the world, these youngsters also learn to recognize their fears and overcome the forces that control their destiny.

The novel was written for a wide audience of young adults and wiser readers. *The Dust That Remains* unfolds in a rural imaginary world, filled with charismatic characters. The narrative is laced with a bit of humor and some down-to-earth reality. Its thematic significance reveals concepts that may provoke readers into a free play of ideas in reading and conversation.

Nearly twenty years of experience studying and teaching English and Spanish literature led the author to craft a novel that intends to teach and delight readers. For the teachers of young and adult learners, this book may be used as a text of choice for the purpose of constructing and deconstructing the various nuances of language and literature. It will certainly stimulate a young mind—as it may become the vehicle to learn and understand language and literature.

The Dust That Remains opens a door, a window for readers to come in and look into the many adventures these young protagonists experienced. Every person has a story to tell. This is John D. Conandes' first attempt to tell one of many.

Happy reading!

Russell

The jagged terrain sloped down from the skirts of the Great Endes Mountains and merged below into the fresh soil of the valley. The crystalline streams that fed the Manso River descended from the melted snow high in the peaks. Waterfalls flowed from crevices and cracks in the mountains and into the river that, once it reached the valley, opened up into numerous, trickling channels, creeks and brooks that irrigated the town of Russell and the adjacent farmlands.

The farmlands extended from the foot of the mountains into the center of the valley, unfurling rows of verdant vineyards and orchards that turned the lush countryside into organized, checkered mosaics, accentuated by hues of almond, apricot, cherry, and olive trees. Fruit of different shapes, colors and tastes hung from trees, like the fecund roundness of Mother Nature's breasts exuding their sweet colostrum. Grapes of all hues and sizes loosely hung from the pergolas in the homestead where the Druetts lived and in adjacent vineyards in Russell. Ripened peaches emitted the scent of vanilla and honey—their mature fragrance permeating the air. Alongside peaches and olives, almond trees stood proudly, perhaps because of the seed and flower they produced. Almonds attached to long and thin rods stemmed from branches connected to the trunks of the trees. And in maturity, the leathery fruits, spread along each rod, opened up like two protruding innocent lips, offering up their distinctive seed, which in its center was as acrid as the freezing winter mornings and in its crust, as rough as the dusty clods in the scorching summers.

During the harvesting season, the scent of the laborers pervaded the farms, as they made their way through the endless vineyards and groves ceasing only at brooks and alamedas, where trees created natural fortresses along the boundaries of the farms and fields in which they worked. The vineyards were depleted of their fruit, ravished by the hands of the laborers. Crews of harvesters assiduously undressed the groves, picking the crops, baring the land of its produce, stripping nature of her foliage and down to her twigs, as a consensual and natural deflowering, as if she were an expectant maiden to be undressed. And she seemed to welcome the strong hands of sharecroppers that gently bent her branches, the soft and virtuous hands of children that caressed the lower shoots of her vines, the tender hands of women that took only the nearest ripened fruit, and the rough hands of men who disrobed her foliage and bare fruit.

The harvest lasted for three months of arduous work. In the fields, sharecroppers and day laborers looked as rugged as the mountain soil, but behind their stern and ironbound looks, these folks were simple, amiable, and honest. They came from all parts of the country and beyond to work the land. Theirs were the hands that plowed and harvested the land, allowing the chocolate aroma of the damp soil to waft upward and evaporate in the air. Their rough hands were the force that pulled the sap from the ripened grape racemes. Theirs was the firm grip on draw hoes and shovels, the protruding veins of their hands swollen by the handles, a furious torrent of blood through their veins that ran like the crystalline streams, like water gushing through the land, like a furious and impatient torrent seeking to escape at the end of each season.

Three generations of harvesters and countless migrant laborers worked the land during this time. Infants wrapped in blankets or bundled in alpaca ponchos were suspended from olive tree branches while folks harvested the crops. At times, mothers carried babies, swaddled in shawls, slung across their backs until the kids were old enough to toddle behind them. Scrambling about the surrounding dusty alleys, lads competed with each other, playing hoop and stick, making a game out of a day's work, a good-natured contest that was as natural and healthy as they were. While they worked, they competed among themselves to prove who was the fastest grape harvester, emulating the movements of their parents and the other young men and women in the crews working alongside the rows in the vineyards. Younger men were the fastest while older folks kept a steady pace. Side-by-side with their families, crews of men worked the fields, each serving its own interest by helping the others make the best of the harvest. A sense of belonging filled the women, children and men as they knew themselves to be part of their crews and part of the earth that nurtured them all.

The graceful silhouettes of women sauntered along the rows of the vineyards. Their long, colorful skirts swayed between the vines. Red and white kerchiefs bobbed sporadically around the vineyards, like colonies of diligent red ants sucking the sap out of the sweet grapes hanging from the vines. Wearing beige aprons, the women worked by the side of their husbands. Most men did the heavy lifting and carried fifty-five-pound tin containers. After filling the containers, the men carried them on their shoulders and shuffled through the clods along the vine rows. As they walked, grape juice seeped through the small orifices in some of the containers and dripped down on the men's backs. The aroma of the grape nectar and scent of the vegetation confused and enticed bees and mosquitos while the men walked into the alley to drop the grapes into the dump truck that waited there.

The truck trailed along the alley as the harvesters advanced, stripping each row of its fruit. Women stayed behind and filled the containers. Sometimes, to give their husbands a break, they carried the containers themselves. Enclosed in the leafy vines, women roughly snapped the stalks of vines and gently pushed the juicy grapes down into the containers. The dripping juice resembled the breaking of water prior to the giving of life, as if the vines were giving birth to the fragile clusters of grapes that fell into the containers.

At lunchtime, the crews ceased their work and sought shelter from the scorching sun under the cool shade of olive trees along the alleys of the vineyards. Women laid out blankets and set down the food. With their sleeves rolled above their elbows, men and children helped each other pour water from jugs to wash the smears of dark soil and the sticky grape resin from their fingers. Men knelt and prepared tea as they talked while waiting for their wives to feed them. Conversation among them ranged from politics to the type of dresses some women wore. Older and middle-aged men initiated conversations about life, and much common sense prevailed among them as they speculated about the effect of the seasons on the crops and the wages they earned. Gossip and trivial banter rose and fell with their emotions, as each of them made their points or told their stories. Women eavesdropped on the men's conversations and lowered their gaze, blushing and giggling when the men seemed to subtly touch upon the unspoken. All of this happened between them and nature: natural men and women who pondered upon nature and their natural right as such. They followed the course of nature, as harsh and simple as nature was, and as harsh and simple as life was for them.

Defiance

"Rise and shine. Birds are chirping. Grandma's getting breakfast ready," Grandpa said.

"Grandpa, I don't want to go to work," said Grasshopper on the bed, removing the sheet from his face.

"School's out and you gotta find something to do," said Grandpa. "Men's gotta work."

"I'm too tired," said Grasshopper, stretching his arms and yawning. As soon as Grandpa came into their bedroom, Alejandro, Grasshopper's older brother, quickly rose to his feet.

"That's because you haven't done farm work yet," Grandpa said as he walked by the window and drew the curtain, letting the morning sunrays sift into the room.

"I don't know farm work," said Grasshopper, yawning, rubbing his eyes.

"Don't worry about that. There's plenty of work to show you the way work is done. You just gotta get up and get started," said Grandpa.

"Look at you, you lazy sloth," said Alejandro. "You can harvest some grapes, so you'll know what work is all about." Alejandro smiled.

"I can do any kind of farm work," Grasshopper said.

"Start by getting up," said Grandpa. He chuckled and exited the room.

Russell was a rural town immersed in the lushness of its sylvan abundance at the foot of the Great Endes Mountains. The town was an agricultural center for farmers and sharecroppers and a hub for wine cellars and olive processing plants. The adobe house where Alejandro, Grasshopper, and their grandparents lived sat on the outskirts of the town beyond the Manso River and well into the verdant foot of the mountains. Grandpa and Grandma Druett had taught the boys what they knew about working the land and being sharecroppers. Since the passing of their parents, the two brothers had enjoyed living in Russell and the life that nature could offer them.

Grandpa was in his early sixties but he looked younger. His tanned, well-defined body was only affected by the passing of the years in that his pace and his stride carried the weight marked by decades of arduous work and habit. A proud yet austere man who sought to educate himself by reading all he could get his hands on, Grandpa and Grandma cherished having his grandsons living with them. Their three daughters worked and lived in downtown Russell and only visited the homestead on weekends. Grandma was a sweet, yet witty woman who spoke her mind without reservation whenever she saw the need to seek the best for her family. The delicate features of her face showed a proud and distinguished semblance, which, together with her personality, made her looks even more appealing. She was short but invulnerable. In her youth, she had won the crown of the queen of the Wine Fest, an honor given to the most beautiful woman in Russell and surrounding towns. But she carried herself humbly and was well-respected by both men and women in Russell. Though her role at home was often submissive, she raised a family of five children, who had already departed the nest.

As young as they were, where Alejandro had just turned fifteen and Grasshopper still at nine, the boys had helped their Grandpa do the finishing work and touches on Mr. Gurua's new house. As the seasons brought all sorts of farm work, Grandpa welcomed the opportunity to teach Alejandro and Grasshopper to work and become resilient and self-reliant.

Throughout the years that Alejandro and Grasshopper lived in Russell, they wondered about the simple notion of playing and just being part of such a lush place, about being born and able to breathe fresh air and run free under the sun and rain. For them, the world at first seemed welcoming, like the offer of radiant, red, and ripened fruit that hung loosely from tree branches in the orchards around them; as they grew and learned the ways of how the world worked, they sensed nature's endowment and its aromas. They also saw the rotten fruit at the foot of the trees. Despite its fetid smell, they realized it was up to them to nurture new soil, perhaps their livelihood, and even the new generations to come.

At first, in their tender minds, Russell offered them a lush playground that they could explore. Grandpa Druett sought to teach Alejandro and Grasshopper the various trades of farm living. He understood their livelihood—a right to exist and a place to call home. This was all that Grandpa Druett wanted for them after the two brothers had lost their parents.

Working at Mr. Gurua's house felt like an adventure for the boys. They felt at ease in his presence—a type of commitment that wasn't forced, even though Mr. Gurua paid them handsomely by the hour.

"You can't eat the desert before the main meal," said Grandpa to Grasshopper. The stern look in his eyes, the drop of his eyelids at both ends, made him look even more serious. He had a deep glimmer in his eyes, a type of depth that only experience and the harsh realities of the world could give a man. His face was tanned, perhaps from working under the scorching sun, and when he laughed, his smile was wide and joyful. There is something about the smile of a man who has suffered. His smile did much more than just beamed; it showed a type of joy as if he had never experienced a happy moment before in his life. But he didn't smile often. Whenever he retold the times he had seen Grasshopper and Alejandro play around the homestead, whenever he recounted the antics his grandsons had pulled on each other, he smiled in such a joyous way. But for the most part, his countenance, his face was often serious and had a harsh semblance that earned him respect by other men in Russell.

"You can't eat the desert before the main meal," said Grandpa again.

"Why not, Grandpa?" Grasshopper asked. "It's all going to the same place."

"You'll eat the dessert once you finish your meal." Grandpa looked at Grasshopper and shook his head. Grasshopper didn't argue. His face looked ashen and grimy from the workings they had been going through in the morning at Mr. Gurua's farm. Behind the smudging on the boy's face, there was a soft and tender semblance, a gentle reminder of youth, the tender face of a child that was waiting to mature.

"It don't matter, Grandpa," said Grasshopper. "I'll eat the dessert later." Grandpa squinted at him as Grasshopper wiped his nose with his sleeve. A vivid light in his light-brown eyes followed Grandpa to see his reaction.

"He means you gotta wait for the best part," Alejandro said as he put an olive in his mouth. His manner was nonchalant and confident. His body was slender but firm. His marked facial features made his face look chiseled and fresh, but the natural aspect of his face and body still revealed the semblance of a child. The light in his honey-brown eyes gave him an air of clarity of mind and purpose. Grasshopper kept licking his fingers as he dipped them into a glass jar with apricot jam.

"Don't do that," said Grandpa. Grasshopper lowered his gaze and retrieved his hand. Then he took a bite of the sandwich Grandma had made for him. Alejandro savored the olives. After chewing the meat out of each olive, he put each pit between his lips and spit the pits into a furrow away from the table where they were having lunch.

"A hardworking man like myself should eat his jam whenever he wants," said Grasshopper. Mr. Gurua chuckled, then laughed at the sight of the boy who kept dipping his fingers in the jar when Grandpa got distracted.

Grandpa eyed Mr. Gurua and shook his head. The gloss of Grandpa's grayish hair glided with the reflection of the sunrays that sifted through the tree branches above them. The shiny tan on his forehead became even more vivid in the summers when they worked outside.

Twenty springs and nineteen harvests had passed before Grandpa could save just half of the money he needed for the two-acre tract he wanted, which was located fifty miles upstream from the homestead. Life at the adobe house in the homestead was quiet, but as a tenant and sharecropper, he could secure only room and board for himself and his family by working on a piece of land that would never be his own. Grandpa Druett oversaw the 15-acre farm that belonged to Dr. Arino Maxim in exchange for living in an old adobe house on the homestead. After Dr. Maxim provided the seeds and fertilizer for the crops, Grandpa received ten percent of the total profits for his work. Any profits from additional sowing and harvesting went to Dr. Maxim.

Dr. Maxim was an engineer of sorts who had inherited his land. He wore thick glasses that made the intense blue of his indigo eyes seem small. He never made eye contact with anyone as he spoke and looked down every time he engaged in conversation, as if to avoid the typical agreement folks show in conversation. His negligible will to talk with others was followed by a smirk, a sign of distrust prevailing over his protruding facial features. He had intense eyebrows, and his demeanor and body language seemed driven but at the same time superficial. But he owned the land and at times acted as if he also owned Grandpa's livelihood.

The piece of land Grandpa wanted upstream the Manso River belonged to Mr. Gurua, who Grandpa often helped with the planting and harvesting of crops in his orchard and with whom Grandpa had become friends. People in Russell respected Mr. Gurua and often called him "Cholo." He and Grandpa had become friends after an oil leak caused an explosion at the distillery owned by the Black Treasure Oil Company. The fire from the explosion scorched Mr. Gurua's left leg and left him bedridden. Grandma also often helped Mrs. Gurua when she needed extra help with house chores and other errands. After the accident, when Mr. Gurua could not work, Grandpa stepped in to help the Guruas take care of the small farm they had and other errands. Their friendship continued as Mr. Gurua built a new home near the homestead, which Grandpa also helped build.

Mr. Gurua worked as an engineer for the oil company on the skirts of the Great Endes Mountains. Trust reigned between the men, for both shared knowledge of masonry, carpentry, and fine woodworking. Mr. Gurua was an educated yet simple man. He had been born a sharecropper so the boundaries, such as occupation and status that at times set men apart, to him were insignificant, at least in the relationship he and his family maintained with the Druetts.

"Boys are growing strong, Mr. Druett," said Mr. Gurua. He inclined his head, as if waiting for Grandpa to say something. His dark eyes revealed a humble gaze. His hair was black and slicked back, with drops of sweat on his tanned forehead. He constantly dried them with a white towel that he kept draped around his neck. He wore a blue overalls that had the initials B.T.O.C. engraved on the left side by the chest.

"Yes, they are," said Grandpa. "The more they grow, the more they talk back to you."

"That's because our tongues grow too," said Alejandro, smiling. Mr. Gurua and Grandpa looked at each other and chuckled.

"My tongue don't grow, only my belly," said Grasshopper, deepening his fingers in the jar.

Grandpa kept his sight on the mountains.

"Soon you'll turn into a fat hare," said Alejandro.

"And you into a chameleon," said Grasshopper.

"You see what I mean," said Grandpa to Mr. Gurua.

"You boys got a good man here. You gotta take care of your grandpa and be good kids," said Mr. Gurua. He looked at Grandpa and then at the boys as he got up and sauntered back into the scorching sun and the furrows in his farm. "Mr. Druett, if we don't get back into the grind, we'll be working under the moonlight."

"That's right," said Grandpa, getting up from the stool where he sat. "C'mon, boys," said Grandpa. The boys put the tea jug and silverware away in their lunchbox and followed Mr. Gurua and their grandfather.

"I can have the boys work on the palisade," said Grandpa.

"That'll be fine. I need your help with the plowing, if you don't mind, Mr. Druett. You think you can get the mare and finish that patch by the blackberry brambles?"

"Sure can," said Grandpa.

"In a few more years, we'll have the boys do the plowing," Mr. Gurua added as he sauntered through the furrows to get his Jenny and plow.

"I doubt it," said Grandpa. "These two can do farm work now but are cut for city living or something like that."

Mr. Gurua grinned.

Conversation between them was amiable, respectful, and honest. Their relationship was built not only on work but also on mutual good will based on their cooperation, a trust they had earned, which they did not need to force upon each other. In the simple essence of their lives, they were simple humble men; theirs was a genuine and natural trust, a trust between free men that transcended their material conditions as landowner and sharecropper.

Most men in Russell didn't befriend one another because of their heritage, occupation, living conditions, or life circumstances, but because of how they worked, how they viewed the world, and how they reasoned with one another. Finding themselves within the common order of nature, they found that nature herself provided an order and space wherein common men of goodwill and reason could cooperate with each other. This vast, amiable arena was the space they needed to seek their livelihood and be free.

Mr. Gurua was sincere. The depth of his eyes and his humility had a lasting effect on other folks, just as Grandpa Druett's did, but without the harsh and direct look in his gaze. Mr. Gurua moved around with a particular bearing. He embodied a humble patience and wisdom reflected by his casual sauntering through the furrows of his property and his respectful manner toward his hired hands. He was often pensive and embodied a wisdom that was collected and natural. On the field, Mr. Gurua worked shoulder-to-shoulder with the men he hired to work his land.

"C'mon, you sweet lil' Lily!" Mr. Gurua shouted at his jenny as he buried the plow along the furrows behind his house. "Bahhh!" he yelled as he cracked the reins against his right leg, startling the mule.

The boys, who sat on the palisade along a path adjacent to the field, looked at him and laughed. They liked the sound of "Lil' Lily" and how the cracking of the reins echoed through the farm. Mr. Gurua would gesture with a smirk of confidence at them every time he did this. He knew Alejandro and Grasshopper liked to hear him yelling at his mule.

Since the boys had come to live with Grandpa and Grandma, they had worked like grown men side by side with their grandfather, Mr. Gurua, and some of the crews of laborers around Russell. He and other people in Russell liked the kids' willingness to work. While the kids called Mr. Gurua "Cholo" because he really didn't mind them calling him by his nickname, they did not do it in front of Grandpa. And Mr. Gurua often favored the two boys over other kids to run errands for him. Alejandro and Grasshopper often competed with each other for this privilege, for Mr. Gurua paid them handsomely, and Mrs. Bianca Gurua, Mr. Gurua's wife, often rewarded their industry with jars of apricot and peach jam that she had cooked in a bain-marie late in the summer.

Mr. Gurua was a good neighbor who requited the hand that helped him. When Grandpa added the toolshed to the back of the adobe house, Mr. Gurua had brought two neighbors, Mr. Campito and Mr. Beneto, to help Grandpa erect the walls. The men came together because they enjoyed their company and trusted their intentions, sense of humor, and will to do well for each other. This is how friendships among them began and transcended into camaraderie and even lasted for years, even after some of them had passed away.

Grandpa and the kids helped Mr. Gurua with errands around his farm and near the homestead, and at times at the lot he owned up in Sweet Heaven. Mr. Gurua's 2.47-acre tract sat adjacent to the Manso River, about half a day by foot from the homestead. Though in the winter the rocky contrasts of the land seemed barren, the soil was fertile and could support a small olive grove and other crops, as it had access and right to irrigation from the Manso River. Prior to offering the lot to Grandpa, Mr. Gurua had tried to work the lot, but because of the distance and the work that his small farm in Russell required, he was unable to take his jenny and tools there. So the day Grandpa and the boys helped him carry rolls of barbed wire, stakes, and a few hand tools to mark the boundaries of the lot, Mr. Gurua offered the land for sale to Grandpa.

"Mr. Druett, the boys would like it here. Look at the river and the trees. It's rough terrain, but they'll enjoy it," said Mr. Gurua in a humble tone.

"I'm sure they would. They'll enjoy it even more when they know it's theirs," rebutted Grandpa. He leaned over his right leg, which rested on a small boulder.

"I wouldn't mind if you paid for it in parts or installments," Mr. Gurua said, lowering his gaze while he talked to Grandpa. Grandpa's right arm laid on his lap while he held a Le Mans. He lit it, and then exhaled its smoke, fixing his sight on the distant highest peaks of the Great Endes Mountains.

Mr. Gurua's tone of voice was humble when he offered Grandpa the land and hoped he would accept it. Grandpa wanted the land, but promising his friend payments in installments didn't sit well with him. He was adamant about accepting favors or loans from anyone, much less being indebted to a friend. He was stubborn and too proud to accept Mr. Gurua's offer. He wanted to own the land in full but without being indebted to anyone.

When Grandpa first saw the land coasted by crystalline streams, he felt himself bound to its rugged purity and startling contrasts. The fiery scarlet flycatcher, the sparrows swiftly dodging through the air, the Picui doves, virtuous, proud, and immaculate as the land itself, and the thriving brown and black ovenbirds, whose melodies heralded the mornings mist, embellished the lushness of trees and grasses that glowed in the sunlight and carpeted the pristine wilderness. The flora and fauna manifested the perfect harmony and prodigious bounty of the range. As Mr. Druett admired the beauty of the property, he looked at his two grandsons standing like two young trees through the seasons. The taller and older tree, with its fresh trunk and solid branches reaching up to the sunrays, with a verdant bark, a kind of soft maturity, embellishing his body. The shorter tree stretched its weather-beaten, light brownish shots, a mix of verdant with long and tender branches, its tendrils springing, curling, like vines aiming to climb to the crown of the foliage—Alejandro and Grasshopper were as young and fresh as the foliage. Grandpa realized that the boys—with their shrill laughter and playful nature—blended with the contrast and fecundity of the land. Saving money to buy the land from Mr. Gurua became even more of an overarching goal for Grandpa: He wanted to leave the boys their own homestead, a home of their own, a legacy to dream and live for.

Grandpa would often ponder that being born into this world did not yield a man a piece of land he could call his own. *Was the earth too jealous and meager to offer each man on this earth a home? Wasn't this a natural right every man deserved for being born on this earth? Who had the meager hand that divided the earth among men and let some of them dictate who could enjoy its riches?* Despite his fears and questions, Grandpa began to view this fertile but undeveloped piece of land as a future sanctuary for his grandchildren.

As the boys grew, they understood Grandpa's dream and helped him as much as they could to gather the money by assisting in the sowing and harvesting at the homestead and other farms in Russell. Alejandro had just turned twelve when Grandpa took him to work for the first time as a day laborer. For Alejandro, school wasn't a priority—work was. After three years of arduous labor, he had grown increasingly fervent and sensitive. During this time, the lad had learned to love, cultivate, and harvest the land. He was becoming a man and one of the most efficient harvesters, perhaps as quick as Mario Lessar and George Reys, the two fastest grape and olive harvesters in Russell.

Alejandro's pace was promising, though not quite as proficient as Mario and George's. As did the seasons in the valley, the boy's temperament evolved gradually. Alejandro had just turned fifteen when the grape harvesting season began, and his dexterity was admirable. Even Mario Lessar looked at him with confidence and respect. They were now working side by side.

During the harvesting season, on a regular day's work at the vineyards on Mr. Lessar's farm, trucks moved out with their purple humps across the fields, carrying grapes to the Pravo Winery in Russell. The trucks took one trip right before lunch time, the other at the end of the day. After lunch, the vineyards became quiet, and men took siestas under the fresh and cool shade of olive trees as they waited for the truck to return. Barefoot children ran through the dusty alleys, climbed the olive trees in the groves, and rambled through the neighboring groves and vineyards. They even crossed over onto adjacent farmlands. But on the farms in the valley, trespassing for kids, young lads, and local folks was permitted as an intrusion of innocent spirits, sometimes folks just took shortcuts to pass from farm to farm.

Away from their parents, children of harvesters knew they needed to return to work with their crew once they heard the sound of the horn and the diesel engine of the truck as it roared into the vineyard. The truck neared the field, and the men roused, and the women whispered and giggled among themselves to signal their return to work. And by the time the truck had returned, lunch break was over.

Martinet, the foreman and truck driver, who collected and transported the grapes to the winery, had a sleek black el bandito mustache and dark glossy hair combed backwards, a slick look that increased the intense darkness of his eyes. His deep, dark, and glossy contrasting appearance and his impressive height often scared the children. After the truck stopped, Martinet stepped out from the machine, the obsidian black in his eyes locked on the tin bins filled with grapes that waited along the alley to be dumped into the receiving end of the truck. Before going to lunch, harvesters would fill their bins and leave them ready for the truck once it returned from the winery. Each container lined up along the alley seemed to be overfilled with grapes. Bees buzzed and butterflies flitted about the grape-filled bins under the scorching sun. As Martinet fixed his fedora and nonchalantly sauntered away from the truck, he stuck his hands to the side of his waist, between his belt and his rounded, protruding belly, which hung over his belt. Proud and in control, he cocked his head while he studied the line of containers that the workers had laid down before lunch. One container in particular caught his eye.

"Whose container is this?" shouted Martinet, with the deep voice of a foreman as he stood next to the container. The sound of his voice echoed along the alley.

Flocks of skylarks flew away from the olive branches of the trees under which the harvesters rested. Some of the men who were still napping were awakened by the man's forceful tone. When they heard the call, they rose to their feet. The men moved toward Martinet, and they looked at each other, puzzled about the container the foreman had pointed out.

The container was a bit smaller than the others; it had been bent, as if it had been beaten up, kicked, and narrowed, as if to fit less grapes in it. A regular fifty-five-pound container had an arched handlebar that was attached lengthwise to the brim. Compared to the other containers, the one Martinet had fixed his sight on had grapes reaching only to the brim of the bin and not to its arched handle like the others.

"Whose container is this?" Martinet shouted again, this time in a harsher tone.

From high above on an olive tree branch, Alejandro answered. "Mine!" he said, while he folded the sleeves of the beige industrial shirt he wore. Grasshopper's eyes grew as he realized the trouble his brother was in. Nonchalantly, Alejandro began descending from the tree. He then jumped and grabbed a branch with both hands. His long, tanned arms swung from it and landed with both feet onto a lower and thicker branch. Staggering and keeping his balance, he then landed on the dusty floor by the tree.

Martinet cocked his head, looking at Alejandro from top to bottom. Alejandro stood erect and assertive, with grape must smudged on his pants and shirt. His light, ragged blue jeans and slender body gave his young age away. His dirty face was still tender and childish. The gaze of his honey-brown eyes waited for Martinet's reaction.

Grasshopper was high up in the olive tree and followed his brother. Alejandro approached the foreman who had craned his head to accept the challenge the boy had posed.

"That container outta be topped to the handle," insisted Martinet. "To the handle or you'll get no token!" said the foreman as he stared down at the boy.

On average, each worker accumulated a total of fifty tokens per day, the equivalent of fifty containers. Half of this number afforded them a few pieces of salami, some loaves of bread, and two pints of beer. Some harvesters like Mario and George surpassed the 70 tokens per day. Sometimes neared 100.

Proud and defiant, Alejandro walked toward Martinet. "Nobody said anything about filling them up to the handle," he replied, looking at the foreman. "This is a fifty-five-pound container when it should be forty-four. Besides, I'm being paid for filling a container, not filling a container to the handle," said the boy, challenging Martinet. He then looked at the other laborers who just stood there. He felt as if he were speaking for all of them, but as he looked around, the men lowered their heads and fixed their eyes on the dust on the alley. Some even shook their heads as if to dismiss and undermine what the boy had said. Grasshopper's eyes were wide as he just stared at his brother and Martinet.

Angered by the comments, the foreman frowned and squinted while Alejandro talked and pointed his finger at the container. The men around them began to murmur among themselves and looked at each other knowingly, some wondering, some even questioning, others considering the validity behind Alejandro's claim without fully acknowledging it. In his mind, the meager pay they received didn't justify the extra effort; in many other farms, owners did not comply with the right measure or wage during the harvest. Some paid more; some paid less, depending on who they were. So Alejandro felt the need to say something. His riposte had overwhelmed the foreman, who looked at the boy and then at the container, in the presence of all of the other workers there.

As Grandpa overheard the exchange, he approached the truck.

Ignoring Alejandro, the foreman directed his attention toward Grandpa. "Mr. Druett, make sure the boy fills it up to the handle," said Martinet.

Quiet and with a passive look in his eyes, Grandpa picked up the container and took it back to a row nearby. He coughed. Grandpa wore leather sandals and the hem of his pants were folded nearly half a foot from his ankles. His stride was submissive, and so was his gaze after Martinet had told him to fill up the container.

Martinet carefully studied Grandpa's calm pace. The foreman's gaze was condescending; the squint in his eyes disdainful.

Alejandro looked at Martinet and frowned at him. "It's got to be done quickly," Martinet said to Grandpa. The boy kept squinting at the foreman. Looking at Alejandro and with disdain still on his lips, the foreman said to him: "Just go ahead and place the container right under the vine, boy. Kneel down there a bit more, and you'll be able to fill it up to the handle."

"I sure will, Sir," replied Alejandro, looking at the foreman with contempt. "The only thing is that when you harvest grapes you don't kneel down. You stand up and work." This was the least he could say after seeing his grandfather being humiliated by Martinet. Alejandro looked back at the other workers as if waiting for a reply, but they either looked down or away. Then turning his back to the foreman, he followed his grandfather.

The angry foreman looked and grunted some disapproving and vague remarks as the rest of the workers witnessed in silence. "C'mon fellows, get to work!" shouted Martinet to the other men.

They quickly dispersed and picked up their containers, climbed up the steps on the ladder by the side of the truck, and dumped in the grapes. Martinet stood by the steps next to the side of the truck and threw a token in the empty containers as each man descended.

❧

As the sun set on the horizon, the harvest had ceased for the day. After a long day's work and upon their return to the homestead, Grandpa eyed Alejandro and noticed the boy's somber face. Adie and Frank, the boys' parents, had been dead for nearly three years and the boys appeared to have coped with the loss. During the few years they had spent living with their grandparents, farm living had grown on them as much as they had grown living on the farm. As they walked along the *callejón,* the long dirt road that led to the dusty road by the homestead, a dispirited Alejandro kept his eyes locked on the ground. Grasshopper walked a few yards behind them, holding a stick that he used to poke and scratch the mounds by the side of the dirt road. Grasshopper's overalls weren't as dirty as Grandpa and Alejandro's clothes. Grasshopper viewed work as a game, for he didn't take it seriously, but he did it because he knew Grandpa would be disappointed in him if he didn't try. Besides, he was more into work to pretend to be a harvester. He often pretended to be older, emulating Grandpa's gestures and movements, especially when he was working with Grandpa in the toolshed. But when he was with Alejandro, he was more his own person and felt free to do as he pleased. He even pretended to make important decisions.

"Here, have some grapes," said Grandpa to Alejandro, taking a cluster of Bordeaux grapes from a burlap bag.

"You took some grapes?" said Alejandro. He smiled.

"Well, a few clusters won't mean much to them," said Grandpa. "You were right!" he affirmed as he also stared downwards, trying to find common ground with his grandson.

"They always want more than what they pay," murmured Alejandro. "Is it always this way?"

"Always," said Grandpa. "And they hope they can keep you thinking about that." Grandpa lit the end of a Le Mans. The tobacco gradually smoldered, consumed by its ember. Grandpa kept his sight fixed upon the tiny light ahead at the end of the *callejón* while the smoke wafted upwards.

"It isn't a forty-four-pound container," said Alejandro. He wanted to know why Grandpa had complied, giving in to humiliation for just a few clusters of grapes.

"No, it isn't," said Grandpa. He coughed. He remained quiet, not knowing what else to say. The taste of the cigarette was bitter. The Bordeaux grapes were sweet, perhaps the sweetest in the whole valley, but the sweetness of the grapes contrasted with the bitter aftertaste of humiliation that day.

The silence along the *callejón* was always soothing in the quiet summer evenings. Yet the intermittent shrill of cicadas filled the void. Alejandro felt as if the quietness of the *callejón* hunted him. As he, Grasshopper and Grandpa continued walking, they saw a man by the road who Grandpa recognized. The man squatted on the gravel and as they walked by him, he mumbled a few words.

"People say I'm, I'm c-c-crazy 'cause I t-t–tell t' truth," he said to Grandpa. Grandpa looked at him and smiled.

"Hello there, Charles," said Grandpa.

"Spare a smo-mo-moke, Mr. Druett?" said the man after Grandpa puffed on his Le Mans. The man was barefoot and his clothes were dirty and ragged. He spoke softly and almost unintelligibly.

"Take a few," said Grandpa as he jerked the pack forward. The man dashed toward Grandpa and quickly took one smoke.

"Thank you k-k-kindly, Sir," said the man, bowing after he took the cigarette. His hands, clothes, and face were dirty, and he smelled like stale urine and sweat. Grandpa pulled out his lighter and brought it close to the man's face.

"You have a great evening, Charles," said Grandpa, lighting the cigarette.

"You do as w-w-well, well, Mr. Druett. May the L-L-Lord, the Lord bless you." The man went back to the side of the road. He walked and wondered and kept mumbling and puffing on the Le Mans. Scared, Grasshopper caught up with them and walked next to Alejandro.

"Who is that?" said Alejandro. "I've seen that man around."

"That's Charles High," said Grandpa. "He was a math teacher once."

"My shoulder hurts," said Grasshopper.

"Why is he like that?" said Alejandro.

"His mind is gone," said Grandpa. "He got bitten once."

"Who bit him?" Grasshopper asked.

"Nobody knows. People say he's crazy. He spends most of his time at the sanitarium near downtown Russell," Grandpa said.

"He doesn't look like he could hurt anyone," said Alejandro.

"He's a very gentle and kind man," said Grandpa. "His mind is just gone. They let him out from time to time."

As they neared the homestead, Kaiser's barks echoed in the distance. The dog wore a leather harness Grandpa had custom-made for him. As Kaiser ran toward them, the sound of the metal latches attached to the harness jingled. His reddish-brown fur and the leader harness made Kaiser look tougher than he really was. Resembling the strides of a small lion but at an amusing pace, he ran about the homestead.

"Hey, you doggish dog," Grandpa said as the dog approached, wagging its tail. As Grandpa stooped down, he stretched out his hand and let his pooch lick it.

Alejandro glanced at Grandpa, then at the dog, and then looked at the vegetation along the dirt road. His mind was sunk deeply in thought. He thought of the years his grandfather had been arduously plowing the land, collecting fruit at each harvest, and working side-by-side with many of the other sharecroppers and day laborers in Russell. Somehow, the work they did was never sufficient for the owner of the land. In general, it was never enough to satisfy the basic needs of the other harvesters and of Grandpa and his family. Alejandro realized that some men wanted more than enough and that those men wanted other men to work more than enough, even when they did not pay enough. *It was that*—he thought—*that despite being humble and good-natured, most men in Russell had to carry this extra weight. It was that some men liked to impose such disgraceful pride on others—a strange pride that meant expecting more from others than they expected from themselves. While for others, it meant a bit more pride for the time being, and for many others, perhaps a place that was worth keeping for a while.* This is all Alejandro understood at first.

A Teamster's Bottle

In the mornings at the homestead, the silence around the toolshed in the back of the adobe house contrasted with the chirps and chirrs that echoed in the olive grove. An early cool breeze pierced through the poplar trees in the homestead while Grasshopper walked around to the back of the old adobe house, along the path that led to Grandpa's toolshed. By the shed, wild rose vines climbed on poplar tree trunks, embracing the trunks and shedding their ephemeral aroma in the surroundings. On one of the trunks, Grasshopper had carved an "I" with Grandpa's Swiss Army Knife, but the "I" had been covered by the vines that formed a natural boundary around the trees that divided the homestead from the olive grove. Once the sun had risen, the morning mist evaporated under the glaring rays that sifted through the pale alameda and lit the metal door of the toolshed. The shed hid a mystery—it intrigued the boy, like the cover of a book, an adventure of sorts, a discovery—one that Grandpa usually kept under lock and key.

As Grasshopper sauntered along, he looked at the field and in the distance, under the cool shade of olive trees, he saw Grandpa tending beds of cucumbers on the west side of the farm. With a firm grip around the handle of his draw hoe, Grandpa removed the wild weeds that grew among the crops and cleared the furrows from clumpy clods to make way for the flow of water during irrigation.

From the distance, the boy observed his grandfather, and then turned to discover that he had left the door of the shed ajar. Cautiously, Grasshopper walked through the doorframe and groped carefully about the wall. The morning light filled the shed, and as the boy stood in the center of the room, he was engulfed by the scent of fresh sawdust, tung oil, and other fumes that fused with the smell of dry dust from the old adobe walls. Amazed by the organization of the shed, he studied the walls that were embellished with an array of hand tools: handsaws, pliers, and planes of many sizes; plows, clamps, adjustable spanners, stripping-knives, hacksaw frames, screwdrivers, and nuts and bolts of all sorts; hammers, axes, a sickle, and rolls of copper and barbed wire, each neatly hung on their designated hooks. In the center of the room, a tool stand was affixed to the floor. Pieces of jagged aluminum and wood scraps, chisels and gouges, Jules Verne's *Journey to the Center of the Earth*, and back issues of the *Reader's Digest* were all scattered about on the stand.

In the winter evenings, Grandpa secluded himself in the toolshed, sheltered from the cold and rain and from the distant shrills of his grandchildren around the homestead. At times, he filed the metal edge of his draw hoe, fixed tools while the rain subsided, and took small breaks to read old newspaper articles and the *Reader's Digest*. He also worked on miniature toys for his grandsons, such as small airplanes and an old teamster leading a wagon of harnessed oxen, which he carved and polished for *Navidad*. Grasshopper and Alejandro sometimes pried through a hole in the metal door and spied on Grandpa.

While the old man worked inside the shed, he glanced at the door, and somehow he knew the boys were there. "Grasshopper? Alejandro? Have you tended the coop yet? Go tend the hens!" said Grandpa, aiming his voice at whoever was outside the door of the shed.

Grasshopper remained quiet, hoping he hadn't been noticed. *He can't see me*, the child thought.

"Go help Grandma!" he ordered as he glanced at the door, uncertain of the boy's presence. But that day Grasshopper stood quietly watching his grandfather work, studying his movements, slowly breathing in the fresh, oily scent of poplar wood, wondering if the objects his grandpa was assembling were finally finished.

With large pieces of wood, Grandpa used large chisels and coarse files; with small ones, he used the fine chisels and files with more caution. At times, his hands moved in tandem with the swaying of his upper torso, toing-and-froing to the rhythm of a saw, hand plane, or tick-tock of a half-repaired old Westminster clock that he fixed only on Sundays. With a paring chisel, he carved the railings of a miniature wagon. He then puffed the shavings from the wood—the sawdust from the pieces—and examined them carefully, from different angles, caressing the edges of the wood with his fingertips and smoothing out the sharp splinters with sandpaper. He puffed again and set all the pieces together on the stand as he studied them critically, hoping to find the flaws imperceptible to any eyes but his own.

Carving pieces of poplar was a hobby Grandpa enjoyed in winter almost more than the children enjoyed playing with the toys he made. He kept the toolshed locked to keep the children from prying inside, perhaps to raise their curiosity until *noche buena* arrived. Then, he finally revealed the gifts and watched the glow of complete amazement and innocent delight in the children's faces.

When Grasshopper wasn't climbing trees along the *callejón* or in the olive grove, he would spend his time wandering around the toolshed. The toolshed was a place of mystery, where Grandpa kept his secrets. To Grasshopper and Alejandro, this place was forbidden. Here, the air was tempered by the morning dew, by the fresh scent of moist soil, by the sweat of clutching the draw hoe in the fields, by the rust of old plows, and by the dust that always remains. But inside, for the boy, a new world emerged. At times, when the door was open, Grasshopper leaned against the doorframe as he watched Grandpa work. The swaying would continue, uninterrupted by the boy's presence.

"Grandpa, can I work with you?" Grasshopper often asked. But when the old man cast a stare upon him, the boy already knew the answer.

"You aren't supposed to be around here, Son," Grandpa replied. "I don't wanna see you around here. These tools are too sharp. They're too dangerous," he cautioned every time as he turned his back to his grandson.

But that morning, the boy entered the shed. He knew that Grandpa would scold him if he caught him inside, but he also knew the old man loved his grandsons and that his words did not always come out right and in accord with what he truly felt.

As Grasshopper found himself in the shed, the stillness of the place revealed Grandpa's absence, and as the boy ventured into the solitude of the shed—his eyes widely amazed and his tender cheeks aglow—he discovered the miniature wooden wagon with its pair of railings pulled by a team of wooden oxen led by the tiny figure of a teamster. *This is the present Grandpa made for us*, he thought.

The wooden pieces were smooth like silk, well-polished, and radiated the magic that children often see in toys. Grasshopper looked around the shed and saw other scattered pieces of wood, sheets of sandpaper, and chisels on the stand where Grandpa had left his work unfinished. The tiny teamster wore a *sombrero,* and had its right arm lifted upwards as if he were holding a bottle. Without thinking, the boy began to make the part that was missing. With sandpaper and a scrap of poplar wood—too small for the chisel—he began to sharpen the contours of a well-proportioned jug, smoothing off its jagged corners to form the neck, shoulder, and body. A cloud of fine whitish sawdust fell like snowflakes over the teamster's hat. The boy's ministrations revealed the volume and proportion of a wine bottle. Then, he grabbed a small spoon gouge and carved out the punt on the underside of the bottle. The miniature vessel looked almost like an authentic bottle of Bravo, the type of Cabernet Sauvignon made from the grapes grown in the vineyards surrounding Russell. A bottle of wine accompanied the teamster as he led his team of oxen. Smudged with soot and polished, the oxen smeared Grasshopper's fingers. As the boy diligently polished the final touches on the bottle, the soot captured their dark color while the teamster on the stand sat quietly covered by fine snowy sawdust.

Unnoticed, Grandpa calmly strode across the pathway to the toolshed. A dry cough outside the toolshed announced Grandpa's presence. In the quietness of the shed, the boy hearkened. He listened carefully and became paralyzed—still holding the miniature bottle in his hands—the sandpaper now shivered between his fingers. The shadow of Grandpa's robust shoulders appeared at the threshold of the shed. His long and stern face turned downward in the boy's direction as his disapproving gaze fell upon the tiny bottle and the sandpaper in Grasshopper's hand. His eyelashes fluttered like the wings of the two *gorriones*, two sparrows that bathed in a puddle of grimy rainwater outside the shed. Grandpa sauntered inside, took the draw hoe off from his shoulder, and hung it on the wall. He then looked over at the teamster and stretched his hands toward his grandson, demanding the new piece.

"I never thought of giving him a drink," he said as he placed the bottle in the teamster's hand. "But I think a little wine will do him just fine."

As Cucumbers Peel

In the field adjacent to the dusty road, Grandpa tended the cucumber beds. He worked intensely. He knew that once he received his ten percent from this year's profits, and once added to his savings, he would have nearly half of the money he needed to buy the land from Mr. Gurua.

In the distance, far along the *callejón* from the gate of the road that led to the homestead, Grasshopper could see a group of five men on horseback surrounded by a pack of greyhounds that cried and barked as they trotted along with the horses. He was still about a few minutes away from the adobe house. Dazzled with fear, he stood in the middle of the dirt road and stared at the dogs and riders who moved toward him at a fast pace.

As the wild cries of hounds approached and sharp hooves pounded against the rocks, Grasshopper shrieked and began sprinting along the *callejón* to the acacia tree by the gate of the farm.

As Grandpa heard Grasshopper along the road, he approached the boundary of the farm and hid behind a patch of reeds. He secretly watched through the reedbed that separated the farm from the stream and the *callejón* and observed what he took to be his grandson's play. He would often laugh at the games Grasshopper played.

Stooped, Grandpa observed as Grasshopper ran along the *callejón* and reached the acacia trees by the reedbed. Grasshopper ran fast; in his chest, the spirit of youth was pumping fear; in his mind, the devil and the hounds were chasing him. As he ran along the *callejón*, the moving pace of his legs could not be distinguished one from the other. Even in jagged and bumpy terrain, he leapt from furrow to furrow, with height, speed, and dexterity, and disappeared through the brush and trees to appear walking nonchalantly and laughingly on the other side of the farm. "Tricky Grasshopper," Grandpa called him every time he found fruit and slingshots hidden high in the forks of the trees. Seeing him jumping through furrows, through the brush, Grandpa had given him the nickname.

"He leaps just like a grasshopper," Grandpa said, laughing at his grandson. But Grasshopper wasn't laughing now. Grandpa knew he feared hounds. The men on horseback grinned and chuckled at him as he climbed the tree.

With a steady trot, the horsemen rode further down along the *callejón* and passed under the tree while the boy looked from above. The smell of horse sweat pervaded the air around the acacia tree. Grandpa looked at Grasshopper and laughed at his awkward posture and expression. He seemed to be transfixed by the scene of rough riders with their harnesses and gear. Lifeless partridges and the elongated bodies of dead hares were tied across the haunches of the horses. The men talked among themselves, and an air of confidence reigned among them after a successful hunt.

"The mare wasn't so tough after all," bragged one of the riders, laughing and staring down the horseman next to him, who rode empty-handed.

"This dapple gray knows who's riding her," said another rider, rearing his horse to the right.

"I thought you were talking about that old lady down the valley," said another rider as he swiftly flicked the reins of his horse. Their chatting broke into a guffaw that echoed along the *callejón* .

Tall, slender and dignified, the hounds whined and growled. They loped softly on tiptoe behind the riders along the *callejón*. The echoing of hooves on the gravel, the crying of the hounds, the jingling reins of the horses, and the laughing and chatting of the horsemen diminished to a murmur as they moved far down the dirt road.

"FFWWEEEEEE!" Grandpa whistled to Grasshopper. As the wind rustled through the leaves of the acacia trees, he recognized the whistling and looked to where Grandpa was standing.

"Grasshopper!" called Grandpa. "Come down from there and help me over here."

"In a flash, Grandpa," said Grasshopper as he hid his slingshot behind his back and tucked it between his belt and the back waistband of his pants. He then jumped from one of the outer branches of the Acacia tree onto the other side of the stream by the reedbed.

"I'm laying another bed of cucumbers," said Grandpa.

"I can help," said Grasshopper. "And Alejandro, Grandpa?" He asked while he dusted his pants.

"He's loading wood into the oven for your grandma. She's baking bread," said Grandpa as they walked through the clods along the furrows until they were underneath a dense and tall olive tree.

"It's getting hotter than heaven," said Grasshopper.

"Hotter than hell," said Grandpa.

"No, hotter than heaven," said Grasshopper.

"How you figure?" Grandpa looked at him and squinted.

"Heaven is closer to the sun, so I said it must be hotter than heaven, not than hell," he said.

"There's fire in hell," said Grandpa.

"Yes, but we can't tell where hell is," Grasshopper said. "Heaven is up there closer to the sun. It's hotter."

Grandpa smiled. "Watch," he said. "Take three cucumber seeds, dig a two-inch hole into the soil with your thumb, and place the seeds there." He had a small burlap harvest-sack with seeds in it and placed it around the Grasshopper's neck. He began to emulate the movement of his grandfather, making the exact movements and gestures Grandpa did as he pushed his thumb into the soil and inserted the seeds. "Do it at the top of the mound, there between the two furrows," he said, pointing as he checked on his grandson. Stooped forward, Grasshopper kept his left forearm pushed against his left leg. With his right hand, he dug the two-inch hole and placed the seeds in it. "Cover the seeds with soil and flatten the area around them—don't leave any air inside the hole, or it'll rot them and they won't grow." Grandpa advised him from a few yards away.

They took short breaks every ten or fifteen minutes to straighten their backs. Then they continued reaching down and planting the seeds.

Some of the adjacent areas in the farm contained beds of tomatoes, but cucumber vines were copious throughout the western part of the farm. Some areas were ready to be harvested, for cucumbers grew fast.

"You wouldn't believe how fast these suckers grow," said Grandpa.

"Some of them are big," said Grasshopper.

"Yeah, we don't want them big," added Grandpa. "Got to pick them small."

"Yeah, I've seen them. They'll be small one day, the next day they'll grow as big as a horse's you-know-what," Grasshopper said.

Grandpa chuckled.

"That's why you and Alejandro gotta help me here. Instead of going around wasting time and playing nonsense," said Grandpa.

"Yes, Grandpa," said Grasshopper. "They won't grow big when I'm in charge. That's for sure."

Grandpa chuckled. "You'll be surprised. They grow at night when the water's out," mumbled Grandpa. One morning, the wide leaves of the creeping cucumber vines would hide the small fruit only to reveal large, elongated cucumbers the next day. Their growth was almost magical. This was why Grandpa was so adamant about reaping them on time.

As Grandpa and Grasshopper finished planting the seeds, they moved through the furrows to the next patch of soil some yards away.

They took a break from the heat at the foot of an olive tree. Grasshopper leaned against the trunk and wiped the sweat from his forehead. Grandpa sat down and took out his red Swiss Army pocket knife and grabbed a large cucumber. Grasshopper squinted at the knife, then at Grandpa, who, with great care, began to peel the skin off the fruit from the blossom end, along its body, and to the stem. Grandpa took two of the elongated thinly sliced skins and gave them to Grasshopper.

"Put them on your forehead. Cucumber skins are as cold as the shade of olive trees. They'll cool you down," said Grandpa.

"Why are they so cold?" Grasshopper cocked his head while he looked at his grandfather's eyes. He patted the slices that rested on his forehead.

"It's because of the water they take. They drink and grow at night when the water is on."

"You've seen 'em grow?" Grasshopper asked.

"I see they change from day to day. One day they are small, the next day they are twice as big. It is the water that makes them grow and be so cool."

"We'll plant cucumbers once we get our land, right, Grandpa?" asked Grasshopper.

"We sure will. And a lot more vegetables and fruits," said Grandpa as he raised his eyebrows. He then got up to continue his task.

"Can I plant some tomatoes?" he asked.

"You sure can. Grandma will help you. She'll make tomato sauce, too," said Grandpa confidently.

"When are we buying the land?" said Grasshopper after he repositioned the cucumber skins on his forehead.

"Dr. Maxim owes us some money, and after we harvest and prepare these cucumbers, we'll have a good chance at getting the land."

"Is it going to be like this farm?" he asked.

"Not as big. Just about two acres," replied Grandpa as he sauntered through a few furrows.

"What's an acre?" asked the boy.

"It's a little bigger than the field where the kids play at school," said Grandpa. "Let's get back to work." Grandpa handed the rest of the seeds to Grasshopper and moved to a patch of cucumber vines. He started reaping some small cucumbers while Grasshopper planted the seeds on another patch of soil.

Grasshopper thought about what Grandpa said but his thoughts were interrupted by the distant echo of an truck engine approaching the homestead. Grandpa cocked his head as if to place his ear in the direction of the diesel engine roaring along the *callejón*.

"That's Dr. Maxim," said the boy while he looked at his grandfather.

"Sure sounds like his truck," said Grandpa. "I've been waiting for him." Grandpa straightened his back and stood up straight, arms akimbo amidst the lush bed of cucumbers. The truck circumvented the farm along the *callejón* and entered the homestead through the gate.

"Stay here and finish the bag," Grandpa told Grasshopper before walking toward the adobe house to meet his boss.

❧ ❧

As Grandpa washed his hands in the concrete basin in the back of the house, Grandma appeared beside him. She stood next to him, holding a bar of soap and a white towel. Her delicate and small frame didn't do justice to the household she administered and maintained, or to her beauty. Her face was delicate and distinguished. Her hair was short. If she had long hair, it would have been difficult to keep men away. Grandpa often said, "When men see a beautiful woman, flies come rushing to the honey." So she kept her hair short to keep bugs from landing on her skirt. Her mouth was also small but distinguished; the wavy shape of her lips matched the undulated and inviting signature of her eyebrows. Her eyes were calm and sincere. Despite her age, the tanned semblance of her cutis was still fresh and appealing. Her delicate and soft face was a vivid reminder of a regnant beauty of years passed.

"The doctor's here," she said, handing Grandpa the towel.

"I know," said Grandpa, walking toward the front of the house. Trying to read the man before talking to him, Grandpa looked at Dr. Maxim. Kaiser came from around the house and started barking and charging at the man.

"Please, please, keep it off me," pleaded Dr. Maxim as the dog growled and threatened to jump on him. Dr. Maxim's son, Herman, had stayed waiting for his father inside the truck.

"Kaiser! Get back! Get back there!" shouted Grandpa, making Kaiser retreat with his tail between his legs. The dog looked apologetic. He walked back and lay down under the front porch of the adobe house, where he observed and remained attentive to his owner and the men Grandpa talked to.

After seeing Kaiser retreat, Herman got out of the truck and approached Grandpa and Dr. Maxim.

"Good morning. I got news for you," said Dr. Maxim with a vague grin, avoiding Grandpa's eyes.

"Good morning, Dr. Maxim," said Grandpa as he walked a few steps toward him, removing remnants of water from his forearms and taking off his straw hat.

"You ought to keep that lion on a leash," he said in a low sonorous voice.

"I'm sorry about that. He's not used to seeing people around the homestead."

"The first barrels of pickles made it to the capital. But the money isn't here yet," said Dr. Maxim.

"Benjamin, my nephew, said it will take at least another month to get it."

"Another month?" Grandpa asked. "We're almost two months into the season."

"Well, I know that," said Maxim.

"Last year, the day laborers were paid in winter," replied Grandpa. "And some weren't even paid. This year I have no one but my grandkids to help me."

"Well, I recall everyone got paid," said Maxim, minimizing the importance of what Grandpa had said. "You gotta get everybody out to help."

Herman cocked his head at his father, as if finding the reason behind what he was saying.

The news about the money felt like a slap on the face, pain that throbbed through Grandpa's body. A deep pain of impotence rose to his face and trickled down to his chest, and then sank within his gut and stayed there. Every time issues about money owed or work unpaid were brought up, Dr. Maxim reminded Grandpa he had to be grateful for having a roof above his head.

"Well, I recall everyone being paid, Mr. Druet," said the doctor again. "And besides, you have no worries about finding a place to live, right? Or having utility expenses to pay, right?" Dr. Maxim looked at Grandpa as if wanting to keep him at bay. Herman listened, trying to make sense of what his father was saying to Grandpa. "I think we'll paint the facade of the adobe house soon," added the doctor. "What color do you think Mrs. Druet would like? Beige? Yellow?" he asked.

"We can fix the front yard and garden for Mrs. Druett, too," Herman said, trying to compensate for not having his money.

"Shut up!" Dr. Maxim said, scolding Herman. Herman's eyes squinted, unable to understand the situation.

"I can bring you some extra buckets of paint I got left over from painting our place. I'm sure you and your family will feel more at ease if we spruce the old adobe house up some. By the way, how is the harvest going? They're not rotting, are they?" inquired the doctor, trying to change the subject.

His son squinted and looked deep in thought for a moment.

Angry, Grandpa looked back at the house, musing on Grasshopper and Alejandro as he stuffed the clay oven with dry olive branches. Grandma held a tin tray with dough shaped into loaves of bread and set it on a stool by the oven. The man turned his sight further into the distance and saw Grasshopper planting the cucumber seeds. Grandpa looked down at the dirt around the doctor's feet and then back up at the man's face.

"We'll harvest the small ones on time. They'll be fine," he said.

"You just keep them coming. I'll be sure to get you your ten percent," replied Dr. Maxim as he shook Grandpa's hand. He then rubbed his right hand, wiping it on the side of his pant, looked over at the oven, and waved at Grandma before he left.

Alejandro kept loading the oven with desiccated olive branches. The wood quickly sparkled and blazed with an ardent fury, just like the anger Grandpa felt in his gut. Dr. Maxim walked back to his truck and once he turned the ignition key, the diesel engine roared like a beast while stalking its prey. Grandpa wiped the sweat off his forehead, raked his fingers through his hair, and slapped his lap with his straw hat as if to dust off his frustration, hoping to free himself from the effect of the greedy man whose land he worked.

The smoke from the oven rose high above the house and the trees. It drifted and dissipated in the evening breeze. Cucumber skins were as cold as the shade of olive trees, Grandpa had said. Long after the conversation with Dr. Maxim, Grandpa still felt the heat in his gut. A burning that not even the coolness of all the cucumber skins or the shades of all olive trees in the grove could relieve. The pain seemed subtle. But it stayed there. It moved through his gut and spread through his chest, down in his arms, and into his hands. Hands that grew cold and that tended cucumbers under the cool shade of olive trees.

Proto Chúcaro

The dusty road that led to the entrance of the farm stretched about one hundred feet from the adobe house to the gate. From there, the dirt road ran adjacent to the stream and along the various other farms neighboring the homestead. Toward the mountainside, the dirt road met the asphalt road that connected the farms to downtown Russell. In the opposite direction, the dirt road continued for nearly seven miles until it and the stream met a crossroad and a canal.

By the gate of the farm, along the *callejón*, the row of acacia trees, where Alejandro and Grasshopper spent their summer afternoons, ran parallel to the stream that descended from the Manso River. The trees and the stream set a natural boundary between the homestead, the dirt road, and the many other farms along the *callejón*. During irrigation rationing and restrictions, the stream became a creek but once the water was released, the currents would create deep pools where Grasshopper and Alejandro would bathe in and play in the summer.

The acacia trees threw their branches over the stream and provided a natural shade. In the summer, Alejandro and Grasshopper would cool down and play on the branches. The area there was as verdant as nature could be. The kids loved it. A scent of fresh fennel and the pungent odor of rabbits and hares' cecotropes permeated the air. At first, the kids did not know the source of this scent, but on autumn nights around the fire, Grandpa talked about how hares ate their own feces and how difficult it was to catch them. Having heard the stories, the kids dreamed of catching the wild hare that was often seen running across the fields and in the farms around the homestead.

"I'll catch that hare one day," said Grasshopper.

"We've never seen one," said Alejandro.

"I've seen one." Grasshopper flustered his eye lashes. He had never seen one but he still pretended he had. Alejandro knew his brother was lying and he didn't mind letting his younger brother's imagination fly. *It was a sort of white lie that wasn't hurting anyone*, he thought. On the contrary, the lie boosted his brother's confidence and gave him a reason to keep looking forward to something greater than his confidence.

The effervescent and crystalline flow of water under the overpass that connected the *callejón* with the dusty road to the adobe house reminded the boys of the boundless possibilities of being vis-à-vis nature. The acacia tree that they often claimed as theirs stood tall and monumental near the entrance of the farm. To Grasshopper, the stature of the trees inspired in him a sense of confidence. The trees were friends with whom to play and, at the same time, they provided shade and a hiding place. To Alejandro, the trees had given him much more.

As the stream flowed beneath the acacia tree, the radiant sunlight against the leafy branches created the perfect hideout for the boys. They could climb up to the crown of the acacias and not be seen by the passersby along the dirt road below. *The trees were true friends to the kids, for they were always there for them,* they often thought. The boys hung and swung from the branches in the same way a small child hangs from the arms of his father—swinging from limb to limb, up and down the tree. They spent countless hours watching birds preening and fluttering their wings and seeing the fish glistening as they slipped away through the current below.

"Do you think Grandpa is gonna like us wasting so much time here?" asked Grasshopper.

"Don't worry Grassy, he will never know," answered Alejandro.

"Yeah, but if he asks? He told us to tend the crops." Grasshopper's eye grew large.

"Then you tell him the truth. Just don't mention we've been climbing trees," said Alejandro.

"You know he wouldn't like that," said Grasshopper.

"Yes, but don't you go telling him about things if he don't ask you. You got that?"

"Yeah, okay. I won't say anything," said the Grasshopper as he blinked and looked at Alejandro.

The two boys spend their days playing and exploring the vineyards and olive groves around the homestead. The Reys' farm was further down the *callejón*, in the opposite direction of the mountain, a favorite spot for the boys because of the sweet muscat grapes, the cherry orchards, and the beautiful horses there. Every time the boys went to the Reys' farm, something had to happen to Grasshopper. Sometimes he would get sick from eating so much fruit.

"I got to run!" shouted Grasshopper as he suddenly appeared out of a tree while he held his belly with one hand and his rear end with the other after eating too many grapes or peaches.

But Alejandro had a lot more at stake. Alvera Reys lived there, and since the last harvest season, he had been climbing to the crown of the tallest olive trees near her house just to get a glimpse of her. From the distance, he observed her as she scrubbed and rinsed towels and sheets in a tin basin. He would watch her with fascination, looking attentively at her waist as she squeezed her laundry and stretched on her toes to reach the rope where she hung white sheets and towels. Her terse, tanned skin, from her tiptoed feet up to her calf, he observed; the white translucent silky dress encapsulating the proportions of her voluptuously refined body, he admired; her outstretched, elegant arms that reached up to hang the sheets, he ambitioned. A silky white dress and soft white sheets enclosed the radiant appearance of a gentle angel in his pupils. The flapping white sheets and dresses on the rope interfered with his view as he sought not to lose sight of her from a distance. He did not know what love was, but he felt some kind of fire, a glow inside his chest, connected to a warm feeling in his loins, that caused his early manhood to rise with the same vigor as the maturing and ripening fruit in the surrounding vineyards and groves. *Is this love?* he wondered. Whatever it was, he kept coming back to the farm for more of Alvera, as Grasshopper kept coming back for more grapes, cherries, and peaches.

One day, floundering through the clods, between the vine rows at the Reys farm, Alejandro and Grasshopper sought to engage a stallion they called *Proto Chúcaro.* The beast ran wildly, galloping along the rows in the vineyard. It charged and ran over anything that dared to stand in its path. It had the stature of a Clydesdale but was more slender and muscularly defined at the legs and thighs. Its jet-dark mane flew in the wind as the horse galloped with a force fueled perhaps by the animal's innate sense of freedom. They boys loved it. They admired the way it seemed to break through reality, as if it wanted to escape the limitation of being a mere animal trapped in space and time. When they were bored, the boys would run through the vineyards at the Reys Farm along the ditches and furrows under the cool shade of olive trees. There, they unleashed their wickedness, their immaturity, and their mischievousness by provoking the stud into a chase.

"Come on, let's get *Potro Chúcaro,*" enticed Grasshopper, pulling his brother's arm.

"Are you crazy?" said Alejandro, looking at him askance but still thinking it would be fun to do. To avoid seeing his brother getting hurt and still allow him to enjoy the thrill of the experience, Alejandro would often take the lead in their adventures.

"You stay here. Climb up this olive tree while I get him," said Alejandro as he cut a thin switch from an olive tree branch and stripped it of its glossy green leaves. Grasshopper quickly climbed up through the branches. Alejandro then moved unnoticed, carefully stalking the stallion, into the pasture where *Potro Chucaro* and the mares were grazing.

"Heeeeee-haaaaaaww!!!" the boy shouted as he waved the stick to get the attention of the beast that stood yards away from the mares. Before Alejandro knew it, with a nervous outburst and snorting in anger, *Potro Chúcaro* began to charge at him.

"Run!" cried Grasshopper from the crown of the olive tree, "Run!" Alejandro ran toward the tree as fast as he could, the wild and muscular devil was now chasing behind him. To the boys, teasing the horse into chasing after them was an adventure, something like a ritual that validated a growing feeling of manhood within them. To the horse, it was a transgression that threatened its territory and ownership of the string of mares.

The difficult terrain, littered with clods between the vine rows, kept Alejandro from running more than a short distance ahead of the charging beast. Head down and bucking at full speed, the horse raced toward Alejandro, who barely reached the foot of the olive tree in time to escape. Grasshopper's heart pumped with fear, desperation, and excitement all at once; his eyes and mouth grew wide in shock.

Once Alejandro reached the crown of the olive tree, the horse, neighing and snorting, ran past the foot of the tree and stamped its hooves on the ground, kicking up the thin gray dust along the path. This was the height of the boys' excitement. They were enthralled by the glossy, almost oily texture of *Potro Chúcaro*'s coat. The boys loved looking at the angry horse within such proximity. Its pelage released a sort of steam from its sweat and a leather-scented tang that the boys could smell from above. *Potro Chúcaro* was a true specimen of his kind. The horse charged toward them once again, arching his neck. Once beneath the shade of the tree, it reared on its hind legs, throwing its front legs and chest upward, slashing at the air with its hooves, trying to reach the boys in the crown of the tree. It grunted viciously, glowering at them, with its head cocked to show its red, glossy eyes filled with anger and wrath. The two boys stared in awe through the branches above. This was the moment that they were after. A moment of fear inspired by the reaction of the horse. For them, this was an opportunity to get something unique out of the horse by making its blood boil, while they watched the torrent that pulsated through the veins of its neck and legs and the drool and foam that dribbled from its mouth, as if the beast could not contain its frustration.

The boys waited to escape the anger of the horse that pawed the earth and prowled below. Time passed, the shade of the tree had moved, and they could not come down from it. The sound of the horse's neighing filled the Reys' farm. In the distance, Alvera saw *Potro Chúcaro* charging at something, but she couldn't tell what it was. The stud ran along nearby rows in the vineyard and came back to the olive tree to patrol the area. Alvera kept her sights on the beast while she approached the foot of the olive tree. The horse—who was still charging toward them—slowed yet maintained a brisk trot along the alley, as if to keep the boys at bay.

"Get away!" the brothers screamed at Alvera as the animal approached her. Recognizing her, *Potro Chúcaro* lifted its head. Its trot settled into a slow and quiet gait until it stopped. It scratched the ground with one of his hooves. Alvera stood by the tree, unaffected by the presence of the stallion as her right hand stretched out to offer the animal a fistful of muscat grapes. The stud began nibbling on them calmly. The beast gently caressed the dust with its hooves as the two boys watched in disbelief. Alvera stroked the horse on the face and neck before leading it away in the direction of the corral.

"Hey!" said Alejandro to her as she led the horse away. She turned, looked up at the tree, and saw the two boys.

"What're you doin' up there?" she laughed. The undulated shape of her lips, her tender gaze, and beaming smile, dazzled the boys.

"Nothing," said a bewildered Grasshopper as he looked up at his brother, who remained speechless. Alejandro's words would not come out, but he gazed at her intensely, bedazzled by her manner, her grace and her beauty as she led the horse away. Everything about her voice entranced him.

"You know my father won't like it if he catches you here," she said before turning away. This time, she squinted upwards until she spied Alejandro. Her tone did not convey much of a reprimand. She looked at Alejandro again, noticing his eyes and how he looked at her, as if discovering something within him. Suddenly, she seemed to become aware of what he felt.

"You'd better come down from that tree before my father finds you here," said Alvera. She turned and led *Potro Chúcaro* to the corral.

"Hey," said Alejandro, "what's your name?" He knew her name.

"Alvera," she said as she looked back at him and smiled.

The colorful hues of summer seemed to reflect the warm tingle in Alejandro's chest as he considered how to approach her once again. After his first direct encounter with Alvera, visiting the olive grove at the Reys' farm was something he would not bring himself to do again. Perhaps out of embarrassment. Perhaps out of respect. Taunting *Potro Chúcaro* had been a way to get her attention, but it was a child's game he didn't want to play anymore.

Short-Legged Lie

In Russell and its surroundings, the land offered a bountiful restitution for the harvesters and farmers' efforts. The area around the town was regarded as the most fertile and productive of the country. Every year, after the harvest seasons, the larger part of the fruit of the land disappeared—trucked off to packing plants, canneries, wineries, and the market—as if the work of the men and women had never occurred. All that remained of the fruits and vegetables were remnants of dried shoots and leaves along the furrows. As Alejandro and Grasshopper grew into the work at the homestead and the many other farms around Russell, it was inconceivable to them that sharecroppers, like their grandfather, worked the vastness of the land to receive little to nothing for the work and harvests they themselves had nurtured.

In the surrounding lands, especially in the Reys' farm, the cherry orchards had flourished into lush swathes of deep green and glowing red. The brilliant crimson in the trees could be seen from afar. For Grasshopper, it was enticing. From the top of the acacia tree, he could see the inviting crowns of trees loaded with bright clusters of cherries. It was a temptation he could not resist.

"Put one seed t-t-there, a-a-nother t-t-there, you'll get n-n-owhere," Grasshopper heard. "Oh, yes, Mr. H-h-high. There'll be a-a-many. Bountiful, Mr. H-h-h-igh..." Grasshopper stood still, trying to discern the raspy voice that moved along the *callejón*. The man behind the voice coughed up a loogie and spit it. Then he hacked again and coughed a little more. Grasshopper came down a few branches so he could get a closer look at the man. "Mr. H-h-high never dies. I've s-s-seen it all, seen it all," the man repeated. Charles High was barefooted and looked dirty. He wore an old and raggedy pair of khaki pants and a faded brown shirt, both torn in parts and stained at the elbows and knees. His face was smudged and long-bearded. His long, curly, dark hair grew backwards as if strong winds were hitting his face and pushing his hair back. He was a slender-looking man, with an assertive yet saddened look in his eyes. He carried a Coca-Cola glass bottle, from which he took small sips while he walked along the *callejón*. After he reached the stream, he squatted beside it and kept mumbling. He then scooped some water and splashed it over his forehead, combing the water through his hair with his right hand.

Grasshopper carefully observed the man taking the water. The air was calm and the day was hot. Mr. High couldn't see the boy above. Grasshopper gradually descended to a lower branch. A couple of trees down the stream, a Picui dove began cooing, adding to the solitude of the moment. The man looked up at the tree branches above and saw Grasshopper, who froze as he met the man's eyes.

"What's that l-l–little bird up there? Little birdie g-g-got no wings?" said Mr. High.

Grasshopper looked at him. "Hi, Sir," he said. "Just waiting for my grandpa." He was scared.

"Little bird f-f-flying...not afraid to fly?" asked the man. A Picui dove suddenly flew away. Mr. High got up and continued on his path, face down, along the *callejón*. Grasshopper's gaze followed the man to make sure he was gone before he came down from the tree. He had heard stories of weirdos around Russell but never about one like that man. He'd seen the man before along the *callejón*, but never made eye contact with him. "Scary-looking man, some kind of stranger from somewhere far away, kinda weird. He's just weird," Grasshopper whispered.

∙⟫⟫⟩ ⟨⟨⟨∙

Scared, Grasshopper ran quickly to the Reys' farm and climbed one of the cherry trees there. The Reys were the only ones who grew cherries in the area. The enticing red glow of the fruit stood out in contrast to the green background of the leaves. He had straddled a main branch, his legs wide open, one foot on a smaller branch, the other on another, which helped him keep his balance. He took each cherry and relished it like it was the last one of the season. When the boy crushed the fruit with his teeth, the sweet and carmine juice seeped out and stained his lips. He savored them, mashing the sweet flesh and spitting the pits onto the ground. He ate one after another and began stashing a few in the small burlap harvest-sack Grandpa had given him, where he carried his slingshot, marbles, some cucumber seeds, and other keepsakes.

As the boy ate and spat, he began spitting farther from the tree to see how far he could reach. Each time, he spat out the cherry pits a little further from the tree. To his surprise, one pit hit the straw hat of a man who had just appeared walking along the rows. Once Grasshopper realized who the pit had hit, he remained still, trying not to be noticed. But when the man looked up to see what had hit him, he peered through the branches and saw the boy.

Mr. Reys was on his way to release the water to irrigate the cherry orchard. He carried a draw hoe on his shoulder. Setting the draw hoe on the ground, he looked up at the tree, and he made an effort to recognize the boy.

"What are you doing up there?" demanded Mr. Reys, in a tone questioning the child's trespass. Grasshopper's mouth by now was dyed reddish-purple by the dark juice from the succulent feast he had just enjoyed. As the boy looked down, he saw Mr. Reys, glaring at him.

Grasshopper's eyes grew larger, filled with fear and guilt as he descended from the tree.

"You're taking what isn't yours," said Mr. Reys as Grasshopper clutched the small harvest bag while he climbed down.

"I wasn't eating them, Sir," he said as his eyelashes fluttered with shame. He rubbed his mouth with his hand.

"You're one of the Druett boys. Aren't you?" His tone of voice suddenly softened.

"Yes, Sir," said Grasshopper.

"Does your grandpa know where you are?" Mr. Reys asked.

"No, Sir," Grasshopper replied as he scratched the area around his mouth and placed the bag strap around his neck.

"Don't you know the fruit belongs to those who grow it? I've got to have a talk with your grandfather about this," said Mr. Reys in a stern but compassionate tone of voice.

"I was just getting a few cherries for Alvera, Sir," answered the boy, even though his wide eyes revealed his guilt and the stain around his lips marked him as the culprit.

"Alvera?" the man frowned. "My daughter?"

"Yes, Sir," said Grasshopper. "She is my friend," he said, assuring Mr. Reys of the reason for his trespass.

"I see." When Grasshopper handed Mr. Reys the bag, the man shook his head. "That's fine. You can keep them." Silence filled the air as he studied Grasshopper's face while the boy hung his head.

"Sorry, Mr. Reys," Grasshopper eventually said, raising his gaze. "But I got to go and help my grandpa now."

"Tell him I'll stop by to visit him soon."

Grasshopper ran with disgrace on his heels. His mouth burned. He felt as if he had eaten chilies instead of cherries. Mr. Reys' eyes followed the boy, shook his head, continued walking along the furrows and the trees in his orchard.

Once the boy left the Reys' farm, he cut across the reedbed that divided the farm from the olive grove in the homestead. A natural spring bubbled among the reeds, creating a fountainhead that overflowed and vanished into the marshy soil. This was another hiding spot for Grasshopper and Alejandro. The clear water was fresh and cold. There was no purer water in Russell. It was so fresh and cool that the boys drank until their bellies became full and wide. "We got watermelons," they said to each other, rubbing their bellies after drinking it. The unique taste of the water was almost addictive in nature. The spring was fed by one of the underground streams that ran "from the guts of the Great Endes Mountain and into the valley," Grandpa often said when he told the boys stories.

As Grasshopper reached the spring, he could not bear the burning and itchiness of his mouth, tongue, and lips. He knelt by the spring and lapped up the water to soothe the unbearable stinging in his mouth. He looked at his reflection in the water and saw that his lips were swollen and surrounded by the livid stain. His grandfather would know where he'd been as soon as he saw him. He scooped up some water with both hands and tried to scrub off the fruit dye. The boy knew he had gone too far by trespassing into the cherry orchard, but the cherries and the gurgling of the pristine water were too tempting. Despite the consequences, the enticing nature of breaking a boundary was also exciting to him. After all he was nine; he was just a kid, playing, trying to get away with stuff, trying to have some fun. If there was a price to pay, the itchiness and swelling of his lips reminded him of this transgression and the consequence for taking the cherries.

The sound of his footsteps in the water and the rustling of the wind against the reeds filled the air as Grasshopper left the spring. The boy floundered through the reeds to reach the *callejón*. From a distance, an outburst of laughter reached his ears and he heard voices of older men talking.

"Ohhh shit, Dad! It was fifteen times more!" said one of the voices. "And we'll make a lot more."

"Well, we'll tell old Druett to do it," said the other man. "He'll break his back for you. We'll make sure to give him a bit of what we make and he'll be happy," said Dr. Maxim to his son Herman in a more somber tone, as they made calculations and wrote down notes for future plans. Grasshopper recognized the men's voices as belonging to the owners of the olive grove and the homestead for whom their grandfather worked.

Alejandro and Grasshopper never liked them. The doctor never looked anyone in the eye as he spoke, and his son always talked with a smirk on his face, beginning and ending every sentence with the word "shit," especially when he addressed the day or migrant workers who picked olives and grapes. Father and son were a replica of before and after, physically and mentally, of each other. Herman had a strong physical frame, curly dark hair, and somewhat of a bulbous face; his father's eyes looked cunning, deceiving and perverse, especially when he laughed and at the same time talked. He had a hooked and protruding nose, with a curved nasal bridge, and a downward-sloping tip.

"Ohhh, shit, boy, you see! Ohhh, shit! Ohhh, shit!" Grasshopper imitated Herman in mockery. The kids called Herman "the Sheeeater," and his father "Dr. Piggie," for he had a protruding belly that cascaded over his belt and he often grunted when he laughed.

"By the end of the season, we'll get plenty from the cumbers harvest," added the doctor. He grunted.

"Benjamin and I made tenfold what we invested. That money will be resting like ten golden eggs in a nest at the bank in town." Raising his eyebrows, Herman nodded and grinned at his father, seeking his approval.

While the two men laughed, they both nodded and looked proud of the money they had and would make from Grandpa's work. It was a deserved triumph for them, which in their poor minds was confirmed by Grandpa Druett's faithful service, a service that multiplied their earnings and their livelihood. And so Dr. Maxim walked away laughing, grunting, and tittering his words, while Herman remained behind smirking, widening his lips, and saying his usual "Ohhh shit, boy." The reed-bed hid Grasshopper from their view. He had heard the conversation but did not know exactly what it all meant, since he was still in pain and distracted by his swollen lips. After Herman left, Grasshopper kept walking until the field met the *callejón*. He reached the foot of the acacia tree. He climbed up to wait for the swelling to cease so he could go back home without revealing his misadventure to his grandfather.

The Old Acacia Tree

At the homestead, Alejandro held a persimmon in his hands. His fingers curled and looked as if his hands enclosed a ball of fire. He ate the fruit vigorously while Grandpa gathered some tools inside the shed. Grandpa was meticulous every time he took up a project. And he wanted to teach each trade to his grandsons on his own terms.

"Alejandro and Grasshopper, come and help me with the handcart," he called from inside the shed.

Alejandro stood quiet, not wanting to expose his brother's absence. He walked immediately toward the shed in response to Grandpa's call.

"Where's your brother?" asked Grandpa as he tightened the last bolt to the axle of the wagon.

"I don't know. I haven't seen him," Alejandro said. His voice moved from a thick semi-strong tone to an involuntary high-pitch squeak. At times, his voice sounded broken and piercing, as if he were calling out wrongdoing. The instability of his maturing vocal chords produced an unpredictable range of sounds that vacillated between hoarse whispers, high-pitched screeches, and baritone croaks. The beauteous change of adolescence was molding him into a man from the inside out. He was becoming that unique creation of nature. His facial features looked as if nature was carving a manly version of him. His docile hair was becoming thicker, the bone structure of his face more chiseled. He was becoming a young man, whose contrasts merged to form an integral whole, like the delighted trilling of a thrush in the morning, harmonized with the mournful cooing of Picui doves in the *callejón*. The cooing was simple and unforced; his physical self looked healthy and tempered by the enchanting traits of alluring nature—youth.

The handmade cart that Grandpa made was finally taking shape after a couple of weeks of work. Despite his age, Grandpa was up to any challenge and did not wait for anyone or anything when he needed something done. He spent hours or even days in the shed contemplating and working on the tools and equipment he needed to do work on the farm, and designing the tools that would suit his tasks. The entire family was amazed by how Grandpa crafted his own tools, carts, and especially toys for the kids for Christmas.

The boys spent part of their play time watching Grandpa work on the handcart. He had designed two wooden hubs that fit tightly within the rubber wheels he fashioned from old tire-treads. Three smoothed poplar poles became handles to steer the new invention. A split and flattened olive oil metal barrel covered the wooden chassis of the cart. Grandpa swiftly spun two glistening ball bearings, rotating around his index finger. Once he had greased them, they were ready to be inserted within the wheels.

With his elbow down on the table and his hand holding the weight of his head, Alejandro watched, bewildered by the complexity of the creation that Grandpa had designed from scratch and constructed from scraps of wood and metal.

"Hold this for a second," Grandpa handed one of the ball bearings to Alejandro while he forced the other into one end of the axel that supported the wheels. He then added the other. He knew his trade well: He was not an expert but was practical and apt at his work, which itself showed him what to do.

"Your work is your best reference when it is done right. When in doubt, let the work show you the way," he often said to the boys. They watched his artistry.

The cart that Grandpa Druett and his grandchildren used to carry firewood to the homestead for winter was finally ready. It could be pulled by horse or manpower, but he wanted to use the completion of the cart as an opportunity to teach the boys about another aspect of farm work. Grandpa didn't force the boys to work, but he tried to teach them about work and life and about good faith and decency, whenever possible.

"Go ahead and pull the cart," said Grandpa. He then took an ax from the wall and other tools in a burlap bag, and they were on their way to collect the wood.

Alejandro steered the cart as Grandpa carried the ax in one hand, while the chisels, hammer, file, and wooden and metal wedges rested in the bag on the chassis of the cart. A manila rope was coiled across Grandpa's shoulder and torso. He lit a LeMans and let it hang from the left side of his mouth.

"Where's your brother?" asked Grandpa, puffing on the cigarette.

"I haven't seen him, Grandpa," answered Alejandro in his distinctive tone, as the two came to the *callejón*. Alejandro kept his sight locked on the gate ahead.

The acacia trees where the boys liked to play were near the gate of the homestead. The vegetation there was dense with lines of acacia trees, small natural mounds, and wild brush that served as natural boundaries, separating the dirt road and the stream from the farm. The stream ran along the dirt road and irrigated the acacia trees, the reedbed and all the vegetation on each side. During the rainy season, the waters rose, turning the stream into a canal, sometimes overflowing it.

Near the gate, Alejandro steered the handcart while his grandfather strolled behind him. They approached an old acacia tree and Grandpa sat down to prepare the tools they would use to bring it down. Alejandro recognized the tree that he and Grasshopper often played on. Grandpa placed the ax on his lap and pushed the file along the edge after dipping it lightly in the water. In the meantime, Alejandro cleared away the brush from around the tree.

High in the tree and unnoticed, Grasshopper just observed Grandpa giving the ax a last touch. Crouched down, Alejandro just looked at his grandfather as he filed the sharp edge of the ax. The way Grandpa worked was steady and meticulous. Standing up at the foot of the tree, Grandpa looked up at the crown, studying it, just as a small child looks up at his father. Not noticing Grasshopper, he looked at Alejandro and pointed toward the rope that lay in the cart.

"Hand me the rope there," Grandpa instructed and turned, squinting, looking at the crown of the tree again.

"What are you doing up there, Grasshopper?" asked Grandpa, surprised to see his grandson. The boy was hiding behind a branch and holding on to another. Alejandro approached and looked up too. He laughed. As the boy descended, Grandpa noticed the swelling on his face.

"Hi, Grandpa," said Grasshopper. "I've been waiting for you."

"What happened to your face? Come down!" said Grandpa.

"I was stung by a bee at the Reys' farm, Grandpa," said the boy as he reached the foot of the tree. His scrubbed face and lips now showed no trace of the dye from the stolen cherries he had relished.

"Let me see," said Grandpa as he held the boy's chin and studied the swelling. "Umm, where did it sting you?" asked Grandpa, growing suspicious.

"You look like a duckling ready to give his girlfriend a kiss," Alejandro said.

"Here," said the boy as he held his upper lip. Grandpa tried to contain his laughter.

"Why is your other lip swollen?" asked Grandpa looking at Grasshopper straight in the eye.

"When the wasp stung me, it hurt, so I bit my other lip," he said. "It hurt like heaven!"

"You mean like hell," Alejandro said.

"No, Grandma said not to say that word," said Grasshopper.

Grandpa took another look at the boy's lips and stared at him once again, knowing the kid was lying and that something did not square it all away. Ashamed, and with swollen lips, Grasshopper watched Grandpa walk a few yards away to unearth a bulb of purple garlic by the streambed. He reached inside his pocket and pulled out his red Swiss Army knife. He shaved a few slices of garlic, placed them on a rock, and smashed them with the end of the knife.

"This will take care of it," said Grandpa as he applied the paste to the protruding lips.

"Wait, it hurts. It stings!" said Grasshopper, making a fidgety gesture with his hands.

"Easy. This will make you feel better," said Grandpa as he thoroughly applied the paste.

As noon was upon them, Grandpa took off his shirt, coiled up the rope and placed it over his left shoulder, and began to make his way up the tree: hugging it at first, holding on to the first branch, then stepping on it, reaching for the one further up, and climbing his way to the top through leaves and branches. Then, he made a loop at the end of the rope and tied it to a thick branch about three quarters of the height of the tree. Intrigued, the boys looked up and watched every movement Grandpa made. They began to understand the plan. Once the rope was secured, the line hung down through the center, along the trunk, to the foot of the tree. Grandpa Druett descended faster than he had ascended. He moved gracefully and with the dexterity of an eighteen-year old boy.

The ax's edge glimmered. Suddenly, it registered with Grasshopper that their favorite tree was really going to be brought down.

"Why are we chopping this tree?" Grasshopper asked. He looked at Alejandro and then toward his grandfather. In an effort to protect the tree, Grasshopper flung his arms around it and hugged it tightly, unable to fully reach around its thickness. Pieces of bark fell as if the tree knew it was about to meet its demise.

"Please, Grandpa, don't cut it down; I'll be good, please," said Grasshopper as tears ran down his cheeks.

Grandpa looked at the boy, puzzled by his reaction. But the old man proceeded to pick up the ax and remove the other tools from the handcart.

"Why do we have to cut this tree, Grandpa?" Grasshopper asked.

"Acacia wood burns longer than any other firewood, Son," he said. "And the tree is already too old. It may fall and hurt someone."

"Are we going to cut down the others, too?" asked the boy as he looked down at the row of trees along the stream.

"No, we only need one tree. This wood should last for the entire winter," he added as he looked at the boy, noticing his shoelaces were untied.

"Stand clear, boys," Grandpa warned as he gave the tree a first hit. With every strike the tree trembled. The dry acacia seed pods rattled as tremors passed through every branch. Bare-chested, Grandpa picked up the pace with every strike of the ax. His accelerated breathing paused and he coughed, ceasing his labor for a moment after going at it for a while.

"Tie up your shoelaces, Son," he said, motioning at one of Grasshopper's leather shoes and extending the ax toward him. "You go now." The words clattered in Grasshopper's head. The tree had been his home, his refuge. He could hear the creaks coming from his noble friend, like pleas not to bring him down. The thought of cutting down his favorite tree felt like losing a friend, like the loss of his parents.

But Grasshopper knew he had to. The serious, intense gaze of his grandfather told him he had to.

"Grab it firmly and give it your best blow," encouraged Grandpa. With tears in his eyes, Grasshopper began chopping at the tree. After every blow, he hesitated to take the next. After about ten thwacks, the ax's edge was six inches from the heart of the trunk. Exhausted, Grasshopper sank to the ground and pushed the ax toward Alejandro.

Alejandro studied the handle of the ax and grabbed it by the end knob with his right and by the shoulder of the handle with his left. He raised the ax as he tilted his weight away from the tree. Sharply, with his whole body, Alejandro bludgeoned the core several times, much harder than Grasshopper and Grandpa had. The movement continued until Grandpa took a closer look at the trunk.

"Hold it right there," said Grandpa. He looked cautiously up the tree and collected the rope that hung from the crown.

"I want you boys to hold on to this rope and walk along the road until I tell you to stop," he said. "Take the cart that way too."

After the boys had trailed about forty yards along the dusty road, they stood at a distance, holding the rope tight as they were told, and waiting for their grandfather's command from afar.

"Now, pull hard!" shouted Grandpa. As the boys tugged at the manila rope, Grandpa struck the trunk with all his might a few more times. A loud crack echoed in the fields around the acacia tree, which, little by little, appeared to tilt to one side. The tree was succumbing. The boys kept pulling the rope. The tree gradually gave in, but it still seemed to resist the force of each blow of the ax. It shook as it gradually leaned to the side, emitting an even louder crack—a cry that must have been heard a mile away.

"Pull harder now!" shouted Grandpa from afar. "Pull harder!" The colossus tree plummeted to the ground. A behemoth cloud of dust engulfed the area around the tree and rose into the air high above the crowns of the other trees there. After the cloud of dust had settled, the tree lay outstretched on the ground. The two brothers stood. Their dusty semblances were two ghostly faces suspended in the air. Grasshopper's favorite tree, his friend, was now gone.

After the dust had settled, Grandpa and the boys began to cut out the branches, beginning with short and narrow shoots, and then the thick logs, cutting them into pieces that they could carry home on the cart. The heavy logs were cracked in half using chisels and wedges. When hammering a wedge into the head of a log and another halfway down, a rip cracked open across the log from one end to the other. Then, the long halves were chopped into pieces. Grandpa gazed quietly as the splintered fragments revealed the core of the logs. The scent of fresh wood, the unique smell of the tree's core, was in the air. The boys, still dumbfounded by the event, looked at their grandfather as he went to work on the logs with a power and energy they could not conceive he had. He displayed a physical force that overwhelmed them, especially Grasshopper. Grandpa looked deep in thought as he reminisced about the many times trees like this one provided comfort for him and his family. He relived the times he had worked the land without receiving a good harvest. *How ungrateful was nature to forget the hand that tendered it*, he thought at times. But how thankful he was for what she provided for him and his family in the end. On the whole, nature had been kind to him all these years. The land had eventually rewarded the calm hand that nurtured it. He sighed. He owed much to the land to which he himself belonged, to the cool summer breeze that comforted him, to the harsh times even when the land only provided a meal, and to the cool shade of trees, which was his sanctuary during hot days in the summer.

The ax struck the head of a log, but it would not split it. It took three wedges to split open the thicker end of the acacia trunk, for its fibers were too firm and compacted, too strong even for Grandpa's experience and adroit hands.

"Give it a stronger blow," Grandpa encouraged Grasshopper. The boy's hand clenched the ax handle nervously and struck the log mercilessly with the fury and impetus of a child. He exhaled a brief squeaky cry from his lungs as he hit it, like the shrill of a boy who had just wanted to play with the tree. Then, Alejandro followed, showing the power and prowess of his age and the training he had received from Grandpa. Once all the trunks and logs were cut and ready to be transported, they loaded the cart and took the wood back to the homestead and repeated the process as it was necessary.

That night at the homestead, Grandpa and the boys took turns chopping the logs into smaller pieces. The creaking of the wood echoed in the fields through the row of poplar trees behind the old adobe house and beyond the foliage of the olive groves. The acacia tree cried as it was ripped open. Its weeping traveled through the air and vanished with the barks of the country hounds in the distance. It didn't sound like wood being cut, or the laughter of kids playing on tree branches, but like a heart-rending shriek from some distant place.

Out of Sunrays and Petals

The thought of seeing Alvera again occupied Alejandro's every waking thought. He had to create the opportunity to see her, especially now that she had become aware of him. He knew that to get home, she would have to walk along the *callejón,* so he thought of hiding along her path until he could muster the courage to speak to her.

Waiting for her had become a routine. Alejandro hid behind the green leaves and shoots of the reedbed just to observe Alvera's elegant stride along the *callejón.* The sound of the gravel under her feet hid Alejandro's gentle rustling in the reedbed. He watched in silence. Without really knowing her, he adored her. He felt so much attraction for her that he did not know how to understand his own feelings. But he was not alone, as the affection for Alvera co-existed in his brother's heart. Grasshopper also liked her, but his love for her seemed fraternal, perhaps filial; Alejandro's was platonic. He did not understand his emotion, but he knew it was something he had never experienced before. Something within the fire in his chest told him this was different. He was becoming a man, inspired by Alvera's arresting physical beauty and the little interaction he had with her.

So Alejandro waited while he and Grasshopper spent their free time on the branches of the acacia trees. Time seemed to stand still in the summer, and the heat of the day made him impatient at times.

"I think Alvera likes me," said Grasshopper.

"She might," Alejandro said, looking at his brother.

"But she's too beautiful," Grasshopper added. "You know what Grandpa said about marrying a beautiful woman."

"I know he said that, but look at Grandma. She was so pretty when she was young and he married her," said Alejandro.

"She still is," Grasshopper said.

"You're right," said Alejandro. "Grandma doesn't really look her age."

"I think sometimes Grandpa just says things to make us laugh," said Grasshopper.

"I think he does," said Alejandro, chuckling.

Alejandro was also inspired by Alvera's graceful simplicity, the same simplicity she demonstrated with *Potro Chúcaro*. As she walked along the *callejón*, the green skirt she wore and her multi-colored blouse, like the orchestrated hues of apricots and plums against the luxurious green undergrowth, embellished her as if she were a queen displaying her royal worthiness. She would have the opportunity to prove how beautiful she was at the Wine Fest at the end of the harvest season during the carnival in Russell. But to Alejandro, she was already a majestic queen gliding down the *callejón*. Nature flourished around her as she stepped delicately along the road: The murmur of Picui doves, the colorful wings of monarch butterflies floating in the air, and the sonorous chirping of crickets heralded her coming and accompanied her steps.

"I love you endlessly," he said to himself, imagining himself in front of her.

Her presence was magical for Alejandro. For weeks, his admiration for her was both overwhelming and unsettling. He observed every aspect of her appearance, as he peered from his hiding place in the reeds. Her purity, the smoothness of her moist skin set off by her delicate green dress, and her narrow shoulders enticed Alejandro's eyes. His hands twitched with a yearning desire to travel down her soft skin along her back and caress her delicate waist. The proportions of her beauty dazzled his eyes as if he were blinded by sunlight. Truly, she was a semblance of the glories of paradise.

She knew someone lurked in the brush, for she had often sensed someone observing her. *It could be that boy,* she thought. She smiled. But she was too noble to pay attention to trivialities. Her proud and calm stride continued. Her scent merged with the aroma of fennel, wild roses, and the lush vegetation as Alejandro's eyes followed her every step until she disappeared in the distance along the *callejón*. When he lost sight of her, he became mad at himself for missing the opportunity to talk to her. Then, he ran with an effort to flee his own impulses and desires. He was a mad *Potro Chucaro* running through the furrows in the vineyards, one who ignored the command of his grandfather to tend the land first before playing.

But dazed, Alejandro was in a musing of sorts, a trance that often ended in frustration and in solitude as he wandered the vast farmlands surrounding the homestead. The fugue would end in breathless agitation for not having Alvera, as he sank between the furrows to feel the simplicity of the soil beneath his hands, as if seeking some cool refuge that could shelter him from the pressure of all the feelings he did not understand and that were mounting in his chest.

"I wish I could hold your hand," he said to her, gazing at her image in his mind, imagining the undulated shape of her lips.

"Why don't you?" her voice whispered in his ear. In his mind the dream of having her was perfect. The thought of being with her surrounded only by nature was magical. During the day, his witnesses were mostly birds that chirped and dodged through the air; at night the stars conspired with him in his infatuation and his desire.

But the reality was that he didn't have her.

He laid there alone within the furrows in the vineyards, facing the stars, and the moon, wanting her. His thoughts were his only comfort. He thought about having her in his arms. He picked a clear muscat grape and placed it between his lips and thought of her, as if he was tasting the sweet of her lips. The juicy taste of first love. He wanted to kiss her lips and her body, taste the grape juice, hold her waist, feel the contour of each grape, and engulf her body, with her breasts against his chest while he fondled clusters of muscat grape in his hands. But he groped about with an innocent and inexplicable desire to clench a mound of fresh soil and feel the proportions of the earth with his hands. Then, he reached up and clasped a cluster of muscat grapes from the vines next to him, bringing the fruit to his lips again, squishing the round fruits until they burst, as if he were softly biting and gently kissing her neck and her lips. He breathed and regained his calm. Then he relaxed, feeling one with nature, and sated his desire with the sweet smell of grapes until the dusk grew upon him.

It was in him, the thought of loving her. The stars above seemed to be part of his whole, while his whole was withering away like minute, tingling pins, like stars fading in every part of his body, as if he were fusing into the dark firmament above him, as the muscat juice dripped down his forearm, elbow, and into the vital soil below—until all subsided. And the vigor of his youth was tempered by the impression he had made on her. He realized something had to be done, and from that moment on, something had changed in him.

⇛⇛⟫ ⟪⇚⇚

One day, as Alvera walked along the *callejón*, she noticed acacia petals falling, like yellow snowflakes, gently on her shoulders and on her path.

It was as if the sun's rays had descended on her, a bed of golden petals illuminated and carpeted her path. When she looked up high above her, near the crown of the trees, she saw Alejandro holding and denuding a bunch of acacia flowers. Curling one leg around a thick offshoot and bracing the other on a trunk, he kept his balance. He wore a playful smirk on his face. Her eyes glistened, resembling her bright surroundings. She squinted as she looked up and giggled. She cocked her head, smiling, and gently signaled for Alejandro to come down.

"You really like climbing trees, don't you?" she asked as she looked up, blocking the sunrays that sifted through the acacia branches.

Alejandro's eyes grew wide at her invitation. "Yes, I do," he said, and with the dexterity of his youth, he began to descend from the crown of the acacia. He leaped from one limb to another, grabbing branches and sliding down the trunk in an effort to impress her.

"How funny!" Alvera said as she saw him quickly descending from branch to branch. He hopped again, misjudging his step and missing the next branch, lost his balance and fell back, tumbling downwards. As he fell through the branches, his pants, and brown leather belt got caught on a sharp protruding offshoot, which fastened him securely to the tree by the seat of his pants. Relieved from the trepidation of the fall, he sought to dissipate his embarrassment by slightly smiling at Alvera and pretending he had it all under control. He remained suspended in midair with his body and face upside down.

"Hey, I'm good," he said. Suddenly, the expression of sheer confidence on his face shifted to imminent panic.

"Holy Jack!" he yelled. A sudden jerk, followed by a gradual descent, caused his pants and underpants to slowly peel off his body, leaving him as bare as nature intended, first revealing the top of his buttocks and finally uncovering both hemispheres, which Alvera could clearly see from below. Then his pointy, jutting manhood sprang into the air and hung downwards in plain sight. Unable to reach up to recover his pants from which he was now suspended by his knees, he looked at Alvera in desperation.

"Please, don't look at my pickle!" he pleaded. A vein pulsed at his temple while he hung helplessly in his shame. Alvera's left hand now covered her mouth and her eyes were wide open, perhaps from the shock of seeing him fall or perhaps in the sudden realization of what she was seeing.

"Oh, don't worry. I have a brother," she responded quickly. "I'm not looking," she added as her right hand slightly covered her eyes. Alejandro was stuck. Then, realizing that he was stuck hopelessly, Alvera began climbing the tree to free him from his predicament. Once she reached the branches where he hung, she stretched her right arm to him, reaching out to him, taking hold of him. Then, he moved his torso upwards and clasped her in an awkward embrace she had not anticipated. Looking her straight in the eyes, less than an inch from her face, Alejandro faced her while his parts down below were still pretty evidently on display to the great outdoors. As he held and looked at her, she smiled and so did he, yet his smile looked a bit apologetic as he reached down rapidly with an inconspicuous left hand to tug up his pants.

The awkwardness of the moment, his desire for her, and his gratitude for her willingness to help, merged as their bodies remained entangled on the tree branch.

"You must really like climbing trees," said Alvera again to fill the void.

"Yes, I love this tree," he said, emitting a sigh of relief, as he was still shaken from the incident. He smiled humbly.

"But it looks like you get in trouble every time," she added.

"Yes, it looks like that," Alejandro said as he looked around and realized the awkward position they were in.

"Let me help you," he said. His efforts to bring her down safely interfered with her attempt to assist him, as both moved clumsily along the branches that supported them. Holding her by her waist, Alejandro once again missed a step, causing her feet to step into the void. Her eyes grew in amazement as she realized they were both now destined to fall. They fell through the leaves that interwove the branches in the acacia tree. A loud shrill of laughter was heard in the surrounding farms as their bodies went freefalling into the water below. As both emerged from the crystalline currents, their laughter drifted away like the shimmering and ephemeral reflection of crimson wild roses on the water along the banks.

Once out of the water, they bathed in the sun to dry their clothes; they played and talked.

"You love me, you love me not..." played the two as they laughed, stripping the leaves from a frail acacia shoot.

During the day, Alvera and Alejandro sat holding hands in the lower branches of the acacia tree. At night, they observed how shooting stars traced lines across the firmament as they recounted their brief life histories, laughing and joking with each other, and observing how the entire universe revolved around them: a universe that would soon prove too rushed and uncertain.

The Told Lie

The morning dew, with a gentle and moist mantle, had coated the fields around the homestead. The sharp chirping of crickets had subsided as the light of the day's break covered the homestead in the typical silence and stillness of the morning. Grandpa's winding footprints had trodden a dark trail on the grass that led to the cucumber beds. Birds chirped, announcing the coming of a new day as the sunlight dappled the foliage of the shrubs and trees.

Grandma prepared breakfast and Grandpa, who gazed out the window, waited at the table in the kitchen, his sight locked on the distant fields, contemplating a far-off memory perhaps, a remembrance that often kept him in deep reflection. Grandpa often got up early and went to work but came back to have breakfast by the time Grandma had gotten up. While he waited at the table for Grandma, he often looked at the 1871 Martini-Henry rifle that he kept as a relic above the threshold of the door. The rifle belonged to Grandma's great-grandfather who had fought in the war. On one side of the rifle, below the cleaning hole, the engraved letters on the metal under a crown read *in pulverem*. Alejandro often sat next to him and had conversations about work and life in general. Grasshopper and Alejandro always wondered why Grandpa looked at the rifle in such a fixed yet dismissive manner, taking his sight away from it, as if he mistrusted it, as if he didn't want to look at it. Alejandro got up and approached the wall where the rifle was mounted. He pulled a chair, so he could take a closer look at the rifle.

"What does that mean?" Alejandro asked, standing on a chair and studying the rifle.

"It means you ought to stay away from it," Grandpa said.

Alejandro's sight and reflection were quickly interrupted as Grasshopper appeared, rubbing his eyes on his way to the bathroom.

"Good morning, Grandpa, Good morning, Grandma," said Grasshopper.

"Good morning. I've already removed the cover from the coop," murmured Grandpa.

"Good morning, Robinson," said Grandma. Sometimes, she called Grasshopper nicknames. Robinson Crusoe, Captain Nemo and other names she used at random in honor of the adventurous characters Grasshopper talked and read about in Grandpa's books, especially those he admired and impersonated when reading his books.

"On my way," replied Grasshopper as he stuck his slingshot into one side of his waistband where Grandpa wouldn't see it.

"Go wash your face first," said Grandpa.

"Good morning," said Aunt Rosy. Aunt Rosy and Aunt Claudia were the youngest daughters, who were in their mid-twenties. They visited Grandma and Grandpa on weekends but worked and stayed in downtown Russell with Aunt Ana. Aunt Ana was older. She had a job in Russell and lived with her son, Rolando, and Uncle Mike, a plump man, who, despite not liking to work, liked to tell jokes. At times, Aunt Claudia helped Aunt Ana while she took classes at the beauty school in downtown Russell during the week.

Aunt Rosy had a towel wrapped around her head and wore a white, translucent dress. She was short and attractive, and this often made Grandpa worried.

"You're not going out like that, are you?" asked Grandpa.

"What's wrong?" she said. Grandpa was too protective at times.

"Is that the dress Ana gave you?" asked Grandma. "It's pretty."

"Yes, it is." Aunt Rosy lowered her gaze at Grandpa and looked upset as she walked back to her room. Grandma just eyed Grandpa.

"There's nothing wrong with that dress, Mr. Druett," Grandma said. Every time she tried to get his attention, she addressed him as Mr. Druett.

"I'm worried about the degenerates looking at her, at that dress," said Grandpa. "She's a beautiful woman now."

"Then say that," said Grandma. Alejandro had never seen Grandma challenge Grandpa. He looked at her and seemed to think deeply.

"Rosy!" Grandpa called after reflecting on what he had said. Aunt Rosy came into the kitchen.

"Yes, Pa," she said. She was crying.

"I'm sorry. I wasn't thinking. That's a pretty dress."

"Thank you, Pa." She came near him and hugged him.

"I'm just worried about you out there on your own." Grandpa seemed sentimental. Grandma came near him and put her hand on his shoulder.

"I don't go around alone, Pa. I know how to take care of myself," Aunt Rosy said. She smiled at him, kissed him on his forehead, and went back to her room. Grandpa sighed and looked at Grandma. Then she cleared the table in front of Grandpa to serve him breakfast.

Grasshopper came back from washing his face and walked back into the kitchen.

"Be quick, your grandma has to go to the market and run some errands in Russell after breakfast," said Grandpa, glancing at the boy.

One of Grasshopper's chores was feeding the chickens in the morning. At first, he did not like the task, for he was disgusted by the smell in the coop. The smell of chicken manure, the sweat-like odor, the dust, and feathers made the boy nauseated at first. But the task grew on him. It became a bit of a revelation, for it taught him about compassion and fairness, and something of malice too.

Every morning, Grasshopper arrived at the coop carrying buckets of corn millings and water. By then, the chickens were hungry and waiting, because they knew he was there to feed them. That morning, carrying the grain and water, Grasshopper walked inside the coop. While waiting to be fed, chickens rioted and milled about as in a free-for-all. The cackling and sudden wing-flapping of the chickens, as they took turns stepping indiscriminately over each other, raised dust and white feathers in the air in the coop. One particular bird lay on the ground in the center of the commotion. Grasshopper could barely distinguish it beneath the chaotic clouds of feathers and dust. The bird was lame. Its splayed legs kept it from walking properly or fending for himself.

The boy observed a mob of corpulent, white-bosomed chickens attacking the bird as it lay vulnerable on the floor. The larger chickens surrounded the crippled bird, pecking at its head, striking it with their claws after each peck and opening a wound on the back of its head, pecking and striking at it again, one blow after another, in a reckless assault.

Before pouring the corn millings in the feeders and water in the waterer, he turned to the flock of aggressors. Taking out his slingshot, he showered them with a handful of the small glass pebbles he carried in his pocket.

"You crazy sons of hen-ches!" shouted Grasshopper as he aimed at the big birds. He targeted the larger ones first, the ones that looked like roosters. He avoided shooting at the small chicks, for he knew the aggressors. But for fear of being shot, the small chicks cackled, jumped, and flapped their wings around in a cloud of dust and white feathers. The smell of chicken shit filled the air. "That ought to teach you a lesson," he said, while hoping the guilty recipients of his pebbles felt the pain they had inflicted on the crippled bird. While he gave each large bird its dose of punishment, the smaller birds kept cackling at his revenge for attacking the coop. Scared and nervous, smaller capons observed from a distance.

He then gently picked up the beaten chicken and drew it close to the waterer, observing as the small bird swallowed the water down in its craw. The wounded bird looked at Grasshopper. Then it closed its eyelids as if he knew it would soon die, but Grasshopper kept petting, caressing, and feeding the chicken until Grandma's call startled him.

"I'll take care of you, my friend," Grasshopper said as he picked up the bird.

"Breakfast's ready!" Grandma's acute voice echoed and reached the chicken coop.

"I'm almost done!" replied Grasshopper, moving the deformed chicken away from where it lay and outside the coop. The large chickens cackled and looked askance at the boy, as if they feared another dose of punishment.

"Why is it bleeding?" asked Grandma as she appeared behind the chicken wire fence and looked at the bird the boy held in his arms.

"Those bad birds there were pecking him." Grasshopper pointed at the chickens that were now feeding at the other end of the coop.

"Were you shooting at them?" inquired Grandma.

"No, ma'am, I wasn't," said Grasshopper, hiding the slingshot that stuck out of his rear pocket.

"Go and have breakfast. I'll finish here," said Grandma while she took the chicken from Grasshopper's hands.

❧ ❦

With both elbows on the table, Grandpa curled his fingers around a cup with hot coffee, looked outside through the kitchen door that was kept wide open, and contemplated the morning mist in the distance. Eddies of steam gently whirled in front of Grandpa's face as he sipped from the cup.

Alejandro sat at Grandpa's right hand-side and Grasshopper across from his brother.

"I need you boys to go and help Mr. Lessar," said Grandpa without looking at the boys. "He's been a good friend and he needs help harvesting the almonds. Just go there and ask what he needs help with."

"Yes, Grandpa," they said almost in unison.

"Can I have a bit more bacon, Grandma?" asked Grasshopper.

"Here, you can have mine," said Grandpa, putting a piece of bacon on Grasshopper's plate.

"You like the oink—oink, don't you?" said Alejandro, smiling at Grasshopper.

"I do very much," said Grasshopper. He smiled. Grandma took her bag and gave Grandpa a kiss on his forehead and left.

"That's the piece that Kaiser gets," Alejandro said.

"Are you calling me a dog?" said Grasshopper.

"Grrr!" said Alejandro.

A distant hum, the horn of a cargo train, interrupted their breakfast. As the boys looked at each other, Grandpa cleared his throat.

"I don't want to see you jumping on that train. You hear me?" commanded Grandpa with his usual straight and serious face.

"Yes, Grandpa," they said again almost in unison.

The train tracks were about half a mile from the homestead, and although the boys could not show their excitement in the presence of their grandfather, their anticipation became more intense by the minute. They heard the distant call again. This time they glanced at each other, resolute, with the intent of getting up from the table. Grandpa sipped one last time from his coffee mug, got up from the table, lifted his straw hat from a rustic tree-shaped coat rack, fixed the hat on his head, and walked outside.

Once Grandpa was out of sight, the boys sprinted out of the house toward the dusty road that led to the *callejón* and then to the railroad crossing. In the distance, in the opposite direction, they saw Grandma's silhouette carrying a handbag. They knew she was on her way to the market.

"C'mon, run, you little snail," Alejandro yelled at Grasshopper as dust rose behind them.

The whistling and chugging of the train neared the *callejón* as the brothers ran toward the train tracks. The approaching clackety-clack of wheels on the tracks was vigorous and solid. The train traveled from the skirts of the Great Endes Mountain to the warehouses in the town. Tankers filled with crude oil and wagons loaded with gravel made the train move slowly around the bend, especially as it reached the farms near the homestead. Once the two brothers reached the tracks, they could see the red and black locomotive engine coming ahead around the bend. They looked at each other. Grasshopper's sparkling eyes revealed he had no intention of going to Mr. Lessar's that day.

"Can we stop by the river?" Grasshopper asked.

"Grandpa told us to go help Mr. Lessar," Alejandro firmly said.

"C'mon, let's go to the river. Let's have some fun," insisted the boy. "It's on the way there anyway. We're gonna ride the train, so we'll get there faster anyway." Grasshopper wheedled.

As the train approached, it decreased its speed. The iron wheels of the heavy train seemed to bend the rails as they rolled along the tracks. Lush vegetation was copious on both sides of the tracks. And as the train neared the *callejón*, it warned passers-by and drivers with three loud whistles. The boys hid behind the reedbed that divided the Reys' farm from the train tracks.

"Let's wait until it slows down a bit more," Alejandro said.

"Let's just jump on it now," Grasshopper replied, as he looked at the train cars in front of him. The boy broke through the reeds and began running along the side of tracks in the same direction as the moving wagons.

"Wait!" shouted Alejandro as he saw his younger brother running.

"C'mon, you big sack of potatoes!" Grasshopper yelled as he leaped onto one of the steps of the ladder on the side of the tanker. With a bit of difficulty, Alejandro was able to get a hold of the ladder of a hopper car two wagons behind his brother.

"Are you all right?" screamed Grasshopper from the dome of the tanker.

"Yeah!" replied Alejandro as he climbed the ladder.

"Oh, this is great!" Grasshopper screamed as he stood and stretched his arms. He was now on top of the tanker on the moving train. For the boys, riding a freight train was like a flight to freedom. The feeling of exhilaration they carried while the train picked up speed, the excitement of having jumped on the moving train, and the certainty that they were going to be in the biggest trouble of their lives if they were caught, filled them with breathless delight and fear. But they just laughed and enjoyed every moment of it.

Waving at Grasshopper, Alejandro shouted, "Get down, you fool! The engineer's gonna see you." Once Alejandro had climbed to the top of the hopper, he staggered toward the tanker to meet Grasshopper.

The train had gone past the bend and it was once again gaining speed.

"We gotta get off before it reaches the river," shouted Alejandro. By now the boys were clambering near each other between wagons. Alejandro held on to the hand brake lever. Grasshopper, his legs wide open and stretching his arms between both tankers, held himself fast and balanced between the cars. The train, heedless of the loads it carried, picked up speed.

As the boys rode, the view of the rural landscape became clear. The train cut across the land, revealing the farming fields, backroads, crossroads, reedbeds, jagged terrain, water ducts, oil pipes, and wells. Laborers harvesting the fields waved at the boys and the boys waved in return.

"We gotta get off the train before the bridge!" screamed Alejandro. "You gotta be careful not to fall!"

"Yeah, like that kid they say that fell and died!" shouted Grasshopper amidst the noise and the metal clanking of the train.

"Yeah, like him, but he didn't die!" Alejandro added, raising his voice. "He got his legs chopped off!"

"Really? Both of them?!" asked Grasshopper.

"Yeah, both of them! We gotta jump before the bridge!"

Grasshopper was now filled with uncertainty. His eyes grew wide and worried. The train kept a constant pace, but it increased by the minute. With the clink-clacking of iron wheels against the rusty rails and the clackety-clack of the railings on the wheels, the train kept a steady momentum and pace and advanced vigorously.

As the train reached the bridge, the lushness of the landscape began to dissipate. The bridge that crossed the Manso River stood as a fortress that connected rural and urban Russell. The Lessars lived about three miles from the bridge on the lush side of the river.

As the train neared the bridge, the boys stood perched on the ladders of the wagons.

"We gotta jump now!" shouted Alejandro.

"It's moving too fast!" replied Grasshopper as his hair waved in the air.

"We gotta jump! Land on the bushes," Alejandro urged his brother. The bridge was less than one hundred yards away. Alejandro held on to the rusty red ladder of the hopper, ready to jump at any moment. Grasshopper hung from a handlebar beside the hand brake of the tanker. The speed of the train kept the boys at bay as they waited for the right moment to leap onto the shoulders of the tracks, hoping to land on a patch of soft brushes that would cushion their landing. The brothers looked at each other. They knew if they crossed the river, they wouldn't have a chance to get off the train. As the train neared the bridge, Grasshopper looked at his brother once again and, with a quick leap forward, jumped for the bushes on the bank of the river. But, he miscalculated the train's pace.

Alejandro saw his brother flying through the air. He knew Grasshopper would land right in the water. Alejandro looked back, but the quick passing of speed and railroad ties below kept him from seeing his brother.

The thought of Grasshopper not knowing how to swim overwhelmed Alejandro with fear, so he took a last look and leaped forward.

After the splash, hundreds of bubbles rose to the surface as Grasshopper heaved for air. His body rose to the surface. Inhaling and exhaling deeply, the boy surfaced, flailing his arms above the water in a desperate attempt to keep his head above the surface. The current moved him along as it dragged him down to the ominous silence under the water.

Alejandro landed on top of blackberry bushes along the opposite bank of the river. He rose from the thorny undergrowth and looked downstream to see where Grasshopper was. Alejandro rapidly rubbed his arms to remove the tiny thorns from the bushes, but he wasn't worried about the thorns, bruises, or the pain of the landing. He loped along the bank to find Grasshopper.

Deep breathing in, sinking below, reaching the surface with his arms and hands, trying to pull his weight out of the water and onto the surface, Grasshopper was down to his last breath.

From the distance Alejandro looked at the area where his brother seemed to be sinking.

With a swift yank, Grasshopper was pulled out of the water. He could barely distinguish a leathered-brown color on the surface. Coughing and wheezing, the boy came to himself again and as he regained his breath, he recognized the brown leather pants of the person who was getting him out of the water. One robust hand held him by the shirt front while the other held him by the underarm. Grasshopper recognized Mr. Lessar's son, Mario, as his savior.

Mario was the fastest harvester in Russell. He was known for his speed, diligence, and charisma. The way the man worked the land and fields was prolific. Whether picking grapes, olives, or any other fruits in Russell, he made an artistry out of harvesting. He was twenty-one and he worked alongside older men. Mario respected everyone: the young, the old, the poor, the rich. Older men admired his dexterity and pace. Grandpa and

Mario were well-acquainted, and they often talked about the land and the crops, people and politics, money, life, and circumstance. He was humble and often laughed at himself. The kids looked up to him. His friends looked up to him. People who met him for the first time looked up to him. A good friend to both Grasshopper and Alejandro, Mario often offered good advice and teased and played with them. "Lies are short-legged," he often said to the boys, showing a friendly grin while the intense turquoise in his eyes captivated the boys.

By the time Alejandro arrived, Mario and Grasshopper were already reaching the riverbank. Grasshopper looked exhausted. His eyes were bloodshot and his lower lip was purple and protruding from exhaustion, but he seemed to be regaining his color. Still coughing a bit, Grasshopper looked at Alejandro and his eyes lit up when he saw that his brother was unhurt.

"I saw you both jumping from that mighty train," said Mario, as he affixed a lure to the hook.

"We were good," said Grasshopper, coughing, as he rested his hands on his knees.

"You sure were," said Mario. "You bad asses."

"Yeah, we're pretty good," said Grasshopper while he coughed some more.

"Shut up! You almost died," said Alejandro.

"Yeah, it takes a lot to jump from a moving train and into a mighty current," added Mario. He laughed and shook his head.

"It sure did," replied Grasshopper, looking at his brother. "You got hurt too."

Alejandro looked at the scratches on his arms and touched the bruises on his face. Traces of blood were scattered on his forearms and hands. But he stood there as if nothing mattered. Mario looked at both of them and nodded, squinted his eyes. He grinned.

"How are you gonna get back to the other side?" Mario asked. The boys were now on the opposite side of the river, across from the farm, where the current had carried Grasshopper to the spot where Mario had been fishing.

"Grandpa sent us to help Mr. Lessar," said Alejandro.

"Dad is still waiting for the big boss to bring him the mighty tarpaulins," replied Mario. "There is not much to do at the farm right now and there are less than two acres left to harvest."

"Have you caught anything?" asked Grasshopper.

"Just a couple of ol' whiskers," replied Mario before he reeled in the line and recast it over the water to find a new spot. "They'll be nibbling over there."

The boys now looked at the area around the river, searching for a spot to cross to the other side. Crossing the river seemed impossible, especially for Grasshopper.

"How about the bridge?" asked Grasshopper.

"To get to that mighty bridge, you gotta walk about a mile inland and trace the train tracks back along to the bridge," said Mario. "The ties on the bridge are mighty dangerous. They are too far apart. People have fallen through."

"So, it's easier if we swim across," added Alejandro. He looked at Grasshopper.

"That's right," said Mario.

"Maybe we could find something that floats," Alejandro suggested.

"We could use those reeds over there and make a raft to cross over," Grasshopper said. Alejandro looked unsure, glanced at Grasshopper, but they had no other option.

"Just be careful with the current," said Mario as he recast his fishing line at a shallow spot by the riverbank at the opposite side of the river.

Grasshopper and Alejandro had spent nearly an hour gathering enough reeds and loose trellis wires to make a makeshift raft. The boys brought a bundle of hollow, dry reeds they found along the banks of the river and tied them together with remnants of old wires used to lead the grape vines into the trellises. They found a dry poplar pole that they attached to the raft and used to steer the vessel.

"Go upstream and then go across!" shouted Mario from a few yards away. "Hold on tight to it. I'll be watching you downstream. Watch out for those mighty rapids by the boulders over there." He pointed at them and followed the boys with his sight. "These little rascals," Mario said to himself as he walked downstream.

"Yeah!" shouted Grasshopper in return as he stooped and helped his brother secure the pole to the raft.

"Let's go," said Alejandro as the two brothers picked up the raft on their shoulders and walked upstream.

"Hey, let's name the raft," said Grasshopper.

"What you wanna name it?" asked Alejandro, eyeing his brother.

"Let's call it Moses," said Grasshopper.

"Why Moses?" asked Alejandro.

"I heard Grandma say that Moses was saved from the waters."

"Name it something, but I'm not so sure about Moses," said Alejandro, dismissing his brother's idea.

"How about Nautilus?" added Grasshopper.

"What's that?" asked Alejandro.

"I read it in one of Grandpa's books," said Grasshopper. "Or let's just name it Nauti."

"Yeah, that makes more sense," said Alejandro. "People would think we've named it after you." Alejandro chuckled. "The naughty raft!"

"You calling me crazy?" said Grasshopper.

"Maybe," said Alejandro as he led the way.

After they had walked about a quarter of a mile upstream, they set the Nauti down and Alejandro pushed it into the water.

"You grab that end and I'll hold this one," said Alejandro to his brother. The ripples on the river moved smoothly along. On the surface, the river seemed calm, but the currents below worried the brothers.

"I heard there are swirls beneath the water," said Grasshopper.

"There are," said Alejandro. "They'll suck you in from below if you aren't careful."

"Damn, I'm scared," said Grasshopper.

"Don't be. You hold on to it, now," said Alejandro as his little brother's eyelashes fluttered, his eyes widened by the second.

"Got it," said Grasshopper in a clear yet shaky voice.

As the boys began their voyage onto the river, both laid their torsos on the raft. Alejandro firmly grabbed the poplar pole with his right arm and put his left one around the reed bundle while he and Grasshopper kicked their legs to propel the raft onward.

"The water is too cold," said Alejandro.

"Yeah, it's freezing," added Grasshopper.

Submerged boulders pushed the currents over the surface from which the flow moved into steep descents to the riverbed.

"Just hold on to it," said Alejandro as the swift current moved the raft and the boys toward the rapids.

"I'm afraid," said Grasshopper, eyeing the rapids ahead.

"Don't be!" said Alejandro, assuring his brother. "You just go with it and you'll be fine. Just hold on to the raft."

Grasshopper's grip tightened as the two boys entered the rapids. The raft went over the rocks' ledges. The current grabbed the raft, sending Alejandro below the surface. Taking control of the pole, Grasshopper was able to perch his small body on the raft. From the other side of the riverbank, Mario stood watching how the kids managed their escapade.

Air bubbles and white foam was all that Grasshopper could see around him as the raft floated downstream, away from the rapids. Alejandro emerged from the pillows of water below by the boulders and vigorously stroked the water in an effort to reach the raft.

Drifting along down the river, as the raft neared the opposite banks, Grasshopper kept hold of the poplar pole and steered the raft ashore. He kept kicking until he ran the raft aground on a sandbar. As soon as Grasshopper was able to touch the shore, he looked back for his brother. In the distance, Mario waved at Grasshopper while Alejandro reached the riverbank.

Soil

Alejandro and Grasshopper strolled bare-chested along the alleyway and the train tracks that led to the road to Mr. Lessar's house. Their clothes were soaking, so they wrung out their shirts and slung them over their shoulders. They found their way back to the train tracks, where they were supposed to land before going across the bridge. Nearly twenty yards away from the tracks, they walked by an abandoned oil well on the opposite side of the path. The well sporadically oozed bubbles that exuded a vapor and a tarred metallic scent of unprocessed petroleum. The glossy and dark surface was perhaps three or four feet down from the dusty ground by the path. On the shoulder of the tracks stood an iron tower, on its zenith a railway signal and a lamp.

"From that ladder up there you can see if the train's coming," said Grasshopper.

"I know," replied Alejandro as he crawled under the barbed wire fence that divided the farm from the strip where the railroad tracks were.

Grasshopper stood near the well and looked up at his brother while he climbed to the top, where the tell-tale arm and lamp were attached. Once on top, Alejandro stood high above the foliage of the surrounding orchards. The air was pure, and the view revealed a clear and lush view. He looked over at where the train tracks disappeared and tried to discern the locomotive in the distance, but there was no train in sight. As he looked back at his brother, he noticed something moving down along the edge of the well.

"Look!" Alejandro yelled, "Something's moving right there!" He pointed his finger toward the well before he descended from the ladder. "Some little critter is moving there!"

"Where?" asked Grasshopper as he scurried toward the well.

"There!" said Alejandro, "by the jagged edge of the well."

"Yeah, I see it!" said Grasshopper. "What in heaven is it?"

"Some kind of critter," said Alejandro, coming down from the ladder. "Whatever it is, it's all covered in oil."

"What the heck is it?" Alejandro approached the well. "Looks like a dog! Let's get him out," said Alejandro.

"How do we get him out? He's too deep in," said Grasshopper.

"Let's get some of them dry grapevine shoots by the barbed-wire fence there," Alejandro said. He used the fibrous shoots to descend to the well while Grasshopper held on to them from above.

"Who would do something like this to a poor critter?" asked Alejandro.

"Maybe he fell there," said Grasshopper.

"Maybe," said Alejandro as he struggled to find a place where he could descend and lasso the dog. If he fell into the well, he would be covered in tar, just like the dog. If he were able to get the dog out of it, he would have to get at least his arms smudged with tar.

"Be careful," said Grasshopper. Alejandro descended to a low bank near the edge and was able to position himself before reaching the dog. Grasshopper held the dry grapevine shoots while Alejandro looped the shoots round the dog's torso. "It's all sticky!" said Grasshopper.

Scared, the dog struggled to move away from Alejandro. He was exhausted and stuck in the mire of petroleum tar. He didn't whimper, for he had accepted his fate. He only shivered. His eyes were heavy with the gloom of terminal hopelessness. He was afraid of anyone who came near him. Alejandro moved closer and pulled the dog near him.

"We need to get all that oil off of him," said Grasshopper.

"We'll do that later," said Alejandro as he pulled.

The pooch whimpered a bit as he was pulled out of the well. Once out, he shivered even more. His eyes were filled with rheum, his back was arched, his tail seemed to be glued to one of his legs, and the gloom in his eyes seemed as dark as the tar that covered his body. He was stiff and shivered as if he suffered from rheumatism. Alejandro wrapped his shirt around the dog to avoid getting the tar on himself. Grasshopper did the same once Alejandro moved the dog to the surface.

"Poor little doggie," said Grasshopper. Alejandro picked up the dog and they went on their way to Mr. Lessars'.

"I wonder what his name is," said Grasshopper.

"I don't know. We won't ever know. Whoever owns the poor thing don't want nothing to do with him," said Alejandro.

"That's for sure," replied Grasshopper. "Why don't we name him?"

"We can't," answered Alejandro. "We can't keep him."

"Why not? All dogs have names," said the boy.

"Yeah, but we are not keeping him," said Alejandro.

"Why would you even help the critter if you are not keeping him?" asked Grasshopper. "We should save him."

"So you just wanna be his savior?" Alejandro contended.

"Yes," said Grasshopper.

"I'll call you Grasshopper, the savior then," Alejandro said laughing at his brother.

"That's blasphemy," said Grasshopper. The dog's sad and glossy eyes went back and forth between Grasshopper and Alejandro.

Alejandro squinted. "You can't go around doing things just because they feel right," Alejandro said.

"People don't do stuff just because. Everybody helps somebody, hoping for something back. Don't you?" Grasshopper gave his brother an inquisitive look.

"Maybe. But what can you get out of helping a trapped dog?" Alejandro asked. He was challenging his brother.

"A grateful dog, a new friend," said Grasshopper.

"Yeah, maybe a friend," reflected Alejandro. "That wouldn't be so bad, I guess."

"I mean, you get a pretty grateful friend," said Grasshopper. "You see, so we can keep him, right?" Alejandro looked at the dog and sighed.

"Why do you always ask so many questions?" refuted Alejandro.

"C'mon! Let's keep him?"

"All right. But I already know Grandpa will say no."

⇝⇝⇛   ⇚⇜⇜

After walking about a mile, Mr. Lessar's house was now in sight. As the two shirtless boys carried the dog and approached, they saw Mrs. Lessar watering her plants on the front porch.

"Well, look at the two of you," she greeted them. "How did you get those bruises?" She looked at Alejandro.

"Hello, Mrs. Lessar. Our Grandpa told us to come and help Mr. Lessar," said Alejandro. "It's nothing. Just got tangled up in the brush."

"What you all got there?" she asked.

"A dog we found in the oil well near the train tracks," said Alejandro.

"We're not sure how hurt he is. He's covered in oil," said Grasshopper. "Can you help us clean him up?"

Mrs. Lessar looked at the two boys and then at the dog. She smiled. "Look at that poor little creature," she said. "Well, it may not be so easy, but take him to the back and put him by the basin."

"Thank you," said Grasshopper.

"I'll bring you some olive oil and soap."

It took a while for the boys to oil and soap the dog, and gradually remove the sticky tar from his fur. The dog was malnourished and his arched back resembled that of a terrified black cat.

"We'll name him Axel," said Grasshopper.

"Why would you name him that?" asked Alejandro.

"It's the name of the guy in my book. He's saved from the darkness," added Grasshopper. "But I think I can call him Moses instead. Yes, Moses was saved, too."

"You keep naming things Moses. You can't name a dog Moses!" said Alejandro. "Besides, Moses was saved from the water, not from the oil, right?" Alejandro added.

"I know. I guess I could call him Soil then," said Grasshopper as he rubbed the soap along the dog's back.

"Soil?" asked Alejandro.

"Yes, Soil, saved from the oil," said Grasshopper. "You get it?"

"You really got some brains," added Alejandro and shook his head.

⇝⇝ ⇜⇜

Soil was finally cleaned and baptized. Alejandro picked up the dog once again from the basin and put him on his four legs so he could take a little bit of sunlight. The dog tried to shake out his fur and struggled to walk at first, but after a few minutes he began wagging his tail. It was a frail but humble-looking mutt. His fur was as dark and shiny as the tar he was first found in. The pooch's brown eyes resembled a glimmer of compassion that often results from having been hurt or abused. He had a pointy nose, which made him look a bit distinguished. The boys looked at him and right away liked his semblance.

"Look at him. He's so cute," said Grasshopper.

"He's kinda cute," said Alejandro. "There're some dumb people out there."

"We won't let anyone hurt you again," said Grasshopper to Soil, patting and gently stroking the dog's head.

Mrs. Lessar brought him a bit of milk in a bowl and some leftover rib bones with meat on them on a plate. The poor animal hardly had strength to eat. He lay down next to the bowl and the plate and began to lick the milk and the remnants of meat on the rib bones. He barely had the strength to stand.

After they had taken care of Soil, they left him to rest by the basin and went looking for Mr. Lessar. In the back, apart from the house, there was a corral and further back a pigsty. As the boys approached, they looked at the horse in the corral and admired its stature. They climbed the rail fence to get a better view of the animal. For an instant they remembered their dealings with *Potro Chúcaro* at the Reys' farm. For them, it was an encounter with strength, with desire, with freedom, and they felt a sense of freedom that transcended all boundaries. Seeing the animal so close inside the corral gave them a feeling of power they enjoyed. Both humbly contemplated the movements of the animal with its majestic to-and-fro pace around the corral.

"Hey, there, we got some visitors here!" exclaimed Mr. Lessar, guiding a mare to the stable. "How are you boys doing? How's Mr. Druett doing?"

"Hello, Mr. Lessar," said Grasshopper.

"Grandpa is good. We're here to help you," said Alejandro.

"Sure," he said, "He sent me the best two workers in Russell, didn't he?" He smiled.

"That's right!" said Grasshopper. "What are the names of the horses, Mr. Lessar?"

"That's Lone Ranger and this is Wild Breeze," he said.

"Why do you call them that?" asked Grasshopper.

"Lone Ranger was the only one left of a herd of seven horses that were brought here by the farm owner. All the others were sold. I'm not sure about Wild Breeze's name. She comes from a farm up there by Sweet Heaven."

"Maybe she just runs like a breeze," said Grasshopper.

"Yeah she runs sometimes. I wish I had the tarpaulins here. Almonds are quite ready," Mr. Lessar added. He scratched his head.

"You just tell us what we're good for, Mr. Lessar," said Alejandro. Just like Grandpa, Mr. Lessar knew that having the boys work would teach them responsibility, commitment, and most importantly humility and selflessness.

"I do need to feed the pigs," stated Mr. Lessar, suggesting for the boys to follow up on the initiative. "I wanna feed them before the truck gets here. They'll be taken to the market later today." Lone Ranger started neighing as it saw Mr. Lessar leading the mare toward the corral.

"We can do that," said Alejandro. Grasshopper gave his brother a little kick on the leg.

"You sure you don't mind?" added Mr. Lessar.

"Not at all," replied Alejandro, ignoring his brother. "My little brother loves bacon, so it won't be a problem for him."

Mr. Lessar laughed. "Horses will be breeding today."

"What's breeding?" asked Grasshopper.

"What animals do before they have babies," replied Alejandro.

"I heard you got a new dog?" Mr. Lessar asked while he looped the reins of the mare to the fence.

"Yes," said Grasshopper. "His name is Soil."

"It isn't ours," said Alejandro.

"What's wrong with Soil?" Mr. Lessar asked.

"We found it in the oil well on our way here," said Alejandro.

"Where were you coming from?" asked Mr. Lessar as he put the reins around the horse's head.

"Well, we went for a dip at the river, Sir," interjected Grasshopper. "We just wanted to jump in the water for a bit, for a bath—to cool off."

"Oh, I see," replied Mr. Lessar. "Mario went fishing this morning."

"Yes. We saw him there," said Alejandro.

"Well, let me get you boys some bran so you can get your hands dirty," he said. "You can stay and watch if you want."

"Let's stay," said Grasshopper. "I've never seen horses have babies."

"There are some hay bales around the front that I gotta bring here for the horses," he said. "You'll find the bran in the storage room by the basin. And when you finish feeding the pigs you may go. I don't have much for you boys to do here today. On your way out, ask Mrs. Lessar for some lemon custard," he said as he raised his eyebrows at the boys. Grasshopper's eyes grew larger and his face lit up.

"Let me show you where the hay is," said Mr. Lessar. Alejandro and Grasshopper followed him as he made his way to the front of the house.

⇒⇒⇒ ⇐⇐⇐

After Grasshopper and Alejandro carried a few alfalfa hay bales to the corral, they carried the bran to the pigsty. The grunting of the pigs was copious when the boys entered the sty, carrying buckets filled with bran.

"They got a lot more little piggies now," said Grasshopper. "A lot of breeding here."

"Hell, yeah!" laughed Alejandro. "You wouldn't even know how pigs have so many piglets," Alejandro said.

"Yes, I know. They call that 'orificial dissemination'. That's when they put little pigs' seeds into the she-pig's snout, then little piglets are born in the pig stomach after some time," responded Grasshopper.

"How do you know that?" asked his brother.

"I read it in a magazine Grandpa has in the toolshed," said Grasshopper.

The boys looked at each other and leaned against the railing. Their gaze was curious and knowing at the same time. They studied how the pigs pushed and shoved one another by the railing of the sty, devouring the bran that the boys had poured into the feeders.

"I guess pigs can have as many piglets as they want," said Grasshopper after he saw a drift of piglets darting quickly after a larger pig. "They'd use a syringe to put tiny piggies in the mouth of mamma pig," added Grasshopper.

"A syringe?" asked Alejandro, holding on to his laughter.

"Yep, a needle."

"You mean that corkscrew needle right between his hind legs?" said Alejandro, pointing at a pig's crotch, unable to contain his laughs. Grasshopper laughed too.

"It seems they never get enough to eat," said Grasshopper.

"A pig is never full," said Alejandro. "If pigs were full, there would be no purpose for Mr. Lessar to raise them. You know, he wants these pigs to be as fat as an egg basket. He wants them to eat all they can and gain weight, so he can sell them for more money at the Sunday's market," explained Alejandro.

"The life of a pig is pretty good," said Grasshopper. "They don't have to do anything but eat, shit, and sleep."

"A grunting pig is a healthy pig, it seems," Alejandro said.

The two boys looked at the pigs pushing and shoving each other for some remnants of alfalfa and bran.

"I'd rather be no pig, but if I were one, I'd be a disgruntled pig and not one waiting to be slayed," said Alejandro.

"What do you mean?" asked Grasshopper.

"I mean I don't wanna be a well-fed, fat, happy pig waiting to be taken to the slaughterhouse," explained Alejandro. "If you were, then it'd be too late. By the time you realized what life was worth, you'd hear all the other hogs screaming their hearts out. They know that a sharp knife will pierce right through from their throats to their hearts. They're smart, too. You gotta be disgruntled so they'll know not to mess with you," explained the older brother.

"How do you know that?" Grasshopper asked.

"That's what happens to them at the market," said Alejandro. "That truck that's coming to pick them up, didn't you hear Mr. Lessar? They'll be taken straight to the slaughterhouse."

"I guess the life of a pig is pretty bad then," said Grasshopper, fixing the intense depth of his eyes on the animals. He opened his eyes first, then he squinted. Suddenly, he looked at his brother with a determined intent to right a wrong.

"Hey, let's set them free!" said Grasshopper. "Before the truck gets here."

"What?" said Alejandro. "You're crazy? We'll get Mr. Lessar in trouble.

"Come on! Let's free these hogs," replied Grasshopper.

"If Mr. Lessar finds out, he'll tell Grandpa, and we're done, you hear?" said Alejandro.

"Yeah, but you said the pigs were gonna die anyway, didn't you?" urged the boy.

"Yeah, but letting them go would be too much," said Alejandro.

"Not for the pigs. We'll be their liberators. Come on!" insisted Grasshopper. Alejandro didn't agree, but he liked the idea. He looked at his young brother and didn't want to disappoint him. They had been partners in crime, going against Grandpa's orders, riding the freight train, getting Soil out and keeping him, and now freeing the pigs.

"Let's go back to the corral and watch the horses for a while and see what Mr. Lessar is doing," said Grasshopper.

⊱⊱⊱⊱ ⊰⊰⊰⊰

Alejandro and Grasshopper approached the corral and waited until Mr. Lessar led Wild Breeze into the corral. The mare hesitated a bit as it entered the corral. Then he tied her to a hitching rail. He wore black rubber gloves and a bucket with warm water and a towel. They saw how she neighed and moved away from Lone Ranger. Mr. Lessar couldn't get her to stand still as he brought the stallion near her. Lone Ranger's flaccid phallus all of a sudden began to stretch, hung loosely, then stiffened before mounting the mare.

"His wanger's out!" shouted Grasshopper.

"Help me out here," he said to Alejandro.

"Right away," he said as he jumped over the railing.

"Hold her still," he extended the reins to him, signaling for Alejandro to grab the reins. Lone Ranger kept neighing and quickly pacing back and forth as Mr. Lessar brought him about to mount Wild Breeze. Grasshopper observed the mare moving away then standing still. Mr. Lessar put Lone Ranger into position and the mare urinated profusely.

Lone Ranger began to neigh, and Wild Breeze's hind legs shook. She seemed nervous.

Lone Ranger got on its hind legs and mounted Wild Breeze, pushing forward, attempting to insert its horsehood into the mare's.

"What the heck is he doing to her?" said Grasshopper while he looked at the scene in disgust.

"They're making babies," said Alejandro. The horse aimed but couldn't penetrate the mare.

"Hold her still," said Mr. Lessar.

"Shhhhh! Shhhhh!" Alejandro tried to soothe Wild Breeze by placing his hand on her pelage until Lone Ranger mounted her. The horse neighed a bit more, now stamping abruptly, behind the mare. The muscles of its hind legs shivered and became more defined. Then Lone Ranger shivered a bit more, peeling its teeth and trying to bite Wild Breeze's mane, while they made babies. All of them looked at Lone Ranger for a moment while it kept itself on Wild Breeze. And then Lone Ranger ceased.

Grasshopper was serious. He had never experienced such an exchange—breeding.

"They'll breed good," said Mr. Lessar. He massaged the area around Lone Ranger's phallus.

"So they have babies like this?" said Grasshopper.

"Oh, yes they will," said Mr. Lessar. "A healthy, strong horse and mare, and you'll have a fine specimen."

"What's a specimen?" Alejandro asked.

"One of its kind," said Mr. Lessar. "We got to let them cool down." Mr. Lessar untied Wild Breeze, leading her out of the corral and into a pasture behind the pigsty.

"We've got to breed them again tomorrow," Mr. Lessar said.

Alejandro exited the corral. "Mr. Lessar, we just gotta pour some water into the tank in the pigsty," said Alejandro.

"Let me take care of that," said Mr. Lessar.

"Are you sure?" said Alejandro.

"Yeah, I got to get some water for the horses, too, and take the mare outback. Don't forget to get some lemon custard before you go. And tell Mr. Druett I said thank you," Mr. Lessar added.

Once Mr. Lessar was gone, Grasshopper and Alejandro ran back to the pigsty. Alejandro looked at Grasshopper and they both knew what was next. As they neared the sty, the pigs began to raise their long snouts, making repeated grunts in the direction of the gate, as if they knew why the boys were there. The buckets that Mr. Lessar carried squeaked, and before he saw them, the boys ducked behind the fence. As he approached, Mr. Lessar whistled just as the buckets squeaked.

"He thinks we're already gone," whispered Grasshopper as he looked over the fence to see the man.

"Yeah, he didn't even look around to see if we were still here," said Alejandro.

"I told you," said Grasshopper.

Mr. Lessar sunk the buckets in a barrel by the door and walked back near the corral and poured the contents of the buckets into a water tank. Grasshopper squatted sideways and threw his right arm over the fence to undo the gate latch.

"Let's not do this," murmured Alejandro. "It doesn't feel right."

"We're doing it now," whispered Grasshopper.

"Let's go now. He'll see us," whispered Alejandro as he motioned for them to find the exit. The whistle of the train echoed afar.

"We need to get Soil," said Grasshopper.

"I'll get him," replied Alejandro. "I'll meet you by the side of the house."

"Get the pie, too," whispered Grasshopper.

The gate of the pigsty was now unlocked, and Grasshopper gave a subtle kick to it, so the swine would follow. The sharp creaking of the gate was now audible and visible to the pigs. He easily slipped away through a couple of loose planks in the fence adjacent to the pigsty. Mr. Lessar didn't notice him, but he quickly realized what had happened.

"Crazy kids left the gate unlocked," said the man as he put down the buckets and approached the sty. He reached the gate, but as he tried to hold back the pigs that were already exiting the sty, pigs and piglets muscled their way out, popping both doors open. Grunting and squealing, the hogs scattered through the yard and around the corral and then disappeared through the rows of grape vines bordering the house.

⟫ ⟪

As the boys ran to the train tracks, Alejandro carried the dog in his arms while Grasshopper hauled a container with the lemon custard in a burlap bag. He ran behind Alejandro, leaving a cloud of dust behind him. They stopped and rested when they were tired. Soil was still too weak to run on his own. They had walked for a long while when they could hear the horn of the train in the distance. As they approached the train tracks, they could hear the slow approach of the steel wheels on the rails.

"Here, hold Soil for a bit," said Alejandro.

"We'll get on the train; it's coming slow," said Grasshopper. "How'll I get on the train carrying Soil?" asked Grasshopper. The same train the boys had ridden on their way to Mr. Lessar's was now returning with empty wagons. On the way back, the train was not loaded, but it slowed its pace as it reached the bends and cut through *callejónes*, making it easier to board.

"Here," Alejandro said, pulling out the plastic container with the lemon custard in it and holding the burlap bag. "Put Soil inside the bag." Alejandro held the bag handle with one hand and made a movement for Grasshopper to grab the other handle, as if to open it to put the dog in it.

"Good idea," said Grasshopper. Once the dog was in the bag, Grasshopper opened the container and took a bite of the lemon custard. He passed a piece to his brother before the train approached. "You get on first so you can catch up with me and pick up Soil," Alejandro quickly said to his brother. As the locomotive passed in front of them, Alejandro began running.

Alejandro ran about thirty yards in front of his brother. Grasshopper got on the train first. Once he was on board, Alejandro ran along the train and handed the burlap bag with Soil in it to Grasshopper. Then he climbed up. Once on the train, they moved through the wagons until they found a space to settle as the train moved along. They laughed, looked at each other, and sat between wagons, petting Soil and eating the custard.

"What are we gonna tell Grandpa?" asked Grasshopper.

"I don't know. We'll tell Grandma first," Alejandro answered.

"What do you think she'll say?"

"That this is a bad idea for sure," said Alejandro.

"I kinda like Soil already. Look at him," said Grasshopper as he petted the dog. "The train's going so slow."

"We'll be able to get off with no problem," said Alejandro, "just like we got on."

⟫ ⟪

The train was now near the homestead. And as it cut across dirt roads that intersected the railroad tracks, the arm gates came down to stop car traffic. The train kept moving at a slow pace.

"You can call yourself 'a hog liberator' now," said Alejandro to Grasshopper, waiting to see his reaction.

"That's right," Grasshopper said. "We've done some good deeds for the little critters today." They laughed.

At first, they were a bit remorseful about setting the pigs free at Mr. Lessar's, then anxious about catching the train while carrying the dog. But as they settled on the train, they felt a sense of ownership of it all, as if life was at their disposal, as if they could control all the forces they encountered in Russell. They fed Soil a piece of lemon custard and ate the rest of it while they sat on the steel surface between the wagons.

The traffic had stopped to yield for the train to pass. It was near noon and drivers hung their arms out of their cars and trucks while they waited. Some of them noticed the boys in between the wagons and began waving at them. They whistled and shouted indistinctive cries followed by laughter. Grasshopper pointed his middle finger at them.

"Those fools are making fun of us," he told Alejandro.

The men laughed even more. Grasshopper got up and held on to the metal ladder that ran to the top of the wagon and waved back at them to get their attention. He then climbed the steps to reach the top of the wagon. Alejandro followed him, carrying Soil in the bag. Then when Grasshopper saw they were looking at him again, he turned around, pulled down his pants and mooned them. "Laugh now, you fools!" he screamed.

He was the center of their attention, and as folks waved, they blew their raucous horns as a sign of amusement, or approval perhaps. Grasshopper made indistinct gestures of prowess, flexing his still languid biceps, exhibiting his faint arm muscles, lengthening his torso, standing akimbo, and hitting his chest to show all of them who was in control. They laughed and pointed their fingers at him.

As the wagon on which the boys stood passed in front of the bar that blocked traffic, a bus with locals from Russell waited at the front of the line. Now with his pants up, Grasshopper kept issuing gestures at them while Alejandro and the others laughed.

"Hey, you there!" pointed Grasshopper at those who laughed and sat in their cars or in the front seats of the bus. He then turned around once again, pulled down his pants, and mooned the front passengers and bus driver, who were staring at him. The pace of the train slowed down even more, making Grasshopper's show last even longer. The passengers laughed while the bus driver shook his head.

In an instant, Alejandro's face turned pale, and the glee that filled his smile was suddenly gone.

"Grandma!" said Alejandro as he tried to reach and pull his brother down so he could sit. Grasshopper was still mooning everyone.

"We'll worry about her later," said Grasshopper as he stood half naked, showing his buttocks, wobbling his rear.

"There, you fool!" rebuked Alejandro, pointing at the bus.

"What?" asked the boy, looking at the bus.

On the front seat next to the bus driver, Grandma was sitting in a comfortable and graceful position as she stared at the boys. She wanted to laugh but kept her composure and looked in the opposite direction. Once she realized the boys had seen her, she squinted and shook her head, indicating the punishment that awaited the boys. Grasshopper covered his face with his hands, not turning around, hoping that Grandma wouldn't recognize him. Alejandro brought Soil closer to him and turned his face in the opposite direction. The train kept rolling along.

"What are we gonna tell Grandpa now?" said Alejandro.

"I don't know. We won't say anything!" said Grasshopper, after the train had gone out of sight.

"Damn, we gotta get off now," said Alejandro as the train approached the bend.

"I'll get down this time and you hand me Soil," said Grasshopper.

"No, you'll hand Soil to me," said Alejandro.

Alejandro got down and ran alongside the train while Grasshopper handed him the dog. Then Grasshopper jumped off from the train and kept running alongside it. As they walked away from the tracks, they were near the homestead, and so was Grandma, who had returned from shopping and running errands.

"We gotta get there before Grandma does," urged Grasshopper.

"She's already seen us," said Alejandro.

They knew that it would be easier to deny what she had witnessed if they arrived first at the homestead. At least for Soil, he had been saved from the dark and sticky mire of oil and tar; but for the boys, they would soon be stuck in a deep mire of trouble.

At the Dinner Table

Thunder rumbled and dark clouds blanketed the sky as the gentle twitching of raindrops on acacia leaves announced the oncoming storm. The boys had arrived before Grandma; they came back running from the train tracks, hoping to avoid the rain, lightning, and punishment. Grandpa was picking cucumbers, so they went and took a nap and pretended to be asleep.

A couple of hours had passed when Grasshopper came into the kitchen.

"Look, Grandma, I got goosamps," said Grasshopper after he entered the kitchen.

"Goosamps? How was work at Mr. Lessar's today?" asked Grandma while she looked at Grasshopper and felt his forehead. "Those aren't goosebumps," said Grandma. She examined the rash on the boy's arms.

"Mr. Lessar told us there wasn't much work to do," said Grasshopper, looking up and staring at Grandma. His eyelashes fluttered desperately like a young, hopeless fledgling, struggling to take flight.

"And your shirt?" asked Grandma.

"Oh, we went and jumped in the river," he replied. "We found a dog." Alejandro came in too.

"What dog? Whose dog?" asked Grandma.

"He's nobody's dog," Alejandro interjected. "Some mean Joe threw him in the oil well. We got it out while we were on our way to Mr. Lessar's. Mrs. Lessar helped us clean him up."

He's ours now," said Grasshopper.

"Let me see your arms again," Grandma asked. She examined the boy's arm.

"Can we keep him?" Grasshopper asked.

"We'll see," she said. "Go and wash off. Dinner will be ready soon. Uncle Mike and Aunt Ana are here."

"Really? All right!" said Grasshopper.

Dinner at the homestead was always special. Grandpa sat at the head of the table, in front of the China cabinet. Whenever they had visitors, Grandma sat across from him at the other end of the table, near the wood-burning stove, where she kept a coffee percolator, a kettle with boiling water, and another steaming pot with aromatic herbs. The pungent aroma of eucalyptus pervaded the kitchen. It was common for folks in Russell to keep steaming herbs at home.

The ambiance in the kitchen was pleasant. When the whole family was gathered, it was an enjoyable time. Everyone was there that evening. Uncle Mike, Aunt Ana, Rolando, Aunt Claudia and Rosy.

"Pa, you want tea right now?" Grandma asked Grandpa while she held a metal bowl and whisked its content.

"Yes, but after you're done there, Darling," said Grandpa. "I can pour it." Grandpa got up and walked toward the kettle.

"The bayonnaise is almost ready," said Grandma and looked at Grasshopper.

"But Grandma, why do you always say bayonnaise? It's mayonnaise," he corrected her.

"I know. I just like saying it that way," said Grandma.

Everyone at the table chuckled. Grandma did too, for she knew and always expected Grasshopper's witty response.

The entire family ate together. Alejandro usually sat on Grandpa's right-hand side. Aunt Claudia, who sometimes preferred to sit next to Alejandro, sat next to Grandma on her left side. And Grasshopper next to Grandma as well, but on her right side. Rolando, the boys' older cousin, sat across from Alejandro and next to Aunt Ana, who sat across from Uncle Mike. Aunt Rosy, who was always late to any family gathering, often sat next to Aunt Ana, who would help Grandma pass out the food and drinks. Though she preferred to sit next to Aunt Claudia whenever she could. No one ever sat next to Uncle Mike, for he always took almost two chairs for himself. Grasshopper and Rolando always picked on him. But it was healthy humor that Uncle Mike welcomed.

"Guess who brought dessert today?" asked Rolando. He was two years older than Alejandro. His hair often covered one of his eyes and he had pimples and redness on his face.

"I did," replied Uncle Mike, laughing.

"What's for dessert, Uncle?" asked Grasshopper.

"Watermelon!" replied Mike, holding his belly. They all laughed.

"Don't eat the dessert before the meal," said Alejandro. Grandpa grinned.

"You ate it already," said Grasshopper laughing. Everyone laughed.

Behind Aunt Claudia was the wood-burning stove Grandpa had handcrafted.

"You flutter your eyelashes just like your mother," said Grandpa to Grasshopper, reminiscing his daughter's childhood. Alejandro and Grasshopper's parents, Adie and Frank, have been gone for a few years now, and the void of their presence was still reminiscent among them. Except for the sound of the coffee percolator and the simmering water on the stove, a deep pause remained.

"You do," said Aunt Ana to fill the void.

"Let's not talk about the accident again," said Grandma.

"Aunt Adie was so nice," Rolando added.

"So was Frank," said Uncle Mike.

"They worked so hard to get what you needed," Grandma said in a nostalgic voice. She couldn't resist mentioning them. Alejandro and Grasshopper just listened. A tear dropped by the side of her face.

"I remember the day after Grassy was born," said Aunt Claudia to ease the tension. "We couldn't get in the hospital, so Frank held him up like he had just won a trophy or something. It was so funny. We could see Frank through the hospital window showing Grasshopper up from the 3rd floor."

Everyone at the table laughed as Aunt Claudia told the story.

"A really nice trophy he was," said Grandpa. Everyone laughed.

"Yeah, Dad felt he had a trophy until he had to change his diapers," said Alejandro. Everyone kept laughing at the table and eying Grasshopper.

"Then he got a real trophy," added Uncle Mike, showing no emotion.

"Yeah, and some of you used to change my diapers, too. How about getting those trophies?" Grasshopper said, laughing and pointing his finger at everyone. It was a lot easier for everyone to talk about the good memories.

"Why do you have to talk about that at the table?" Grandma reproached, drying her eyes.

"Grandpa, tell us the story about the mountain lion," Grasshopper said. Reading, telling stories, getting into mischief were Grasshopper's ways of blocking the memories, the fact of not having his parents around anymore.

"Yeah, Grandpa," said Alejandro and Rolando.

"Finish eating," said Grandma.

"Can I have some more chicken?" Grasshopper asked. "And some cornbread too?"

"Me too!" said Rolando.

"I want some more too," said Aunt Claudia.

Grandma passed along the basket with cornbread and the bowl with pieces of roasted chicken.

"Can I get a leg this time? Last time I got the bum," Grasshopper complained before Grandma added a piece on his plate.

"Got the chicken butt again?" asked Aunt Claudia.

"I don't like that," said Grasshopper.

"Here," said Alejandro, holding up the wishbone and hoping to break it with Rolando.

"I know why you wanna win it," said Rolando.

"You know nothing, you brat," replied Alejandro.

"A wish for a girl!!!" chanted Rolando, looking at his cousin and raising his eyebrows in a suggestive manner.

Grasshopper gave both of them a stare.

Grandma looked at Alejandro. Although Grandpa didn't say anything, he cast a look upon him as if they both knew what Rolando was talking about. Aunt Claudia and Ana chuckled while Uncle Mike coughed after sipping on his wine glass.

"How's work?" asked Grandpa. Uncle Mike eyed Grandma.

"Well, you know. It's good," replied Uncle Mike. "Pretty good stock!" he added, lowering his gaze. He then took the last bite out of a piece of cornbread.

"Why don't you tell the truth?" said Aunt Ana.

Grandpa cocked his head, raised an eyebrow, and looked at Uncle Mike. Grandma passed around the basket with cornbread.

"Well, I've been laid off. Most of the workers have," said Mike. "There is no need for hand labor. No more sorting olives."

"These people are always making promises they can't keep, and then they just let you go. They just replace you like a broken crate," said Aunt Ana.

"With the new machines they are bringing, there is no need for workers anymore," said Uncle Mike.

"Just like they did with Carlos. They made him travel a thousand miles, promising work. And for what?" asked Aunt Ana.

"What are you gonna do?" asked Grandpa, looking at Uncle Mike.

"How did Uncle Carlos die?" asked Grasshopper.

"Sshhhh!" said Grandma. "Don't speak when adults are talking."

"Well, I'm looking," said Uncle Mike. "I've talked to the foreman at the refinery, and he said he'll let me know as soon as there's an opening."

"You can always come and work around these parts," said Grandpa as he coughed.

"Thank you, but I'm not cut out for farm work," said Uncle Mike. "I just gotta have a clock to punch in and out."

"Yeah, we all do," said Grandpa, squinting at his son-in-law.

"They'll soon be hiring for the Wine Fest," said Grandma.

"Oh, yeah," said Aunt Ana. "We ought to try that."

"Speaking of work," said Grandpa. "How did you guys do with Mr. Lessar?"

"We did really good," said Alejandro.

"We found a dog," said Grasshopper. "We got to see how horses have babies, too."

Grandma looked at Grandpa.

"What did you see?" asked Aunt Claudia.

"It was nothing surprising. I read all about breeding and sex seeds in the *Digest*," said Grasshopper, with an air of confidence.

"What about the dog?" said Grandpa.

"Yeah, his name is Soil," he said. "Can we keep him?"

"You brought him here?" asked Grandpa.

"Yeah," said Grasshopper. "He's in the back by the basin. Mrs. Lessar helped us clean him. Can we keep him?"

Grandpa just looked at Grandma.

The day had grown dark at the homestead. Aunt Ana, Rolando, and Uncle Mike had left. Grandpa sat near the stove—Grasshopper and Alejandro by his side—and Grandma prepared hot coffee and tea. Aunt Claudia and Aunt Rosy had gone back to downtown Russell.

"Were you there when the lion ate that man?" asked Grasshopper, looking at Grandpa. Grandpa had told the story before, but every time he told it, he seemed to add a new detail that made it more interesting. And he didn't mind doing that. The kids liked it.

"Yes," said Grandpa. "But I didn't see it."

"How did it happen?" asked the boy.

"It was too dark," said Grandpa.

"Tell us, please!" Grasshopper begged him.

"It's already too late," said Grandpa.

"Please, Grandpa, tell us again."

"It's time for you to go to bed. He'll tell it to you tomorrow," said Grandma.

Disappointed, the boys got up and went to their room.

"It would be good for them to have a pet of their own. Don't you think?" said Grandma.

"Maybe," said Grandpa. "A bit more responsibility may be too much."

"They're always working. Having to feed the dog will give them more of a reason to be at home. They spend too much time wandering around the farms," said Grandma.

Kaiser was Grandpa's dog and didn't seem to require much care. Soil, on the contrary, was still a frail young pup that would suit the boys well, especially Grasshopper.

"Sounds like a new dog will be good for them," said Grandpa.

Fallen Souls

In the stillness of the night, Alvera and Alejandro rested on the roof of the adobe house. There was something special about being on the roof. They knew Grandpa or Grandma wouldn't come around, especially at night.

"Do you love me?" Alvera asked Alejandro. She rested her arms and head on his chest and looked at him.

"I do," he said.

"How much do you love me?" she asked, smiling at him.

"I love you as the flowers in the fields love sunlight," he said.

She gently closed her eyes and kissed him.

The fertile soil and lush foliage of the valley converged into a perfect and consensual union. The beauty of the valley resonated. It was exalted by its hues, shapes, aromas, by the natural whispering of the winds, the chirping of birds, and the murmurs of farmworkers embedded in the lush foliage during the harvesting seasons.

The land had been generous to the hands that harvested; it was an imperfect body waiting to be nurtured once again. And while the men tended the land year after year, the land bore its promise. Land, oh sweet land, how sweet this land was, how sweet this land was to give herself up to the hands and arms that caressed her. The pressing hands that caressed the luscious and plump clusters of ripened grapes exuded their sap in the vineyards around Russell. This was maturity's mettle, making the fruit and its imminent taste enticing.

Before the spring, the grape buds were dormant, but then they burst out into full blossoms, dropping their calyptra in the early spring. Birds and bees coasted from field to field, transferring the pollen grains to the stigma of the brightest and most colorful flowers. And all grew well and all in due time yielded its fruit. In the stillness of the landscape, light pappuses of dandelions drifted aimlessly and free through the air and fell as softly as the morning dew on the furrows between the blossoming buds and leaves of the grapevines.

Late in the summers, the hands of laborers seemed to fondle the contour of each grape cluster that was as delicate as the skin of the women in the fields. The men snapped the fruit from the vines in the summer and disrobed the vineyard of its verdant dress. They left behind rows quilted with dead leaves, withered remnants under the force of decay that waited for the cold, rain, and wind of an inclement autumn to do its part.

Along the banks of the main streams that irrigated the vineyards of the valley, beds of wild roses hung their scarlet blossoms over the water. Their docile petals kissed the ripples of water on the surface, like the fresh crimson lips of young lovers, driven by the impatient current below. The opaque rocks and sediment on the stream bottom contrasted with the transparent petals on the surface. And the soil, water, and vegetation became one amalgamating force that unified all the land.

In the summer, clusters of grapes glistened with the fresh morning dew. Gleaming droplets dripped like pearls from each grape cluster. As the dew receded from each cluster–like the melting snow high in the peaks of the Great Endes Mountains, like the condensing sweat on the harvesters' foreheads and backs— it burst onto the jagged, cloddy soil below, absorbing its moisture.

Plowed and immaculate furrows opened to receive the new seeds together with the rain and hail that pelted and softened the land. Rainwaters became shallow streams that irrigated the fields and parcels down in the valley. Carmine petals and other vegetation were sent adrift by mad and impetuous streams that surged through the clods. Water and earth merged into one to nourish the crops and to quench the thirst of life in the dry and dusty fields once again.

Gentle thrushes with their elongated beaks, pierced the grapes, figs, and cherries left behind by the harvest. They sucked out the sweet sap and dropped the seed to impregnate the soil below. A wild thrush sings, wailing through the foliage, through the vineyards, and through a land that announces life's bliss. Thus the land receives the seed and gives form to its fruit, to its offspring.

The rain, thunder, and winds came pushing their way in. The land nurtured the seeds and the crops flourished, and so did the grapes and the women. And once the rain subsided and the fields rested, languid and uncluttered, silence abounded. All in nature came together as one. All was redeemable. All merged into water, wind, soil, and work within the stillness of the opulent vegetation around Russell.

Vines revealed copious clusters of grapes as the generous hand of nature offered its bounty. The lushness of the land burst open to uncover the raw, naked furrow and the aroma of moist soil wafted upwards, pervading the air. Delicate grape clusters dangled loosely in the wind, slightly rubbing against each other with flirtatious ease, at times offering their naked beauty to the natural world around, at times covering it with their leafy foliage. Trunks and branches of grape vines stretched out like elongated, muscular, and venous arms, legs, and tendrils, as if reaching for comfort and warmth from the sun; as if reaching down through their roots to the plump and damp soil; the impending forces of nature at work intertwined all at once through the rows in the vineyards like the fiery embrace of young lovers.

Days went by and the atmosphere was inebriated by the sweet aroma of ripened grapes that scented the air. The days transcended and dissipated rapidly into a climatic trance. The chirping of thrushes announced the sunrise while the twilight drew flocks of birds into the sunset.

With every dawn, the sunlight expanded over the farms again, beckoning the day like the gentle awakening of two eyelids to the morning light. Thus, the morning dropped its drizzle onto the vines, onto the soft unsullied neck of the shoots that hadn't yet been snapped. The vines surrendered themselves to the warm rays from above to begin each day anew. The stillness of the mornings became palpable as the fresh dew dropped its soft blanket on the vineyards once more, like a tender mantling, a peaceful copulation that was repeated through the days, the weeks, the seasons, and the years.

In the fall, the winds blew through Russell and insects and birds took whatever shelter they could find in the vines and trees that the harvesters had not stripped away from their fruit. The fields were barren and bleak amidst the tawny hues of the seasonal foliage. Remnants of vine shoots left behind from the pruning season stuck erected out of the plowed soil of the furrows. And until the next season, the land waited to be nurtured again. The cycle took place every year at the same time, like a rendezvous of young lovers gone mad and intoxicated by ripened nectar, trapped in an endless swirl, in a desperate impulse to coalesce in body and spirit with the elements and with themselves.

The cycle began as rough gusts plunged down the marble slopes of the mountainside, following along the chiseled skirts of the Great Endes Mountain, and sweeping into the valley. Reaching the farming fields, the winds shook the fragile blossoms, dancing swiftly and swirly, carelessly caressing the clusters once again.

"I better get going," said Alvera, smiling. Alejandro stretched out his hand to touch her, to caress her skin before she left, as she got up and smiled at him, and then climbed down one of the ladders Grandpa used to harvest olives. Their eyes met once again under the moonlight before Alvera departed.

Alejandro kept looking at the stars. The whole world was perfect for him. What else could he ask for? Alvera, the girl he loved, loved him immensely. He sighed and contemplated the quiet night and closed his eyes to feel that spirit that unifies it all.

"What are you doing up here all by your lonesome?" Grasshopper said as he suddenly popped his head by the side of the roof.

"Alvera was just here," Alejandro said.

"Look at the stars. They're so bright tonight," said Grasshopper, climbing on the roof and lying next to his brother.

"That's Delphinus," Alejandro pointed out, as both of them contemplated the night sky.

"I wonder what's behind the stars," said Grasshopper.

"That's just a mystery we've gotta live with," said Alejandro as he stared at the sky with his arms folded behind his head.

"Some are brighter than others," Grasshopper contemplated. "Some seem to take away light from the others. You see? Some are more brighter than the others!"

"They sure are." Alejandro kept his sight fixed on a bright star.

"All of them are bright and beautiful. They all have a place in heaven," said Grasshopper.

"They do," said Alejandro, sighing. "Some seem to dim while others become brighter."

"That's true. The brighter ones dim too."

"They sure do. That's the balance they keep, I guess." Alejandro looked at his brother.

"I wonder if Mom and Dad live in those stars we see," said Grasshopper.

"They do. They're watching us now," said Alejandro.

Grasshopper sighed. "They're always watching us. I wonder what would happen if all the dimmer stars would fall," said Grasshopper.

"We wouldn't have as many stars up in the sky at night," replied Alejandro.

"I wonder what the sky would look like if there were only a few bright stars and all of the other stars that are not so bright were gone?"

"I guess it'd be pretty dark," Alejandro concluded.

"We probably wouldn't have such a pretty sight tonight."

"We probably wouldn't. It's getting a bit late. I've got to help Mr. Reys in the morning. We've got to be at the market by three," said Alejandro as the two brothers stood and came down from the roof.

"I won't have to get up so early. You're gonna have a long day tomorrow," said Grasshopper.

"I sure will. Mr. Martinet is picking us up at seven," explained Alejandro.

"I hope Grandpa lets us keep Soil," said Grasshopper.

"I think he will."

Unforgiven Debt

Mr. Reys had asked Mario and Alejandro to go with him to unload and deliver crates of cherries at the market. So he and Mario picked up Alejandro early in the morning.

The truck moved slowly. With approximately 300 crates full of cherries, it seemed to stagger under such weight. A truckload of 300 crates per day at the market was common during the harvest season. In Russell, men would load trucks full of grapes, apples, cucumbers, almonds, tomatoes, and watermelons, as well as crates of olives, peaches, bell peppers, cherries, and an array of other fruits and vegetables. The air at the market was filled with the fresh, dense scent of the crops.

On their way to the market, Alejandro rode on the canopy of the truck while Mr. Reys and Mario were inside the cabin. When they arrived at the market, they joined a caravan of trucks that waited to unload their cargo. Dawn had not yet cracked, so the men caught up on their sleep while they waited for their turn to unload.

The roaring of truck engines and the smell of diesel fumes pervaded the air as they gradually moved up the line. Mario dozed inside the cabin while Alejandro lay on the canopy. After a while, Mr. Reys unfolded what looked like a bill and paperwork and walked up the line toward the gate of the market.

"Gotta move this old clunker up!" said Mr. Reys upon returning, waking up Mario and Alejandro. Mario got out of the cabin, pulled a long yawn, stretched his arms, and lit a cigarette.

"You got caught sleeping on the job," said Alejandro to Mario. He smiled.

"I wasn't sleeping," said Mario, rubbing his eyes. "I was just counting some mighty sheep with my eyes closed." Alejandro laughed. Mr. Reys mounted the cabin, pressed the gas pedal, and steered the truck through the gates.

"You gentlemen watch me while I park it," said Mr. Reys as he pushed down the glass on the driver-side window with one hand and cranked the handle with the other.

"Let me do it, Mr. Reys," suggested Mario.

"You think I'm too old to do this?" he replied, laughing at Mario and looking in the driver-side mirror. The engine of the truck roared.

"Not at all, Sir. Just giving you a break from driving," said Mario. The truck moved forward.

"He won't let nobody else drive the truck," Alejandro said.

"I know. I was just giving him a hard time," Mario laughed, grinning at Alejandro.

"Old timers tend to hold on hard to what they have," replied Alejandro.

"They do. I drove his truck once," Mario said.

"You did?"

"Yeah, one time he lent it to us to pick up a crew near Sweet Heaven."

"How did you pull that one off?"

"My dad convinced him."

"All right, brave men," interrupted Mr. Reys. "Let's get this baby started. I know Martinet is picking this young fellow here up at seven."

"Yes, he is," said Alejandro.

It took the men exactly one hour to unload the truck. By the time they had finished unloading, the stars were still out, and the fresh scent of the morning combined with that of the fruits and vegetables at the market was enticing.

"I gotta run an errand for my Grandma and get me one of the red ones over there," said Alejandro as he walked over to a green, wooden stand topped with glossy red apples.

Mr. Reys nodded and smiled at him.

On his way there, Alejandro noticed Mr. Rollies' meat stand. He was a butcher and a friend of Grandpa. Alejandro approached the stand. When Mr. Rollies saw him, he smiled at him and said his common phrase about the Druett boys. "How are little mischiefs doing?"

Alejandro smiled, "Good, Mr. Rollies. How about yourself?"

"Oh, I'm doing great! Just one day at a time," he replied as he shaved a few filets of cow tongue with the edge of his knife. The pinkish tongue looked languid on the cutting board. The blade of the knife slid softly and smoothly through the soft texture of the meat, revealing its red, dark insides.

Mr. Rollies was quite a character. He was short and baldheaded and had long patches of glossy dark hair right above the ears. He had a thin pencil mustache right above his upper lip, which made him look deceitful, cunning, and funny. He held a toothpick he fiddled with from one side of his mouth to the other, then to the center between a set of gapped teeth that were all too noticeable when he smiled. He had a humorous smile. His face emitted a kind of amusement that entertained his customers, which kept them coming back for more meat and laughter.

"This cow right here didn't get to say a thing before she died," he said, slicing the tongue filet. His customers laughed.

He also liked to pick on the kids, but his humor was friendly and healthy. Grasshopper often joked and said that the shiny spot on Mr. Rollies' bald head was a sign of his brilliance.

"He's a brilliant man with a bright future and head," Grasshopper often said.

The kids often joked about the man who always teased them when they went to the market, but they never openly disrespected him. The jokes were more of a secret kids' play to laugh about between themselves.

The inside of the market was well lit. The radiant glare emitted by the neon lights reflected an arcoiris, a rainbow of lively hues of the fruits and vegetables there. Dawn had not yet broken into the clarity of day, but the voices of men calling out the various fruits and vegetables, prices and offers, made the morning as lively as if the sun had already risen. The black price tags stood out among the colorful displays of the fruit, while the price and weight were written on them with white chalk. Alejandro looked at a pile of apples, picked one up, and admired its contour. He puffed a couple of breaths on the glossy skin of the fruit and then rubbed it against his shirt before taking a bite. He savored its sweet-tart and sandy nectar as its crisp pieces crunched in his mouth. Cutting across from among the other fruit stands, a short, plump man wearing a dark green apron approached Alejandro.

"That'll be two silver coins, young lad," he said. Alejandro just stood there serious, about the whole situation.

"Two coins for one apple?" said Alejandro. "I only got one."

"That's right," affirmed the man as he got closer and looked at Alejandro.

"An apple don't cost no two silver coins," Alejandro replied. He squinted.

In Alejandro's mind, two silver coins was too much for an apple. It did not reckon with what he, his grandfather, and other laborers earned in the orchards. It did reckon with what the landowners paid sharecroppers for harvesting the fruit.

"The sign says it," said the man.

"Well, I don't have no two silver coins, Sir," replied Alejandro.

"Well, my young fellow, you won't pick and eat a piece of fruit here and not pay for it," he replied.

"Those apples where I live," Alejandro said, pointing to the fruits, "don't cost that much. You just pick them from a tree."

"Let him have it," said a gritty voice behind Alejandro. The voice was deep and commanding. Quietly obedient, the plump man returned to tend the other piles of fruits on the stands adjacent to Alejandro as he wiped his hands on the apron. Alejandro turned and looked as far as the row of fruit stands ended. There in the darkness, he fixed his sight on the point from where the voice had come. He could distinguish a few dark silhouettes in the shadows far beyond the eaves of the market roof. The shadows faded away, but they were still visible due to the stark darkness in that area and the imminent rise of the sun in the distance. Among the three shadows, he recognized the voice.

"I know him," the voice said. He grunted.

"If I could sell the air we breathe, I would," said a different high-pitched voice. "I don't know why you gave that apple away."

"It's just an apple. And I'm not giving anything away. That lad works for me," said the deep voice. As Alejandro got closer, the three shadows appeared to turn in his direction. They whispered to one another. Alejandro recognized the deep voice and the grunting.

"Dr. Maxim?" he asked into the darkness.

"Don't they get enough already?" said a third voice whose shadow seemed to make hand gestures of disagreement toward the other two.

"You got to let them have a little something. If you don't, they start crying," replied Dr. Maxim.

"That's right, that's right!" the high-pitched voice agreed.

In an effort to figure out who the men were, Alejandro moved closer to the three shades.

"Dr. Maxim? Is it you?" Alejandro asked again. Dr. Maxim had come far enough into the light for Alejandro to distinguish his face. The other two shadows remained motionless and attentive.

"You better carry some money with you the next time you come to the market," the doctor said, looking down.

"We haven't been paid yet," said Alejandro. "The little money I had from some of the work I've done, I gave it all to my Grandma for groceries. I only got one silver coin left."

"You do good, boy, by helping your grandma," said the doctor. His eyes showed a measure of disdain mixed with embarrassment and guilt. His tone didn't convey the trust and goodwill that most men in Russell had when they talked about work and money with one another, nor could he bring himself to look Alejandro in the eye.

"I've been thinking that once we're paid, we'll have enough money for half of the payment on a land lot," said Alejandro.

"What?" inquired Dr. Maxim, he seemed surprised and a bit amused. "What do you need a lot for?" Dr. Maxim's eyes wandered from side to side, avoiding looking at Alejandro, but studying his intentions.

"My Grandpa is getting old and I want to take care of my family," he said.

"Listen, as long as you work my farm, like your grandpa, you will have a roof over your head," replied Dr. Maxim.

Alejandro squinted and looked at him. "I can get and start a farm too," said Alejandro, raising his head at Dr. Maxim.

"You ought to stick to what you are already good at," Maxim added. "Besides, land is way out of your reach."

Alejandro didn't answer him this time. But an overwhelming weight of impotence pressed on his chest. Discouraged, he looked around and saw the profuse emissions from the trucks behind the gate that were waiting to unload. The loud acceleration of the trucks filled the air just as Dr. Maxim and the two other men became fully visible. Alejandro did not recognize the other two men, but they studied him and stared at his clothes and shoes.

In the light of day, the market became livelier by the minute. Many of the trucks had unloaded and were now driving away. The bounty of produce the market displayed, and the price tags that stated the value of a long season of hard work, mirrored an opaque image of the labor of the men and women in Russell. Men and women, who in the whole of life, had to take part in it all: from preparation of the soil to planting of the seeds; from germination to sprout; from nurturing to growth; from flowering initiation to trying patience; from prime maturation to arduous harvesting; from capricious prices to fruitful profits.

But in the same fashion the men and women in Russell depended on the soil and their livelihood to survive, there were men who depended on the effort of others so they could co-exist. Men in their whole made the market prosperous and whose labor and intentions defined their worth and their profit. No matter who they were, they carried with them a number on what they could produce, as long as they could simply work and maintain the cycle as it was.

"My grandpa is getting older. I ought to help, you know," said Alejandro to bring the talk to an end.

"You let me know when you are ready to take over the farm," said Maxim. "I'll make sure you can help your family."

Alejandro looked at Dr. Maxim, who spoke to him but looked at the fruit displays in the market.

⇝⇝ ⇜⇜

As Alejandro wandered through the fruit stands, Mr. Reys approached him from behind and laid a hand on his shoulder. "We'll be getting ready to leave soon, Son," said Mr. Reys in a calm and fatherly tone. Alejandro felt apprehension at first, but then relaxed when he recognized Mr. Reys.

"I'm sorry," he said. "Sure, Mr. Reys. I've got to get something for Grandma, if you don't mind waiting a bit."

"Not at all. Meet us by the truck when you're ready." Mr. Reys looked at him and noticed Alejandro's discomfort, but he kept walking toward Mr. Rollies' stand.

While Mr. Rollies kept cracking jokes and fiddling with a toothpick on the side of his mouth, he cut and wrapped meat for the customers. He struck the cutting board with the knife. The customers laughed as they listened to Mr. Rollies' usual wisecracks.

"Here's the best piece of this happy cow you can get, my queen," he said to a woman who stretched her arm to receive the meat wrapped up in white butcher paper.

"Thank you," said the lady, smiling.

He kept hitting the board as he placed cuts of meat on it. Every time he struck the board with the knife, his hair, which was combed over his bald spot and looked like a disheveled toupee, rustled and flopped out of place. People watched him chop the meat and laughed at his jokes, yet they glanced slyly at each other as the shock of hair moved askew to reveal his shiny naked pate.

"This bull died standing up," he said as he hacked out a cut of roast. The customers laughed and called out their orders.

"Be careful now!" he said, "Little mischief is back," as he looked at Alejandro.

Alejandro smiled. "Yeah, my grandma..."

"Yep," he interrupted Alejandro and reached under the counter, pulling a large and already well-wrapped package that he handed to Alejandro.

"You tell Mrs. Druett that Mary Lue loved the socks she knitted for my little Johnny."

"I sure will," said Alejandro, stretching his arm to hand Mr. Rollies a folded envelope.

"No, no need," said Mr. Rollies, rejecting the envelope. "Tell Mr. Druett my grandson sleeps tight in the new cradle," he added. "And let me tell you, he's a sleeper." He sounded so proud.

"I helped Grandpa make that cradle," said Alejandro, smiling.

"I know. He told me," replied Mr. Rollies. "You boys are as talented as your grandpa."

"Thank you, Mr. Rollies," Alejandro said while Mr. Rollies' customers called out their requests. After he received the package, he then looked over at where the truck was waiting and saw Mario gesturing for him to hurry.

As Alejandro walked back to the truck, the cries of young sellers contrasted with the calls of older greengrocers who sold fruit in the market. He noticed that boys were working side by side with grown men and were competing with one another for customers.

"Two for one! Sweet deal here!" called out one of the boys as he held three large peaches in each hand. His voice was high-pitched and youthful, but his hands were as adroit as any man's. He juggled the fruit in the air near the stands.

Another boy used a cleaver and swiftly carved a triangle into the side of a watermelon, piercing the cut triangle in the center, and then pulling out a crimson, juicy triangular slice of the fruit. He showed off his dexterity with the cleaver as he enticed customers to approach the stand and try a piece.

"Sweet peach! Sweata peach! Sweet peach! Sweata peach!" another seller squawked as he sunk both thumbs by the stalk and into a peach, prying the fruit open, and showing the pulp and seed inside. Customers relished the samples before buying the fruit.

"What the hell do you think you're doing?" said a tall, well-dressed man, who made a commanding gesture with his hand at what the boy had done.

"Customers buy more after they see it, Sir," he replied as a pile of donut peaches tumbled down at the foot of the man.

"Well, you will give away no damn peaches here. So just stick to selling them, understand?" The man reprimanded his employee as he kicked and stepped on a couple of donut peaches. It was obvious the man had a certain degree of authority over the boy.

"Yes, Sir," the boy said. "What do you want me to do with these peaches?" he pointed to the peaches on the floor, while he kept his submissive eyes locked on his boss.

"Pick them up! Put the good ones on the stand. We'll feed the others to the pigs down in the Landing," the man said. Alejandro and other men there looked at the scene while the boy picked up the bruised and smashed peaches. They were all looking at the boy, and they were all silent. The honk of the truck caught Alejandro's attention, and a market that seemed to have stopped for a few seconds was back in full swing. He firmly clenched the packet he carried and jumped on the back of the moving truck.

On the way back from the market, the wind hit Alejandro in the face while the squeaking and jerking of metal locks and chains hit the tailgate of the truck as it ran over potholes and humps. He firmly grabbed the sidebars while the to-and-fro of the truck thrusted his body about. He held the package of meat Mr. Rollies had given him with one hand while he held onto the rails as tight as he could with the other.

Far in the distance, the bright morning sunlight lit the Great Endes Mountains, but Alejandro's sight was turned inwards. His hopes and vision seemed to have lost something that early morning and his mind seemed to have gained some deep insight about himself, other kids who worked at the market, and the fruits of their labor.

A Fist Full of Dirt

Harvesting grapes was perhaps one of the most demanding jobs in Russell and its surroundings. In addition to all the conditions of the job, harvesters had to keep up the pace as the vine rows were depleted of their fruits. That day, by the middle of the day, the truck had gone to unload its first load of grapes. It was a bright day with the scorching sun radiating its heat onto the dry clods along the rows and the dusty alleys in the vineyard at the Lessar farm. That week, Grandpa, Alejandro, and Grasshopper had been harvesting grapes at Mr. Lessar's and the heat was suffocating. The rows of grapevines there extended for at least forty yards; in some parts of the vineyard, some rows were even longer. Alejandro carried his metal crate as he walked past the row where he and Grasshopper were harvesting.

"What you crying about?" asked Alejandro when he saw Grasshopr squatting between the rows. Tears dubbed the ashy coat of dust on Grasshopper's face, mixing into a washed-out smear beneath his eyes.

"I lost all the damn tokens," said Grasshopper, sobbing, rubbing his eyes, and clasping a yellow token in his left hand.

"The whole pouch?" Alejandro asked.

"All of them," said Grasshopper.

"When did you see them last?" asked his brother.

"I don't know. I dumped the grapes into the truck, and after Mr. Martinet threw the token in the crate, I couldn't find my pouch to put this token in anymore." In anger, he held a couple of clumps of dry dirt and smashed them against his lap.

"I did all this shit for nothing," Grasshopper cried. "And my shoulder is all bruised up."

He had lost a pouch full of tokens, a half day worth of work. The feeling of losing his pouch amounted to nothing after half a day of hard work. His crate was a bit smaller than the others but still a bit too heavy for him. He was strong and carried it with difficulty but did his best to hide it, especially from Grandpa. But it was common. At times for the day laborers, an entire day of work amounted to a handful of tokens in their pouches and little money in their pockets, especially when the harvesting and climatic conditions were poor. Grasshopper felt sorrow for what he no longer had.

"You didn't draw the string tight enough, did you?" Alejandro asked.

"I did," said Grasshopper as he continued sobbing. "I had about fifteen tokens in it."

"Did you go back and ask Martinet if he'd seen it?" asked Alejandro.

"He was gone already by the time I took the crate back to the row and got my token. Whoever found it is not giving it back," said Grasshopper.

"Don't think the worst just yet," said Alejandro. "Let's take a look." Alejandro walked back to the rows where Grasshopper had been harvesting to look for the pouch. Harvesters had gone to eat; the stillness and silence around the vineyard brought a sense of peace. *If Grasshopper had lost the pouch while he was harvesting, then it would be there*, Alejandro thought.

"We'll look for it after lunch," Alejandro said, walking back to where Grasshopper was. "Everyone's gone to eat lunch now. We'll come back to check before everyone is back."

The olive trees cast their shade over the vineyard alley and as the midday sun shined, the cool shade hid just under the trees and provided a cool place for the harvesters to eat and rest during their lunch break. The shade, the food and the chit-chatting of entire families under the trees made the heat more bearable while harvesters had lunch and laughed, making the day easier and calmer.

"Imagine if we didn't have to work," said Grandpa, looking at Grasshopper. He scooped some sugar out of a small jar and put it in his tin cup and added tea from a stainless steel thermos. Alejandro lay against the trunk of an olive tree, eating a glossy red apple Grandma had gotten from Mr. Campito's farm. Grasshopper ate some cornbread and bacon.

"It'd be great, if it wasn't for all the work we do," replied Grasshopper casually. "Just play and eat a bit and sleep all day."

"Don't know about that. Life would be boring without having something to do," said Grandpa, unfolding the cloth Grandma had used to wrap the breaded beef steak sandwiches they brought for lunch.

"You'd like that," Alejandro said, looking at Grasshopper.

"Yeah, and we wouldn't have to worry 'bout those damned tokens," Grasshopper said, touching, rubbing his shoulder.

"Without those damned tokens you wouldn't buy a damned thing," Alejandro replied as Grandpa handed him a sandwich. "We can eat a bunch of grapes for free here, but in the city you gotta pay."

"You gotta have your dreams, and money can help with that," said Grandpa, giving Grasshopper a sandwich.

"Dreams aren't real," said Grasshopper. "Besides, 'money earned is money spent.' I read that in a book." He pulled the neck of his shirt and aired and looked at his bruised left shoulder.

"You haven't worked hard enough to be talking about money earned," Alejandro said.

"I have. I just lost all my work," said Grasshopper, angry. "Look at my shoulder." It wasn't common to see Grasshopper angry, but Grandpa picked up on it right away.

"What do you mean, you lost all your work?" Grandpa asked.

"He lost his pouch," said Alejandro, "with all the tokens in it."

"How many times have I told you, you have to take good care of what you have?" Grandpa said.

"I know, I just lost it, Grandpa," said Grasshopper, "I'm sorry."

"You gotta pay attention," said Alejandro.

"I have," said Grasshopper, looking down in frustration.

"I wonder how a few hours of work can turn into a piece of plastic so quickly," Alejandro added.

"And then turn into nothing." Grandpa shook his head as Grasshopper spoke. "We can go look for it now," Grasshopper said, getting on his feet.

"No. You're gonna have lunch first," Grandpa said as he took a bite from his sandwich.

"But what if somebody finds it?" said Grasshopper.

"Then that's the lesson you gotta learn," Grandpa said, raising his eyebrows.

"Damn tokens," said Grasshopper. "All this work for nothing."

"That's right," Alejandro interjected. "You got to take care of your things or you'll be left with nothing but a fist full of dirt."

"I hope one day I can have all the money in the world and have nothing to do, no work, just play," said Grasshopper.

"And eat bacon," said Alejandro, laughing at Grasshopper, hoping to let go of the tension.

Grasshopper smirked, trying to hide the disappointment.

"It's good to work for what you want. Money gotten the wrong way very soon runs out,'" Grandpa said.

"What does that mean?" asked Grasshopper.

"Like the money they're not paying us for the work we've done," said Alejandro, keeping his gaze fixed on Grandpa.

"It means that you gotta do right no matter what to earn your keep." Grandpa had a stern look in his eyes.

"Doing right?" Alejandro raised his eyebrows.

"Yeah, do right no matter what or to whoever," Grandpa said. Alejandro's eyes wandered in doubt.

"I see people doing right, working their lives off, and for what? To do right for others more than for themselves?" Alejandro added.

Grasshopper squinted. "Just like you helping me find my tokens," said Grasshopper. Grandpa smiled at him. "If people do right no matter what, it would be really good, but that's not real," he added.

"Where did you lose your tokens?" Grandpa asked.

"I don't know," said Grasshopper.

"We're gonna look for them after lunch," said Alejandro, eying Grandpa.

"You see, you're gonna do right no matter what to help me find my tokens," said Grasshopper. "But if someone else finds them first, it would be no use."

"You ought to take good care of your money. Look how hard you work, carrying those heavy crates. One day you'll want to have a family, and a real man has gotta help his family," said Grandpa as he coughed and rubbed his right eye. Alejandro looked deep in thought.

"Yeah, one day you'll have a lady to take care of, Grasshopper," said Alejandro, breaking his silence. "Isn't that right, Grandpa?"

"Oh yeah, the whole milk and honey," Grandpa replied, coughing, laughing, and struggling to talk. They laughed.

"And the bee stings and cow dung, too," said Grasshopper.

Grandpa and Alejandro laughed.

"My lady is sweeter than honey," added Grasshopper. The mood of the conversation had shifted. It seemed as if there was no need to cry over spilled milk, but to rather make the best of the moment.

"What was that?" asked Alejandro as he drank some iced tea.

"Yeah, my lady is as sweet as the muscatine grapes," said Grasshopper.

"You mean muscat grapes," said Alejandro.

Grandpa laughed under his straw hat. "How long have you got a girlfriend?" Grandpa asked.

"Yeah, how long?" asked Alejandro.

"A true gentleman," he said as he savored the breaded steak sandwich, "don't go around talking about his lady, but you know her." He was now in better spirits. Talking about Alvera and eating the sandwich had taken away the irritating thought and sour taste of lost tokens.

"Who is she?" asked Alejandro. He winked at Grandpa.

"I know Mr. Reys likes me, so I'm not worried about it," said Grasshopper, putting a muscat grape in his mouth.

"Alvera?" questioned Alejandro.

"That's my lady," said Grasshopper. "We've been friends for some time now."

"There's your dream now," added Alejandro as he eyed Grandpa, who also nibbled on some grapes.

Grinning, Grandpa looked at Alejandro.

"Well, she's very real to me. She likes me, I know," affirmed Grasshopper. "Dreams aren't real. And now I don't have any tokens. That's how real it is." He rubbed his shoulder.

"Well, if you don't want them to be real, they just won't happen," Alejandro said. "But that piece of land of ours that we want looks pretty real to me," he added and took another bite off his sandwich.

"That's a dream," said Grandpa, finishing his tea.

"Dreams are just ideas people put in your head," said Grasshopper. Grandpa sighed.

"When I was a boy, I always dreamt of snaring a hare," said Grandpa. "But it was hard to catch one because out in the fields you seldom see one, until it appears like a flash and then, as fast as it appears, it's gone. You gotta be very lucky to see one running for a long while. You may watch it as it nibbles and grazes on the pretty fields, but they know better than to come around people."

The boys sat and listened as Grandpa talked. "They're really pretty, right Grandpa?" asked Grasshopper, opening his eyes. He was excited now to hear Grandpa telling a story about the hare. "Did you ever catch one, Grandpa?"

"I did, when I was a lad," he added. "It's kinda tricky to catch one."

"You caught it with a snare, Grandpa?" asked Grasshopper.

"I did. But before I caught one, I set about a hundred lassos," said Grandpa as he raised his eyebrows. He played with a small olive twig between his lips while he told the story.

"So what's the secret for catching one, Grandpa?" asked Alejandro.

"The secret's learning to think like one," replied Grandpa, forcing the words out as he coughed.

"I'll be thinking about eating fennel and carrots," said Grasshopper.

"It's not so much what they eat, but the trails they go on," answered Grandpa.

"They're pretty smart," added Alejandro.

"I'd be changing my trails every time to not let people catch me," added Grasshopper.

"Little critters come and go. You hardly ever see one near you," said Grandpa, dissuading the kids about the hare. Grandpa lowered his straw hat and the kids understood that as a sign for him to doze off after the meal.

"We're not gonna find it," said Grasshopper. He trailed behind Alejandro along the row and the spot he had harvested last before lunch. This time, Alejandro retraced his brother's steps while Grasshopper lagged a few yards behind. He kept walking, looking down, and kicking chunks of dirt-soil along his path in an effort to find the pouch.

Overwhelmed once more by a feeling of loss, Grasshopper stopped walking and squatted. Seeing his brother crying on the ground, Alejandro frowned at him. Then, he stood straight and looked around the other vine rows. "What the hell are you doing there on the ground?" Alejandro asked.

"They're gone," Grasshopper sobbed.

"Stand up and shut up!" Alejandro demanded.

He looked up at the row where Grasshopper had been reaping the vines and walked back, trailing and checking the path along the row.

"Crying isn't gonna get your tokens back," he said, leaving his brother behind. As he kept walking among a few jagged, dried, and dusty lumps of soil, he found a small, grayish, folded drawstring bag. The dusty pouch was camouflaged by its gray color and the dry clumps on the ground, but Alejandro could see it. The bag contained several yellow plastic tokens tiered in stacks. He picked up the bag and put it in his pocket. As Alejandro returned to the front of the row, Grasshopper still sobbed.

"I hate this, hate this!" he said, kicking against the clods.

"Did you have any tokens before today?" asked Alejandro.

"No," said Grasshopper.

"Then why are you crying?" said Alejandro. "Don't be so upset about a few tokens," said his brother. "At times, we lose a lot more than a few tokens. In the end what really matters is that you've done all you could do to make the day right."

"You sound like Grandpa," said Grasshopper, drying his eyes with the sleeve of his shirt. Grasshopper stopped crying and looked up at his brother.

"Grandpa is right," said Alejandro. "You gotta keep looking forward."

"Yeah, that's easy to say. You didn't lose nothing," said Grasshopper.

"Here," said Alejandro, giving his little brother the dusty pouch. "No money is worth crying about."

"Where was it?" said Grasshopper, opening his eyes.

"Right there where you were kneeling down," Alejandro replied. "There, under the clods."

"How did I not see it?"

"Here, take a few of mine. I've made nearly sixty tokens today so far," said Alejandro, putting two stacks of tokens inside Grasshopper's pouch. "It isn't so bad after all."

Grasshopper's eyes lightened, and he regained his usual charisma. His cheeks regained their usual color. He stood up and hugged his brother while he tightly held the dirty pouch in his fist.

They came back under the shade of the olive tree where Grandpa was napping.

"This is the tallest tree in this farm," Alejandro added as he looked up. Grasshopper looked at him, nodded, and pointed his lips at the crown of the tree. Alejandro approached the trunk and signaled for Grasshopper to climb the tree with him.

They quietly climbed and reached the crown of the tree. They enjoyed the breeze hitting their faces at the crown of the tree. From above, their half-bodies, upper torsos stood out at the top of the dark green foliage and the several olive trees along the alley in the vineyard. As they looked over the farm from the top of the olive tree, they felt in control of everything around them. Nature had a special way of making them feel they own their destiny and surroundings. There was a special harmony in having such a position. Birds seemed to acknowledge the fact that Alejandro and Grasshopper were there, at the top of the tree, as if they were in charge of it all. It was a quiet, peaceful moment, a moment of reflection about their worth, about harvesting grapes, while all of the harvesters were napping. The kids felt a presence that told them that they were part of the whole of nature. It was a fact that no one could change, that no one could take away from them.

After lunch break was nearly over, the men and women around the vineyard murmured and prepared to return to work. Some men stretched their bodies while others walked toward their crates.

"We gotta dump the bins when Martinet gets here," said Grasshopper.

"From up here we can see everything," said Alejandro, looking at the lushness of the vineyard. From above, Alejandro and Grasshopper watched the dump truck park in the alley and saw all the harvesters gathering below. They had a bird's-eye view of everything and loved to have this sight.

Lunch was over and the men were getting ready to dump their metal crates full of grapes into the truck. Martinet kept squinting at the crates, and firmly observed the men around him, as if he were trying to catch any form of deception among the crates.

⟫⟫⟫ ⟪⟪⟪

The day was almost over, and the dump truck had already left for the second and last time for the winery. The harvesters, Grandpa, and the boys waited for the truck to return so Martinet could take them back to the homestead. Grasshopper and Alejandro waited, sitting on their crates. Their clothes, faces and bodies were smudged with grape must and juice. Their hands and bodies were as sticky as the sap of the acacia tree. There was a feeling of confidence and fulfillment after a good day of work. With his straw hat covering his face, Grandpa sat near the boys, dozing against the trunk of an olive tree at the entrance of the rows.

"You know, what you told me is true," said Grasshopper.

"What's that?" asked Alejandro.

"I can't take your tokens. It don't feel right," said Grasshopper, stretching his right arm toward Alejandro, holding the two stacks of tokens his brother had put in his pouch.

"Why not?" asked Alejandro.

"Cause they're yours," said Grasshopper.

"Yeah, but I'm giving them to you. They're yours now."

"You said not to worry about it," said Grasshopper.

"Yeah, I said that," said Alejandro.

"Well, I guess I can think about something else when something bad happens," said Grasshopper.

"Yeah, that works sometimes, but you can't hide forever if you have a problem," replied Alejandro. "Sometimes you go down that road and when there's nothing you can do, you just gotta let go, move on and keep looking forward. Like losing and then finding new tokens. Nobody and nothing can change what is waiting for you."

"Yeah, maybe I should think about Alvera," said Grasshopper.

"That's a good idea," Alejandro said. "Alvera is a sweet girl and a bit too wise for you." The thought of Alvera being Grasshopper's girlfriend amused Alejandro and Grandpa. Alejandro knew his brother liked to tell lies and there were some lies that didn't hurt anybody or bother him, especially coming from his little brother.

"Yeah, when I think about her, I forget everything," said Grasshopper.

Alejandro squinted and smiled. "How long have you liked her?" Alejandro asked.

"For a little over two weeks," said Grasshopper.

His brother smiled. "Have you talked to her?" Alejandro asked.

"No, not yet."

"Have you done anything special for her?" Alejandro asked, hoping not to downplay his brother's intentions.

"Yeah, I gathered some cherries the other day for her," said Grasshopper. "But I couldn't give them to her yet. But I know she likes me."

Alejandro looked at him. He listened as Grasshopper kept talking about Alvera.

"Yeah, she is like an angel from a dream," Alejandro said. Grasshopper looked at him and smiled. He began counting the tokens he had made.

"I know you like her too. But she loves me," said Grasshopper.

"I know she does," said Alejandro.

"What would you do if you had a lot of money?" Grasshopper asked as he counted the tokens.

"I would buy a piece of land of my own," said Alejandro, narrowing his eyes and looking at the silver lining of the clouds far in the horizon.

"That's just like Grandpa's dream," Grasshopper said.

"Yeah, but like you said, sometimes dreams pass us by just like days. There is a day today and tomorrow is no longer that day. Like a picture you look at and then you move on to look at another."

"Yeah, and pictures get old, too," said Grasshopper. "I think I made forty crates today."

"And one all beaten up," said Alejandro. "Martinet got real mad."

"I'm sorry about that," said Grasshopper.

"I think I got a little more than yesterday," replied Alejandro.

Grasshopper poured the token from his pouch together with Alejandro's. Grasshopper felt relieved. He squinted and smiled at his brother.

"Now we can give the money to Grandpa for the new place," said Grasshopper. "I think we have a lot." He looked at the tokens with the hope that they would be enough.

"Yeah, that's a good idea," said Alejandro.

"But it won't be enough." Grasshopper squinted, looking again at the tokens.

"But little by little we'll have enough," said Alejandro.

"Look!!! Look!!!" screamed Grasshopper, jumping, getting on his feet right away. "Look at it!!!" The alarming sound of his high-pitched voice scared other harvesters there. Grandpa was still asleep while he waited for Martinet to return. But he was woken up by the commotion.

"There's that damn rabbit!" said Grasshopper.

"That's a hare," said Alejandro.

"Whatever," said Grasshopper.

Alejandro stood up and looked at the hare as it hopped through the rows and slipped away through the grape vines. With a swift spring, its hind legs boosted its body forward in the air, a quick pass, a zigzag, right to left and vice versa. Its long, wide, aerodynamic ears slashed through the air as the creature zigged-zagged across each row. Grasshopper took out his slingshot and one of the pebbles that he kept in his pocket. Alejandro took control of the slingshot.

"Let me shoot it," said Grasshopper. Grandpa pretended to be asleep and just looked at them, squinting his eyes.

"It's too quick," replied Alejandro, giving the slingshot back to Grasshopper. "We're better off just looking at it."

"Yeah, but I still wanna get that critter," said Grasshopper as he ran after it.

"Don't bother," said Alejandro, "you're not catching it."

"I still wanna try it. It's fun!" screamed Grasshopper as he ran through the row where they last saw the evasive little beast. The hare was too quick for them. It moved from row to row, only appearing in instants, and finally zigged-zagged and faded away through the lush foliage of the vines. Grasshopper aimed a pebble a few times at it. Even though his shots did pierce through the vines near the hare's path, the critter was too quick for the pebbles.

"Man, I almost got that damned hog," said Grasshopper as he returned to where Alejandro was. "It was huge."

"I told you so, but it wasn't no hog, you fool," replied Alejandro.

Grandpa just glanced at them under his straw hat.

"I know, but it was as big as a hog. I'll get it next time," said Grasshopper. "Maybe we can set a snare."

"Yeah, a snare loop may work," said Alejandro.

"Yeah," said Grasshopper. "We'll get it."

"I don't think Grandpa wants us to hurt critters, though," said Alejandro. "You know that's why he doesn't like you shooting slingshots."

Grandpa just observed with a little twitch of a smile.

"Yeah, but he used snares himself. It won't matter. He's asleep anyway."

"We'll get it next time."

"And when Grandpa wakes up and sees we got the critter, he'll be proud of us," said Grasshopper.

"Maybe one day he'll show us how to make snares," Alejandro said.

The Origin of Wrath

Kaiser used to run wild and aimlessly around the homestead early in the mornings after Grandpa unleashed him. Sniffing the fresh soil in the furrows, the hound would stomp through the clods, running headless to where his intuition would lead him. At night, his thick collar was connected to a leather harness that Grandpa had made to keep him secure to a chain and wire that ran along the chicken coop. Kaiser was the guardian, protecting the chickens from small predators. In the pitch darkness of the homestead, he would even bark at the psithurism in the poplar trees on a breezy night or at the misty fog during the early mornings before Grandpa unleashed him. As the hound bucked and ran loosely around the homestead, the metal rings of his harness struck each other, sending a ding-a-ling melody in the distance.

Grandpa had given in about the idea of keeping Soil to the point where even himself was feeding the pooch, giving him milk and shredded chicken. The dog was still pretty weak. It trembled every time it tried to stand up. It was gradually regaining its strength but wasn't strong enough to follow Kaiser around the grove.

In the morning, Grasshopper spent time carrying Soil around the homestead, carrying him in his arms and asking him what he wanted to do.

"You wanna play now? You wanna climb some trees," Grasshopper would ask, whimpering like a puppy.

Kaiser sniffed Soil and began jumping on Grasshopper as he carried the small dog.

"Get away, Kaiser!" Grasshopper screamed as the big dog wagged his tail, jumped, and tried to put his front paws on him. He avoided the dog as he walked to the front of the adobe house, where Grandma was getting ready to light the clay oven.

Soil's solemn brown eyes idly gazed at the boy without expecting anything from him. Its black fur shone as scattered sunrays beamed on his pelage. The pooch laid his head on the angle of Grasshopper's arm and licked it as it rested there.

"You'll be good in no time, poochetty pooch," said Grasshopper. "Look Grandma, isn't he a nice little doggy?" Grasshopper asked Grandma as he walked by the clay oven. Alejandro was stuffing the clay oven with dry olive branches.

"Kaiser!" Grandma screamed to call the dog's attention to make him get away from Grasshopper. "There goes that crazy fool again," said Grandma as Kaiser ran away, erratically and wild, enjoying the freedom the open spaces provided at the homestead. He would sniff at the clods and then lift his head to sense and follow the air, perhaps smelling other hounds in the area. Then he stopped, picked up the scent of a bitch in heat, perhaps, and like that, following his instinct, he'd be gone for days.

"He likes to look tough but he's really a playful dog," said Alejandro.

"So is this one," said Grasshopper while he kept walking, carrying Soil to the other side of the adobe house.

"Crazy dog," said Grandma. "Grandpa is not well this morning."

"If I could have another job, I'd get more money," said Alejandro as he contemplated Kaiser in the distance. "If I could have a job, Grandpa wouldn't have to work so much."

"You're still a boy to go and work on your own with grown men," said Grandma, dismissing Alejandro's idea. She then lit a match and carefully placed it below some bark and wood shavings inside the clay oven.

"Kaiser!" shouted Grandma again. "Hwiiiisss!" she whistled. "Every time I see him acting like that, the fool runs away for days."

"Grandma, I need to help Grandpa. I'll be sixteen soon. I have already gone to work with him," he added.

"Aren't you helping Mr. Gurua?" asked Grandma in an effort to divert the conversation.

"Yes, but he only gives me small jobs. I need a real job," said Alejandro.

"He'll give you more responsibility if you stick around," Grandma said.

"I know, but I think he will once I'm older," said Alejandro.

"Why are you wearing your good shirt?" asked Grandma, looking at Alejandro's black shirt.

"Why can't I, Grandma?" he responded. "I'm gonna go ask for work."

"Look at those clouds. Rain is coming," she said. "There he goes again. He's gone now," she added, making gestures after whistling toward the dog in the distance, and hoping to dismiss Alejandro's claim for finding work.

"I'll get him," said Alejandro. He ran through the furrows to reach the dog.

Kaiser jumped from furrow to furrow like a wild hare and disappeared beyond the reedbed. Alejandro could hear the splashes the dog made along the swampy boundary by the reedbed that led to the train tracks. Following the dog's path, Alejandro reached the reedbed and trudged through the brush and water.

"Get over here, you crazy pooch?" he said. He felt the cold water inside his shoes. His job-hunting day had been ruined.

"Kaiser! Kaiser!" The dog kept running. Kaiser's heavy breathing and the high-pitched tinkling of the metal rings kept Alejandro aware of the dog's whereabouts. Alejandro followed him to the train tracks and realized Kaiser had already crossed the reedbed.

"Kaiser! Come here, you fool!" he called one last time, but the sound of the collar faded beyond the vineyards in the distance while Alejandro continued walking through the reedbed.

"He did her really good!" A voice traveled indistinctly from far beyond the reedbed, on the other side of the *callejón*, near the railroad across from the Reys' farm. The boisterous voices of drunk men with their chatter and guffaws resounded in the quietness as Alejandro got closer. Unable to recognize the voices, Alejandro stopped his stride and eavesdropped on the conversation.

"Hell, I did too," said another voice as the pristine sounds of the water from the spring nearby filled the void.

"Now you owe me a big one," said one of the voices.

"Shit, you can come and work for us if you want. I don't owe you nothing," replied another voice that Alejandro recognized. Next to the gate of the Costar's farm, the farm across from the Reys', Herman and two other men stood in an open field next to a stack of wooden crates that contained ripened persimmons. By the crates sat a few bottles of *Bravo*, the cabernet produced in Russell.

"Shit, we'll have a lot more comin' this season, boys," said Herman while holding an open bottle.

"You'll pay me good for it?" said one of the men next to him. He was short and stocky, light skinned, with dark eyes.

"You'll get a good deal," affirmed Herman, looking askance at the man. "Shit, boy, we'll have to hire a lot more hands, though."

Alejandro's eyes widened, and his interest grew as he heard Herman's words. He moved forward and made his way through the reeds. The men stopped the conversation as they heard the cracking from the reedbed and saw Alejandro emerge from it.

"Who the hell is that?" asked the stocky man.

"That's one of old Druett's boys," said Herman as he kept his sight on him.

"He sure wanna draft of good ol' *Bravo*," said the other man, a large man who seemed more intoxicated than the other two.

"Hello, Mr. Herman," said Alejandro in a polite tone as he approached.

"Hey there, boy, what are you up to?" Herman contended.

"I was looking for my dog. I heard you say that you'll need to hire more hands this season," responded Alejandro.

"We sure will," said Herman as he eyed the other men. "Shit, boys, the boy wants a job."

"He be looking for men, boy," said the short man as a smirk rose to his face.

"I'm up for it. I really need work to help my grandpa," said Alejandro, ignoring the man.

"Yeah, a real man like you, kid," added the large man as he laughed.

"I just need to work. I'm a hard worker," said Alejandro.

"You wanna work, boy?" said Herman.

"I do, Sir," replied Alejandro.

"You gotta work hard. The pay is good, you know?" said Herman. Herman looked at Alejandro and brought his hand down to his crotch. The alcohol made his speech worse.

Alejandro looked Herman in the eye.

"What do you mean, Sir?" Alejandro asked.

"Shit, you just gotta be nice to me," he said while he kept touching his crotch. His neck was sweaty, and he had a vague and fiery look in his eyes, a type of vile heat, as if the spirit or ethanol in the wine had possessed him. He took another deep draught of *Bravo*. The men laughed.

"What do you mean, Sir?" Alejandro asked again, looking puzzled, but now more serious.

"*Bravo* is the best wine you'll find in this area," interjected the large man.

"He means you gotta come close to him so you can play with his cherries," said the short, stocky man, who now leered at Alejandro. They continued to laugh, embarrassing Alejandro who was standing in front of them.

"You want a job, don't you, boy?" asked the large man.

"Yes," said Alejandro.

"Then you gotta earn that right," said the large man as he looked at Herman and smiled wantonly.

"You gotta play with Mr. Herman's fruit piece," explained the stocky man, inciting more laughter from the others.

"You're all drunk," said Alejandro, redirecting his sight to Herman.

"He's right," said Herman, leering at the boy with a lewd smile. "Are you willing to do that?" Thunderous clouds were gathering and roaring above them.

"What do you take me for?" demanded Alejandro as he leaped forward and grabbed Herman by the flap of his jacket. "What are you saying to me?"

The other two men took hold of Alejandro and pulled him away from Herman. One pulled back Alejandro by his hair and right arm while the other held his left one. Herman gulped down the dregs of the *Bravo* and cast the bottle aside as he lunged toward Alejandro.

"Let me go, you bastards!" shouted Alejandro.

"Shit, boy, you dare to put your hands on me, you filthy rat," said Herman. His eyes were bloodshot, and the irises of his eyes had a strange color in them, like the blazing reddish-orange of a few overripened persimmons in the crates by his side.

"Let go of me." Alejandro pulled and tussled, forcing his way out of their grasp.

"Now, you're gonna learn some respect, you little shit," said Herman.

As Alejandro tussled with the men, his new black shirt was a bit torn at the edges and one of his shoes came loose. The large man overpowered him, repositioning and holding him by the wrists while the other two men slapped Alejandro across the face and punched him on the rib cage and stomach. The drunken men laughed as they pushed the boy about.

"He wants a job," said Herman. "You wanna have a job?" he slurred, redirecting his sight toward Alejandro.

"Let him have a swig of *Bravo*," said the large man as Herman wrenched the cork off another bottle and forced it into the boy's mouth.

"Let go of me, you sick pigs," said Alejandro, bursting in anger, spitting out blood, wine, and saliva on Herman's face.

"You bastard! Grab him tightly!" said Herman. "You nasty rat!" His fist landed on the boy's cheek. Herman grabbed an overripe persimmon and smashed it against the boy's face. "So you wanna a job? Shit, boy!"

"Look how pretty he looks, with all that red from the *Bravo* and kaki on his face," said the stocky man as he held the boy up to see his face.

"Yeah, he's got some rouge on his pretty lips," added the large man, slapping the boy across the face.

"Pretty sight of a girly boy, isn't she," said Herman, grabbing Alejandro by the face. Blood and saliva dribbled from Alejandro's lips, mixed with the *Bravo* that also dripped from his mouth every time Herman forced the bottle past his lips, leaving streaks of crimson down the boy's chin.

"She sure is," added the large man, laughing.

"Shit, we should make her pay, then," added Herman, pouring more *Bravo* into Alejandro's mouth.

"I think she's ready," said the stocky man.

"Oh, sure she is," added the large man.

Alejandro was almost unresponsive.

Nature had been so kind to provide its lucrative bounty. Many of the persimmons in the crates were ripe. But maturity didn't reach the minds of vile men in the same way. The natural course of maturity had been breached in a vicious assault, all on the account of a boy looking for work. It did not mitigate any existent conflict; it fed the fire with unbridled rage and wrath.

Some of persimmons had not only become overripe but also turned rotten by the meager hand that neglected their care and harvest. A fruit with promise but spoiled. The indistinct blazing reddish-orange sparkle that gleamed in the iris, the rotten thought that traveled through the spine, a distorted order that thwarted innocence in its disarray, to the young fruit that was ripe for the picking. The incongruity of the rotten persimmons alongside the ripe ones in the crate accelerated their process. The lack of control and power—a glint filled with malice, an unrepentant and perverted enthusiasm unveiled.

"We'll call this one 'the pretty boy who loves persimmons,' woo-hoo! " screamed the stocky man.

"Shit, let's call him 'kaki eater,'" said Herman. "He'll taste it, all right." He stuck the persimmon, smashing the boy's face.

"Oh, yeah!" replied the large man as the other laughed wildly in the solitude of that misty morning. Their voices echoed and guffawed in the void.

After they had tussled with Alejandro, he lay on a dusty spot in the middle of the field. The men laughed, still swilling the *Bravo,* and stood over him, smashed and bloody, badly beaten, and nearly unconscious on the ground.

The sight of Alejandro's body brought the fat man back to reality. With his eyes wide open, he looked at the boy and then at Herman and the stocky man. "What do we do now?" he asked. His face seemed to have regained its sobriety.

"Let's throw him in the ditch," said the large man. They positioned themselves to carry Alejandro to the ditch in the reedbed. As they lifted him, they heard the clacking of metal rings striking on Kaiser's leather harness. The dog's heavy breathing was approaching. Suddenly, he was in sight, growling and charging furiously toward the men.

The men dropped Alejandro and dove behind the crates to avoid the dog. The fat man jumped on top of the crates as the stocky man plunged into the reeds. Herman managed to climb onto a persimmon tree, but the twisted branches and boughs impeded his efforts. His legs and arms wrapped around the branches made the rest of his body hang, leaving his half-ass butt crack exposed to Kaiser's bites and snaps. His round and ruddy butt crack glowed brighter against the tawny hues of the persimmons while the dog kept at it.

Alejandro lay beaten on the field. After taking several bites at Herman's rear end, Kaiser sniffed the air, looked back at Alejandro, and returned by his side. Kaiser then sniffed Alejandro and started licking his bloody face. The dog turned and growled at the fat man and Herman as they ran off through the reedbed to the adjacent orchards.

The day was gloomy. The breeze from the west brought dark clouds and rain over the reedbed. Kaiser kept licking Alejandro's face while the rain fell.

The raindrop would cleanse his wounds. The wounds would heal. The humiliation would not. Disgrace would linger, stripping a young man of his innocence and pride. The feeling of powerlessness and offense would fester, threatening his ability to free himself from others. How much rejection and abuse he, and many like him, had to endure to have a place in the world. His fifteen years of dignity and manhood were tarnished in a moment by a lesser kind, who would toy with a young man's very soul and need, all on account of their patrimony, vice, and influence. Why was it so easy to violate a young man's integrity when they could have just denied him the job? Or just paid him for his labor? He just wanted a damned job. And he had to pay the price set by the kind of men who obviously had never merited to be in that position.

In the face of such circumstances, the lad had to learn to accept his fate. With his innocence shattered, he had no other option than to collect himself, pick himself up, and fight the sons of the devil.

Puma

In the evenings, Grandpa and Grandma sat in the kitchen by the cast-iron stove in the two sofa chairs Grandpa had made. The chairs were comfortable and positioned next to each other. He and Grandma were the only ones allowed to sit in them. In the summer, Grandma only lit the stove to boil water for tea and coffee. There was always an atmosphere of comfort and peace in the kitchen. After she had served Grandpa a cup of tea, she sat comfortably on the chair and took naps.

As Grandma's chin dropped to her chest, she would doze off while Grasshopper and Alejandro talked to Grandpa. Sometimes she sat up straight after being startled, opening and closing her eyes and then falling asleep again until Grandpa's sonorous, guttural voice woke her up again.

"Mrs. Druett?" Grandpa asked while she was sleeping.

"Yes, dear, in a little bit," she would reply from her slumber, her eyes still closed.

At other times, Grandpa pretended he was laughing, and then the kids started laughing too, just to see her wake up laughing as if she were taking part in the conversation and knew the reason for their laughter. Whenever she realized they were pranking her, she got serious and rolled her eyes at them. Grandpa and the kids would cackle.

"Don't you have something better to do?" she would ask. Then, Grandpa and the kids would laugh even harder.

The end of summer brought with it the end of the grape harvest, the beginning of the olive harvest, and the Wine Fest celebration in Russell. On weekdays, Grandma spent part of the evening in the kitchen, guiding Alejandro and Grasshopper with their chores. In the summer months, they worked alongside Grandpa. Grandma did too at times. Whether she harvested grapes, olives, or any other crop, her pace was admirable. She was prolific and quick. Despite her age, the manner in which she worked was graceful and assertive. Every day, Grandma prepared their lunch for the next day at work when they were harvesting. But she stayed behind at the homestead doing house chores and harvesting the crops that she could while Grandpa went on to work on adjacent farms in the area.

Alejandro and Grasshopper would help Grandpa with the olive harvest deep into the fall, until all the collection of fruits subsided. But Grandpa handled the bulk of the harvest at the homestead. It wasn't an easy job having to carry heavy wooden ladders and move them around the olive trees.

"What happened to your face?" asked Grandpa when Alejandro came into the kitchen that evening.

"Oh, I got all tangled up in the blackberry shrubs by the undergrowth," said Alejandro. His gaze seemed resigned and despondent. Bruises at times are necessary in the playful day of a child, but these were bruises he didn't want, bruises that would remind him what life was worth. These bruises on his cheeks and arms were engraved marks that had been imposed on him, carved out on the fresh and soft texture of his skin. He remained deep in thought as Grandpa tried to talk to him—his downward gaze stared into space and into a void of despair.

"You're all wet," said Grandma. "Leave your shirt so I can wash it. Did you find anything?" Grandma whispered to him.

"And how do you get all bruised up in the shrubs like that?" asked Grandpa. "And your shirt is all torn up. What happened to you? Where have you been all day?"

"I was chasing Kaiser through the brush. It's raining, so I fell a couple of times. The shirt got caught up in some shoots," he said.

Grandma looked at him. "You didn't go look for a job, did you?" she asked.

Grasshopper observed him quietly. He knew his brother wasn't telling the truth.

"Go and change that shirt," said Grandma.

"Grandma, my head hurts," said Grasshopper.

"You've been under the rain all day playing with that dog," said Grandma. "Have some water. I made some lemon pie. Do you want a piece?"

"No, I don't feel so good."

"Let me see," said Grandma, feeling Grasshopper's forehead.

Alejandro came back into the kitchen after he had put on a dry shirt.

"Grandpa, tell us about the mountain lion," Grasshopper said, trying to hide any signs of distress.

"You got a little fever," said Grandma.

"No, I'm fine. I feel better now," said Grasshopper as he positioned his chair closer to Grandpa.

"Are you sure you're okay?" asked Grandpa. "I know when you're lying to me."

"Yes, Grandpa, I'm fine," he said. Alejandro remained quiet and serious.

"Once the story is finished you both go to bed," said Grandma. Grandpa coughed and cleared his throat. The boys were quiet and attentive. Yet Alejandro's face looked unexpressive and stoic. Grandpa kept looking at him, trying to figure him out.

As Grandpa began to tell the story, Grasshopper's eyes grew larger. Grandma served Alejandro a piece of lemon pie and hot tea and then sat on a chair next to Grandpa.

"The nights in Sweet Heaven were always freezing, with the type of cold wind that pierces the skin," said Grandpa. "We were in a crew of four, right off the skirts of the Great Mountain near Indian Houl. Anders, who we called Chico; Julian, who was a mason by trade; John, who had only one eye; and me, a jack of all trades. We all had come from the valley to seek a better fortune for ourselves." Grandpa kept telling his grandsons.

"We were afraid to go outside the cabin after dark," Grandpa continued. "Word from the locals was that in the farms near the foot of the mountain, a lion had struck cattle and a teamster during daylight."

"Was it a big lion?" Grasshopper asked.

"Yes," said Grandpa. "The nights up there were colder than nights here during winter. But this night was even colder. No matter how much you bundled up, you could still feel the freezing cold in your bones. We were drinking coffee inside the cabin. And the night was quiet and calm." Grandpa squinted intensively at Grasshopper.

"We were all afraid of the lion," Grandpa continued, "but none of us showed our fear. We even joked with each other about going outside to get water or to take a piss. The well was about thirty yards from the cabin, into the brush." Grandpa eyed Alejandro.

"Did you go out?" asked Grasshopper again.

"Let Grandpa tell the story," said Grandma.

Alejandro listened as he indifferently ate the pie and sipped on the teacup. He was eating just to eat. His gaze was still fixed on something on the table; his face appeared overwhelmed by a pensive semblance and gloom.

"Yeah, stop asking dumb questions," said Alejandro in a slightly angry tone. Grasshopper frowned at him.

Grandpa continued. "No one went outside at night. It was just too dark and cold. One night while we were playing cards, we ran out of water for coffee, so we decided that whoever lost the next hand would go out and get water." Grandpa coughed and took small sips of his hot tea. He lit a LeMans before he continued. He puffed some smoke out one side of his mouth as he talked while he held the cigarette with the other. "We often joked about coming face to face with mountain lions or other creatures."

"Did you ever?" Grasshopper asked.

Grandpa didn't answer; he just looked at the boy and carried on with the story.

"'Remember that time we were coming down the mountain?' I said to Chico and the others."

"'That's the day you saw the lady of your dreams!' John said to Chico."

"'No shit! That's the time I shit my pants!' Chico said to all of us," Grandpa said it in a squeaky voice, emulating Chico's voice. Grasshopper and Grandma laughed. Alejandro smiled but pressed his lips.

"Did he really?" asked Grasshopper. He laughed again.

Grandpa gazed into the distance and continued. "'Remember that night we're coming down the mountain, when we heard some chirping in the shrubbery?' said John." Grandpa kept telling the boys. "'We stopped to see if there was a bird or some other animal. It was pitch dark that night. We were all silent. I saw a flare of red sparks that faded within the bushes. They musta been a couple of fireflies.'"

"'It looked like that,' said Julian. 'It looked like *el diablo* himself.'" Grandpa opened his eyes wide as he told the stories. Grasshopper moved onto the edge of his seat.

"Beyond the brush, there was some type of clear cloudy stain floating in the air. It's hard to explain what we saw. None of us could explain it," Grandpa said, raising his eyebrows. "But we all agreed that it was a clear, white-stained fog floating in the air. It had long white threads and looked like it had long hair. John said it looked like Chico's old lady. We all laughed."

Grasshopper laughed. Alejandro remained deep in thought.

"You were all really good friends," said Grasshopper, smiling.

"Very good friends," Grandpa said and continued narrating the events. "'You keep peeing on my shoe and telling me it's the angels,'" said Chico. "We knew all the tricks John had under his sleeve. But you wouldn't believe what we saw that night. 'Oh, man! Oh, man! Oh, man!' Chico kept saying." Grandpa kept imitating Chico's voice. Grasshopper laughed. "Why did he keep saying 'oh man?'" Grasshopper asked, laughing. Grandpa didn't answer. Every time he retold a story, he would add a new detail, a new expression to it.

"'Man, what we saw that night made all of us shit and pee our pants,' said John while he glanced at the cards on the table. 'When we looked, that apparition looked more and more like a woman,'" Grandpa told the kids.

"Or like an old man with long hair," Grandma interjected. She pretended to be asleep. They laughed.

"Could you see her face?" asked Alejandro. His eyelids showed he was tired and beaten, but he made the effort to ask.

"Yes, she looked mad and was wearing a white silky robe," said Grandpa.

"'Her hair was sticking up,' said Julian. 'Her eyes were black and glossy. Then she just hovered away.'" Grandpa kept telling.

"What?" said Grasshopper. His eyes grew big.

"'That's pretty much the way every man's wife looks in the morning,' said John." Grandma gave Grandpa a light kick in the shin. Grandpa laughed.

The kids laughed.

Grandma chuckled and shook her head and dozed off again. Grandpa loved to tell ghost stories and liked to watch the boys' faces as he told his tales.

"What happened to the ghost?" Grasshopper asked.

"After that, it was gone," said Grandpa, looking at Alejandro.

"What did Chico and Julian say?" Grasshopper kept asking.

"Nothing," said Grandpa. "We were just quiet. The ghost had scared us to death. The best part of seeing a ghost is seeing one. The ghost won't do a thing to you; it would only manifest."

"Manifest?' said Grasshopper.

"Yes. It would just show itself," said Grandpa.

Grasshopper just stared at Grandpa as he said this. "Tell us another one," said Grasshopper, hoping to keep Grandpa engaged.

Alejandro embraced the cup of tea with both hands and remained quiet and eyed Grandpa to show him he was listening.

"When I met Chico for the first time, I didn't like him," said Grandpa.

"Why?" said Grasshopper. Grandpa continued.

"'Let me ask you something, Sir,' I asked him one day. 'Do you always fart in front of people?'"

Grasshopper laughed again. Alejandro chuckled while he looked at Grandpa.

"'What do you mean?' asked Chico. He looked all too serious," said Grandpa.

"'That you always fart in front of people,' I said again and looked him in the eye."

"'Oh man you got me! How do you know I'm farting?' he asked me."

"'You keep balancing side to side on the chair,' I said. 'You let one go when you tilt sideways. It goes out silent. You can't fool me. I know when you're lying to me,' I said to him. From that point on, we called him "whiff thief" because he would let one go in silence through the back door. But he didn't like the nickname."

Grasshopper laughed loudly and Alejandro seemed to be in a daze and tried to laugh. Grandpa noticed his discomfort. The laughter startled Grandma, who sat up and blinked next to Grandpa. She burst out laughing too, then she immediately rolled and closed her eyes and dozed off again.

"Then Chico looked at me all serious. 'Oh man! Breaking wind is a natural process,' he said."

"'That's a real discovery,' I told him." Grasshopper laughed again. "The nights in Sweet Heaven were often like that. We worked during the day and told stories and played cards at night. That horrible night we were playing cards." Grandpa continued.

"What happened?" asked Grasshopper as his eyes widened.

"'You ready to fold?' asked John." Grandpa kept telling the story.

"'Not yet,' said Chico as he kept looking at his cards. 'Oh, man! Oh, man!'"

"'We're out of water,' I said. 'One of us is gonna have to get water from the well.'"

"'You all heard 'bout the pumas?' asked Julian."

"'Yeah, it attacked a man and some cattle near Russell,' I said."

"'Puma or no puma, we gotta get some water,' said Chico. 'There is no damn puma 'round here.' He got up from the table, picked up the coffee kettle and walked outside. That was the last that we saw of him. We kept playing cards for a while longer. The wind began to rustle and whistle outside. The temperature outside the cabin dropped as the wind picked up speed and we kept playing."

"All of the sudden, we heard a high-pitch yowl, a type of snarl of a big cat followed by a piercing 'Aaaaaahhhhh!' outside, echoing a long, horrible cry."

Grandma woke up, her eyes were wide open and looked around the room like a sleepwalker after Grandpa had mimicked the sound of the cat and Chico's cry. "We all looked at each other and were paralyzed."

"What happened to Chico?" asked Grasshopper.

"No one knows," said Grandpa. "We all went outside with torches and sickles, but Chico was gone."

"And did you call out for him?" Grasshopper kept asking.

"We did, but we only heard the whistling wind in the darkness."

"You didn't see anything?" asked the boy again.

"No," said Grandpa. "He just disappeared into the pitch darkness. The next day, at daybreak, we walked to the well and found the kettle and a trail of blood. We followed it for about a mile, and it led us through a grove. The trail disappeared as it moved uphill. We lost track of it in the jagged rocks above the skirts of the mountain."

"That must have been a big cat," said Alejandro in a somber tone, looking at the floor as he enclosed the cup of tea around his hands.

"It must have been at least two hundred pounds," said Grandpa.

"What did you do then?" Grasshopper asked.

"Nothing. We came back," said Grandpa.

"Poor Chico," Grasshopper said.

Alejandro just kept silent. Nothing was known about Chico, as nothing was known about what Alejandro had endured that day.

"Well, there's the story," Grandpa concluded, getting ready to get up and go to bed.

"Tell us another one, Grandpa, come on?" Grasshopper asked.

"No, it's time for you to tuck into the envelope and be sent adrift," said Grandpa.

"How about tomorrow?" asked Grasshopper.

"Maybe. We won't be going to work tomorrow. It's too wet," he said as the boys got up from the table and were on their way to bed.

Blood and Betrayal

When inclement weather happened, days of work were lost. Dark clouds hovered balefully low and overwhelmed the skies upon the homestead and its surroundings while Alejandro and Grasshopper walked along the dirt road. The deep green foliage on each side of the road swayed with the wind in a to-and-fro motion, which contrasted with the dark and gloomy shades that grew in the sky and marred the lushness of the surrounding trees. From each side of the road, the gloom of acacias, poplars, and other trees widened there. Where Alejandro and Grasshopper stood, the dirt road opened wide and the adjacent trees formed a cave-like tunnel that gradually faded into the distance, where its furthest point down the *callejón* became a tiny glimmer of light.

Raindrops dripped on the vegetation: poplar and acacia trees sprung vigorously from among the crimson wild rose beds in the undergrowth by the stream. Storm clouds and thunder felt as close above Alejandro and Grasshopper's heads as the lower branches of the acacia trees were to the ground. Picui doves and sparrows cut through the rough wind gusts and sought shelter in the thick foliage of the branches and parts protected from the wind. Sparrows muscled their way through the air with riotous chirping, announcing the thunderous showers. Other birds darted from branch to branch and populated the leafy acacia shoots. Sonorous thunder shivered the branches as the wind swayed the trees in a unified tandem.

It was near dusk and the water of the stream along the dirt road had been cut off. At times in the summer, irrigation flows were diverted, and the water supply was rationed throughout the valley. The boys didn't hesitate to jump to the opportunity and explore the bottom of the stream, which was still rocky and muddy from the rain. They dug out old glass bottles and jugs of all shapes and colors: Bromo-Seltzer, Bovril, Coca-Cola, milk, wine, and other bottles of every kind. The lads unearthed rocks, arrowheads, and rotten logs buried under the mud in the creek bed.

Alejandro carried a walking stick that he used to poke and turn over rocks. In his back pocket, Grasshopper kept his slingshot ready to shoot at any critter that might come around. When both of them went out on adventures, the older brother had the right to the first shot.

"C'mon, let me take a shot!" demanded Grasshopper, who stood on the side of the *callejón* and looked at Alejandro below. From the bottom of the creek, Alejandro signaled to his brother for the slingshot and a pebble and aimed it at the crown of tree branches that hung over the creek. The mourning of Picui doves and the raindrops falling on leaves resounded and kept the birds from noticing the two brothers who lurked beneath the trees, searching for targets.

"Someone's coming over there," Grasshopper said. In the distance, along the dirt road, he saw a silhouette of a woman who sauntered along in their direction, but Grasshopper could not distinguish her from afar.

"I'm gonna kill one of those birds and eat it like Uncle Carlos used to do," said Alejandro as he aimed at the crown of acacia trees. There was something in the gleam of his eyes that was different. He had the same stoic face he had when Grandpa told the story about the puma. Behind his face there was anger, fear, and a thirst for seeing something suffer. He now knew how to feel pain, but he didn't know how to inflict it upon another. He unconsciously wanted to see if the feeling of retribution was as strong as the pain of an attack, like that sweet release that many talk about brought about by revenge.

"Yeah, but Uncle Carlos used the rifle, remember?" said Grasshopper.

"You don't need a rifle to kill a little critter. You just have to aim right, and you'll get one—watch!" said Alejandro coldly, while they heard the roar of a diesel engine reverberating in the distance.

"That's Doctor Piggie," said Grasshopper, as he looked back at Alejandro.

"Sounds like him," said Alejandro. "How did you get all broken out like that? What happened to your arms?"

"I don't know," said Grasshopper. "I think it's poison ivy."

"Yeah, let's go!" said Alejandro as he climbed back onto the dirt road. "It's starting to rain."

The two boys took shelter from the incoming rain and hid under a leafy acacia tree among the lush vegetation by the road.

"Wait! Look over there!" shouted Grasshopper. "A snake! Shoot it!" A dark-scaled and white-patterned snake glided across the dark glossy stones on the dirt road.

"Where?" asked Alejandro.

"Over there!" pointed Grasshopper. "There!!!" screamed the boy as he stooped to reach a rock from the ground.

"Wait!" said Alejandro as he reached down for a couple of round pebbles on the ground. "I'll get it!"

"C'mon! It's getting away," shouted Grasshopper again. The elongated dark and thick reptile slithered swiftly across the gravel. Its skin glinted brightly under the lightning in the clouds as it tried to reach the undergrowth near the dry stream.

As Dr. Maxim drove down the dirt road, the woman that Grasshopper had seen walked down in the same direction of the truck. She wore a white dress, and her stride was proud but seemed exhausted. There was only one woman in Russell who had that stride and distinctiveness. Alvera. Her distinctive figure would make any man stop what they were doing. If Alejandro could have stopped breathing for her, he would have. He fell into a trance every time she was around him. As Dr. Maxim approached down the *callejón*, he slowed down and pulled the truck alongside Alvera.

"Hello there, Miss Reys," said Dr. Maxim while he stuck his head out of the window to seek her attention.

"Good evening, Dr. Maxim," said Alvera.

"How is Mr. Reys these days? Would you like a lift?" asked Maxim as one of his eyebrows raised in a wanton innuendo. Folks in Russell were courteous and good-natured, but her intuition told her to be cautious.

"He's fine, thank you," said Alvera, lowering her gaze. She looked indifferent, as she continued walking under the rain.

"Come on, I'll give you a lift," he said as his truck moved along with her.

"Thank you," said Alvera. "But I'd really like to walk."

⇝⇝➤ ⫷⫷

By now, Alejandro was about ten yards away from the snake when one of the pebbles he had aimed at it deflected from the scales near its head, making some of its scales come loose. As Alejandro reached down for another pebble, the snake suddenly charged toward him. The reptile made an awkward movement, bracing its back, throwing its body swiftly forward. Grasshopper's eyes grew wide when he noticed the snake was now charging toward his brother.

"Watch out!" he screamed in a high and girly pitch. Alejandro aimed at it again but missed. Its fast pace made the reptile look as if it could walk, dive quickly forward, or even run toward Alejandro. He grew nervous and desperate. His shaky hands were unable to reach down for another round pebble to fasten within the leathered end of the slingshot and aim at the snake again. He stood paralyzed as he observed the animal charging toward him. The few pebbles and the forked stick that held the rubber bands suddenly fell on the ground, leaving him unarmed. The skin of the snake turned glossier with its speed and the rain.

"Get away!" Alejandro screamed at Grasshopper while his sight was fixed upon the snake. As quick as the lighting above them, Grasshopper, picked up a wide, jagged rock from the side of the road and pitched it at the snake, hitting it halfway along its back, instantly flattening and breaking its spine, just a couple of feet from where Alejandro stood. The snake curled over, not knowing what had hit it, and then became calm. It stopped zig-zagging its body; its tail slowly curled over from side to side, unable to move forward. Alejandro was overwhelmed by the nearness of the animal that lay twisting at his feet.

"That was close," Grasshopper said.

Alejandro was just shocked by the moment and the nearness of the reptile.

As the rain began to pour, Grasshopper jolted his brother's arm, and both moved back beneath a leafy branch of the acacia tree by the dry stream.

Meanwhile, the sprinkles on the green leaves soon became heavy drops that plunged down on the opaque windshield of Dr. Maxim's truck. Alvera fixed her gaze on the *callejón* and occasionally raised her sight at the flashing lightning in the clouds above. Thunder continued roaring and shaking the trees along the dirt road.

"Come on!" said Maxim. "You're getting soaked out here." The man's eyes gleamed with the same greedy delight his eyes had the day he told Grandpa that he wouldn't get his ten percent. The glimmer in his eyes reflected his greed, like a desire for profits, a wanting of possessions, that looked at the ripened, hanging fruit as if he could only smell its monetary value and not its sweet fragrance.

Alvera's eyes widened as if she faced a terror greater than the lightning and thundering above. As lightning struck the crown of a poplar tree by the road, she felt the flash and impact right above her head and reconsidered. How many men had conspired to be as close to her as Dr. Maxim was now? And how much wealth and abundance they had insisted upon her and her family to convince her? And all because of her beauty. Or how many times had the most prominent men in Russell offered her the world as if they were spoiled, entitled, and greedy children desperate to possess yet another new toy, just for her to turn them down every time.

The end of the harvesting season was approaching, and folks were already talking about crowning Russell's Wine Fest Queen. Dr. Maxim squinted.

"You would make a perfect queen of the Wine Fest," said Dr. Maxim as he leered at her breast. Given the intensity of the rain and lightning, Alvera looked at the skies while she was sitting next to Dr. Maxim.

"Thank you," she said in an indifferent and firm voice.

The downpour rapidly inundated the *callejón* as Dr. Maxim drove along. The rattling of the diesel truck and the crunching sound of tires on the glossy gravel passed by the boys. As the vehicle ran over the remnants of the snake in the middle of the dirt road, Grasshopper noticed Alvera sitting on the passenger's side. They waved at her as they watched from underneath the acacia tree. She looked back and waved at them, too. She was gone now into the dark tunnel down the dirt road. The raindrops on the back window of the truck smeared the image of her face, making her look sad, as if her whole face were crying, and unable to return after reaching the minute dot of light, that distant glimmer, at the end of the *callejón*.

Once the rain had subsided, the boys stepped out from under the acacia tree and into the *callejón*. The dirt road was clear, and any vestiges of the snake were now washed away. Picui doves began their soft cooing once again as if they were quietly mourning. An unusual peace spread through the hot, humid air, which mixed with the scent of rain, emitted a deep and fresh fragrance of soil, chocolate, vanilla, ripened cherries, olive oil, and fresh fennel.

"I see one right there on that branch," whispered Alejandro as he leaned next to Grasshopper and pointed at it. "You see it?" He said softly.

"Where?" Grasshopper asked. "I don't see it. Where is it?" he asked.

"Shhhh...That white and gray one up there," whispered Alejandro as he picked up a sharp and jagged rock and placed it in the leather pouch of the slingshot. He aimed by outstretching his arm and stretched the rubber bands of the slingshot. As he released the leathered end of the slingshot, the rock swiftly ripped through thin foliage of leaves above, piercing them all at once. Then, as some of the leaves fell in disarray through the branches, a puff of white and gray feathers, like tender snowflakes, gently glided down through the air. They heard the sound as the weight of the bird plummeted through the branches and finally fell on the undergrowth on the beds of wild roses and fennel by the stream.

"You got one! You got one!" Grasshopper screamed as he ran toward the bank.

"Wait up!" said Alejandro as he trailed from behind. "Yeah, I got it!" he said. His honey-brown eyes widened as he found the body of the Picui dove in the undergrowth. Blood was still pumping from the bird's heart, flowing from its neck, and its body still shuddered with terror for a few seconds until its legs gave a last kick and it became stiff.

Grasshopper's eyes were now as big as Alejandro's as he stared at the gory scene. The shot had decapitated the bird and the boys stood there watching it like two cowards trembling with terror and shame. Grasshopper didn't feel that way about killing the snake. Alejandro's face turned pale as he processed the impact of the shot. His wan face had a sad resemblance, with an already downcast gaze, plus the impact he felt after taking the fragile life of a harmless dove. The memory of the dove's bloody bosom tainted his mind, as the blood had tainted the dove's white and gray bosom. He had never intended such vicious violence but had only meant to prove his claim that now he could shoot one down. Now he could kill something. Shame rose to his tanned face, darkening his cheeks and forehead. The intense carmine hue of the blood flowing from the dove— the crimson glow kept flowing from the bird's neck, as blushed as Alejandro's shame and as crimson as the wild roses on the bed by the undergrowth.

Uncle Carlos' Dream

By the end of that day, Grasshopper was running a high fever and the bumps on his arms had spread over most of his body. Grandpa and Grandma fixed a makeshift cot in the toolshed because they thought it best to keep Grasshopper isolated from the rest of the family. Despite the fever and itchy skin, he was happy to stay in the shed, enjoying all the adventure books there: *Simbad the Sailor, Twenty Thousand Leagues Under the Sea, Journey to the Center of the Earth, Around the World in Eighty Days,* various issues of *The Reader's Digest,* and other books and magazines that Grandpa enjoyed reading.

By dusk, Grasshopper had gone to bed. Crickets chirred outside the shed once the rain subsided. Grandma sat by the cot, her voice crooning and singing a melody that put the boy to sleep. As she put chamomile compresses over Grasshopper's arms and back, she cooed a song:

Baby dreaming,
Baby dreaming,
On the fields all birds are singing.

Baby dreaming,

Baby dreaming,
In the sky the stars are gleaming
while my boy's sweet asleep.

Grassy's dreaming,
Grassy's dreaming,
Now my boy's sweet asleep,
Kiss his tiny little feet,
While in dreams he's running free.

Baby dreaming,
Baby dreaming,
All the boys are now dreaming...

"I'm not a baby anymore, Grandma," said Grasshopper. He was nine years old but he had the impetus and mischief of a twelve-year old boy.

"I know. I just like to sing that song to you," said Grandma.

As Grasshopper pulled up the quilt, he dropped Verne's books by his side, looked at the cover, and mused about the adventurous Hans Bjelke. His gaze fell upon a picture hanging next to the cot. The thunderous rain resumed outside the shed, and the weak flame emanating from an oil lamp lit up the blurry, black-and-white photo of a slender man with a stylish mustache, carrying an old Martini-Henry rifle over his shoulder. The man stood by the massive eucalyptus tree trunk in front of the adobe house. He looked nonchalant and assertive. His fedora, tilted to the left over a cocked eyebrow, gave him an air of pride and confidence that many men would have envied. Grasshopper's gaze now disregarded the spider cobs in the corners and the clusters of tools in the shed as he focused on the image of his favorite uncle wavering and fading with the reflection of the lamp light. As the image of his uncle disappeared, he fell into the numb lethargy of slumber with his damp hair on the pillow, succumbing to the trance of memory. His head rested softly on the white pillow Grandma had propped behind his head, as if the dreams rested there, enclosed in it, waiting to come true, waiting for Grasshopper to set his consciousness at rest. He didn't believe in dreams, but the images in his mind came and went.

The photograph of Uncle Carlos was distant now. "Up 'n the air you go!" said Uncle Carlos while he held Grasshopper up. He was a small child; he recalled. Uncle Carlos lifted and threw him up through an opening in the untrimmed vines on the arbor that surrounded the adobe house. The voices and giggles in the dream arrived to Grasshopper's ears like the humming of bees that surrounded the ripened grapes on the arbor. Grasshopper giggled, and Uncle Carlos laughed as the boy bounced up and down through the leafy opening. He slept and woke as the photograph of his uncle kept wavering and fading.

In the darkness, Grasshopper could talk, and he could hear his uncle's voice in the distance.

"Let's play in the toolshed, Uncle?" said Grasshopper.

"Grandpa don't like that," he replied.

"Yes, he does," replied Grasshopper

"Tell the truth, Grasshopper. Don't go around telling little lies," Uncle Carlos's voice echoed in his dream, "Lies are short-legged." The sound of oily gun pellets panning out on a skillet...his photograph kept wavering and fading...as uncle Carlos aimed the rifle toward the crown of the leafy eucalyptus in front of the adobe house.

"You see it up there?" Uncle Carlos whispered.

"No. Where is it?"

"Right there!" whispered his uncle again while he pointed the rifle. He smiled at him.

"I see it, I see it!" Grasshopper screamed.

"Shhhh!" warned his uncle as he made way for the boy to see a plump partridge near the crown of the tree. "Do you wanna shoot it?" He handed the rifle to Grasshopper, but the boy wouldn't take it.

"That's a pretty bird," said Grasshopper. "Poor little dove."

"Sure is. And tasty, too," said his uncle. He looked at the boy and smiled. He quietly loaded the rifle, aimed, and shot. A sharp buzzing hummed in Grasshopper's ears while a thunderous boom roared outside the shed.

"Noooo!" the boy screamed—his eyes ungluing—and then burst into tears as he sat upright on the bed, his sweaty palms and fingers clutching the blanket. The ringing in his ears continued as he looked at Verne's books on the bed. The sheets and his pajamas were soaked. The spots on his arms were as red as the wounded chest of the partridge he recalled falling through the branches of the eucalyptus tree.

"What's wrong, Robinson?" asked Grandma, who had entered the shed carrying a tray with a dinner plate for Grasshopper. After putting the tray down, she placed her hand on his back. She comforted him.

"Grandma, I saw Uncle Carlos," said Grasshopper as he rubbed his eyes.

"Your uncle is in heaven now, Grasshopper. Why don't you eat something?" asked Grandma as she gently stroked his hair and cheek.

"I'm not hungry, Grandma," said Grasshopper. "Can I eat it later?"

"Yes, but you ought to eat something or you won't get better," said Grandma, putting down the plate with small chunks of fried partridge.

Uncle Carlos had been gone for three years now. Grasshopper didn't like to talk about him being gone, and he often missed him. While he remained sick in the shed and Grandma tended to him, images of his uncle continued to pass across his mind. As his fever faded, the thunder and rain finally subsided outside the shed.

See Us Fall

R ight before the beginning of the olive harvest season, prominent men and foremen in Russell held meetings to set the prices for labor; auction and barter machinery and other items; discuss profits and strategies to double and triple their earnings; determine interests for loans; and be updated on the latest outlines and plans of corporate bodies in the big cities. They had a tendency to repeat the words, practices, gestures, habits, and the demeanor of men who in their mind were higher up in the chain. They looked up to them as if they were golden petrified sphinxes, despite never talking to or seeing them with their bare eyes, except for on the pages of the booklets and pamphlets that showed graphs, photographs, diagrams, and charts that displayed the upward trends of their earnings, their photographs in their dark Cheaton suits, and their expensive Italian shoes, with their Cuban cigars clenched between their teeth and their shiny bald heads all printed on glossy paper. These men were untouched by the rigorous effort of manual labor. They lacked the callous hands, the peeled and tanned skin, the bruised shoulders from carrying eighty fifty-pound tin crates a day. Their eyes had never been poked by twigs or pierced by the sharp tips of olive tree leaves while harvesting. They knew nothing about the bleeding lacerations on harvesting hands by the sharp grapevine shoots hidden in the foliage from the pruning of of the previous season. But they preceded the meeting; there was a stark contrast between them and the men and women who worked the land.

As the men and women from Russell arrived at the gathering, a large-framed man sat asleep on a low stool leaning against a post by the gate. Here, the *callejón* that led to the homestead, joined the asphalt road that connected all the farms to downtown Russell. This was where the roads crossed. The heavy man's mouth was wide open as he snored lustily. The air and the force of his breath scared the flies that crawled in and out of his mouth. His hands entwined over his large belly bobbed up and down as he breathed. A half-empty bottle of Bravo lay next to the stool. Landowners, farmers, foremen, and some sharecroppers walked by and looked at him. They shook their heads; others laughed at the sight.

The brisk breezes of the fall were upon Russell and felt as cold as the pebbles Grasshopper carried in his game bag. Dr. Maxim had asked Grandpa to go, but he was still nursing a cough. Grandpa had sent word to Mr. Gurua instead, asking him to go with Alejandro in his place. Grasshopper, as always, had overheard them talking about the meeting and snuck in. No longer contagious, Grasshopper followed Alejandro everywhere he went.

That day, Grasshopper trailed behind Alejandro along the dirt road, playing with pebbles to hide the fact he was following his brother. He lagged behind pelting pebbles with pebbles, seeing how the crystalline, glossy, and colorful balls would roll in the smooth areas of the road as he struck one after the other. Ahead, along the dirt road, a boy, who Grasshopper recognized as the son of one of Mr. Campito's seasonal workers, played with a stick and poked and traced lines on the road.

"You staying at Mr. Campito's, right?" said Grasshopper.

"Yes," said the boy.

"Didn't all the workers leave already?"

"We're moving north next week," said the boy.

"Do you wanna play?" asked Grasshopper, showing the marbles.

"I don't have any pebbles," he said.

"I can lend you some," said Grasshopper.

"I'm not good at it," he said.

"It's easy. You knock it right on the head. You win right away," said Grasshopper.

"Okay, but I just play for fun," said the boy.

Grasshopper handed him three pebbles. "If you can get your marble close enough to mine, within a span of the hand, you get another shot to knock it right up close."

"I just wanna play for fun," said the small boy in a passive voice.

"You gotta play for something," said Grasshopper.

"I don't wanna play like that. I always lose," said the boy.

"You gotta play to win, to triple what you have," said Grasshopper. The little boy just looked at Grasshopper and took the pebbles.

As they moved along the dirt road, the kids kept playing. Once they reached the gate, they saw Mr. High, who stood puffing the smoke of a cigarette into the air. Playing pebbles this time was different for Grasshopper. He looked at the boy's humble nature. The game no longer had its escapism, its excitement. It was no longer a game but an opportunity to show the boy the game, perhaps help him feel or experience the good and excitement in it.

When he was at school, Grasshopper played with other kids in the yard. No other kid at school enjoyed playing marbles more than he did. His teachers would often summon him to go to class, but he ignored them and kept striking pebble after pebble in the dust. "I'm goin', I'm goin'," he would say while Ms. Martha, his fifth-grade teacher, waited by the doorframe of her classroom. *Two plus this one, now mine*, he thought as he took every pebble from the other kids in the yard and then put the round, glassy ones in his swollen game bag. He always won. He never hesitated to play when kids were playing. At first, he took the pebbles from every kid he played with. But he had learned the lesson. A tiny trail of cat eyes halfway buried along the dust followed him one day as he left the schoolyard to go to class. A tiny hole in his bag—the price of his ambition—became larger and larger with every pearl he collected, so that most of the pebbles fell through the opening, leaving him with just a few. The realization came to him when he put his hand in the bag, and then in his pocket, that he had nothing left but three large pebbles, plus the smeared dirt and dust his hands had collected in the process. That day he came home crying for what he had lost.

Back along the dirt road, every stroke of the pebbles took the two boys closer to the yard outside the warehouse where the meeting was held. The crispy leaves in the crown of the acacia trees rustled noticeably. Autumn, with its cool and majestic breeze, had arrived and had brought with it freezing nights in Russell.

Prominent men at the gathering talked over one another, often interrupting and imposing their will on each other. "I can ship in a few thousands and we'll be good...," said a man who sat behind a panel. With an air of confidence and conviction, he gestured his reasons to the men next to him.

Alejandro sat next to Mr. Gurua and listened to the men talking. Mr. Gurua leaned a bit to the left and told Alejandro to pay attention. "Listen carefully to every single word they say." Alejandro looked back at the men and squinted. Mr. Reys, Mr. and Mrs. Campito, Mr. Beneto, Mr. Lessar, and other farmers and sharecroppers were there.

"Let me start with the bad news first," said Joaquin Tiele, the owner of Bravo Wines, a man with soft, long hands and a semi-tanned complexion, who had gotten up to preside over the meeting. The plump man that had been sound asleep by the gate approached Mr. Tiele and handed him a stack of papers. "In light of some of your choices not to fumigate your orchards and vineyards with anti-parasitics," said the man, "and based on our analysis of high and low-yielding grapes, we'll reduce," he coughed as he glanced at the papers, "we will reduce the price for each bin for next season. The price will be set at two silver coins per bin," said Mr. Tiele. The crowd murmured.

Alejandro raised his hand. The man first ignored him, but as the other men at the panel saw Alejandro, Mr. Tiele could no longer ignore him. "Yes, the young lad there," he pointed at him. Alejandro got up. Mr. Gurua cocked his head.

"How full should the bin be to get the two coins?" asked Alejandro bluntly. Mr. Tiele looked at him, his eyes wandering about the room. The men in the audience lightly shook their heads.

"Hmm, the way it has always been, full!" he said. The men in the panel laughed and looked at each other. The men in the audience scratched their heads. After a moment, those in the panel directed their full attention to Alejandro.

Mr. Tiele coughed a bit again as if something had stuck in his throat. "I'm sure the child just wants to get away with as little work as possible," said Mr. Tiele in a more serious and dismissive voice, turning to the men on the panel.

"Youngsters are always trying to avoid responsibility," said another man who sat next to Mr. Tiele and who smiled as he spoke.

"My grandpa says I should always work hard, no matter what," said Alejandro.

"That is great," said Mr. Tiele. "You should do what your grandfather says."

"I do, and I wanna know if a full bin has to be filled up to the brim or to the ring?" Alejandro's voice sounded agitated, as if anger were little by little overtaking him. The men in the audience started murmuring to one another again while the men at the panel stared at Alejandro.

"A bin full of grapes is a bin full of grapes, no matter how you look at it," said Mr. Tiele. "Besides, bins are provided for you, your only responsibility is showing up to work and filling them up."

Alejandro looked at Mr. Tiele and then at the men in the audience. He tried to reply to Mr. Tiele, but the man went ahead and began discussing how parasites had taken hold of the crops and had pervaded and damaged the vineyards in some distant farmlands.

"Botrytis and peronospora farinosa," Mr. Tiele continued, hoping to leave Alejandro's question behind. The men in the audience looked perplexed.

"That's gray mold and downy mildew," said Mr. Gurua so the men in the audience could hear him. The men turned their heads toward Mr. Gurua, then looked at Mr. Tiele.

"Pretty soon you fellas won't have to worry about harvesting the fields," he added. "The hard work you do won't be necessary. We will provide you with new technology that will assist you in harvesting your crops. Technology is changing the way we live, and soon you will be able to increase your profits without much labor. You'll be able to spend more time with your families and less time in the fields."

Outside the warehouse, Mr. High squatted as he watched Grasshopper while he and the boy played with pebbles. The man's hair was wild as usual. He had an afro-like hairstyle, protruded cheekbones, thin lips, tanned skin, weather-beaten by the sun, wind, and dust. He wore ragged dusty pants and a shirt with rolled-up sleeves. His tanned, long forearms rested on his knees, and he had on worn out leather sandals. He sat on his heels. He took five round and glossy rocks from his shirt pocket and laid them out on the dust. He picked one up and threw it in the air while he collected another one of the four that remained in the dusty ground. Then he tossed the two up and grabbed another, continuing in this fashion until he picked them all up. Grasshopper and the boy looked at him.

"What are you playing there, Sir?" Grasshopper asked.

"That's the g-g-game of chance," he said without looking at the boys. "The bigger the h-h-hand, the larger the outc-c-come."

"Those are some pretty round rocks. Where'd you get them?" asked Grasshopper.

Mr. High took out a cigarette butt from his other shirt pocket and a red matchbox that had the icon of a raging bull exhaling fire and smoke through its nostrils.

"A single one w-w-won't stay up too long without f-f-falling on the ground," he said after he struck a match and lit the cigarette butt. Then he played the game again.

"You got to pick up the others at once," said Grasshopper. The younger boy just looked.

"It n-n-needs the others to complete the w-w-whole operation. C-c-coordination, number of pebbles in a h-h-hand, how many o-o-one can hold, all that g-g-good stuff," said Mr. High. The cigarette burned but it did not smoke until the smoke would come profusely out of Mr. High's nostrils. He puffed, exhaled the smoke and played with the rocks. Thick gray smoke wafted in the air above him, just like the smoke out of the nostrils of the raging bull on the matchbox.

"Where'd you get them?" asked Grasshopper.

"The r-r-river carries round r-r-rocks like these," said Mr. High. "You j-j-just can't see them. They're at t-t-the bottom."

"All the rocks in the river are jagged," said Grasshopper.

"It only t-t-takes one round one to know," said Mr. High. "One p-p-plus one, two p-p-plus two, three p-p-plus three, and you have a h-h-handful of round ones that c-c-could go up and down....Let's j-j-jump, yeah, let's jump, j-j-jump, jump, more up than down, j-j-just like the rocks, more down then up, that sh-sh-should be enough to e-e-elevate us and j-j-jump." He had gotten up and started to leap on one leg, taking a long stride to land on the other.

The boys looked at him and laughed nervously. Grasshopper smiled at Mr. High at first. "I think the man is a looney," said Grasshopper, whispering to the boy. The boys stood there looking at him. Grasshopper was suddenly scared and slowly walked toward the warehouse. The boy followed him as Mr. High continued his dance of hops and leaps while puffing his cigarette.

Inside the warehouse, Grasshopper and the boy trudged through the rows where folks sat alongside Mr. Gurua and Alejandro.

"It's a dead end with these fellows," said Mr. Gurua. Alejandro cocked his head.

"Mr. Reys, you only got two choices," said Mr. Tiele.

"Well, Mr. Tiele," said Mr. Reys as he removed his hat and held it humbly before him, "last year my crops were protected with the natural fertilizers we use around these parts."

"Mr. Reys, technology's here to stay. If you want your crops to grow, you have to fumigate with Raging Bull pesticide."

"The crops I produced this year were healthy and large, Mr. Tiele."

"But not large enough to increase production."

"We take what the land gives us," said a voice from the audience.

"A fellow down in Wooden Cross mixes natural herbs that work well to protect our crops," said Mr. Reys.

"That's right! He uses nettle, inch plants, rocoto chile, and some other stuff, and fruits grow fine," said Nora Campito.

"This fellow knows what type of herbs to mix to protect our crops," said Mr. Reys.

"Mr. Reys, we always hear about people trying to reinvent the wheel. These concoctions you talk about have already been established and scientifically approved," said Mr. Tiele. "It's a nine out of ten win in an acre, studies show."

"I don't produce any crops, as you all know, but my friend Mr. Segovia's been using these raging chemicals in his orchard and they have caused more harm than good," said Mr. Gurua.

"Well, where is Mr. Segovia?" asked Mr. Tiele. "Shouldn't he be here to speak for himself?"

"He's sick," said Nora Campito.

"Grandma said Mr. Segovia's beehives have died too," a squeaky voice clearly echoed in the room.

"If you are concerned with the potency of the fumes, you can fumigate at night," said Tiele. "Besides, fumes kill plagues, produce larger and better fruit, and you'll get more money for your crops."

Alejandro picked up on the exchange and said, "I remember last year it killed all the bugs around the vines. The fruits grew the same as before, and my grandpa and the crew weren't even paid for all the work we did."

"Yeah," a raspy voice from the crowd said, "the more crops we harvest the less we get paid for them at the market."

"Listen, Gentlemen," began Mr. Tiele, just to be interrupted.

"In low years, fruits are sold for more money and we get paid the same," said Mr. Campito.

"In good years, fruits are plump everywhere and we get paid the same three silver coins for a bin," said Alejandro.

"Listen, Gentlemen," said Mr. Tiele. "I understand your concerns. We can leave the price of the bin indefinite until the beginning of the harvest." The men and women in the audience looked at each other. "Mr. Reys, if you don't fumigate, Brava won't buy grapes from you anymore. You got only two choices."

"I can sell my crops in Grape Valley," said Mr. Reys.

"Listen there, Mr. Reys. You'll have to drive three hours to get there; you'll spend more money on gasoline; you'll use time you don't have," said Mr. Baker, who sat next to Mr. Tiele. "Take it from me that I own trucks."

"Your other option is to put your farm up for sale," said Mr. Tiele.

Mr. Reys frowned. "I'm selling nothing. My family was born and died on this land."

"Mr. Reys, you've always been a friend and contributor to Brava and Brava Markets. We love you; we love your family. We wouldn't like you to sell your farm, but you can always talk to Mr. Baker here and ask for a loan," said Mr. Tiele.

Mr. Reys looked at the man, gave him a sarcastic smirk, and left the meeting.

⤞⟫⟩ ⟨⟨⟨⤝

Under the pretext of progress, some men with rapacious visions had procured the earth, the very water and soil. Contracts were left indefinite, infinite like the darkness of the night, and harvesters and farmers were kept in the dark about the value of their labor, so in due time their visionary bosses would pay them a meager lump sum after farmers, harvesters, and sharecroppers had pulled entire harvests, after the harvesters' entire families had moved from vineyard to vineyard, from orchard to orchard, from field to field, from province to province, and from country to country. At times, the disparities caused massive exoduses of native peoples leaving the area to be replaced by another influx of native folks who were just seeking an honest day's work.

"Is Mr. Reys going to lose his farm?" Alejandro asked Mr. Gurua.

"I doubt it. Mr. Reys is a hard worker and an honest man. He won't lose it." said Mr. Gurua.

"If my Grandpa is paid what he's owed, we can buy the tract in Sweet Heaven," said Alejandro.

"That will be good. I told Mr. Druett I will give him the land for a good price," said Mr. Gurua.

"I'm not asking for a gift," said Alejandro.

"I'm not giving you one. You're even more proud and stubborn than your Grandpa," said Mr. Gurua, smiling.

"I just don't want to owe nobody nothing," said Alejandro. "Some people are born and die owing something to somebody."

Mr. Gurua noticed the seriousness and cold tone in Alejandro's words. "Son, in this world, you gotta owe somebody something to live, to survive," said Gurua. "I owe a lot to your Grandpa."

"Why do you owe him so much?"

"When I got burned, I couldn't work for a whole year," said Gurua. "Your grandparents took care of us."

"When was that?"

"Many years before you came to live with him," said Gurua.

Their brief exchange was interrupted by folks who got up from their seats and began to exit the warehouse. Once those in the audience walked out, the men in suits followed them outside.

On his way out, Mr. Tiele ran into Mr. Gurua.

"How are you doing, Cholo?" asked Mr. Tiele. "How are things running at the refinery?"

"It's all right. How are you, Joaquin?" asked Mr. Gurua, his words were shielded with an invisible armor that kept the two men from engaging in deep conversation.

"Who's the young lad?" he asked.

"This is Alejandro, one of Mr. Druett's grandsons," said Gurua. "Carlos' nephew."

"I see. He even looks like him. Hopefully this one won't turn into a troublemaker," said Mr. Tiele as he walked past Alejandro.

Alejandro squinted at him. "I don't trust that man," said Alejandro after Mr. Tiele had walked outside.

"If you listen closely to these people, you won't ever be fooled by them," said Mr. Gurua again.

"He knew my uncle?" said Alejandro.

"Everybody knew your uncle. He was an honest and hardworking man," said Mr. Gurua. "Most of the things these people say are half-truths."

"What's a half-truth?" said Alejandro.

"Something that sounds like it's true but isn't," said Gurua. "You just got to find the part that's missing."

"A lot is missing here," said Alejandro.

"Yes, that's why you have to pay attention."

Mr. High squatted outside and examined a cigarette butt while farmers and sharecroppers exited the warehouse and ignored him as they passed by. Grasshopper and the boy continued walking and playing marbles along the dirt road. To Grasshopper, the meeting didn't mean much. In his mind it wasn't much: Two silver coins per crate. It was three coins the year before. It had always been plastic tokens in exchange for grapes. In Grasshopper's mind, it was grapes in exchange for jars of apricot jelly. Grapes in exchange for bread and sausage in the minds of workers. Grapes in exchange for beer and a loaf of bread in the minds of seasonal workers. A small plastic token in exchange for profits in the minds of business owners. Work in exchange for dreams in the minds of some sharecroppers. Coins in exchange for crumbs of dignity in Alejandro's mind.

Alejandro and Mr. Gurua stopped at the entrance of the warehouse and kept talking.

"Why did Mr. Tiele say my uncle was a troublemaker?"

"Your uncle never stopped demanding what was due," said Mr. Gurua. "He wasn't a troublemaker."

"Then why did he say that?" said Alejandro. He looked Mr. Gurua straight in the eye as if demanding the truth, as if something was owed to him.

"Because Carlos was just a man who didn't take crap from anyone," said Mr. Gurua.

"How come nobody knows what happened to my uncle?"

"We'll never know. What we know is that your grandparents received his body one day and nobody knew what had happened to him."

"Why?"

"He took the risk of leaving Russell. He was lured to the big city where there was more opportunity, I guess," said Mr. Gurua. "Not everyone that leaves makes it." Mr. Gurua looked at Alejandro. A direct and honest look on his face. "There are people who paint a pretty rosy picture of what life is like elsewhere but when you get there, it is worse than what you had to begin with."

"I could see why they would risk it all," said Alejandro.

"Carlos was too smart to stay in these parts," said Mr. Gurua.

"What do you think happened to him?" Alejandro asked.

"I don't know. All we know is that he's gone now."

Alejandro looked serious and saw his brother walking down the *callejón*. Mr. Reys walked farther down the dirt road until he became a tiny dot in the distance where the road was no more.

Grasshopper parted with the boy, gave him two pebbles for him to keep, and took a shortcut through the farm adjacent to the homestead. Alejandro was within some distance and followed his brother through the shrubs, a passage Grandpa and the kids often used to avoid circling through the *callejón* to the homestead.

After Grasshopper got through the shrubs that separated the dirt road from the farm, he saw Alvera picking herbs by the side of the shrubbery, so he picked some daisies for her.

"She loves me, she loves me not, much, little, or nothing," said Grasshopper as he plucked each petal of one of the flowers.

"You like daisies?" asked Alvera when she noticed Grasshopper was near her.

"I do."

"A flower is a bit like a woman," said Alvera.

"I'm holding a bunch of womans in my hand," said Grasshopper.

"Not like that, you silly boy," she said.

"I know what you mean. A woman is pretty like a flower," said Grasshopper.

"Yes, women are pretty and delicate like flowers," said Alvera.

"Here!" said Grasshopper as he stretched his arm, giving Alvera the tender bouquet.

Alejandro appeared through the shrubbery behind them and walked toward them.

"Oh, thank you," said Alvera. "I was just saying."

"I wanted to give them to you anyway," said Grasshopper.

"Thank you," she said. Alejandro's somber look was lighted by his brother's action. Alvera smiled at him after Grasshopper had handed her the daisies.

"Are you all right?" Alvera asked Alejandro, but she was interrupted by Grasshopper.

"Do you like them?" Grasshopper asked.

"I wonder if women are as pretty as flowers, what happens in the fall when all flowers become old and dried?" asked Alejandro.

"I do," Alvera said. She frowned and squinted at Alejandro, trying to figure out what he had said. "A woman's beauty can last forever; some daisies are beautiful only one spring and summer," she said.

"Sometimes people last for only a few springs. Then they die. They disappear," Alejandro said.

"People are as fragile as the petals of a daisy," Alvera said.

Alejandro remained deep in thought.

"Grandpa says that women are as fragile as the petals of a rose," said Grasshopper.

"Grandpa is a wise man. Women liked to be protected and respected," said Alvera, looking at Alejandro.

Alejandro looked at her, his usual smile slightly hidden. "I got to see if Grandma needs me," he added.

"I think I can protect you," Grasshopper said.

Alvera looked at Grasshopper and smiled at him in a maternal way. Alejandro grinned at Alvera and kept walking toward the homestead. Alvera looked at him, trying to figure him out.

"I know you can," said Alvera. "You and Alejandro are really nice folks."

"If you'll be my girlfriend, I can get you everything you need: cherries, daisies, grapes."

"That's very sweet of you," said Alvera. "What kind of grapes do you like?" she asked in a soft and maternal voice.

"I like the muscadine grapes. Alejandro calls them muscat grapes. They're very sweet," said Grasshopper.

"Me too. I like those too. When was the last time you got a present?" Alvera asked.

"Sometime time ago. Grandpa got me a teamster."

"If you could ask for something, what would that be?" she asked.

"My Mom. My mom's gone to heaven. My Dad and Uncle too." His eyes watered.

"I know." She approached him and hugged him.

"I really miss her," said Grasshopper, looking up at Alvera.

"I know you do. Listen. Whenever you want to talk about your mom, you can always talk to me."

"I feel you really understand me," said Grasshopper. He hugged her harder. His head was against her bosom. She was at least one foot taller than he was. Grasshopper closed his eyes as if he tried to love her with all his might. *I love her*, he thought. He thought she loved him too. And he felt comfortable with that thought. But Alvera thought of him only as a younger brother, as Alejandro's brother.

"You know you don't have to worry about your mom. Wherever she is, she is good now."

"Sometimes I feel I need her. Like needing a friend," he said.

"I can always be your friend," said Alvera. "It must be hard for you not to have friends around these parts."

"Sometimes I wish I had someone special to talk to," Grasshopper added.

"You can talk to me or Alejandro," said Alvera.

"I know. Do you have a special friend?"

"No," she said at first. Then said, "Yes, I do have a special friend," she said and thought. The depth in her eyes glimmered, a type of contentment that only the promise of love could bring.

"Can I be your friend, too?" Grasshopper asked.

"Of course you can be my friend," Alvera said.

"I knew you were the one. You are so nice," Grasshopper sighed.

"I'll be your friend forever," she said, in a maternal tone.

"Forever?"

"Yes. Forever."

Scent of Sky Light

The olive harvest season had arrived with showers of light rain that keeps sharecroppers and seasonal workers at bay, making their stay shorter than usual. At the homestead, the rain had subsided, and the sun was now setting in the horizon. Grasshopper yawned, stretched his arms, clenched his fist, rubbed his eyes, and removed remnants of sleep. He stayed in the toolshed for at least a week after he had fully recovered from the pox. Grandpa sat on a solid wooden stool outside the shed while he patiently carved a new handle for his ball-peen hammer. He got up and walked into the shed to look for sandpaper so he could smooth the contour of the handle. When he went in, he looked at Grasshopper and lifted his chin at him, making sure the boy was awake. Grasshopper looked at him and knew what his grandpa meant.

"Why do fireflies light at night?" asked Grasshopper. "I dreamed with fireflies."

"You gotta get up," he replied as he looked and raised his eyebrows at him. The toolshed was Grasshopper's favorite place in the house, and he wanted to stay there. Grandma and Grandpa didn't mind, for they thought it was good for the boy to read the books Grandpa kept there.

"How do they glow in the air?" asked Grasshopper, as he removed the sheet that covered him.

"They breathe," said Grandpa. He cleared his throat.

"Grandpa, can we make a balloon? Do you think I can travel to the stars one day?"

Grandpa had been bedridden for a few days but was now in good spirits. "That's a crazy good idea," he said. Grasshopper stretched his arms.

"I know." The child squinted.

"Everything is possible though. The only thing mankind can't do is give birth," said Grandpa.

"I'd like to fly to the stars one day."

"The stars are too far away."

"But in Sweet Heaven you can almost touch them. I'll be near mom and dad there."

"Yes, in Sweet Heaven stars look close, but you gotta get up now."

"I'd like to make something fly. I think if I make a balloon, I can see how far it flies. Do you think I can make it fly?"

"Yes, but first, you wanna ask yourself about the reason for making one," Grandpa said.

"Why?" he asked.

"A man has got to know and understand the reasons why he does something," Grandpa replied.

"I know," he said, erecting his posture. "When I see a star, I always ask for a wish."

"What wish?" asked Grandpa as he coughed and paid attention to the boy.

"To go to the stars one day and see mom. You ever seen stars when they fall?"

"Stars don't fall," said Grandpa.

"What do you mean? I see them falling all the time at night."

"They don't."

"But they do. I've seen them."

"What you see is just a piece of dirt in the sky."

"Dirt?"

"Yes, dirt that falls to the earth."

"But I see a light cutting across the sky."

"You do because it burns when it touches the earth's skies."

"I think I read that in the *Reader's Digest*, but I don't think it's true. To me, it's just a falling star. I don't want stars to fall to the earth; I like them there."

"Well, if you wanna make a balloon, I can help you make one," said Grandpa and he continued coughing. Since the beginning of the harvesting season his coughing had worsened.

"Really?"

"Yes. When there are good reasons behind what you want to do, other people will always help you get them done," added Grandpa.

"Well, I want to make one for mom and for my friend Alvera."

"Whenever you do something, you have to know why you do it, and do it for the right reasons."

"She's my good friend and I like her too."

"Well, if she's a friend, then that's another good reason to make one," said Grandpa, looking at Grasshopper. "You're gonna have to gather some materials."

"I can get all the materials we need," said Grasshopper while his eyes widened and blinked with excitement. He jumped from the cot and put on his shirt and shoes.

"When are you going to give it to her?" Grandpa asked.

"Her birthday is the day of the Wine Fest."

"Good. Maybe you wanna give it to her the night of Wine Fest Day, then." He coughed. "That's a great idea!"

"Grab a pencil and paper. Look there by the stand," pointed Grandpa. He sat down and began to list the items Grasshopper needed for this project.

"You can get these from Grandma. Some of them I have here. But write them down anyway. Get about ten pins, scissors, half cup of cornstarch...."

"Cornstarch?" asked Grasshopper. "What are pins?"

"Yes, cornstarch," said Grandpa. "I got those here."

What on heavenly earth you want cornstarch for? Grasshopper thought, but he did not want to question Grandpa. "Aluminum paper," continued Grandpa. "Write this down. Parchment paper, get about eight dried twigs, get thick and thin ones."

"Wait, eight twigs?" wrote the boy.

"Yes!" said Grandpa. "Cotton, kerosene, a small tin container, one of those small sardine cans will do, and pieces of thin copper wires too. Gather these materials and leave them here on the stand. I have copper wires here," he pointed at some wire skeins he kept in wooden boxes under the stand.

"I can get the kerosene from the stove. I've seen Grandma pour it in it."

"No, I'll get the kerosene, too. You can ask Grandma about the other materials."

Grasshopper grabbed the paper and ran outside, excited about his project.

❧ ❦

Alvera had come to the homestead to visit grandma to ask her for advice about participating in the Wine Fest contest, and how she could prepare for it. She had thought about what Dr. Maxim had said to her. Folks in Russell often talked about how Lisa St. Agustin had been the prettiest of all Wine Fest Queens. It was often talked about that the richest man in Russell, Leo Vidal, had offered Grandma his patrimony if she would marry him. But she refused. She refused to live a life of comfort and wealth and chose her love for Grandpa instead, so he could steal her from the St. Agustins.

Grandma's brother, Raul St. Agustin, a man feared and respected in Russell, had broken his leg after falling from 21-Miles, an Arabian white horse that was known for running long distances at top speed. While Raul was at the hospital recovering, Grandpa stole Grandma. So the day Uncle Raul had recovered and could walk again, he went out, gun in hand, to look for Grandpa. Grandma smiled every time Grandpa told the story. "You wanted to be stolen," Grandpa often joked with her. She smiled. When Grandpa and Uncle Raul came face to face, Grandma got between them and confessed to her brother that she loved Grandpa and that they had already been married and were expecting their first child, Grasshopper and Alejandro's mother. Seeing that Grandpa was now connected to him by blood and love, Raul put his gun down and embraced his sister and welcomed Grandpa. When Adie, Grasshopper's mother, was born, Uncle Raul pledged to be Adie's godfather, and whatever dispute or quarrel there was between him and Grandpa, it was finally resolved and forgotten. When Raul visited his sister every year for his niece's birthday, he brought the prettiest tulips for Adie in addition to food and other gifts.

"If I have to think of a flower name for you, it will be a zinnia, my dear," said Grandma to Alvera. Alvera smiled.

"There are so many other pretty girls in Russell," said Alvera in a humble and soft tone while she sat on a chair and Grandma braided her hair.

"Maybe, but it's all about personality. And you are already the prettiest girl in Russell."

"Oh, Mrs. Druett," Alvera blushed.

"No need to be embarrassed. You got to own and take what's yours. A woman can never doubt herself for being a woman," said Grandma. "We're created to shine, no matter in what colors and shapes we glow, my dear."

"Do you think Alejandro would like me to be in the pageant for Wine Fest Day?" She looked uncertain.

"Of course he will. He'll be drooling for you when he sees you."

"Ha, ha, you're funny," she said, smiling. "I hope he likes it."

"And I'm gonna make sure you look your best."

Grasshopper ran inside the kitchen and interrupted the conversation. He looked at Alvera's chignon on top of her head. Breathing heavily, he couldn't hide his laughter, so he lowered his gaze to avoid looking at Alvera. Between outbursts of laughter, he said: "Grandma, you got some twigs for my balloon?"

Grandma frowned and looked at him. "Why are you running like a crazy mad dog? I was about to bring you some breakfast."

"Grandpa told me to get up."

Grandma just looked at him. "What are you laughing about?" asked Grandma.

"He's laughing at my chignon," said Alvera, smiling and looking at Grandma, and then looking at Grasshopper's rosy cheeks. Grasshopper couldn't contain himself and burst out laughing.

"Ha, ha, ha. It just looks like a tomato," he said while he held his belly.

"Your face looks like a tomato," replied Alvera, laughing at him too.

"What balloon?" asked Grandma.

"I just need a few twigs, Grandma, please," said Grasshopper. He laughed.

"Go beyond the tomato bed, there by the dry olive branches, near the foot of the poplar trees, and you'll find some twigs," said Grandma. "You ought to know better not to walk in and stick your nose into ladies' businesses."

"No, I don't want any ladies' business!" yelled Grasshopper, running outside.

❧

Dry olive branches, with their long, dark, and golden dry leaves, formed a tangled pile along the foot of the poplar trees on the other side of the adobe house. These were the remnants of branches Grandpa and Alejandro had collected from the last season after they pruned the olive grove. Grasshopper picked up a pole and walked around, poking along the pile of dry wood. He put his right foot forward first to keep the tangled branches from coming apart. Then he reached to pull a stick from below the branches.

He stood still for a second and locked his sight on a glossy branch that was coiled around some twigs. Two elongated, bright red, fork-like appendages with protruding tines tasted the air in the surroundings. Grasshopper froze as the creature remained still, sensing his presence. Grasshopper stood still. The animal drifted, coiling through twigs and shoots, in an intimate spiraling with its terse and tanned scales through the branches. Its skin was tanned brown as if it had been going through the fields on a hot day. It slithered away through the lower branches. Grasshopper realized the creature needed to be there as much as he did. This time he was not going to poke it with the stick or throw a pebble or a rock at it. This time, he would let it go because he enjoyed seeing it slithering free. It was a beautiful creature when it slid away free.

After he had gathered the twigs, Grasshopper could see Grandpa hammering a piece of steel in the distance outside the shed. The clacking of the hammer and steel contrasted with the sweet, melancholic melody of the bandoneon that played on the old Phillip battery radio Grandpa had near him outside the shed. Grasshopper could hear the melodies of the old tunes in the distance.

"To be the queen, you must have the presence of a queen," said Grandma. "Be dressed like a queen. Be the queen," Alvera just looked at her.

"I want to be the queen," Alvera said.

"You are already the queen," Grandma affirmed. Alvera Smiled. "You just need a crown. Every queen wears a crown."

"I'd like a crown," Alvera said.

"We can learn how to make one—a natural crown with flowers and olive branches," said Grandma, looking at Alvera and waiting for her answer. "You are gonna look wonderful."

"Yeah, I'd love to make one," said Alvera. "What kind of flowers should we use?"

"Well, we have options. A woman always needs options, my dear," said Grandma. She smiled. "For the frame of the crown, some fresh olive branches, even better if we use a thin branch of eucalyptus with flowers on it. Some white spray roses. We'll also need some fine copper wires. Oh, and a pair of scissors."

"How many roses?"

"No more than ten."

"It doesn't look too difficult to make one," said Alvera.

"Not at all. It's quite simple. So, olive branches, eucalyptus flowers, and white spray roses."

"I think we have plenty of those."

"Yes. You want to use the eucalyptus flowers; they'll make you look heavenly. Just be careful with the leaves; they are a bit rough on the skin. But they'll make you look heavenly. Don't you want to look heavenly, my dear?"

"Yes, I want to look my best," said Alvera. "I love the strong scent of eucalyptus."

"It's so fragrant. Come with me," said Grandma and the two of them walked outside.

⇝⇢⇢ ⇜⇜⇜

After gathering the materials he needed, Grasshopper walked inside the shed. He carried some of the materials that Grandpa had asked him to gather. The harmonic vibration and the distinctive marcato of the bandoneon kept reverberating around the shed. Grandpa lowered the volume on the radio and then turned to direct Grasshopper.

"Put some old newspapers on the stand so we have enough space to work. Then lay all of the materials on one side," said Grandpa.

"I know," said Grasshopper as he grabbed a few newspaper sheets from under the stand and laid them over the surface.

"The first thing you wanna work on is the burner," said Grandpa after Grasshopper had covered the stand.

"Why not the paper first?" asked Grasshopper. "It's easier."

"Start from the base and up," said Grandpa. "The foundation is always the most important part." Grasshopper folded his arms and laid them on the stand, then he leaned and rested his body on it while he observed Grandpa.

"So, you first wanna grab the empty can." Grandpa cleared his throat. He rearranged the organization of the materials on the stand.

"I had to wash that can a thousand times. It smelled pretty stinky," said Grasshopper.

"I saw Kaiser licking it earlier," said Grandpa. Then he gave the can to Grasshopper.

"Yeah, the crazy dog didn't wanna let go. I had to take it from him. I think he was a mule in his past life."

"Looks like you and him are of the same kin," Grandpa said. He smiled as he unmounted a couple of chisels from the wall and laid them on the stand.

"He's pretty smart, you mean right, Grandpa?" replied Grasshopper.

"And stubborn too," Grandpa added. "Take that small hammer and that half-inch nail there." Grandpa coughed and gave Grasshopper a nail. He then took out a whetstone from one of the wooden boxes under the stand and a small plastic bottle with water and placed them on the stand in the center of the shed.

"Done! Now what?"

"Now go ahead and pry four holes in the can," said Grandpa. "This is where the fine copper wires will go." Grandpa pointed where the first two holes needed to go and observed how Grasshopper placed the can on the table and perforated the first hole in the can.

"Is this good?"

"Yes," said Grandpa. "Now make another hole on the opposite side of the can. Be sure the hole is near the top edge of the can." Grandpa kept eyeing Grasshopper's work.

"Across from the other?"

"Yes, right across." Grandpa grabbed the can after Grasshopper had made the first two holes. With a carpenter's pencil, he marked where the other two holes needed to be.

"Oh, so it's like a cross," said Grasshopper, studying the marks.

"Yes. Something like that."

After the can was perforated in four places around its contour, Grandpa handed the aluminum paper to Grasshopper.

"Right there," he pointed out, "you wanna grab a piece and place the can on it. Cut a square shape."

"A big square or a small square?"

"A small one." Grandpa coughed. "One that will wrap around the can." Grandpa licked his lips.

"Like this?" Grasshopper looked at the paper. He concentrated on the task and emulated Grandpa's movements and demeanor, as if he were a little master of his craft. But he wasn't there yet.

"No, that's too small," said Grandpa after Grasshopper had cut a piece. He took another piece.

"Should I wrap it all around it?" Grasshopper studied the foil and the can to find ways to wrap it. He squinted and thought about different ways of placing the foil, moving the foil about. He looked at Grandpa for approval.

"Yes, but just so the foil can be molded around and into the inside of the can. Cut another piece." Grandpa just gazed at the boy and his work. He then took a chisel and began sharpening it against the whetstone, adding a splash of water on the stone as he honed the chisel against it.

"Like this?" said Grasshopper as he placed the new piece of foil and molded it over the can. The grinding sound of the chisel irritated Grasshopper, making him clench his teeth with every vibration.

"Yes, like that. Now, press the foil inside it. Be sure the foil covers all around and over the edge of the can."

"I'm gonna add the kerosene right away," said Grasshopper, his eyes suddenly growing in excitement.

"If you do, it will be gone by the time you're ready to fly the balloon. You can put a piece of cotton in it after you finish wrapping the aluminum paper."

"Why cotton?" The boy frowned.

"Cotton will keep the wick lit, so the smoke can waft and fill the inside of the balloon. That'll make the balloon fly," said Grandpa as he studied and caressed the sharp edge of the chisel.

"I thought the air would make the balloon fly," said Grasshopper.

"Once it's all ready, you'll add the kerosene, then you'll light the wick and the hot gas from it will make the balloon fly," said Grandpa.

"What gas?" asked Grasshopper.

"The gas inside the balloon," said Grandpa.

"The balloon has gas?" The boy grinned. "That's pretty funny," said Grasshopper laughing.

Grandpa, with his usual stern face, just gazed at him. "Now that you have the holder ready, let's make the frame," said Grandpa. "Take the thicker twigs and cut them into four even pieces."

"Only four?" said Grasshopper.

"Yes, four thick pieces and four thin ones. Be sure they are all of similar length."

"What do you mean by thick?" Grasshopper said.

"The thicker ones should be as thin as a match," said Grandpa, putting one chisel down and picking up another.

"And all the others should be the same?"

"Yes, exactly the same." He struggled to swallow as he coughed.

"Should I measure them with the measuring tape?"

"No, just quickly see how long they are," said Grandpa. Grandpa took the measuring tape from the stand and placed it on the side by his waist.

"But it won't be exact," said Grasshopper.

"It don't matter. You gotta trust your eye there," said Grandpa. "Aim for half a foot, six inches. Then make a square shape, glue the corners with cornstarch, and wrap each corner with a small piece of tin foil after the cornstarch dries. You're gonna mix that cornstarch with water in a minute." Grandpa put the tape back on the stand.

"How much is an inch?" asked the boy.

"You see my thumb?" replied Grandpa, putting the chisel down, then showing his left hand and moving his left thumb.

"Yes."

"One half of your thumb is an inch," said Grandpa, holding the middle and tip of his left thumb with his right index finger and thumb. "That's an inch."

"How about the thin ones?" asked Grasshopper.

"The thin twigs will be attached to the square shape you're making. But wait until the frame is glued together." He held up the chisel so he could see the sharpened edge against the light, a gleaming line across the metal surface of the tool shone. Grandpa kept one eye close the other open to bring the edge of the chisel into perspective.

"Like this?" asked Grasshopper, holding the thin twigs parallel to the length of the thick ones.

"No, like this," says Grandpa, turning directly toward Grasshopper and holding the thin twigs vertically to the joining corners of the frame. "Like the beams in the pergola," said Grandpa.

"What's a pergola?" asked Grasshopper.

"A frame like the arbor by the house, where the grapes are."

"Like this?" asked Grasshopper, "Like a little cage."

"Yes, something like that, like a frame, but upside down," said Grandpa.

"How do you know which side is up?" he asked.

"You'll know once all of it is ready," said Grandpa. "Go ahead, add a bit of water to the cornstarch." Grasshopper grabbed the cup with cornstarch and added some water. "Now mix it. When it is all mixed, glue the corners. Do one end at a time, and hold it until the glue is solid."

⇶ ⇷

Once Grandma and Alvera had returned from getting the flowers, Grandma made some tea. "We'll have some tea and pastries before we start. We're gonna use these little pieces of copper wire to attach the flowers to the branches," said Grandma. "I can already tell this will be a great royal crown."

"You want me to lay all of them on the table?"

"Yes, please," Grandma said, making room for Alvera to put things down and then setting two teacups on the table. She took some sweet pastries she kept inside a jar that was covered with an embroidered cloth on top of the china cabinet. "If I don't hide them, Grasshopper will eat them all," she added, setting the kettle on top of the cast iron stove.

"He's such a sweet tooth," said Alvera. She poured half a tablespoon of sugar in her teacup.

"He is. Pretty soon he'll start school."

"I don't think he likes school," said Alvera.

"No, he won't, but he likes sweets," said Grandma. They both laughed. "He's been bedridden sick." Alvera squinted. "That's why we still have some pastries left. He'll be here soon when he remembers he hasn't had breakfast. So, you gather a few spray roses first," continued Grandma and then placed the roses in the center of the table.

"Before I forget, be sure to gather the flowers on the day of the fest," said Grandma.

"Withered flowers won't be any good," said Alvera. "Should I cut them right here?" Alvera made the cut near the neck of one of the roses.

"You probably want to leave at least two inches from the neck, my dear, so you can later coil the wire around the shoot." Grandma got up and removed the steaming kettle from the stove and poured hot water into the teacups.

"Like this?" asked Alvera.

"Yes, be sure you coil the wire well around the shoot, enough times for it to be secure to it." After she took a sip of tea, she put down her teacup.

"I see. You can put two flowers on each end of the wire, can you?"

"Yes, you can. You see, you're not only the most beautiful girl in Russell, you're also the smartest."

"Oh, Mrs. Druett, it was just a simple question."

"Do you see that longer piece of wire there?"

"This thicker one?" Alvera asked.

"Yes," said Grandma. "We're gonna use that to coil the eucalyptus and olive branches."

"Should we finish attaching all the spray roses to the wires first?"

"Good idea!" said Grandma.

"We'd better drink the tea or it'll get cold," said Alvera, looking at her teacup.

"We should," said Grandma while she smiled at Alvera. Then she pushed the plate with pastries toward Alvera.

"I could add different colored roses."

"Yes, of course. You make it the way you want it."

"I think white roses and eucalyptus flowers make it look better."

"I agree. They'll make you look like an angel," said Grandma. "Angelical is the word."

"But a little plain, too. Don't you think?" Alvera showed how the flowers contrasted with the olive branches. "I can add a colorful flower with every other white flower," she added.

"Yes! That will make it look even prettier," said Grandma, approvingly.

"I can see this is going to turn out very pretty. "

"It is supposed to and it will be even much prettier once you wear it as a crown."

"Should I bend the wire yet?" Alvera's soft hands curled around the leaf branches and flowers.

"Not yet. Just be sure to wrap the wire around the shoots for now," said Grandma.

"Like this?"

"Yes. Do you see the ends of the wires?"

"Yes." Alvera stretched the wires, pulling their whole length.

"We want to keep them completely coiled around the shoots or the endings will stick upwards."

"I see. We don't want those sharp endings stuck in our hair, right?"

"Yes! It should be delicate, almost flawless," said Grandma, approvingly.

Grandma had been showing Alvera how to make a royal crown while Grasshopper continued working on the balloon. Grandpa went to the water gate to release the water and irrigate the olive grove. By the time he returned, Grasshopper was still inside the shed, browsing a magazine. Grandpa had told him to wait for him before working on the balloon.

"Are we getting the envelope ready?" asked Grasshopper.

"Yeah, that sounds like a good idea," said Grandpa.

Grasshopper smiled. "I'll get the paper," he said, reaching over the table to pick up a few sheets of parchment paper.

"These sheets should be light enough to make the envelope fly," said Grandpa. He opened the sheets and stretched them out on the stand. Then he handed one sheet to Grasshopper. "Fold the sheet in thirds."

Grasshopper smiled. "Do you think it will fly?" asked Grasshopper.

"Of course it will," said Grandpa. "Fold each sheet in three equal thirds."

"Fold the paper in equal turds," Grasshopper quietly voiced. He eyed Grandpa.

"If you aren't serious about what you're doing, nobody will ever respect your work," said Grandpa.

"Like this?" asked Grasshopper in a more serious and loud voice.

"Now fold the corners to about half an inch from the line of the first and top thirds," added Grandpa. "Be sure the top and bottom ends of the diamonds are of the same length as the twigs.

"A diamond? Oh, I see."

"Yes, a diamond, an octagon," said Grandpa.

"What's an octa-gone?" asked Grasshopper.

"That is an eight-fold," said Grandpa. "Eight times. Eight parts."

"So if it's a ten-fold is it a tentagone?" said the boy.

"No, a tenfold is decagone, that's a ten-fold," added Grandpa.

"Now it makes sense; octagon, decagone it's all gone," said Grasshopper.

"Yes, a decagon," Grandpa clarified.

"All parts will be gone. An oc-ta-gone means the balloon will soon be gone in the air, right Grandpa?" asked Grasshopper.

"Sure will," said Grandpa. He chuckled. Then he coughed. "Now fold the other edges about half an inch. Do that to all the sheets."

⤳⟫⟩ ⟨⟨⟪↢

The white spray roses that now lay on the table seemed more numerous now that they had been attached to the wires. The combination of multicolored roses seemed to make all the flowers, white and colored, stand out even more.

"Do you think the roses add a nice touch to them?" She picked up a few and showed them to Grandma.

"They look wonderful. Wait until we attach them to the long wire with the eucalyptus and olive branches," said Grandma. "You'll know then."

"That's true. They remind me of how wild rose vines climb branches in a garden."

"They look wonderful. Now you can take the spray roses and attach them to the long wire," Grandma said.

"Should I make a circle with the wire yet?"

"Not yet, but that's a good idea. We wanna make sure the crown fits you before we go on."

"Yeah, I wouldn't want to be wearing a necklace instead," said Alvera, smiling. She coiled the roses around the wire.

"Or a hula hoop," said Grandma. They both laughed. "We want to tie the roses every two inches along the long wire."

"I'll look like one of those Hawaiian ladies on the cover of *magazines*," said Alvera.

"You'll look like no other, my dear. You see how the olive green makes the colors stand out even more?" Grandma said. She put the roses and eucalyptus flowers next to the dark green branches.

"I don't think we'll need any more flowers," said Alvera.

"I don't think so either. It's all about how you feel about it."

"It looks pretty the way it is."

"Now, take an olive branch and make a circle with it, like a ring," Grandma said.

"Like this?" Alvera asked while she made the circumference of the crown. "Now I'm gonna try it on."

"Now you do that," said Grandma. She grinned. Alvera fit the fresh halo slightly above her forehead, around the top of her head. "Looks heavenly, my dear," said Grandma in a sweet tone. Alvera smiled. The crown made her look heavenly as Grandma said, giving her a majestic air, even with the crown still unfinished.

"You may weave in the shoot along the wire once we finish attaching the roses," added Grandma.

"Maybe I should lace the crown with the eucalyptus shoots too."

"Yes, you do that," said Grandma while she helped Alvera attach the last set of spray roses to the long wire.

"I love how the roses and eucalyptus look together," said Alvera, holding the roses and branches all in a circle.

"They're lovely, my dear. Just remember, pick the flowers on the day or the day before the fest."

"Yes. The scent will be so fresh."

"Yes, it will be so soothing."

⟫⟫⟩ ⟨⟨⟨

The sheets had been glued together. The balloon looked like it had eight sides, but in the shape of a diamond. All ends had been sealed, and Grasshopper held a box of matches in his hand.

"Are we tying the burner to the frame now?" said Grasshopper.

Grandpa studied the other tools mounted on the wall, trying to decide which tools he needed to sharpen. As his eyes moved around the tools on the wall, he sighed and looked back at Grasshopper. He coughed.

"Not yet. We're gonna get the burner ready now," said Grandpa. "We'll then attach it."

"Attach it to what?"

"To the frame. Go ahead and hand me those pieces of copper wires there," pointed Grandpa.

"You want me to get the burner?" Grasshopper asked.

"Yes," said Grandpa. "Take four of those wires and lace them through the small holes you made earlier."

"So the wires are attached to the frame."

"Yes," said Grandpa. "If the burner feels too heavy, we'll have to do it without it."

"I think it will be just right," said Grasshopper.

"Take the twig frame and attach the wires through it midway on each side."

"And attach the holes with?"

"Use the wire itself." Grandpa coughed again.

"What's wrong, Grandpa?"

"I need to sit down for a while," he said while he kept coughing.

Grasshopper moved closer to Grandpa. He held him by the arm and helped him walk to the cot where he lay down.

"You go ahead and finish it. We'll try to make it fly when it is done," said Grandpa.

Grasshopper continued attaching the wires. He was focused on his industry, for he thought that his Grandpa would feel better if he was able to finish making the balloon on his own.

The balloon was ready to be set on its course. But Grasshopper wanted Grandpa to be present, so he waited. He would have to wait until nighttime on Wine Fest Day to see it lit in the air. In the darkness of the night, the balloon would glow like a glimmer of hope, with Grasshopper flying it, with hope in it, to the shivering stars, so Alvera could see it; so his mother could see it, too.

Alvera had woven a few Queens of the Night and a few blossoms of jasmine to the crown, adding a honey-like scent to the fragrance of spray roses, olives, and eucalyptus. Grandma told Alvera to do this the night of Wine Fest Day so she could smell the fresh scent of their aroma. And the colorful and august crown would be ready before the day of Wine Fest, and so would the queen.

Grasshopper had written a few phrases of poetry on the balloon. The phrases looked like ephemeral free birds that, once released into the glowing light at night, would brighten Alvera's eyes, perhaps reminisce the memory of his mother in his heart and mind. Grandpa had said this to Grasshopper, and the boy loved that thought. The balloon was ready, and the Wine Fest was just days away.

The Ax's Edge

At the end of the summer, almost all of the fruits had already been swept away by the harvesters. Except for the trees in the olive grove, most of the trees were starting to show signs of decay, and the fall season was now imminent in the shades of the reddish and brownish colors of the tawny foliage in Russell. At times, warm and cool winds blew during the days, sending adrift dried leaves and twigs left behind from the harvests into tumbleweeds across the fields. The fruit was gone, almost all the day laborers were gone, and the natural vibe of lush farms was gone. Orchards and groves became desolate while the trees seemed to shiver in anticipation of the cold and menacing winter ahead.

The forceful sound of a tractor engine roared and ripped as it approached the homestead. Puffs of smoke and the sound of metal chains announced Dr. Maxim and his son's arrival. Kaiser started barking and trotted toward the dusty road as if marking his territory. Soil made an effort but could only work up the energy to bark under the porch. Dr. Maxim was behind the wheel while Herman rode standing on the lift arms behind the machine. They laughed as they approached at full speed. But this time, they had not even come to tell Grandpa about the profits from the last cucumber harvest and the money they owed him. Dr. Maxim brought him no news, for in his mind Grandpa didn't deserve his share of the cucumber harvest. He turned off the ignition key, and they walked toward the adobe house.

"Mr. Druett, please keep that devil away from us," said Dr. Maxim while he and Herman approached Grandpa, who was sitting on the front porch. Kaiser was charging at them, showing his teeth and growling, not letting them move ahead.

"Kaiser!" Grandpa yelled at the dog. He coughed and stooped a little. The dog, with his tail in submission, retreated behind Grandpa as he walked toward the men.

"Mr. Druett, we're bringing down one of the old acacia trees by the reedbed," said Dr. Maxim. "You're not feeling well, are you?" Dr. Maxim studied Grandpa.

"I'll be all right. We brought down an old one with my grandsons already," said Grandpa.

"Well, some of the others are getting too old too and we're just gonna take one down. Send your boy over. We'll need an extra hand to chop the tree once it's down."

"Have you heard anything about the money?" Grandpa asked. The last thing Grandpa would do was to give up on a legacy and dream that he could leave for his grandchildren. Somehow, he knew his time would be due soon. He knew he needed to plant a seed so his grandchildren could thrive and grow their own crops and be under the cool shade of olive trees planted by their own hand in their own land. The coughing, the humiliation, the pain, the cramps in his gut, he could take; the notion of leaving nothing for his grandchildren, he could not.

"The sooner we forget about this money Mr. Druett, the better we'll all be," Dr. Maxim said, hoping to null any sense of hope that would give Grandpa reason to keep demanding his share of the profits. Herman looked down as Grandpa looked at him; Dr. Maxim never made eye contact.

Grandpa coughed, ahem, and swallowed whatever pressured his throat. Then his throat tightened. Demanding his grandson's help was adding spit to injury after much injury had been already added to the whole insult of taking from an honest and old man who had done his part.

"Well, Mr. Druett, we'll be by the reedbed," Dr. Maxim said as he and Herman walked away, laughing, not even feeling what Grandpa felt, not even for a second. Instances like this, this callous disdain, had aggravated Grandpa's condition, causing him to fall into bed and break out in a fever. It wasn't just about taking Grandpa's money; it was like a beast wanting to take the man's health, his whole livelihood, and his peace of mind. And everything else it could take. After they were gone, Grandpa went inside the house and lay down.

⤜⤜⤜ ⤛⤛⤛

"Why do Grandpa's eyes look like that?" asked Grasshopper. Grandpa's eyes were somnolent and appeared to lack the usual luster in them. His body sank in the bed.

"He's not feeling well right now," said Grandma. "He's been running a fever since last night."

"Again?" asked Grasshopper.

"Yes," said Grandma.

"He got more sick when that man came here," he said.

"No, Grandpa hasn't been well for days now," said Grandma.

Grandpa coughed.

Grandpa had relapsed into a weakened state that would keep him bedridden for days. Then he was well again for another few days. When he learned that the money he expected wouldn't come in, his health deteriorated even more. And what else could he have done to be paid? Asking for his dues was like hoping that a cucumber's seed would germinate in the middle of winter in the tarry asphalt on the road that led to downtown Russell. It was useless to keep asking. He was sick and had no energy, and this worsened his condition.

The harvest at the homestead wasn't done. Cucumbers needed to be snapped before they grew larger, and with Grandpa being ill, Alejandro had to take care of the farm. He picked up where Grandpa had left off when he got sick. Alejandro was able to pull off the job and even advance and finish the last reaping. The small cucumbers were often picked first, for these could be sold faster and provided higher profits. Grandpa and the Maxims knew this and so did Alejandro.

When Alejandro walked back from the fields to the homestead, life around the homestead seemed to have fallen into a brownish decay. It was perhaps the fall settling in. Remnants of crops were dying. Untrimmed vine shoots sprung eagerly and violently in rampant disarray. At the roots, the furrows had become bleak with a thick crust of soil left by the water flows and then dried by the scorching sun in the peak hours of the day. Loose soil patches on the surface turned into dusty swirls that roamed like dust devils wreaking havoc and traveling over the land to adjacent farmlands down the valley. Others whirled across the rows, alleys, and roads, gathering small twigs of crops, the reminiscent aroma of ripened fruit, lifting the ashen dust that remained on the ground. It was a swift sweep through the valley of Russell.

When Alejandro arrived from the field, he asked immediately "How's Grandpa doing?"

"The fever is back," said Grandma, sitting down by Grandpa's side with her sight locked on the olive grove outside the window. She stirred some peppermint tea in a tin cup with other ingredients she had concocted for Grandpa. Her eyes had an opaque gloss, like a prelude of sadness. The hoot of an owl echoed in the grove while the wind gently whispered. The fold of her eyelids dropped heavily over the outer edges of her eyes, but her face was smooth and tanned. A tiresome mood had overtaken her face as she watched her husband's health deteriorate. But Grandpa kept her on her feet, and even when he wasn't well, he cheered her up.

"How's my sweet damsel?" Grandpa got a hold of her hand as she passed by the bed holding the teacup. Grandma looked at him and went back to the kitchen.

Alejandro was in the bathroom washing off his hands. He came back to ask Grandma for a towel.

"Did Maxim come by?" Alejandro asked.

"He did, but no news," said Grandma. "They haven't received no money yet. And I don't know when they will."

Grasshopper stood on the threshold of the bedroom door, eavesdropping.

"That son of a bitch!" Alejandro muttered to himself.

Grandma looked at him, aghast.

"That's a lie," interrupted Grasshopper as he walked in. "I heard both of them talk about making money and that the money is now in the bank."

"When did you hear that?" asked Alejandro. He looked at his brother intensely. Grandma listened.

"The day we chopped down the big tree," said Grasshopper.

"How do you know they were talking about Grandpa and our money?" asked Alejandro again.

"Cause they talked about the harvest and Joaquin and the money. 'Tenfold' they said."

"Are you lying again?" Alejandro asked, staring at his brother.

"No, tenfold means ten times," said Grasshopper. "A decagon!"

"Why didn't you say anything before?" said Alejandro, charging at Grasshopper.

"I didn't know—" said Grasshopper. "I didn't know they were talking about Grandpa—I just remembered."

Grandma remained deep in thought and didn't even blink while Alejandro scolded Grasshopper.

"Damned bastards!" said Alejandro.

"You won't talk like that in front of your grandmother!" Grandpa's voice echoed in the house. Grandpa had been listening to Alejandro and Grasshopper.

"Dr. Maxim brought a tractor and left word for you to help him bring down one of the trees by the reed-bed," said Grandma in a serene tone.

I'm gonna kill that bastard, Alejandro thought.

Grandpa knew exactly what Alejandro was thinking and called him in. "You aren't gonna do nothin' 'bout da money, you hear!" said Grandpa as he gasped for air.

"But they gotta pay, Grandpa!" said Alejandro. His eyes were filled with impotence.

"Yes, they gotta pay. but you will not be the one settling justice here. You hear me?" demanded Grandpa.

"And who will then, Grandpa?" retorted Alejandro, now projecting his voice. His words were no longer those of a child who conformed to authority and accepted this fate. He spoke with the steady, firm, and resounding tone of a man. His voice had echoed through the room, causing Grandma to come in.

"And who the hell do you think you are? Our savior?" Grandpa's voice cracked. "You will honor Dr. Maxim as you would honor me and say nothing about the money." Anguished and exhausted from the tussle, Grandpa sank back on the pillow.

Alejandro remained speechless, lowered his gaze, and accepted his grandfather's order.

Grandma was now spreading a white cloak seamed with golden double stitching over the bedspreads that covered Grandpa. With her finger, she signaled Alejandro to hush. A dense silence filled the bedroom. To Alejandro, it was yet another wrong that had to be addressed, one that stifled Grandpa within the four walls of his room, a wrong that had stifled his family's chances through four generations, like the disease that was now suffocating him. Alejandro's resounding voice had emerged and reverberated through the thick silence in the room, through Grandpa's mettle and his sick livelihood. But no act of vengeance was to be done by his grandsons, no matter what was at stake. Alejandro understood this. No money was ever worth the life of a man, especially that of a young man.

Angry, Alejandro stalked out of the bedroom and back to the bathroom, where he scrubbed his face as if washing off the frustration. He felt nauseated. He looked in the mirror, observing his face in detail. A trait he had never noticed before emerged from the image that looked back at him. The image was real, but it wasn't his face. It was no longer the tender face of a child with its soft and fresh skin. The gleam of childhood in his honey-brown eyes was gone. His face had turned rough, chiseled, and weather-beaten. The bones of his cheeks protruded and the orbs of his eyes seemed to have sunk deeper, perhaps somewhere within his mind or soul, as if he had carved some sort of truth or a new man out of himself, perhaps in the same fashion as Grandpa had carved toys out of poplar wood for him and Grasshopper for Christmas. His image was that of a man with the rough visage and blistered, callused hands of a sharecropper. It revealed rough years of toil and sweat, and a soul hardened by experience and circumstance. He looked and sounded like a man. He thought like a man. And he had learned to feel anger like a man.

As he walked outside, the air around the adobe house had lifted, causing a few dust devils to spiral along the dusty road and dissipate through the tree crowns in the homestead. Grandpa could no longer fend for himself. And it was up to Alejandro now to step up and be the stronger man.

Before sunset, Alejandro went to the toolshed. He unmounted the ax from the wall and lightly caressed its sharp edge with his thumb. The ax was sharp, like every other cutting tool that Grandpa kept in the shed. This edge reminded Alejandro of how some men push others to a definite and sharp edge, forcing them to accept, to conform to their ill will. An edge that most men accepted generation after generation, so they could survive with the bare minimum, so they could belong to the tumultuous flow of men who were thrown into existence to conform and accept such fate after being born; it was an edge that many grown men did not want to face and ran away from. And the few that would step to the edge wouldn't leap for the fear and consequences attached to their needs and their livelihood. And others who would know about the edge and were well aware of how it came about, at times being face to face with it, wouldn't leap forward simply because they were just afraid. And some were just ingenious, some ignorant or absent, and others simply just didn't give a damn.

Outside the shed, the tawny hues of an autumn sunset contrasted with the dark and flat shadows in the orchards. Alejandro threw the ax over his left shoulder and walked to meet Dr. Maxim and Herman. His firm grip on the ax handle revealed Alejandro's resolve. Anger ran through the young man's veins and gnawed at his soul. His blood boiled and throbbed as pulsations became evident on the veins at his temples.

It was almost dusk when Alejandro made his way to the acacia trees by the reed-bed. The sunrays on the horizon had dissipated upon the fields and the evening was growing as dark as the thoughts overwhelming his mind. With a firm stride, Alejandro walked along the reed-bed to meet Dr. Maxim. As he neared, he could hear the voices of the two men as they struggled to find an angle to begin bringing down one of the acacia trees.

"Pull it harder, Dad," said Herman.

"Goddamn it!" Dr. Maxim screamed.

"Harder, Dad!" His son insisted.

"This shit!" Dr. Maxim's bellows echoed around the field as if the two men were wrestling with a giant. Their voices and the sound of the tractor engine reverberated. The machine emitted forceful roars and dark billows of smoke.

"Let's hold it this way," said Herman while the tractor struggled.

Alejandro cut through the reed-bed to observe the two men fighting with the tree. He ground his teeth as he looked at the two men he despised and to whom Grandpa had ordered him to help. He again softly tested the sharp edge of the ax with his index while he kept a firm grip on the neck of the handle.

Dr. Maxim wanted to bring down an acacia tree, but not in the same fashion as Grandpa had done with Alejandro and Grasshopper. The tree wasn't as tall as the old acacia tree Grandpa and the boys had brought down. This one had only two branches, and it was no higher than both men's height put together. A tree that looked old and decayed, covered in fungi. He used a tractor to prove the might of the machine or perhaps to assert his own power. He had chained the acacia tree and attached the chain to the tractor, giving the tree repeated yanks that made Dr. Maxim angrier every time the tree refused to yield.

"Son of a bitch!" said Dr. Maxim. He yanked it again.

"Oh Shit, this damn bastard won't give in," said Herman.

"We probably need to ax this sucker a bit before it'll come down!" shouted Dr. Maxim as the tractor kept charging. In some places by the reed-bed and the trees, the swelling ground bulged into small mounds that made the task of the machine even more difficult. Maxim pressed harder on the accelerator, hoping to rip the tree's massive root out by brute force. Then he slowed down to make sure the chain was still attached to the trunk. But the tree remained rigid. The mound by the trees kept the tractor at an awkward angle position, throwing its front wheels up in the air while the machine kept charging. Heavy smoke from the exhaust rose above the crowns of the trees. He stomped on the accelerator, forcing the pedal, and pushed forward again.

"I told these people to come by and help us," griped Dr. Maxim. The dripping sweat from his forehead was now steaming into his glasses and blurring his sight. Initially, he had intended to show his son how to bring down a tree, but the difficulty of the task had turned his moment of bravado into a frustrating test of strength and wits. Alejandro did not rush to assist them. Why would he make haste to comply with their demands if they did not value the work his family did for them?

"Pull that damned chain tight!" shouted the doctor, looking back, as he kept one hand on the steering wheel and the other on the mudguard of one of the wheels. His disheveled hair fell over his forehead and eyes, blocking his eyesight. His glasses were fogged by the steam of his sweat and profuse breathing, just as his mind was clogged by his boiling rage. The dark emission of the tractor kept rising to the crown of the trees adjacent to the one that he was trying to bring down. The smoke coalesced with the dimness of the evening, darkening the sky.

As Dr. Maxim attempted to drive over a small swelling of the ground, the tractor roared once again and one of the loose chains rumbled and then clacked sharply against the rear gears of the tractor, making the machine jolt forward over the mound.

Alejandro observed how Dr. Maxim was gradually losing control of the tractor. As the machine jumped over the mound, it seemed to stand on its hind wheels with both front wheels in midair. As the rear wheels dug into the ground, the tractor tilted to one side while its front wheels remained suspended in the air, halfway over the hump, and still charging forward into an irrigation ditch.

"Hold it right there," said Herman. "Don't push it anymore." But as he said this, Dr. Maxim jammed his foot on the gas pedal once again, pulling the chains completely loose from the tree and thrusting the tractor forward over the mound. For a second, Dr. Maxim lost control of the steering wheel, but then he regained it and swerved to the left to avoid hitting the guide wires and end posts of the vine rows near the trees.

"Wait!" screamed Herman as he saw his father and the tractor roll over and down to one side, causing the machine to rest on the man's torso and face as the engine kept running and one of the thick rubber wheels kept spinning. It all happened in a second, and then time seemed to slow down and stretch out indefinitely into the gloomy night.

Alejandro rushed out of the reed-bed and ran to where Herman was struggling to remove his father from under the tractor. "No, no, no, no, Pah, Pah, nooo...," cried Herman. Dr. Maxim lay semi-conscious as the engine continued running with his foot stuck, still pressing on the gas pedal. The wheel kept spinning while the smoke from the engine dimmed the already tenuous dusk.

"He's still breathing," said Alejandro as he approached the tractor and looked underneath.

"Get him out!" cried Herman. His effort to push the weight of the tractor out of his father's body was useless.

After Alejandro had disconnected the gas pedal, the engine gradually subsided. Herman just stared at the tractor squashing Dr. Maxim's torso. He just looked at his father.

"Push it over here," said Alejandro, urging Herman to take action.

The tractor was still tilted on one side of the mound with that side's mudguard pressing against Dr. Maxim's chest. The other wheel remained spinning slowly in midair until it gradually ceased.

"Keep pushing!" insisted Alejandro, nervous and moving quickly around the tractor while trying to find a way to free the man. Herman was petrified by the sight of his father, who by now seemed to have lost consciousness completely and bled profusely from the mouth and nostrils. Alejandro and Herman were able to use the weight of the tractor to push it down from the mound and release Dr. Maxim. The man's breath was ragged, as if his lungs were struggling, gasping for air.

"Run back for help!" said Alejandro. Herman stood transfixed by the gory scene. He didn't move.

"Go get help now!" shouted Alejandro, bringing Herman back to his senses.

The nebulous twilight was upon them. Dr. Maxim lay outstretched by the foot of an acacia tree, while Alejandro knelt by his side.

Dr. Maxim seemed to have regained consciousness. His eyes opened and closed. He coughed out a burst of blood, gasping with short and brusque breaths. Alejandro took his shirt off and put it behind Dr. Maxim's head, making his position a bit more comfortable.

"I can't feel my body," whispered Maxim as he groped for Alejandro's hand.

"Be still. Help is on its way. Just wait," said Alejandro, holding and pressing the man's hand.

"Don't leave me here, please!" begged Dr. Maxim. "Why…you helpin'… me?"

"I won't leave you. Don't say anything. Help is on the way," said Alejandro, encouraging the man to stay put. For the first time, Dr. Maxim's weak voice retained no trace of his former commanding and disdainful tone. The dying man no longer had control over Alejandro or Grandpa's livelihood, the farm, and the livelihood of their family. For the first time, he looked directly into Alejandro's eye and moved his lips in an effort to speak. He turned his eyes toward the mound and reed-bed. His gaze seemed lost as he stared into nothingness.

"I…, I…," he gasped. "I…," said Dr. Maxim while he tightly gripped Alejandro's hand. Then he let go. He let out another ragged breath.

"Don't worry. Help will be here soon," said Alejandro, comforting the man.

The twilight quickly dimmed the vineyards and the orchards around the homestead. The approaching darkness cast a shadow over the young man and the motionless body of Dr. Maxim. Sunlight had passed all the way beyond the setting sun that now cast a darker shadow over Alejandro and the Dr.'s deceased body.

Alejandro stayed with him until someone from the neighboring farms could arrive. Dr. Maxim's eyes remained open and their natural shine became an opaque and dark luster. The presence of life was no longer reflected in the gleam of his indigo pupils. His eyes remained locked in, an intense stare into space, a terrified gaze into vanishing eternity, as if they were seeking an explanation of something that couldn't be explained: the fate that he, like the rest of mankind, had to face.

Dr. Maxim was no longer able to tell Alejandro or Grandpa what their fate would be. He lay by the mound, as if his body had instantly become a chunk of old flesh and bones that would soon turn into dirt. As the darkness slowly overcame the adjacent farms, Dr. Maxim's remnants could not be distinguished from the furrows of soil in the area.

As the darkness there grew, the tiny glint of a crescent moon thrust its minute albedo on the sharp edge of the ax and on Dr. Maxim's opaque indigo eyes. Alejandro looked at the edge of the ax and pushed it away.

From the distance, the sound of Mr. Reys' footsteps and the glow of his lantern grew as he approached the site. Upon seeing the body, he lay his hand on Alejandro's shoulder.

"Son, go home now," said Mr. Reys. "Your grandma would want you to go back now."

"He's gone," said Alejandro, picking up the ax, looking at Dr. Maxim's deceased body, which had become visible by the light of the lantern. He stepped back, looked at Dr. Maxim's body again, and his eyes wandered. Then his sight fell to the side on the acacia tree that remained tall and intact.

The Harvest

With Grandpa sick, and no other hands on the farm to help with the olive harvest, Alejandro knew he'd need to live up to the responsibility. Days before the gathering of olives, the harvest was scheduled to end, but Grandpa was still bedridden. Grandma reached out to neighbors from nearby farms so they could lend a hand with harvesting the olives at the homestead. Alejandro had done well keeping up with the last rips of cucumbers. Cucumbers grew at night when the water was out, and a day without picking amounted to losses that would have made Dr. Maxim angry and more demanding. Many of the cucumber vines were slowly drying, but remnants of the fruit remained hidden under the vines that were gradually withering in the autumn. Alejandro kept himself busy snapping the last fruits from the tender stems. His work became monotonous, lifting the vines and snapping mini-cucumbers one by one. The mind of a harvester often found itself wondering, not about the job, which had become repetitive, but about sustenance, about the comforting thought of the woman he loved, about hope for the land he wanted. But there was no room in his mind to think about games or a child's play or to understand why his body was changing, or why he felt the way he did. Thoughts about helping his ailing grandfather occupied his mind. On his mind was also the brutality of the abuse he had experienced and the abuse his grandfather and the whole livelihood of his family had to endure. And after all the thoughts that ran through his mind, he remembered the imperative that irrespective of the circumstances, he must honor his boss.

Harvesting olives was a job for an entire crew, and now that Dr. Maxim was gone and Herman was in charge, there was more uncertainty about the future for the Druetts. Alejandro wondered what their future would bring; he worried about the harvest, the conditions they were in, and whether Herman would force Grandpa to harvest the olives while he was still sick.

For Grandpa and Grandma, Dr. Maxim's death created much uncertainty. Grandma knew that without Grandpa, she wouldn't be allowed to live in the adobe house, unless Alejandro took over the farm. This was a strange and a rather shameful reality of their existence. Grandpa knew that drastic changes would happen if Dr. Maxim was no longer present. Alejandro realized that this imminent change could take place at any moment.

Days after the death of his father, Herman had gone on a drinking binge. The last day of the harvest, as Alejandro was picking the last olives, Herman showed up at the homestead.

Everyone came to harvest the olives at the homestead. Mr. Campito and even his wife Nora, who were landowners, lent a hand. They had finished their own chores the day before so they could help Grandpa. Mario Lessar, Mr. Reys, his son George, Don Segovia, who was also sick but in good spirits, and Mr. Gurua were present as well. Many of the day laborers who worked for Mr. Campito knew Grandpa and came to lend a hand, too. Herman eased in early that morning, just to make sure the olives had been collected before the last day of the season.

"Olives ought to be picked today," murmured Herman as he neared the olive tree where Alejandro stood on a ladder, deep in the foliage of an olive tree while he collected clusters of olives from the branches above. The ladder leaned securely against the branches that formed a natural cushion around the contour and all the way up to the crown of the tree.

"And they will be!" replied Alejandro, swiftly plucking olives from the branches without glancing at Herman. Now Alejandro had the dexterity and swiftness of Mario and George. Smoothly, showing great dexterity with his hands, he gracefully raked the olives from the branches as if he were caressing the hair of the woman he loved.

The olives, with bright green, semi-brownish hues and sporadic gloss and dark tones, created a vivid contrast with the dark green shade of the olive leaves. The scent of the olives remained on Alejandro's hands and was reminiscent of fresh and oily herbs. As he combed through each branch, his hands were filled with the bounty of the plump fruit that he funneled into his game bag.

Unsteady and dazed, Herman stumbled through the clods and furrows—his perplexed eyes sunk within their sockets—as he gawked into the branches where the men and women worked. His puckered lips looked dried and chapped. He had never witnessed this level of diligence and wondered why laborers didn't work as hard for him and his late father.

"You don't expect me to pay these men for the work your grandpa should've done?" Herman muttered.

"No, they're my grandpa's friends," said Alejandro indifferently.

"Shit, boy," said Herman, looking at the workers there. He didn't know what else to say.

Alejandro, day laborers, and the neighbors had worked persistently for a few days to bring the harvest to an end. The tall wooden ladders allowed the harvesters to circle around the trees, reach the crowns, and stripped the tree of its prolific fruit. The olives hung as copiously as grape racemes did in the summer. With the straps of their game bags around their necks, men and women balanced high up on the ladders, while the children stripped the lower branches that almost kissed the clods of soil below. Not a single fruit was left behind. The work was prolific, and as olives were poured into the wooden crates, harvesters removed leaves and twigs from their bounties. Olives just glistened on the surface as they lay in the crates.

Some of the workers heard Herman's remarks and wanted to see what was happening, so they came down from the ladders and stood by the crates underneath each tree while they cleaned the olives in the crates.

"Mr. Maxim, we're here to help Mr. Druett," said one of Mr. Campito's day laborers.

"Mr. Druett is my friend," Don Segovia said as he leaned against a pile of wooden crates while he held a frail olive twig by one side of his mouth. He artfully poured the contents of his game bag into one of the stacked crates and combed the olives for leaves and twigs.

"Shit, what's to you, fat old mouth?" slurred Herman. "You must like working for free. Shit," added Herman with a snarl and his usual curse. Don Segovia lowered his gaze and ignored Herman, as he realized the man was drunk.

"Please leave that man alone," said George Reys in a soft but biting tone as he descended from the ladder with his game bag full of olives. Once he reached the ground, he kept speaking.

Herman continued with his remarks. "You ought to fill that up," he said in a sad and deep voice. The crates were already full. After pouring the olive in the crate, George gestured with one of his long, delicate hands, the other resting on his hip, like a confident young girl, his words towards Herman. "You ought to leave that man alone," he said again, approaching the ladder to continue the harvest.

"Oh, shit, what the hell on earth are you?" said Herman in a condescending tone.

"They don't want no trouble," said Alejandro as he looked down at Herman from the crown of the tree.

"Don't you talk to me like that!" George replied to Herman, with the same scathing attitude.

Herman turned beet red and lunged toward George as he tried to climb back up the ladder. Worried about the exchange, Alejandro came down from the ladder carrying the heavy game bag filled with olives.

"Who do you think you are talking to?" said Herman, pulling George down by the back of his fragile neck and tossing him to the ground.

"You let go of me," blurted George, attempting to stand.

"Shit. I'll set you straight, you damn, filthy 'bomnation," Herman bellowed as he slapped him across the face.

The rest of the harvesters nearby came down from the trees and then circled Herman. George sat sobbing on the ground, holding his game bag. Alejandro approached and stood in front of George to stop Herman from hitting him again.

"You didn't have to hit him," Alejandro said, clenching his fist. He then helped George stand. "What would Dr. Maxim have said about this?" said Don Segovia.

"Not a damn thing! Dad never liked no queer shit." The smell of Bravo pervaded around him. Herman hiccoughed and burped. For a moment, the work had ceased and the orchard was silent.

"Don't let the bad olives get in the crates now!" Mr. Reys' voice aired through the foliage. He must have been thirty or forty yards away and had not heard the commotion but knew Herman was around.

Alejandro heard Mr. Reys' voice and eased his posture before Herman. George climbed back up the ladder, mumbling some insults toward Herman. Anger and impotence seemed to keep him from clearly voicing what he felt and wished to tell Herman. Alejandro, Don Segovia, and Mario stood by the foot of George's ladder to keep Herman from reaching George again.

"It's not right," said Mario, looking at Herman. A man's mettle is measured by his words and his actions in comfort and in distress. The death of his father, his personality, and the spirit in the wine he drank all played a part. And in the face of the events that day, Herman's words and actions coincided. Realizing the men kept him from reaching George, Herman floundered across the furrows and inspected the trees the harvesters had left behind. Don Segovia, Mario, and Alejandro looked at each other but they didn't say anything before they returned to work.

⟶⟶⟶ ⟵⟵⟵

Mrs. Reys had sent Alvera to the homestead with mint and dry chamomile leaves for Grandpa and flowers for Grandma. On her way there, Alvera cut through the olive grove and approached Alejandro.

"You look like you've seen a ghost!" said Alejandro, descending from the ladder. "You look as pale as a full moon!"

Holding the mint and chamomile, she lowered her gaze, as if hiding the reason for her discomfort. "I've been unwell since yesterday, but it'll go away," she replied. "I'd better get these to Mrs. Druett. I hope Grandpa feels better soon," she added as Alejandro squinted and studied her.

Alejandro pulled the leather strap of his game bag over his head and dropped it. "You oughta be resting," said Alejandro as he held her by the elbow and looked into her eyes. He held her hand, helping her walk toward the adobe house.

On their way to the house, Alvera stooped, holding her belly. She rushed into the bushes and retched. From the distance, Herman squinted and observed the two of them.

⟶⟶⟶ ⟵⟵⟵

In Russell, it was usual that farmers celebrated the end of a bountiful season with a barbeque party. Everyone was welcome. Workers would bring their families, and most landowners provided meat, bread, beer, and wine. The harvesters looked forward to this celebration at the end of the season, for it provided them with an opportunity to talk to one another without the stress of making a profit for their bosses. The men talked about the harvest, made commitments for the next year, had amicable conversations, and in general just had a good time eating and drinking in the company of their fellow workers. In instances like this, men and women came together, and all their differences subsided. Understanding and goodwill prevailed among them.

The women's part in the conversation was vivid too, and often challenged the men, who never won an argument and were always outwitted by their wives. Most of the families chipped in by bringing their own food. It was a potluck of sorts. Women brought homemade dishes and desserts, and men brought drinks and sometimes chipped in on the meat and whatever else was needed for the feast. But many of their bosses and landowners seldom ate with the laborers, unless they worked alongside them or lived in and cared for their own farms.

The last day of the olive harvest at the homestead, all the neighbors gathered to celebrate the end of a season. Knowing Grandpa's condition, the families had brought food and drinks to share with one another. This wasn't a gathering to discuss profits, half-empty crates or bins of olives or grapes, and unfulfilled promises, or how much a token would be worth the next season. This was a fraternal gathering to celebrate the common good that transcended the worth of each man's labor.

The sun set early that evening and a cool breeze passed through the homestead. Mr. Gurua and Mr. Campito stayed after all of Grandpa's friends, day laborers, and other acquaintances had gone home to wash off the oily resin of the olives and to change clothes for the celebration.

The women made their husbands arrive late, the men often said, hinting at their wives' vanity, for the women needed to scent their skin with the essences of rosa mosqueta and vanilla. Their silken, dusky hair was embellished with extracts of dried walnut leaves and brushed with drops of olive and coconut oil. The scent of these fragrances pervaded as they kissed on the cheek or hugged each other as they arrived at the party in their bright skirts and lacy shawls.

It was common to set a row of grills with dry firewood. The flames crackled into sparks that sent miniscule particles of fire adrift, like diminutive fireflies hovering aimlessly in the darkness. The men poked the fire with long fire irons to spread the incandescent embers evenly below the grates.

Nora, Mr. Campito's wife, stood stoutly proud. She had arrived early to help Grandma make bread and carry the trays of roast and flank steak, rib beef, chicken breast, blood sausage, and other prime cuts of meat. As she carried the meat to a table by the grills, Grandma followed with tin trays loaded with rounded portions of dough that she took to the clay oven.

Nora and Mr. Campito were an unusual couple. She was robust, at least two feet taller than her husband, and a foot taller than the average height of men in Russell. She could pick up a tin crate overfilled with grapes with one hand and lift it with no effort. Her stature demanded respect. Her breast was wide; her presence commanding and her face, though stern, was soft and distinguished. Although her voice was gentle, she spoke in an assertive and firm manner—hers was the commanding voice in the marriage. Mr. Campito had more of a malleable and happy disposition. He was a hard worker, who owned his farm, who worked side-by-side with his workers. Nora did too, and she was the mind and strength behind their operation.

"How's Mr. Druett?" asked Mr. Campito as Grandma lay the dough board near the mouth of the clay oven.

"He's feeling a bit better," answered Grandma.

"He's as strong as an old oak tree," Mr. Campito said.

"Yes, he is, but he ought to rest tonight, excuse me Don Benito," said Grandma as she turned to walk back inside the house with Nora.

The murmurs of folks along the *callejón* grew in the darkness as they approached the homestead. The meat sizzled on the grills as folks started to arrive at the homestead. The scent of barbecued meat was enticing.

Men and women arrived carrying their children and bags with food and drinks. The men looked sharp and shaven. Their glossy hair and neatly pressed shirts transformed their normal roughness into a suave, elegant, and fresh appearance. The women looked dignified and festive in their regular day dresses adorned with handmade necklaces and colorful shawls. In the darkness, the voices of men walking along with their wives and children sounded clearly and lively in the distance. And as their voices grew, their silhouettes became visible against the glowing light outside the adobe house.

Kaiser usually barked at anything, but something was wrong with him, he was quiet and tired. Grandpa always said dogs were very much like their owners. Clement Baynes, a short man who lived a few miles down the *callejón*, was skinny and short and had a squeaky voice that made him stand out every time he took part in a conversation. He couldn't be quiet and intruded on every conversation. It seemed like no coincidence that he owned a chihuahua.

Kaiser was brave and stubborn, but he looked unwell. Before anyone started arriving at the homestead, Grandma had seen him roaming around the house, chewing at patches of grass and laying down alone by the toolshed. The hound couldn't even bring itself to bark or run after the folks arriving for the barbecue. Although Soil wasn't eating much, he was gaining vigor and would often be around the adobe house, sniffing, wagging his tail, getting to know the place.

Bedridden, Grandpa called for Alejandro when Grandma gave him word about Kaiser. After washing off, Alejandro went straight into Grandpa's bedroom.

"What happened to Dr. Maxim?" asked Grandpa.

"His tractor fell on him," said Alejandro. "He was trying to root out one of the old acacia trees. It was an accident."

"Where were you when that happened?" Grandpa asked.

"I was watching them," said Alejandro. "He tried too hard."

"Were you helping them?" Grandpa asked.

"No. They were using chains and the tractor, so I just looked from afar."

"And then what happened?" Grandpa fixed his sight on Alejandro.

"The tractor tipped over and smashed him. I tried to help Herman to get him out from underneath it, but he was in really bad shape. Then he was gone."

Grandpa's sickly eyes wondered. "Where's Kaiser?" he asked with effort.

"It's back there alone lying down by the toolshed," said Alejandro.

Grandpa got up and put on his sandals. He sighed and tried to regain his strength. He took a lamp and walked out of the back of the house toward the toolshed. Alejandro followed him. When Kaiser saw Grandpa, the hound tried to wag his tail against the dusty floor, but intermittent spasms kept the dog at bay. As they tried to make him stand, the dog appeared a bit stiff. His body was becoming more rigid and a line of white foam outlined his dark lower lip. Kaiser shivered as Grandpa observed him. Grandpa looked as weak as the dog, but he leaned forward and picked him up anyway.

"Strychnine" said Grandpa as he examined the dog. "Let's take it to the washbasin. Ask Grandma for a jug of hot water and mustard powder," he said to Alejandro. He coughed.

"What's that?" asked Alejandro.

"It's poison. Get the water now," said Grandpa as he carried the dog in his arms. By the time Grandpa neared the basin, Grandma had asked Mario to help Grandpa. Mario, who was one of the first to arrive at the feast, was in sight, talking to one of Mr. Campito's workers. He dashed to meet Grandpa.

"Mr. Druett, how are you doing?" asked Mario as he approached the basin. "You're looking mighty strong. Let me help you with that poochetty pup?" he asked, taking Kaiser out of Grandpa's arms. "Mightly heavy hound, isn't it?"

"Yeah, thank you," sighed Grandpa. "Is Mr. Lessar coming to dinner?" Grandpa asked.

"Yes, my old man's around the front talking to Mr. Gurua and Mr. Campito," said Mario. "What in mighty heaven's wrong with this doggie?" Mario asked.

"It's eaten something poisoned," said Grandpa. "Strychnine."

"He sure looks mighty bad," replied Mario as Alejandro came running with a bottle containing the yellowish powder in hot water.

"Some of the foremen in these parts lay chunks of poisoned meat near their coops to rid them of rodents and other critters," said Grandpa.

"Yeah. Some of them loose hounds be stealing hens around our homestead, too," added Mario.

"Hold him up," Grandpa said to Mario and Alejandro. Grandpa coughed. Holding the dog's muzzle, Grandpa poured about half a bottle of water into the dog's mouth. With a few fits, spasms, and whines, the dog swallowed the water. Grandpa massaged its belly after the dog had taken in the water.

"Keep him up," said Grandpa, pouring the remaining water in the dog's mouth. Mario and Alejandro laid the dog down on the ground. With a few coughs, Kaiser brought himself up on four legs. Alejandro looked at Grandpa, who looked as decayed as Kaiser. He understood his fear. Seeing his grandfather sick, Alejandro also understood that Grandpa may soon be gone; seeing Kaiser sick, dying by poisoning, reminded him even more of the circumstances his grandfather had to withstand. And although his own set of circumstances occupied his mind, he could still see the predicament his grandfather was enduring.

"That'll get him straight again," said Grandpa as the dog staggered away, shaking its body, retching, and vomiting up the water and some other gooey secretion. Weak and humble, Kaiser looked at Grandpa and tried to wag its tail. Mario picked up and carried Kaiser to the front porch, laying him down under a table near the threshold of the door. At first,

Kaiser seemed to bare his teeth at Mario, but the dog's gaze was submissive. Grandma brought two blankets, one which she put on Kaiser, the other placed on a chair to keep the light away from the dog. When Mario laid him down, Kaiser hit its tail against the ground and then licked its front paws. Soil calmly approached, sniffed, and licked the side of Kaiser's ears. Then, it suddenly erected his posture, looked into the darkness, and started to growl.

⇢⇢⇢⇠⇠⇠

Grandpa had gone back to bed. As the men gathered around the fire, they heard the crackle of branches and the rustling of leaves. Something was lurking in the darkness. Soil started growling and barking as if it wasn't sure what lurked there. They turned and remained still to see who or what was there. Grasshopper called the dog with a quick whistling, asking him to come near him while a mumbling Herman stumbled into the light.

"I hope you're not expecting me to pay you for taking care of all of Druett's responsibilities here," said Herman to the ones gathered in front of the adobe house.

The men looked at each other. Some of them lowered their gaze and raked their fingers across their hair as if embarrassed by Herman's question and unsure of what to say or make of him.

"No need for that, Mr. Herman, Sir," said Mario. "Mr. Druett's our friend and the good man's fallen sick. A mighty fellow ought to help a mighty friend in need. He'd have done the same favor for us."

"Yeah, but you don't need to be here doing his work," said Herman, trying to win the men over.

"That's not a problem; we wanna be here. He's a mighty good friend. Money is not an issue," Mario responded as the other men followed suit, murmuring their approval and nodding. Mr. Murua and Mr. Reys smiled.

Herman squinted and then directed his sight toward Alejandro. Kaiser tried to growl but was too weak to stand up. Grasshopper grabbed Soil after he started growling and barking at Herman and took the dog near the front by the eucalyptus tree.

"What you all know anyway," Herman replied as he looked around with contempt. "Where are the new harnesses my father brought here last week?" he demanded.

"What harnesses?" said Alejandro, stepping forward. "We never got no harnesses."

"My father brought two harnesses to gear up the mares he was about to buy and now you tell me they were never here? Shit, sounds to me you don't wanna tell where they are," said Herman, snarling with distrust as the stench of stale Bravo pervaded the air around him. He looked around, but nobody looked back.

"Mrs. Druett, if you allow me, I'd like to say a few words," said Mr. Campito, trying to change the subject.

"Go ahead," Grandma said.

"Mr. Druett and his family are our friends and when our friends need us, we help them." The crowd there made approving gestures, nodding and affirming what Mr. Campito was saying.

Herman looked annoyed but remained quiet.

"Suit yourselves," he interrupted. He stayed there looking at everyone and then lowered his gaze as if he was reflecting on what to say next. Everyone looked at him. "I won't argue against that," he said in a humbling voice as he was interrupted by Mr. Campito.

"Now that we're all gathered here, I'd like to say to those who help us with our work," interrupted Mr. Campito, trying to ease the tension. "I've got a bit of an announcement. Hmm...well, you all know," he stammered while raking his hair with his right hand and looking at the workers who work for him and then at his wife. Since they were all gathered, it was the best moment to tell them the bad news, but he could not bring himself to continue.

"Just tell it like it is, you silly man," said Nora as she stepped forward. "The bank has not paid us yet. Moneys from the harvest has not yet arrived, so we won't be able to pay you today. We're sorry, but you'll have to wait until the end of next week," said Nora Campito. Her hearty figure summoned respect and her voice was sincere and soothing.

For a moment, the crew of men and women who worked for the Campitos murmured among themselves. As Nora looked at them, one of the men, Mr. Riverain, came forward.

"Mrs. Nora, you and Mr. Campito have been good to us. We wouldn't mind waiting a few more days. I mean, I wouldn't mind at all," he said softly. "I can't speak for the others." He looked around to seek their consent. The men nodded.

"Be sure to give us the money, Mrs. Nora!" said Yolanda in a squeaky voice. She was the wife of one of the workers. The whole crew laughed.

"I'll make sure Mr. Campito does that, Yolanda," said Nora as the men and women chuckled.

"If you do that, Ms. Nora," said Yolanda's husband, "Mr. Beneto's store will be empty by next Friday."

The men laughed and nodded in agreement with a few "Damn right's," "Oh yeah's," "Hell yeah's," and the like.

"And your dinner plate and bed will be cold by the time you come home," said Yolanda. The women laughed. They all laughed.

"All right," interjected Mr. Gurua. "Let's eat then," as he hoisted a slab of meat from the grill.

"Yeah, I'm mighty hungry now," said Mario as he rubbed his belly and walked toward the long table that was set under the porch of the adobe house.

Unable to make his presence felt, Herman told Grandma to give him a lantern and wandered off to check the olive crates again.

The Hand That Feeds

Racks of ribs continued to sizzle on the grills. Folks sat on the porch around the table that Grandma, Grasshopper, and Alejandro had assembled. It felt like family when all the harvesters were home or when people were invited to a feast. Under the porch, the table was long and narrow, and it was usual to have an after-meal chat that extended for hours.

Bowls with cooked potatoes and salads with fresh tomatoes, onions, garlic, and olive oil were common on the dining tables in Russell. The stinging aroma of fresh cilantro filled the air. The bread had been baked right before the feast, and as they broke its crispy crust, hot steam wafted in foggy silhouettes from the table. The men had finished grilling the meat, and an array of side-dishes and desserts had been placed on the table.

"Got you some lemon pie here, Mrs. Druett," said Joanna Ballivian, the wife of another of Mr. Campito's day laborers.

"Mrs. Nora told me about your good hand at making desserts."

"Thank you," said Grandma. "Watch out with Grasshopper." They laughed.

"Let me borrow your cutting board," said Mario to Grandma as he prepared to slice some homemade salami he had brought.

"Bought sweets and pastries for the boys," said Aunt Rosy, who had arrived from downtown Russell.

Grasshopper cocked his head. Alvera sat under the porch and looked enticingly at the pastries, too.

"Here are some 'tatoes with bayonnaise," said Grandma as she came out of the kitchen and onto the porch, setting the bowl of potatoes on the table. She loved to mispronounce the names of foods and things in general. She liked to tease kids, especially Grasshopper. She knew he would correct her.

"Mayonnaise, Grandma!" said Grasshopper every time.

"Bayonnaise!" she would reply just to get a reaction from the boy.

Alvera laughed.

"These hog ribs look mighty good," said Mario. He licked his lips and looked at Aunt Rosy, who blushed and smiled.

"Mrs. Druett, you think I can take half of that loaf of bread?" Mr. Gurua asked.

"You sure can, Mr. Gurua," said Grandma while Aunt Rosy helped her set a stack of plates on the table.

"Let me help you with that. They look mighty heavy," said Mario, getting up to take the plates Aunt Rosy was carrying to the table.

Aunt Rosy was short and she had some of Grandma's facial features. She was in her mid-twenties and although she dressed like a city woman, her gestures and demeanor were very nonchalant and simple. "No need for that," she said after Mario insisted and beamed. She went back to the kitchen to help Grandma.

"Looks like the young man practicing for marriage," murmured Mr. Gurua, looking at Mario. Mario laughed and eyed Mr. Reys and Mr. Campito. Mr. Lassar just smiled. The other men laughed and congratulated Mario.

"Looks like it," said Mr. Reys.

Mario stopped. He set the plates on the table and looked at them. "You know if I do, I won't be picking those mighty grapes too far from where all of you are at, gentlemen," said Mario.

The men nodded and agreed, laughing.

Mario winked at them while he entered the house to grab some more plates. Aunt Rosy smiled as she came back from the kitchen, not knowing what the men had said. Mario was single. He had a predisposition to help others and was the kind of person who would go great lengths to help his neighbors. He was kind to women and children, fair to other men, and outspoken.

The laughter and conversation during the meal revealed an uncommon congeniality: Such quality was perhaps the will among men when they look beyond the value of their labor and they see themselves for who they really are. One could sense a spirit of mutual compassion, friendship, and solidarity in the air that night. After the meal, Grandma and Nora paraded in and out of the kitchen holding saucers with lemon and cherry pie. Grasshopper helped too. He knew being around the kitchen would get him an extra piece of whatever sweet there was, except for cherries. The wives of other workers carried out spoons and steaming cups of tea and coffee. The strong scent of the cherries and lemon filled the air while the women moved in and out of the kitchen. A brief breeze whistled through the porch, and the conversation rambled pleasantly. The men laughed and the women chattered.

"Has Mr. Druett eaten anything?" asked Mr. Reys.

"He did. He ate a bit of meat and potatoes," said Grandma. "He's sleeping now." There was a pause in the clatter of plates and spoons followed by a deep silence.

"Yeah, let him rest, Mrs. Druett," said Mr. Reys, easing the tension and filling the void of Grandpa's absence from the table. "He's as strong as God's will. He always gets back on his feet," added Mr. Reys.

"Damn right. He'll stand strong like the almighty. He'll be fine in no time," said Mario confidently. He patted Alejandro on the back.

"I remember Mr. Druett talking to Mr. Beneto about marriage one time." Mr. Reys reminisced and continued lighting up the conversation. He looked at Alejandro.

"Oh, yeah, those conversations they had," said Mr. Gurua.

"Mr. Beneto was telling Mr. Druett that his son—you know the tall one, Benny—wanted to get married and his wife-to-be did not want any dogs in the house. Benny wanted a few dogs that could watch the orchard to keep trespassers out at night. Mr. Druett just looked at him and kept smoking his cigarette," Mr. Reys recounted.

"I remember that," said Mr. Gurua. He started laughing.

"Well, Mr. Druett gave Mr. Beneto the best piece of advice for his son. He said that if Benny really wanted to keep trespassers out of his orchard, he should marry an ugly wife. 'Why should he do that?' asked Mr. Beneto. The man scratched his head. Mr. Gurua kept laughing." Everyone listened and waited.

"'Well,' said Mr. Druett, 'having an ugly wife, no man would ever come near your house or your orchard.' We laughed so hard. Even Mr. Beneto couldn't stop laughing," said Mr. Reys.

"He sure didn't follow his own advice," said Mario while he cut the salami and passed it around and then gazed at Grandma.

"Thank you, young man," Grandma said.

"Is it true you were once the Wine Fest Queen?" asked Joanna Ballivian.

"Yes, she was," said Nora. "And the prettiest ever."

"Oh, come on, Nora," said Grandma. "Alvera will be the prettiest ever this year."

Alvera blushed.

"These cherries are quite strong and tasty," said Mr. Gurua after he savored a spoonful of pie.

"And even more tasty too at the orchard!" said Grasshopper. "Mr. Reys grows the sweetest cherries."

"They sure were," said Mr. Reys. He smiled. Then he eyed Grasshopper.

Alejandro looked at Grasshopper and squinted. Mario laughed. "I heard all about you at the cherry orchard," Alejandro said to his brother.

"You heard nothing," replied Grasshopper. "That lemon pie looks so good."

"Now I remember," Alejandro said. "The day we chopped down the old tree, you were gone for a while. Then we found you in the old acacia tree."

"I did. I was collecting peaches for Alvera."

"I thought you said cherries?" Mario asked.

"Oh, yes I was. Cherries," said Grasshopper.

"Where were you collecting cherries?" asked Alejandro.

"Oh, I was on my way to see Alvera, so I picked a few for her."

Alvera looked puzzled. The men looked at each other and smiled. Grasshopper looked at them and said, "Taking a few cherries don't hurt anyone. right, Mr. Reys?"

"That's right!" he replied. "As long as you ask."

"You're taking what isn't yours if you don't," Alejandro reprimanded his brother.

"A few cherries don't mean much," said Mr. Reys.

"A little man taking a few cherries is no mighty crime," Mario added and winked at Grasshopper.

"Some men take a lot more than a few cherries and nothing happens to them," said Alejandro, who looked around toward the darkness. "Still you just don't take what isn't yours," said Alejandro, looking at his brother. Mr. Reys and Mr. Gurua eyed Alejandro.

"Your brother is right," Mr. Reys said.

"I guess we shouldn't take what isn't ours even if we don't get what's ours, right?" said Grasshopper.

"If you do, then you'll lose something somewhere down the line," added Alejandro. "Some way, somehow, it catches up with you."

"Like what? You'll lose something if you don't too," replied Grasshopper, looking at Grandma.

"Lippy here always wanna have the last word," interjected Grandma.

"Well, I'll take another piece of pie before I lose my appetite, if nobody objects to that," said Mr. Gurua. They laughed.

"I want a piece of lemon pie, too," said Grasshopper.

"Go right ahead," said Grandma, handing the lemon custard over to the others so they could pass it to Mr. Gurua and Grasshopper.

Grandpa had always advised them to honor what was right. Even honor Dr. Maxim, the hand they served. "We won't take what isn't ours," Alejandro declared, not letting the issue go. "If you do, you're a thief and we are no thieves."

The men looked at him, for everyone knew Dr. Maxim had not paid Grandpa for the cucumber harvest. Suddenly, the soft and pleasant breeze became chilly and the air thickened. The men turned silent.

"If they owe me, I would take it," mumbled Grasshopper after Nora offered the men coffee and tea. The conversation seemed to have stopped.

"It was pretty sad what happened to Dr. Maxim," said Mr. Reys, trying to change the topic of conversation.

"He was in mighty bad shape when he got to the hospital, right?" said Mario.

"He was gone before I got there," said Mr. Reys. "Alejandro was there."

"May he rest in peace," said Grandma.

"His poor wife, with all her health problems. And now this," said Nora.

"They're going to cremate his body," said Mr. Reys. "That is what Herman wants."

"They're holding a mass service at St. Vincent," Grandma said.

After helping Grandma with picking up the dishes and putting away leftovers, the men and their wives wound up the evening with trivial comments and anecdotes about their lives and work. The light outside the adobe house was little by little losing its glare. A large moth and few mosquitos tumbled through the air, as if they were inebriated by the light and then crashed against the lightbulb. The light dimmed intermittently.

Still weak and laying down, Kaiser sniffed the air and started barking toward the dusty road. Soil barked too and charged into the darkness but hesitated, seeing that Kaiser lagged behind. The growling and barking got more intense. Kaiser was still too weak under the porch, and Soil appeared to see something in the darkness as well. The small dog charged back and forth.

"Damned shit, get out of here!" the voice screamed while Soil barked, running back and forth. Then, Herman's semblance became visible. He was holding a bottle of Bravo and the lantern, which light had gone out.

"I told you to keep these damned dogs on a leash," he said, staring bleary-eyed at the people around the table. "What? Is this party over?" he asked while he staggered toward the porch. The men looked at him. The women got up nervously and moved closer to the door of the house.

"I wanna talk to Druett," he slurred. His words were drawn out longer than usual. In his eyes, there was the usual fiery gleam of a drunk, a glowering of hate and rage that only a troubled and inebriated soul could carry.

Grasshopper was the first one to approach him. Alejandro stood by Kaiser while Grasshopper held back Soil. "My grandpa's asleep!" said Grasshopper. "You stink!"

"I stink?" said Herman, coming within inches of Grasshopper's face. He stared at him, rocked his head from one side to the other, and opened his eyes wide like a mad man.

Grasshopper took a couple of steps back. Alejandro pulled Soil back toward him.

"Shit, you're wrong if you think I'm paying you for this work," he shouted to the men on the porch as he made a weird gesture with his finger.

Alejandro signaled for Mario to take hold of the dogs. Mr. Gurua, Mr. Lessar, and Mr. Reys just watched. They knew it was useless to talk to a drunk.

"You're drunk!" Alejandro said as he stepped forward between Herman and Grasshopper. Kaiser's growl intensified while Soil snarled and bared its teeth.

"Shit! You all got sixty-eight something crates and I was expecting 150," he said.

⟶⟩⟩⟩⟩ ⟨⟨⟨⟨⟵

Meanwhile, in the kitchen, Alvera suddenly took a seat and felt sick.

"Oh, sweetheart," said Nora. "Let me bring a bit of water and some raisins."

Grandma and Nora looked at each other.

"Where does it hurt?" asked Grandma.

"Just right here," said Alvera, touching the lower part of her belly.

"It's just a bit of discomfort," Nora said. "That's all."

"That means the baby's healthy," said Grandma, looking and smiling at Alvera. "Go outside and take a breath of fresh air."

"Do you think they'll notice?" asked Alvera.

"They won't even realize," said Grandma. "You'll be the last one waving your hand. You'll be the finest queen. I promise you."

"Take that from the queen herself," said Nora.

"It'll be nice if I win. We'll have a bit of money before the baby's born," said Alvera.

"You'll see to it that she'll have exactly what she needs," added Grandma.

"Or he," said Nora.

They smiled as Alvera blushed and went to sit outside.

The women stood on the porch. The men had gathered near Herman to keep him apart from Alejandro. Herman glared at him with the same crazed rage he had directed toward Grasshopper. Soil growled. Though weak, Kaiser kept pulling the harness in Mario's grip and snapping its teeth at Herman. The dog began coughing and vomited some remnants of meat folks had thrown under the table during dinner. In an effort to calm the dogs, Mario patted Soil while he held it.

Once Alvera was outside, she sat down under the porch, but then she stood up and scampered toward the side of the house. She leaned against the vines under the arbor, retched, and vomited toward the darkness. Some of the women ran to assist her while the men kept their eyes on Alejandro and Herman.

"The dog and the bitch's puking too," said Herman. He looked at Kaiser and then at Alvera.

"You come 'round here talking like that...." said Alejandro.

"So, what're you gonna do about that, Little Shit?" Herman taunted. The stench of *Bravo* on his breath brought back the sense of helpless anger Alejandro had felt the day he had asked for a job.

"You got the nerve to say it's just sixty-eight damn crates," Grasshopper burst out. "What about the ten tenfold you got from the cucumbers my Grandfather harvested for you?" Everyone looked at Herman.

Herman's face turned beet red and then squinted at Grasshopper. "You insolent, snotty nose," sputtered Herman. He lifted the boy by his shirtfront with both hands.

Grasshopper's eyes grew big and fluttered in fear while his fragile body and legs hung above the ground.

"You get your hands off him!" yelled Alejandro, stepping forward and pulling his brother from Herman's grip.

"First you stole the harnesses and now you wanna cheat me of almost 100 crates! Shit, I'll be damned," yelled the man in anger. "You gonna pay for that."

"You took a decagon!" Grasshopper shouted again.

Herman could no longer hide his guilt. Blood rose to his face. Some people in the crowd didn't know what a decagon was. His glazed eyes roved helplessly over the men gathered behind the two brothers. Time seemed to stop. Everyone was quiet and they stared at Herman. He and his father had a part at sapping Grandpa's livelihood, just as the disease was now consuming him. The harvesters were uneasy, but everyone knew what Grasshopper had said was true. Everyone knew the boy told lies, but what he said sounded like it had come from the heart. And Herman didn't deny it.

Herman grabbed his head with both hands, as if keeping his conscience from escaping into the open. He grabbed the side of his head, his hair, and clenched his teeth, as if he couldn't contain the thought of his guilty conscience, perhaps the stupor of his own drunkenness.

"I'm gonna teach both of you a lesson, insolent rats," said the man, losing his balance as he raised his fists and stepped back into position to fight. Alejandro thrust Grasshopper back toward where the laborers and neighbors had gathered.

Herman was taller and more robust than Alejandro, but Alejandro was more agile and had the strength that farm folks usually have. His calloused hands and knotty muscles were seasoned by the grueling hard work in the fields, the vineyards and orchards. Herman threw a clumsy punch that grazed Alejandro's cheek. Kaiser and Soil were growling again and straining at Mario's hold.

"That ought to teach you," snarled Herman when he saw Alejandro lean back slightly from the blow. Mr. Reys and Mr. Gurua craned their necks at the same time. Everyone knew that Alejandro had to fight this fight. In Russell, men had to defend their own. Alejandro and Alvera's pride and dignity were at stake. The men and women looked at Herman aghast. His face scarcely seemed normal; it looked so distorted with rage and drunkenness that he didn't look like himself.

Alejandro watched as Herman's appearance shifted from that of a drunk child to a decisive man. He was intoxicated but stood firm as he dropped into a relaxed fighter's stance with his guard up and ready. In a blink of an eye, Alejandro shook off the punch and moved forward.

Alejandro was smaller but quicker than Herman. He approached him with a few feints that led the heavier man to lower his guard. With a quick thrust, Alejandro struck him between the mouth and nose, startling and sending him backwards onto his behind. Herman bled from the nose. The taste of his own blood combined with *Bravo* made him even angrier. With an outburst of impotent rage, he stood and rushed toward Alejandro.

Alejandro sidestepped and deftly avoided the lunge. Herman was a raging bull and Alejandro dodged him like a matador, but he finally got a grip on Alejandro and caught him with a headlock. Alejandro kept moving, grabbing Herman by the waist, and struggled to release himself from the man's arm. Even though Herman had him by the neck, Alejandro kept Herman moving at a fast pace. In the struggle, Alejandro lowered his chin to free himself from the headlock. He was more elusive than Herman and was able to now take control of the fight, slipping behind Herman and freeing himself from his grip. He then grabbed Herman's shirt, and, with a to-and-fro, he untucked and lifted it up, making Herman turn, struggling to escape him.

The men and women stood by in awe. No one said anything, except for Mr. Reys, who told the others to let the men fight it off. He could have done it himself after Herman had insulted Alvera, beaten George, but he knew that this time, Alejandro had to defend more than just his pride and Alvera. Mr. Reys knew that if anyone ever needed to fight this fight, it was Alejandro. What was at stake now was the livelihood of those who would come after him.

Mario made a signal to Grasshopper so he could come and take hold of the dogs, who continued growling and barking. "Hold them here, little man," said Mario.

Alejandro kept Herman at bay. He had a firm grip on the shirt and, as Herman moved, Alejandro kept pulling it up the man's back. Folks there could see Herman's leather belt but could not see the sheath and the dark hilt of a dagger he hid in the underside of his pants. With the hustle and bustle of the fight, the top, metal end of the hilt shined with the reflection of the light above. Being drunk was slowing Herman down, but it gave him the bile to continue fighting. In the struggle, Alejandro pulled Herman's shirt completely over his head and arms, blinding and trapping him as he began to twist the shirt collar around Herman's neck. Herman was not only blinded and trapped by his own shirt but also cuffed by the buttoned sleeves at his wrists. The button at the collar was also fastened so it kept the shirt from peeling off from the man's head. Both men were panting like two spent beasts trapped in a mire of wrath, mud, misery, and fermented must: one struggling to survive; the other quenching his prideful arrogance.

"You let me go, you damned rat!" Herman growled from inside his shirt. Angrily crying, he tried to force himself out of Alejandro's lock. Still holding Herman's shirt in a fist by the side of the hem with his right hand, Alejandro began pounding his left fist into the man's side and head. Blow after blow, Herman kept growling and screaming.

"Get him off of me!" he cried as Alejandro kept delivering blow after blow, moving with a quick step around him every time. Herman was in the center of the yard in front of the porch of the adobe house under Alejandro's control. He directed his boss' son any way he wanted to land more punches on him. Hearing the commotion, Nora and Grandma came out of the house.

"You let that man go!" Grandma screamed, but Alejandro couldn't hear. Caught in a trance of rage, he kept pounding at the head within the shirt.

"It's all right now!" the men yelled. Mr. Reys and Mr. Gurua approached to separate the two men. Alejandro stopped when he realized Mr. Reys had him by the shoulders while Mr. Gurua tried to wedge his way between Alejandro and Herman.

Alejandro allowed himself to be pulled back, while Herman managed to free his head from the shirt. "You bastard!" he screamed. His nose and mouth were bloody and the orbit around his right eye was cut and swollen. Circumventing Mr. Gurua, Mr. Reys and Mario, Herman rushed headlong toward Alejandro and pushed him to the ground. Alejandro's back hit the dirt as Herman sprang on top of him. In the struggle, Alejandro held Herman's hands and kept him from reaching his face.

Grandma became even more agitated, and the other women there began to scream for the men there to stop the fight. Holding the dogs, Grasshopper neared Herman while the dogs barked and whined. Kaiser somehow had regained its strength, while Herman had managed to tuck Alejandro's hands under his knees, leaving him at his mercy.

The night sky seemed suddenly darker. Stars shivered in the distance. Moths fluttered around the light post. The edge of the blade shone above Herman as he raised it over Alejandro. An ominous silence pervaded the air. The women covered their eyes and the men's faces were filled with terror. Herman's eyes were fixed on Alejandro. While his weight kept Alejandro from moving, he held him by the neck with one hand; the other held the dagger above him. Frowning, his nebulous thought attempted to focus on the perceived wrong he needed to redress. Alejandro closed his eyes.

Grasshopper's eyes grew bigger, and he let go of the dogs.

"You're gonna fight a clean fight," shouted Nora, grabbing and lifting Herman by the wrist that held the dagger.

"You let go of me, you old hag," the drunken man sputtered while Soil and Kaiser lunged forward, snapping at his ankles and tearing at the legs of his pants. Nora lifted the man higher. Her robust figure looked monumental next to the arm that dangled from her hand, as if he were a dead hog hanging from a rafter. He hung loosely as Nora looked at him, while the dogs chomped at his legs and buttocks. The dagger fell from his hand and Grandma snatched it as soon as it hit the ground.

"Get them off me!" he screamed, trying to kick the dogs away. "Keep them away!" he shouted. The men intervened and took hold of the drunkard.

"You all gonna pay for this." Herman made threats as the men escorted him off the homestead. But as he saw himself overwhelmed, he began to cry, realizing the wrong he had done.

Alejandro stood and walked toward Alvera. She brushed away a tear as she wrapped her arms around his waist.

"Your Grandpa will be very disappointed in you," said Grandma, reprimanding Alejandro.

"I'm not letting that man walk all over us anymore," Alejandro replied quietly.

"You gotta start setting a good example," replied Grandma.

"Why? For who?" he asked. "I can only worry about myself. Everyone looks after themselves here."

"You're gonna be a father," said Alvera as she grabbed Alejandro's hand and placed it on her belly. Grandma looked at her, then at him.

Alejandro fixed his sight on Alvera's eyes, which were still glossy with tears but hopeful and joyous. Alejandro looked at Grandma, then back at Alvera, and smiled. He turned and gazed around at the dark sky above, settling his vision on the sparkly trail, a river of stars in the night sky. He suddenly knew the direction he needed to take now. Nothing else mattered. He knew that things would work out somehow. Fighting Herman was something he needed to do no matter the consequence. He had to set the limit and draw the line that would tell any prominent or common men in Russells that he was now a man to be reckoned with. He knew this and accepted his fate after the fight.

After folks chit-chatted about the night's events, many of them congratulated Alejandro and Alvera for the new life in her womb. Some of the men patted Mr. Reys and Alejandro on the back and offered help for anything Alvera and Alejandro needed. Mr. and Mrs. Campito were some of the last ones to leave. Mr. Reys waited for Alvera so he could take her back home, but Alejandro offered to walk her back to the farm before midnight. Before he went inside to say goodbye to Grandpa, Mr. Reys approached Alejandro and Alvera. Mr. Reys gazed at them. He seemed satisfied but couldn't shake off the worry. Alvera picked up the saucers with remnants of lemon pie, got up, and went inside the house. Perhaps Alvira had told him. Perhaps he was already aware.

"You gotta be careful now how you go about doing things, son," said Mr. Reys. Mr. Reys looked resigned, but after witnessing Alejandro standing his ground, he knew his soon-to-be son in law could protect Alvera.

"You don't have to worry about that," he said to Mr. Reys. "I can earn my keep."

"I know you can," Mr. Reys said. "I can help you and Alvera get settled."

"I wanna earn my way," he said. "Soon I'll have more than a family to look after."

Mr. Reys understood and nodded. He looked Alejandro in the eye. "Bringing a life to the world has to be right in the eyes of God," Mr. Reys said.

"I'm gonna marry Alvera," said Alejandro. "I love her."

"I know you do."

"It is right in our eyes too," said Alejandro, looking at Mr. Reys straight in the eye.

"This is no child's play," said Mr. Reys.

Alejandro sighed, squinted, and thought deeply. A reflection perhaps. A notion of reality crossed his mind and turned into fact—another layer that felt right and at the same time overwhelming was added to his life. The heavy lifting and carrying of crates full of grapes or olives didn't compare to the weight he carried that night.

Alvera came back from the kitchen and sat next to Alejandro. Mr. Reys looked at her and smiled. He then kissed her forehead, put his hand on Alejandro's shoulder and left.

Alejandro and Alvera stayed on the porch with Kaiser and Soil at their feet for a while longer. Then, as they walked back to Mr. Reys' farm, Alejandro wrapped his arm around her waist while she rested her head on his shoulder and both disappeared along the dusty road and into the night.

"Grandpa doesn't look well at all," said Alvera as they walked.

"I know," Alejandro said in the dark silence of the night.

She wanted to know his plan. What would they do, being so young and having a child?

"I'll find work," he said, looking at Alvera.

She smiled but was uncertain of it all.

"Grandma and some of the other folks already know," said Alejandro.

"They do, and they expect a lot more from us," she said.

Alejandro stopped for a moment, hoping to find some answers in the darkness all around him. "I'm too young, but would you want to be my wife?" Alejandro asked, not knowing how to really say it. He said what he felt; he was at a crossroads. He knew which road he wanted to take, but still felt much uncertainty.

"Are you really asking me?" she said.

"Yes!" he said. They embraced in the darkness.

"I don't care where you take me if I'm still with you," Alvera whispered to him.

"Mr. Gurua offered me work and a way to buy a lot in Sweet Heaven," he said.

She held him tight. "I'm sure my dad will help us too," she added.

"Yes, but we don't need anybody's help. We can make it on our own," he said.

"You keep saying that, and look how people here have helped you to pull the olive harvest," she said. "And you keep saying that you don't need help."

"I know," he said and remained in silence. His pride kept him hostage from himself and from fully accepting what Alvera was saying to him.

"It's a good thing to have folks who can give you a hand and advice when you need it," she said.

"Yeah," he said, acknowledging the kind nature and goodwill of most folks in Russell. He thought about Mr. Gurua's offer and the other folks who had gracefully helped him. He was a man now who could decide for himself. They kept walking. Their presence, being next to each other was enough for their peace of mind. They loved each other without words, just by looking into each other's eyes, walking side by side, being near one another while holding hands. As they arrived at Mr. Reys' farm, they stood by the gate, facing each other, like lovers do, waiting for and hugging each other before departing, but with neither of them willing to do so.

"It's three of us now," said Alejandro.

"And Grandpa, Grandma, and Grasshopper," Alvera said.

He gently held her face and kissed her soft lips. "I'll be heading back soon," he said.

She hugged him and they kissed again.

They were lost in thought, imagining the new life inside of them: a new life that would rise brightly like the sun at daybreak or like an ascending full moon in the night sky.

Farewell

As Grandma walked by the bed, Grandpa stretched out his hand, lightly grasping and pulling her dress, inviting her to sit by his side. Grasshopper stood by the light table and looked at Grandpa.

"Go to bed," said Grandma.

"I want to be here with Grandpa," said Grasshopper.

"I'll wake you up for breakfast," she said.

"I really don't want to go to school," said Grasshopper.

"Grandpa has to rest now."

"We'll plant tomatoes next season, right Grandpa?" said Grasshopper. He looked worried.

"Yes, we will. We will," said Grandpa, gasping for air. He had a gentle smile on his face. "We'll have our own place soon," added Grandpa as he grasped Grandma's hand. His eyelids were lazy, and his eyes looked drowsy as they drifted into space.

"Yes, we will soon, my handsome gentleman," said Grandma as she put some basil leaves on Grandpa's forehead. His hands were warm, and he breathed with difficulty.

Kaiser sniffed the air inside the bedroom as it approached Grandpa. The dog licked Grandpa's listless fingers that rested on the side of the bed.

Grandma propped a pillow behind Grandpa and, with difficulty, he sat up on the bed. "This will put you in better spirits," said Grandma. With his hands trembling, Grandpa reached for the drawer of the night table, took out his Swiss Army knife and a piece of paper, and cut a piece of smoked bacon that lay on a plate with leftovers of the food that Grandma had brought for him for dinner. He then placed the bacon on his hand and stretched out his fingers toward Kaiser. The dog smelled the bacon, looked at Grandpa, and licked his hand. He took the bacon delicately with his tongue and snapped it down his throat. Grandpa closed the knife and placed it in Grasshopper's hand. As he sunk back into bed, he gasped for air and kept coughing.

"I want no ceremony. No priest. No church," he whispered with difficulty. He once again held Grandma's hand and gave her the piece of paper.

After eating the bacon, Kaiser whined and stood, looking at Grandpa, as if the dog anticipated his departure. Kaiser remained still, as if he were waiting to chase something, with his eyes locked on Grandpa.

"Grandma, what's happening?" Grasshopper asked while his eyes watered.

"Keep your sight on the horizon," Grandpa said with difficulty, looking at Grasshopper. His voice faded in and out. "We'll have a tomato patch next year," he added as he breathed heavily. He reached out and took Grasshopper's hand.

"Yes, we will," affirmed Grandma.

"Grandpa, are you gonna die?" sobbed Grasshopper. He wiped his eyes with his sleeve.

"Son, things must change," said Grandpa, making an effort to speak clearly.

"But I don't want you to leave me, Grandpa. Why do you have to leave? Why?" asked Grasshopper, kneeling by the bedside and sinking his face into the bedcover.

Grandma took Kaiser outside. Kaiser and Soil's howls now echoed in the homestead. She then brought a pot with steaming eucalyptus and other herbs from the kitchen and began to rub it on Grandpa's chest.

"Please, let me go...let go...," Grandpa said. His words had an ease in them, as if he didn't feel any fear. He sighed. His breathing had the sound of relief, of letting go perhaps, with an ease like a breeze, smooth like the wind. He wanted to be free and be taken like the wind takes dry leaves into swirls in the orchards in the fall. His eyes wandered around the room. He gasped, taking in any bit of air he could.

"Here we go again," said Grandma, looking at him with compassion.

"You'll lay the seed...keep your orchard tight," Grandpa whispered to Grasshopper. "We'll grow red, plump tomatoes." He cleared his throat.

"We will, Grandpa," replied Grasshopper, sniffling.

"That's my little Grasshopper. My little hard worker," Grandpa whispered. He looked at Grandma and now there were no traces of pain on his face.

"Where's Alejandro?" whispered Grandpa.

"He's gone to walk Alvera home. He'll be back soon," replied Grandma.

⇝⟫⟫ ⟪⟪⇜

Alejandro could hear Kaiser's howling from a distance. A bright shooting star ripped across the dawn as he approached the homestead. Stars still dimmed on the dark side of the sky, but those in the East were still visible. Nebulae swirled, like the wind taking a trail of dust aloft and dancing with it through the air. A star-filled sky stretched out endlessly—a glittering path of constellations that were quickly fading in the cold morning—as the sun appeared to announce a new day and lit the way home.

"I've had many dreams in this life, my darling," said Grandpa, gasping.

"Yes, you have. Life with you has all been a dream to me, my handsome gentleman," Grandma said softly.

"Wherever your sight goes, mine will be there too."

"I'm always gonna be here by your side," said Grandma. Time stood still.

"I'm sorry I couldn't do better. You deserved so much better," he said and looked at Grandma. His tender eyelids eased in the moment.

"All I ever wanted was to be by your side," Grandma said as his hand eased into hers. "But you gotta rest now."

Grandpa closed his eyes as tenuous particles of dust sifted through the morning sunlight, as sunrays cast a gentle glow on his face. Thousands of dust motes, like a radiant breath of serenity, floated upwards within the light beam that crossed from the window and into Grandpa's face. Grasshopper followed the particles as they traveled gently through the air.

"Grandpa?" whispered Grasshopper as Grandpa's body seemed to sink deeper into the pillow.

Kaiser and Soil's howls continued outside, reaching the farms around the homestead.

Sitting by his side, Grandma cried while she held and kissed Grandpa's hands. She stood and put her gentle hands on her grandson's shoulders, and both walked outside for a moment into the refreshing morning mist.

Alejandro's steps left dark footprints along the dew-soaked alleyway by the adobe house. Olive tree leaves left behind by the neighbors and laborers lay dried along his path. The sun now rose through the poplar trees in the homestead and glanced into the young man's eyes. Seeing Grandpa's health deteriorate so rapidly, Alejandro knew that Grandpa could be gone at any moment, and he accepted this loss, for the thoughts of Alvera and his child's well-being occupied his mind. The boy in him was gone. He would be the only one to look after the Druetts and his own family. He was no longer an innocent child. Folks in Russell would now respect him and refer to him as Alejandro Druett, though only his mother carried the Druett's last name. Although still a child in years, he had no choice but to become a man.

Alejandro set his sight on the red sunrise that morning, where there was a new place to dwell for him, Alvera, and the life she carried inside her, Grasshopper, and Grandma. He looked at the dew that coated the dusty road and contemplated his tracks that winded back to the *callejón*.

As he approached the door by the front porch and entered the adobe house, Grandma was waiting, holding the folded sheet of paper Grandpa had given her.

"How's Alvera?" she asked.

"She's all right," he replied. "Still a little nauseated but resting. How's Grandpa?"

Grandma looked at him. She cast her glance through the window and then to the floor.

"Your Grandfather left this for you," she said, giving Alejandro the paper. He stared at her and knew Grandpa was gone. He unfolded the paper and read:

Son,

I see a man in you now. Your heart is that of a man. I say farewell to the child. Your heart says farewell to the child. The commitment was never with me or other men. It is not with the money you receive from your labor but with the land that you live on and that you call home and with the life that you want to live. Men spend their lives giving excuses for what they don't do, for what they do, and for the life they may or may not choose to live, but many do not see the generous path before them every day. One thing remains true. In the morning when you get up and see the sun is rising, you rise with it and work during the day, making the effort to do your job well. Your commitment is not with another man but with the opportunity to do good. This goodwill you take home with you, a confidence no man can take away, and a goodwill that no man can ever steal or buy from you. After a good day's work, you go home and give thanks that you got yourself and your family, that you got your hands, your arms, your strength, and your intelligence to be a better man the next day. That's the commitment.

Enclosed, on the other side of the sheet:

A Virtuous Path
Let faith and goodwill show the righteous path,
A child is born among a thousand men,
A man will remain after our Lord's wrath.

Spring showers cleanse our souls, in the aftermath,
Foes will cast the stones just because thousands can,
Let faith and goodwill show the righteous path.

Dignified hands, souls enclosed in the rath,
Greed of some succumbs by the virtuous hand,
One man will remain after our Lord's wrath.

Be your brother's friend from mountain to strath,
No matter the toil, together you must stand,
Let faith and goodwill show the righteous path.

And honor the promise of the Great Bath,
When rivals clasp a cheek with a fierce hand,
One man will remain after our Lord's wrath.

Rest in my words when the vile stone is cast,
Be patient and strong, the work has just begun.

Let faith and goodwill show the righteous path.
One man will remain after our Lord's wrath.

He folded the paper, placed it in his shirt pocket, and lowered his gaze.

"What did he say?" he asked.

"How much he loved you."

Alejandro remained deep in silence. He paused and sat down under the porch for a moment. There was nothing he could do about Grandpa's death. The impotence he felt was an all-too familiar feeling. He wanted to cry but he didn't. He wanted to say something but he couldn't.

He lifted his eyes and fixed them on the orchard. The singing of thrushes and sparrows on olive branches merged in consonance with the rustling of leaves in the poplar trees. And with that cool breeze that morning, Grandpa was gone.

The Dust That Remained

At the homestead, after Grandpa passed away, there was a scent in the air that rose out of the soil in the orchard and vineyard, like a soft lifeforce, which passed inconspicuously, carrying with it the freshness and mist of the morning.

By the toolshed, the crooked pile of rusty iron, zinc sheets, and brass rods were illuminated by an almost fluorescent red glow from the morning sunrays. Grandpa was gone, but his essence seemed to linger: his distant words seemed to echo through the trees and the shed; his footsteps were heard rustling on dry leaves; and the presence and sound of his pace seemed to echoed in the paths where he used to walk on at the homestead.

The morning light grew, and the golden hues of dried grasses and the late blooming of wild zinnias filled the fields of the valley. The decaying and dried foliage of olive trees looked like standing bronze statues over the furrows. For a brief time, the resting soil seemed to have flourished with new life as the sunlight embroidered the fields with tawny, brown hues that extended from field to field to the foot of the mountains.

❧ ⟫⟫⟫ ⟪⟪⟪ ☙

Grandpa was a patriarch. For the most part, he was respected by farmers, day laborers, and sharecroppers alike. Grasshopper had never seen so many people walking along the *callejón* to pay their respects to Grandpa. An era had ended. No generation before Alejandro had drawn the line between themselves and those they worked for. Every generation had to learn to fend for itself, and either learn anew or repeat history. It had to decide whether to remain stuck in the mire of misery and monotony, handed down to it by its own circumstance and landlords, or to design its destiny by its own hand.

With Grandpa's passing, there was a new air at the homestead. The autumn breezes had taken the tranquility and abundance of the summer. The air was frigid and, although the changes seemed to have brought much bleakness and desolation, the lives of sharecroppers were dignified by their work and the lives they lived.

The day of the funeral, frustration overwhelmed Grasshopper. He had run about the homestead after seeing Grandpa take his last breath. His anger turned into tears, for he did not understand why people had to die. He grabbed his slingshot, Grandpa's Swiss Army knife, and leather bag from his hiding spot in the toolshed and headed toward the Manso River.

On his way there, Grasshopper observed mourners walking along the *callejón*. Folks came from the farms around the homestead and even beyond the Great Endes Mountains. Some well-dressed men whom neither Grasshopper nor anyone at the homestead had ever seen before were there to attend Grandpa's funeral. Day laborers from beyond the valley arrived with wreaths embellished with gladiolus and white chrysanthemums arranged on creosote vines. Women brought fresh bread and jars of apricot and grape marmalade, and some even brought red wine to spice and mull during the cold night ahead.

As Grasshopper reached the river, he rambled by the rocks along the bank. He sat on a boulder and took out Grandpa's Swiss Army knife and began sharpening a stick that was stuck out of the sand. "Why do people have to die?" he asked. The boy could not understand why Grandpa was gone. *Grandpa was old but why—of all people—did he have to die? Is that it?* he thought. The boy sobbed. *If I sleep when others are awake, then am I really asleep?* He began tracing a line across the sand, wondering about these ideas. He wondered what else there was to life. It was a meager mystery that assured that in the end, good and lesser men had the same fate. No matter the circumstances, in the end, all exited in the same way.

But not for Alejandro. To him, men left behind a legacy, good memories for others to reminisce and rejoice, and learn from. To him, a life worth living meant a life worth dying for. He was no longer afraid, for he finally understood his place in the world where he was destined to be.

Back at the homestead, the silence outside the adobe house pervaded the air with the stillness characteristic of misty daybreaks in the grove. Everything seemed to stop. In the distance, birds were no longer tweeting and chirping. Solemnity descended on the people gathered together as they spoke, murmuring their accounts about Grandpa.

"The day my child died, we had no money to give him a decent burial," recounted Mr. Gaseto, with his eyes locked on the ground as he recalled the painful memory. Other neighbors listened and nodded. "Mr. Druett arrived at our home and brought with him a hand-made cedar coffin," continued Mr. Gaseto. "I told him I couldn't pay him, but he asked us to accept it as a token of condolence for our loss. My wife and I couldn't find the words to thank him."

"That's the kind of man he was," murmured another man.

"Yeah, one Christmas Eve, the year of the drought, we had no food. The only thing left on our table was some remnants of melted wax and the burnt wick of a candle. He brought fresh bread, honey, and milk, and even hand-made toys for our little ones," said a tall, lean man as he puffed on a cigarette.

"They say he used to drink a lot," said Mr. Cavoni, the owner of the largest store in Wooden Cross. "But I never heard the man say one bad thing."

"He did drink as a young man, but he quit when his grandsons were born," said Mr. Reys, who was also among them. "Mr. Druett was a good man. He wasn't perfect, but he was a good, proud, and honest man. A good neighbor. He took nothing from nobody, and whenever someone needed help, he found a way to be there."

While the men continued talking, Alejandro and Mr. Gurua stood near the porch of the adobe house. Alejandro seemed to take the news of Grandpa's death very stoically as if it had not really sunk in yet.

"You may take me up on the offer I made to your grandfather. He was my friend, you know," Mr. Gurua suggested to Alejandro.

"About the land in Sweet Heaven?" Alejandro asked.

"Yes. Your Grandpa wanted the lot up in Sweet Heaven for you and Grasshopper," added Mr. Gurua. "You could easily find a way to pay for it."

"Thank you Mr. Gurua, but I can't accept that," said Alejandro while Grandma walked out of the house. He thought about what Alvera had said to him.

"Please have some hot coffee," said Grandma as she set down a few coffee mugs and a kettle on the table. The steam of the tin kettle swirled slowly upwards and wafted away, merging with the stillness of the morning.

"Let me help you with that, my dear Lisa," said Bianca, Mr. Gurua's wife, as she passed the mugs and picked up the kettle to serve those who were there.

Grandma went inside the house to bring back some pastries.

⌁⌁⌁ ⌁⌁⌁

The men continued to talk as more people arrived. "Heard the doctor had not paid him yet," said Mr. Godsends, another of Grandpa's friends who stood with the others outside the house.

"That happened to me one time," replied Joe Needleman, a slender man, whom Grandpa had helped secure a sharecropping job at the Segovia's farm. "You ought not to deal with that kind of folk."

"It's a bad deal to work for men who won't keep their word. It's a bad deal," said Mr. Bejusto, who held a mug of coffee between his hands. He was an older man who made and sold reins and other farm and household items. Grandpa used to say he was an artist.

The men suddenly became quiet as they saw Herman approach the house. Alejandro and Mr. Gurua had walked by the clay oven on the side of the house. When Alejandro saw Herman approaching the house, he squinted at him and approached the porch. Herman saw the crowd standing outside the house. He looked disheveled and chagrined.

"Good morning, gentleman," he said. His voice was calm. He had sobered up.

"Good morning," all of the men said.

"I'm sorry about your father, Mr. Maxim," said Mr. Needleman.

"Thank you, we appreciate that," said Herman.

"I'm sorry 'bout Mr. Druett too," Herman said, addressing the crowd in a subdued tone. Then he handed an envelope to Grandma. "Here's a part of the money Dad owed you. I figure you'll be needing it for the funeral."

Grandma looked at Alejandro, who was now standing next to her. "Thank you," said Grandma.

"You ought to give us the ten percent you owe us," Alejandro said. His voice was now firm as he looked Herman in the eye.

"You ought to see this family get all the money you owe Mr. Druett," said Mr. Gurua. "You ought to honor Dr. Maxim's word." The others murmured and nodded.

"I'll pay as I receive the money. Right now I got to straighten out some of my father's businesses," said Herman in a shaky voice.

"Yeah, you ought to pay them their due," said Mario, who overheard the exchange from the porch.

Something in Alejandro's gaze made Herman lower his sight. Perhaps it was a type of recognition that some men were whole and others broken, or that one man possessed dignity and another vanity, or the realization that greed would make a man deny himself by taking from those who might have helped him, or simply possess a kind of blindness that brought darkness where light needed to abound.

Alejandro was serene. He did not owe Herman a thing, and he could look his boss' son in the eye without shame, for he knew he wasn't the one beholden. The Druett's livelihood needed to be redressed; Alejandro held the knowledge that showed how one man can be better than another, even after a sad soul had tried to toy with his and his family's dignity.

"I'm afraid I won't be needing you on the farm next season. I've been thinking I might better hire day laborers from now on," said Herman.

Alejandro had fully expected this turn of events and he felt relieved. The announcement somehow freed him; he felt at peace, a peace that was reflected in his unwavering gaze and the silence he kept after hearing a drunkard's empty excuses.

Herman couldn't hide his shame. He looked about haplessly. No one spoke except for Grandma, who brought him a cup of coffee and said, "I'm really sorry about your father."

Herman looked down as he held the mug with both hands, took a few sips, and put the cup on the table. He then attempted to look at Alejandro once again but turned around and walked away.

"Where's Grasshopper?" Grandma asked before going back to the kitchen.

Mario cocked his head and looked around. Mrs. Gurua carried trays with round loaves of bread and slices of cheese for the guests.

In the face of such circumstance, Mr. Gurua looked at Alejandro and approached him. He tried to persuade him to buy the land. "The offer for the land still stands," said Mr. Gurua to Alejandro. "I wouldn't offer it if I thought you couldn't pay for it."

"I don't want to owe money to anyone," said Alejandro. "I want to be like Grandpa and not owe anything to anyone."

"We all got to owe someone something if we want to offer our families a better life," said Mr. Gurua.

Alejandro seemed downcast. "If I owe someone something, I will always be bound to someone. I couldn't ever feel or be free. How can I think and live as a free man if I'm bound and indebted to another?" said Alejandro.

"But son, everyone has to do it that way. We couldn't survive another way," Mr. Gurua insisted. "I have saved my money through the years, but I still owe the bank. I depend on them."

"I don't want to depend on no one but the land and my work," replied Alejandro.

"When things don't go well, the bank can help you," he said.

"Yes, but only to get more money out of you, right?" Alejandro questioned.

"Well, yes, that's true, but they can get you out of a bind when things don't go so well."

"Or they can take all you have if things get worse," said Alejandro. "I can't take risks. Alvera is expecting. I'm gonna be a father."

"Well, that's great news!" said Mr. Gurua. "Now more than ever you need to think about the land." Alejandro smiled but that sparkle of joy in his eye was also filled with worry.

"I have to think about a new home for everyone. Herman won't need us next year," Alejandro said.

"Look. I had told Mr. Druett that I would give him a good deal for the land up in Sweet Heaven. And you are just like him," Mr. Gurua said.

"How am I?"

"Stubborn like a mule," said Mr. Gurua. He shook his head. Alejandro smiled. "Now you think about it, son," said Mr. Gurua. "I'm not giving you anything. This is a fair deal. Your Grandpa did a lot of things for me without ever asking for anything in return. So, I do it for that reason too. You think about it and let me know. You could pay part of it and the remaining you can pay with work next year. Just know that I'm not giving you anything." Mr. Gurua had a stern look on his face, he looked Alejandro straight in the eyes and Alejandro did the same.

Alejandro understood that he and his grandfather were not alone in the world. That being around like-minded and good people could make life more bearable. He took time to reflect and realized that it was no longer about his pride. He thought about his child. About Alvera. About Grasshopper and Grandma. About Kaiser and Soil. And about having a roof over their head and the tools he needed to provide for them. If he had been offered a hand, he needed to accept it and make the best of it. Perhaps he needed to wait for his turn to help someone like him one day and finally understand that all men and women are connected, that everyone matters, that everyone could be exalted in his or her own measure and circumstance.

"A grown man has to do what's right for others before he does for himself," Mr. Gurua said as they walked away from the front of the adobe house.

"There are grown men who don't live up to that idea," said Alejandro, referring to Herman as they saw him walking away. "Some grown men who have plenty to live a good life still want something from others. It's like a thirst they can't quench."

"Look, I don't know what else this man has done to you, but whatever it was, you gotta let that go," Mr. Gurua said.

"It's hard to let go of bad memories," said Alejandro, looking directly at Mr. Gurua.

"A bad memory is like a prison. It confines you. It's like having a prisoner in your head, unable to escape." Alejandro squinted. "You gotta let that memory go. You bring that child into this world with you reliving that memory every time you have a chance. And that child somehow, someway, will relive that memory, too."

Alejandro cocked his head and looked at Mr. Gurua. He sighed. And then fixed his sight into the distance, not looking at anything. He realized Mr. Gurua was right. He felt somewhat relieved and thought about the prison and the prisoner in his own mind.

"Look at it this way," said Mr. Gurua, "Every time you open your eyes and look for something better, you are letting that memory go," said Mr. Gurua.

Alejandro's eyes watered. And he looked down, not to show Mr. Gurua that he was crying.

"It's all right if you cry," he said, firmly placing his right hand on Alejandro's shoulder. None of the other mourners were in sight as he and Alejandro had moved by the side of the house by the clay oven.

"My Grandpa is gone now," said Alejandro. A deep sigh and sob sunk in his chest.

"He died a proud man because of you and your brother," said Gurua. "Listen, you gotta take things like a man now. You and Grasshopper got so much going for you. You're hardworking and smart. You know how to work the land and some of the trades your Grandpa taught you."

"I know." Alejandro was now regaining himself again.

"Once the funeral is over, we'll set things up so we can sit down and talk about Sweet Heaven," Mr. Gurua said.

Alejandro nodded. "Thank you," he said sniffing, sighing, and whispering.

Grasshopper sat under the bridge at the Manso River that separated Russell with the outskirts of the Great Endes Mountains. He wondered about his grandfather, about everything that lives and dies. He observed how the currents of the Manso River cascaded downstream, forming foamy swirls that seemed to turn on themselves and switch direction. What thoughts may have crossed his mind? *Must water flow in one direction? Could it change the course of nature? Could life turn against death? What would this natural change be? Could death change back to life? Can a river turn against its own current? Could life? Could death?* he thought.

Mario parked his truck near the bridge and descended to the riverbank. He jumped from boulder to boulder, finding his way down.

"Grasshopper!" he shouted, as he looked around. "Grasshopper!"

Grasshopper got up and walked to the bank by the bridge, where he began to skip rocks off the water.

"Hey, Grasshopper," said Mario as he approached him.

Grasshopper kept casting the stones over the water, ignoring Mario's call.

"Hey, little man," said Mario in a low voice. "You okay?"

Grasshopper just cocked his head to one side.

"I'm sorry about Grandpa," said Mario. "He was a good, mighty man."

"Why does it have to be this way?" blurted Grasshopper. His eyes watered.

"That's just the way it is," replied Mario.

"So why even bother?" said Grasshopper.

"What do you mean?"

"Why bother doing anything?"

"We got no choice."

"It's like a trap," said Grasshopper while he threw another stone across the water. "Why did Grandpa have to die? First my mom and dad. Now my Grandpa."

"We all do," replied Mario as he squatted next to him. "Your grandpa loved you. He talked about you all the time."

"I know. I loved him too," Grasshopper said, sobbing.

"Sometimes that is all we can take."

"What do you mean?" said Grasshopper. "Take what?"

"The good memories, I mean," he said. "The mighty love we have for each other."

"That's it," said Grasshopper.

"It's the best we have. A pretty mighty thing. We just gotta keep pushing."

"Don't people get tired of pushing? Grandpa was tired of pushing."

"We spend our lives pushing," Mario said. "A mighty fight we gotta put up."

"Grandpa spent his whole life pushing." He gazed at the sand by his feet.

"He did, and he was respected and loved for that," said Mario.

"It don't matter no more. He's gone."

"It does matter, because the mighty things he did, he did them for Alejandro, for you, for Mrs. Druett, for everyone in the family. And I'm sure he'd have wanted you to remember that." Grasshopper gazed at the sand and reflected upon what Mario had said to him.

"I need to go back. Grandma is gonna get worried." Grasshopper had regained his composure.

"Listen, Grasshopper. You and Alejandro are in charge now. You gotta go back and help Grandma."

"I don't know if I can," said Grasshopper.

"You're a mighty little man, you and Alejandro," said Mario. Grasshopper listened in silence as he looked at Mario. Then he began to make his way back up the riverbank.

⇥⇥ ⇤⇤

Although it was obvious to everyone that Alejandro and Alvera were a couple, Grandma had known about them for some time, and Grasshopper had known even longer. Alvera confirmed her membership in the family the last few weeks since Grandpa had been sick. The night of the funeral, she had arrived early to help Grandma with the house chores and with serving the visitors.

"Do you like the name Franco?" asked Alvera.

"I do," said Grandma. "Or Frances. Do you know what it means?"

"Yes," replied Alvera. "Either way, it means frank, honest."

"I think it will be a good name for the baby," Grandma added as she kneaded two loaves of dough on the table.

Alejandro came into the kitchen and saw Alvera striking her belly and looking pensive.

"You all right?" asked Alejandro, approaching her.

"Yes!" she said. She smiled, grabbed Alejandro's hand and placed it on her belly.

"He moved! She moved!" he said. His eyes lit with excitement.

She giggled and said, "Not yet, silly, it's too early!"

He led her to Grandpa's seat and said, "She did move. She moved. I felt her."

Alvera looked at him and laughed.

Outside, folks kept talking. The day was a bit cloudy, but the warmth of the gathering seemed to take the chill from the air. If not for the solemn expressions and mourning clothes, the guests might have been enjoying one of the festive gatherings they held at the end of each harvesting season.

"There is a wager offered to the winner of the Wine Fest," said Alvera to Alejandro.

"There is?" he asked, surprised.

"I think I can win it," said Alvera, looking at Alejandro.

Grandma grinned and looked at them.

"You will," said Alejandro.

Grandpa was buried on a piece of land that wasn't even his. The remnants of his body would remain at the homestead. Dust would remain in that spot, on a soil that had absorbed his sweat, his blood, his tears, and his whole mettle. If all the men and the families that were gone after each season could talk. If the dust could talk, if the seasonal laborers' calloused hands could talk, if their passing through the fields could talk, if the hardships they had endured generation after generation could talk, if the Druetts could talk, if humanity could talk and if it all had a face, it would blush for ages and ages into perpetuity.

Of Fire and Dust

When Grandma and Grasshopper arrived at the carnival during the Wine Fest, Alejandro was in sight. The noise and lively colors of the event lit the entire mood of the night. He and Alvera had arrived early to get ready for the pageant. Grasshopper carried the balloon and was ready to let it go so Alvera could see it. He had written a few words on it.

"I'm ready to let it go," said Grasshopper, holding the balloon.

"What did you write on it?" Grandma took a closer look at the balloon.

"*With you to the stars,*" said Grasshopper.

"Who is the 'you'? Grandpa?" asked Grandma.

"No, my mom and Alvera," said Grasshopper.

"Alvera loves your brother," Grandma said, looking Grasshopper in the eye.

"I know," he said as he lowered his gaze. "She's my good friend. She's like my big sister."

Grandma smiled. "Here!" she said, handing a box of raging bull matches to Grasshopper. Grasshopper smiled. Alejandro stood next to them and just watched. Grandma held the diamond-shaped paper octagon while Grasshopper placed a lit match inside the holder, but a gentle breeze of cool air blew the flame off.

"I want Grandpa to see the balloon, too," said Grasshopper.

"He'll see it," said Grandma, making a gesture for Alejandro to hold the balloon.

"Can you hold it for me?" Grasshopper looked at his brother.

"Sure," said Alejandro.

"Do you think Grandpa will see it?"

"He will. He's looking at it right now," Grandma said.

"How do you know he sees it?"

"The minute you light it, he'll see it."

Grasshopper lit the wick. As a few twinkles sparkled, the flame gained vigor. Dark smoke and the pungent scent of kerosene wafted upwards, in and around the balloon. Grasshopper took the balloon from his brother's hands. There was a subtlety in the exchange. The wick under the balloon lightened the young boy's face, and as the balloon glowed, it lifted itself upwards and hovered above their heads. Little by little, the balloon gained its form and ascended in the air. Grasshopper gawked as his balloon climbed into the twilight and then through the darkness of what looked like a promising starry night. It traveled above to the fields, away from the festivity. And it flew away, perhaps taken by a cool and calm breeze high above, or perhaps by the high spirit that at times changes it all.

Grasshopper looked at it and smiled at Grandma.

"I told you it'd fly," she said.

"I hope Alvera, Mom, Dad, and Grandpa see it."

"They will," she said. "Let's go now. We have a party to go to."

The carnival of the Wine Fest had started early that evening. Floats embellished with fruits, flowers, and other decorations filled the streets in downtown Russell. Right before twilight, children dodged the adults and sifted through the crowds. Women called for them, but the sound of bass drums, cymbals, and trumpets blinded their senses.

The scent of fermented grapes pervaded the air along the cobblestone streets of the town. It was a tangy scent that gave the evening air a taste of cabernet sauvignon and sherry and inebriated both the atmosphere and the crowds. Folks had come from out of town to support their contestants. Many strangers were there just to watch the procession of the parade.

"I'm so nervous," said Alvera to Grandma from a distance. She stood next to fourteen other contestants, all wearing long evening dresses of different colors that glittered and were adorned with sashes embroidered with the names of the towns they represented.

"You'll do just fine," she said, approvingly. "Remember what we talked about." Then she waved at the Queen.

The contestants boarded their respective floats. Alvera wore a shimmering gold dress. The stars and the glittering of the dress coalesced into a golden banner that contrasted with the darkness of the night. With her beautiful dress, makeup, and the lights reflecting on her whole self, she looked arrestingly alluring. She stood as if a golden rose had somehow blossomed in the middle of the night; the radiance of her presence was a spring morning that had suddenly awoken and scented the air with the aroma of peaches, almonds, honey, and vanilla as she glided through the town on her float. Her crown embellished with white spray and colorful roses distinguished her among all others. She was not only the queen of the wine fest, she was also a natural queen by her own natural right.

The men damned their own existence upon seeing her transcendent poise and calm. Women looked at her regnant beauty with reverent and jealous admiration. With golden bracelets around her wrists and a thin gold chain around her neck, like the glittering trail of a snail crossing a glossy apricot leaf, she beamed with genuine joy.

The streets of downtown Russell were decorated with fresh palm leaves and wild olive branches. The spirit of drunkenness filled the air. Many drank. Even some children who ran unsupervised drank the dregs of cabernet sauvignon left by the adults and hid their stupor by playing innocent games. Some children were eerily happy. Others cried inconsolably and laughed at the same time. All while the crowds celebrated.

From a moving crowd, Grasshopper came running followed by a small swarm of kids.

"Something's wrong with them, Grandma!" he exclaimed as he ran toward his grandmother.

"Ma'am, he told us we were drunk," said a boy, pointing his finger at Grasshopper.

Grandma looked at the boy. "Are you?" she said.

The boy and his entourage of drunken little mobsters stood still and looked at her with wide-opened, watering eyes. Then he squinted and they all darted away without a word. Alejandro chuckled and looked at his brother while Grasshopper stood close behind Grandma.

In the alluring stupor of the carnival, men and women appeared in all manners of flamboyant costumes. Some wore striped pants and jackets. Others wore tight-fitting suits with patchworks of red, green, and blue diamonds and pointed shoes. Some women wore motley dresses that exhibited their breasts as if extending irresistible offers to the drunken men on the streets. Their tits seemed ready to cascade over the seams that propped up their busts. Everyone wore masks and hats of all kinds, colors, and shapes.

In some dark alleys, there were women just wearing a couple of pieces of attire on their natural bodies, an addition to the festival that made it even more appealing to some celebrants. Grasshopper looked at the crowds while he held on to Grandma's hand as they moved along with the crowds. A man dressed as a harlequin stood in the middle of the street and made gestures as he held a puppet. As onlookers passed by, they laughed. Some stopped to look at the performance. Grasshopper pulled Grandma in the direction of the show.

"Lil' Johncy, lil' pupp, he can dance!" said the puppeteer in a high-pitched, twangy drawl as he advertised the show. "Look at 'im! Look at 'im! Look at 'im!" The puppet smiled as he moved its legs to and fro. "Ask if he can dance," said the harlequin as he saw Grasshopper approaching.

The boy right away approached and laughed and asked the puppet. "Can you dance?"

"Yes, I can! But I have no candy," said Lil Johncy in a squeaky voice as he dropped his jaw and stretched his right hand out to the boy. Grasshopper smiled at the puppet and then at Grandma.

"Grandma, can we give him some candy?"

"Well, I have no candy with me now."

"A lil' coin will do," said Lil' Johncy. "But no lil' coin, no lil' candy, no Lil' Johncy dancing," said the puppet, now crying.

Alejandro looked askance at the harlequin and then redirected his sight at Grasshopper.

"Grandma, you got a coin?" asked Grasshopper. The puppet kept crying.

"Give Lil' Johncy a lil' candy, come on, keep Lil' Johncy dancing," said the puppeteer, pulling the strings as he looked around to passersby.

"Here," said Grandma. Grasshopper took the small silver coin and put it in a hat that the harlequin had placed in front of the puppet.

"Lil' Johncy dancing now," said the puppet again, recovering his good humor.

Grasshopper laughed and was enthralled by the dance moves of the puppet for a few minutes. But he became bored after Little Johncy kept repeating the same moves.

"Yeah, just a lil' coin, just a lil' coin, just a lil' coin, to see Lil' Johncy dance," the harlequin kept repeating while he pulled the strings and veered his sight to other onlookers.

"Let's go now," said Grandma.

"There's Alvera!" Alejandro yelled as he pointed at the float that carried her.

The floats were embellished with apricots, avocados, peaches, cherries, and watermelons imitations as well as water lilies, Darwin's slippers, zinnias, and ceibo flowers. Alvera stood on a platform decorated with royal palms, pillows of apricots, and a bed of flowers that emulated the embroidered contour of a field. Russell's float had the most decorations. It featured a paper mache sculpture, a robust bust of a man holding grape vines loaded with clusters of glossy blue grapes in his arms. His face was that of an unrefined, bearded farmer with a cigar hanging from the side of his mouth. He was an impressive brute that gave the float a commanding presence.

As the party continued, each town's float cruised by in front of the onlookers to showcase its queen. The contestants waved their hands at the crowds. Alvera smiled at them. Her posture was natural and majestic. Grandma held up her palm and twisted it to remind Alvera of the proper way to wave. *Remember to always smile and twist your hand*, Alvera told herself to appease her anxiety.

Grandma smiled and Alvera smiled in return as the procession carried her away.

"Is that Alvera?" asked Grasshopper.

"That's her!" said Alejandro, keeping his sight fixed on her. He looked at her and realized how much more beautiful she was that night. She looked so majestic and unattainable, cruising on the float. He realized how men's eyes can be so easily rendered to a beautiful body, and face, how much a simple smile can do to alter the life of a man. And at times he couldn't believe that, that beautiful woman loved him. One thought told him how imperfect and insignificant he felt about not being good enough to measure up to her. But reason, courage, and youth reassured him of his worth and his good presence. He realized that in the perfect universe of a woman, Alvera's, she knew him, knew his heart and his afflictions, and only wanted him to be by her side. There were hundreds in the crowd, but Alvera's gaze was only for Alejandro, and his for her. He felt at peace as he gently smiled back at her as the parade moved along.

"Is she gonna win?" said Grasshopper, tugging his brother's arm. "Is she gonna win?"

"Oh yes, she will!"

The crowds became even more tumultuous. The heated festivities were in full swing as the parade continued down Main Street. Grandma, Alejandro, and Grasshopper stayed together as the crowds appeared intoxicated by the excess of wine and the excitement of the celebration. Many men and women laughed and drank freely, forgetting who they were, and drowned themselves in the abundant burgundy. Grape residue, a liquid purple dye, ran down from the wine *bodegas* and into the ditches on the side of the streets in downtown Russell. Life's trials at that moment seemed altogether conquerable. A bottle of Bravo and a bit of entertainment sufficed to assuage even the worries of the poorest celebrants, while everyone seemed entranced by the beat of drums and cymbals that announced the end of the harvest season.

In the meretricious hype of the night, in the darkest corners of town, libidinous men made haste to amorous encounters with the unrestrained spirit of women who seemed eager to be ravished by their partners' lust. Their breasts hung loose as men backed women against alley walls, devouring their lips and necks, with hands ascending to reveal the women's upper thighs and buttocks. Grasshopper looked at these carnal displays, aghast, until Grandma covered his eyes and directed his attention back to the floats.

In the hype of the carnival, such displays were common. Three judges in disguise stood alongside the three finalists on Russell's float in front of the town square. Alvera and the other two contestants smiled nervously.

"This year, we've surpassed our goal," said the drunken voice of one of the judges whose eyes and nose were covered by a mask shaped in the form of two black diamonds.

"Good money, good money," said an older man in a nebulous tone. The contour around his mouth dropped at each end and below his lower lip; there was a painted smile on his face, which did little for his bulbous, sad countenance. He had a mask that depicted the eyes of a puma. Grasshopper stood right below them and looked up at their coarse faces.

"Shiiiit, boy! As long as we have good money coming," said the man in the two diamond-shaped mask.

"Yeah, as long as we got it coming." The whiskers above his sad mouth fanned out as he spoke.

"We'll have it coming, all right," he replied. "Look at her. Offer her a few coins and you'll take her home with you," said the man in the diamond-shape mask.

"Nah, this one may not be worth your troubles." The man behind the puma mask leered at Alvera and then glanced mockingly at Alejandro who stood behind Grasshopper but could not hear the conversation among the roaring and the celebration of the crowds. A third judge, a man who looked distinguished and well-dressed, appeared to have some kind of authority, and stood over to the left side of the float to oversee the contest.

"You'll have to show us something. You wanna win, right?" said the sad-faced man to the two contestants beside Alvera. His feline resemblance looked in the direction of the drunken men. His eyes shone like the glass of red wine he held.

Alvera looked confused by what the man had said to the other contestants. "What does he mean?" Alvera asked the other contestants.

"He means you gotta let him touch you and grab you," said the young woman next to her.

Alvera looked sick as she stared at the other contestant with disbelief. His cat eyes glowed with excitement while he bit his lower lip and opened his eyes as a sign for a salacious and unwanted invitation toward Alvera.

Russell's governor was standing behind them and nodded as the third judge whispered something in his ear. "Don't listen to these drunks," said the third judge to the contestants before the governor began to speak to the crowds that had gathered in front of the float.

The governor paused for a moment and signaled to two other men to approach the float. He then told the two drunkards that the finalists will be chosen by the crowd present there.

The two drunkards squinted at him. "You're a damn disgrace," one of the drunks slurred toward the third judge.

"Escort the gentlemen off the float," said the governor to the other two men who had approached the float. He proceeded to address the crowd, who didn't notice the affront.

"You'll suffer for this," said the man who wore the puma mask. The two drunks mingled with the crowd below as they descended from the float. However, they quickly moved away into the crowd, cursing and insulting every family member possible.

⇥⇥ ⇤⇤

Before the governor announced the finalists, he signaled for Alvera and the two other contestants to move forward. The crowd cheered and chanted "Russell! Russell!" in honor of Alvera. Alvera glanced at Alejandro and smiled at him. Grandma's eyes watered as it became evident that Alvera was the winner.

"Alvera Reys, Queen of the Wine Fest!" said the governor with much approval. The crowd screamed and broke into an outburst of joy and shrill whistles. Alejandro looked at her with pride and smiled broadly as the governor replaced the natural crown of flowers on her head with a sparkling golden crown, which had a colorless diadem in its front. He handed her a golden envelope with black embossed letters: "Queen of the Wine Fest."

Of Ashes and Dust

Every year, the tumultuous roar of the celebration in town continued and lasted until the wee hours of the morning, sometimes extending into the next day. Families would take part in the celebration until the queen had been crowned. Folks then returned home, retelling the night's events on their way back. Grandma, Alvera, Alejandro, and Grasshopper walked in the pitch darkness of the night, reminiscing and laughing about the best moments of the night. Other families strolled along the road as they made their way back home after the celebration. As they conversed about the night's event, an intermittent, distant glow lit their faces in the dark.

"Did you see that, Grandma?" asked Grasshopper.

"That's lightning in the Valley," said Alejandro as he squinted into the distance.

"They grow watermelons there," said Grandma. "There's always lightning there."

"I think it's gonna rain. Did you see the balloon?" asked Grasshopper as he looked at Alvera.

"I saw it! It was so bright. It went so high. You made it happen," she said.

"No, it was Grandpa! It was really bright," replied Grasshopper. The high pitch of his voice conveyed his excitement.

"As bright as Alvera's crown," Alejandro said. The diadem that adorned Alvera's headpiece shone in the darkness with every flash coming from the valley.

"Yes, it was as bright as my crown," she added as she reached up to adjust it. The flashes in the distance made the image of their faces come and go in intervals. Alvera removed the crown and gave it to Alejandro, who held the wreath of flowers she and Grandma had made. They stopped for a moment. He kissed her on her forehead and then placed the wreath on Alvera's head.

"My forever Queen of the Wine Harvest," he said to her. She smiled and kissed him. Grandma and Grasshopper kept walking and then stopped to wait for them.

"Grandma," Grasshopper said, "she just took your crown."

"Oh, don't be silly, that's the way it's supposed to be," said Grandma.

"The governor removed the judges," said Alejandro and cocked his head and looked at Grandma.

"Every year those two try to ruin the celebration," Grandma said.

"Not this year," said Alejandro. "It was as clear as spring water that Alvera was the queen."

"That's right," Grandma said. "No one can take away what's waiting for you." Alvera smiled.

"That's no lightning," said Alejandro. The volume of the voices of the families in front of the Druetts increased. A worrisome murmur passed along the groups of folks who walked along the dirt road.

As they approached the homestead, blazes rose beyond the crowns of the olive trees. Grandma stopped and watched in disbelief. Alejandro ran toward the homestead and joined the men who directed each other to put out the fire and who were running back and forth in the same direction. Filled with worry, Nora Campito, Mrs. Gurua and other women rushed to the site to help the men. Mr. High squatted by the side of the gate that led to the dusty road and murmured incoherently.

"Six little b-b-birds dodging through st-st-storm gusts," he said. "Don't y-y-you love t-t-that spirit?" He looked at Grasshopper. "The t-t-two plus t-t-two equals a handful o-o-only under dark c-c-clouds of smoke." A bottle of Bravo stood half empty next to him. When Grasshopper reached the gate, his face had a golden red from the reflection of the fire. His eyes widened as he stared toward the rising flames and the sparks that hovered in the darkness. Mr. High continued to rave, making signs like calculations with his fingers in the air. The reflection of the fire made his hair glow yellow. Then with his index fingers, he massaged his temples as if he were meditating. He made a bowing gesture toward Grandma when he saw her. She greeted him in return.

The smoke that rose in the sky was darker than the night, but with the flames the *callejón* was brighter than daylight. The blazes consuming the crowns of the olive trees sizzled as they burnt the oily leaves and branches, which sparkled and crackled while the plumes of smoke and fire looked like desperate evil spirits trying to escape hell itself. Some of the trees adjacent to the farms around the homestead began to catch on fire, but the men there were able to stop it from spreading beyond the homestead.

"Keep out, Mrs. Druett," said Mr. Reys to Grandma. He ran and directed men to put out another patch of fire by the reedbed.

Neighbors and folks from adjacent farms carried metal crates and buckets of water from the stream. A human chain relaying water in the buckets and tin crates that they used for harvesting grapes reached the trees by the side of the *callejón* and into the dusty road that led to the adobe house. The splashes of water didn't reach as high as the crown of the olive trees, and the fire soon overwhelmed and consumed most of the trees in the grove around the adobe house.

"What's gonna happen now?" asked Grasshopper. The tawny orange of the fire dwindled and reflected on his tender face.

"Nothing will happen," said Grandma. She stood serene as she succumbed to the loss. She put her right arm around her grandson. A greater loss can at times diminish the prospects and hopes of the ones that seem essential, especially when those who seem essential can become dispensable. But there was something in them, in the Druetts, that couldn't be diminished. They knew about need and about being content with the little they had. The soul of the poor can be rich in so many ways; it can bring about such an overflowing and overwhelming peace and tranquility that often turns into patience and humility. In want, a constricted soul appreciates the minimum; in plenty, a grateful soul shares his bounty, accepts the generous hand, and gives thanks for such abundance. But the thoughts that clouded Alejandro's young mind after the fight and fire had much to do with finding a place for Alvera, Grandma and Grasshopper.

Grandma knew that her family would be helpless, especially now that her husband was gone. The men who had fought desperately to extinguish the glaring beast had stopped too as they realized their efforts were futile in stopping the fire that consumed the olive grove. Hundreds of years of work were incinerated. The living memory of the laborers' sweat that had moistened the land, the trace of the hands that had caressed the tender branches and glossy olive leaves and the will of the hearts and muscles that had kept the covenant intact for so long were incinerated within the grove. Alejandro returned to his brother's side and put his right arm around Alvera.

⇢⇛ ⇚⇠

As the sun rose in the horizon, the adobe house appeared untouched by the fire. The poplar trees outside the toolshed remained intact. The tree bearing the names of Mom, Dad, Grandma, Grandpa, Alejandro, and Grasshopper was still intact. Their names were carved out, engraved on the bark, like gaping wounds, that looked like scar tissue that remained open for decades and that would perhaps heal one day.

The fire had brought everything else down to ashes and dust. In the morning, the ground was covered with a layer of embers and ashes. What remained of the burned tree trunks stood like petrified dark figures exhaling blue smoke that wafted upward where lush branches had once grown. There were no longer olives or fruits to harvest. There were no longer beds of cucumbers to pick. There was no longer a promise or obligation to the land itself.

Alejandro realized that as long as there was land to work, that as long as there were olives to harvest, that as long as men could have their own land to work on, they would fully honor that promise and the obligation to life itself. For the Druetts, there was only one path to follow now. In spite of it all, the *callejón* looked promising, as if it invited them to walk on its path.

"Accept Mr. Gurua's offer," the road said. "Sweet Heaven," Grandpa's voice whispered in Alejandro's ear.

In the desolate remains of the olive grove, the chirping of the birds was gone. The rustling of leaves was gone. And the Druetts would soon be gone too.

Of Sunray and Chicken Scratch

Time had transcended since the fire. Fall had set in once again. Tree leaves along the *callejón* had lost their luster and looked crisp, dried and inert. Their glossy texture and their motley contours had become weak and brittle. The rustling of dried leaves rattled as the winds caressed the branches high in the trees. Loose leaves flirted with the wind before gliding and gently touching the ground of the schoolyard. Flocks of sparrows tweeted and erratically fled the tree branches, gliding through the air, gently falling on the tawny blanket of leaves on the ground, and then hopping to scavenge the seeds or whatever remnants they could find. The guttural caw of crows high in the trees filled the empty schoolyard as the birds preened their feathers and looked down at the sparrows.

It was Grasshopper's first week of school. The memory of Grandpa was still fresh in his mind and in his heart. School didn't matter to him. It only mattered when he thought about playing pebbles with other kids, and near the end of the year when he needed to pass and complete homework assignments and tests, which he only did because Grandma forced him to.

The family would be moving soon, and he didn't see school as something he needed. He had learned a lot more from working with Grandpa. After Grandpa died and the olive grove burnt, the feeling of desolation had pervaded into the child's feelings and thoughts. He understood that death was a circumstance of the living, but the memory of not seeing or having Grandpa near him affected him.

"So, why haven't you finished your composition?" asked Ms. Helen as she approached Grasshopper and touched his shoulder. He had his head down, sleeping. He raised his head from the desk. His right arm had engraved a red mark across his face, and his eyes were bloodshot and watery.

"My grandpa's gone to heaven," said Grasshopper.

The teacher's eyes softened as she looked at the boy and then eyed the writing on his paper.

"Can I read that?" she asked.

"It isn't done," he said, pulling the paper toward him.

"That's okay. Can you read it?" asked the teacher.

"I don't really want to, but I guess I can." He gazed at the words on the paper. "It's not really a polygraph like you wanted," he added.

"You mean a paragraph," she clarified. "Just read it."

He brought the paper closer. A weak beam of sunlight sifted through the window and fell on the page.

little bird. dry leaves. grandpa gone. sing song. sweet grapes. juicy grapes. blue grapes. red grapes. grapes are gone. by the truck take away. sore shoulders. bruised shoulders. it don't matter. anyway. they don't care. they all gone. at the bodega. mom gone. granny's home. bread loaf. hot milk and honey. kaiser, soil's friend. barks at the wind. wagging his tail like he wants money and bacon. rusty nails. toolshed by the hare's trail. lassos and snares. where he keeps his tools. grandpa stares. grandpa. a mark. starry skies. like the path of a happy snail. windy poplar leaves. hours and will for sale. and in spring. grandpa shoes under the bed. cold and empty day like a dead bird's nest...

Grasshopper looked up at Mrs. Helen. She smiled and took his paper.

"Are you finished?" she asked.

"I don't know. I'm not sure it's right."

"It's a very good start," she said. "But you ought to write in complete sentences."

"Sentences?"

"Complete ideas."

"So, those are not complete ideas?"

"Well, they are, but ideas need to be in complete sentences so people can understand them."

"My grandpa died. Isn't that an idea?"

"Yes, it is. Do you want to finish reading what you have on the page?"

"Yes. I wrote some other ideas," he said as he lifted the paper.

...why, why, why do people, die a life, I wanna bring back, grandpa is sitting, on his chair he made with poplar wood, in the spring we played, with black oxen, a teamster drinks wine, a bad man robbed him of his pride, he works with cucumbers, vines big and small, thorny little things, we pick, a harvest, not, at night we rest, laugh and eat grandma's tarts.

"Well, those are good ideas, but you need to add some punctuation." She glanced at the page as he put the paper down.

"Punctuation?" he asked.

"Yes, periods, commas, and capital letters to organize your thinking."

"I don't want to organize my punctuation and my thinking. It's more like a feeling I got."

"Well, those feelings won't mean anything if you don't follow rules," Ms. Helen said.

"Rules? Feelings don't mean anything? I don't understand."

"Yes. Rules!" said the teacher as she stared at the boy's work, her gaze heavy upon the paper.

Bewildered by Ms. Helen's explanation, Grasshopper looked down at his paper, then at the teacher, and pushed the paper away from him, leaned back on the chair, and shrugged. To him, the words he had written seemed to have vanished like a flock of ephemeral sparrows fleeing the gloom of the fall, like old tree leaves taken adrift in swirls by the autumn wind. When the school bell rang, the children sprinted to the yard in an innocent and soft madness among screams and shrills. In an innocence of disheveled hair and uniforms, untucked dusty shirts, with shoelaces flailing free like the reins or manes of a hundred unbridled *protros chucaros*, reigning and charging into freedom, like drawing lines in the dirt, or making chicken scratches on the dusty dirt of the schoolyard—the children ran finally home.

Of Fennel and New Trails

A few springs had gone by, where a weeping willow tree dipped its branches and green leaves on the shallow banks of the Manso River, as if it were cleansing its branches in the currents below. The tree branches and shoots touching the water resembled the shape of Alvera's silky hair, as if she were bathing and washing her hair in the river. The foamy trails formed by the branches touching the crystalline, gentle currents, splitting the waters into swirls that looked like the unearthing of new soil in the furrows, like slicing open the earth with the shining share and moldboard of a plow, revealing the earth's coppery clumps of soil, rocks, and roots of fennel and other weeds. But the waters of the Manso River were crystalline and pure.

The Manso ran adjacent to the strip of land that Grandma, Alejandro, Alvera, and Grasshopper had bought from Mr. Gurua. The tract had been cleared of brush and weeds, and it slightly sloped easily down to the river. Mr. Reys, Mr. Gurua, and even Mr. Campito and Don Segovia had helped the Druett boys build a cabin, using rocks and wood from the land on the lower skirt of the Great Mountains.

Red tomatoes glowed on a hand-hewn cedar table Alejandro and Grasshopper had made with Grandpa's tools. The sunrays reflected off the thin skin of the fruit. The plump tomatoes seemed fragile as they sat inside an osier bowl. In the field, Alvera picked herbs and wiped her forehead with her wrist. She waved at Alejandro, who held the reins of *Potro Chucaro,* who helped him plow the land adjacent to the tomato patch. The horse showed signs of prowess, but it was no longer in its prime. Mr. Reys had trained the horse well to withstand farmwork and other chores. And the beast responded well to the small load of work on their tract.

Grasshopper took a break from work and ate apricots while Grandma sat next to him, chopping a handful of cilantro and garlic into thin slices. At times, she stopped to contemplate Alejandro and Alvera while they worked the land. Franco had been born a few years back and he sat next to Grandma at the cedar table. They called him Little Steps. Grasshopper pried open an apricot and shared a half with the child.

"You wanna play, Uncle Grassy?" said Little Steps.

"I gotta work now, my little friend," Grasshopper said.

An *Alameda* of tall and spiked poplar trees that Mr. Gurua and Grandpa had planted marked the boundary of their tract. The trees were too young to be carved on by Grasshopper's Swiss Army knife. But on the willow tree by the river, Grasshopper had engraved their names with his Swiss army knife:

Mom

Dad

Grandma

Grandpa

Grasshopper

Alejandro

Alvera

Little Steps

Kaiser

Soil

With time, the carvings would protrude through the bark and look like thick open wounds that had healed. Unlike the carvings on the poplar tree in the homestead, the carvings on the willow tree were not made out of childish pride at seeing their names engraved on something, but as a reminder that they were now working on a piece of land they could finally call theirs, and that they would honor and be there for the rest of their lifetime.

After Grandpa died, Grandma was never the same. He had taken part of her spirit with him. The shine in her eye was gone. Even her memory seemed gone at times when she contemplated the sunrise or dusk in Sweet Heaven. Much of the memory of the old life in Russell was gone as well.

Mario took a city job and kept winking his eye at Aunt Rosy. Eventually, Aunt Rosy accepted Mario's offer in marriage and moved to the capital with him. Aunt Claudia moved in with Aunt Ana and lived in downtown Russell.

Grasshopper was gradually leaving the child behind and Alejandro was now a man. His voice thickened and his shoulders broadened. His stature had increased, and his upright posture made him seem taller and proud. A mettle, not made out of pride, but from the struggle he had endured. Grasshopper never lost his sense of childish humor. The child in him still enjoyed telling lies as much as he could, but good and funny lies that didn't hurt anyone.

"The first time I died, I didn't like heaven," said Grasshopper.

"You went to heaven Uncle Grassy?" Little Steps asked.

"Yes, I did once, but I didn't like it."

"Why you didn't like it?" he said. "You silly."

"It was too boring up there. I had to be a really good kid all the time," said Grasshopper, looking at his nephew. "So it was really boring."

"You did?"

"Yes. So I decided to come back. When you're really good in heaven you can come back."

"You can't die like that!" said Little Steps.

"But I did," said Grasshopper.

"Really?"

"Yes, really. The first time I came back I was a hare," said Grasshopper.

"Really? Like a rabbit?" said Little steps.

"Yes," said Grasshopper, then imitating the squealing sound of a hare.

"Ha, ha, ha....That's funny," said Little steps.

"Then I came back as a grasshopper. And here I am," said Grasshopper. "You see, I was a hare once."

"That's silly Uncle Grassy," said Little Steps.

Inside the cabin, Grandma and Alvera prepared cheese and meat pies during the snowy winters and reminisced about the old days in the adobe house. The dough rolled out soft and fresh on the smooth cedar table, just like the good memories they recounted about the Wine Fest, the harvesters, and friends and other folks in Russell.

Early in the evenings, Alejandro and Grasshopper checked the lassos they'd set up in hope of returning home with some game before sunset.

"Uncle Grassy, you catch the hare?" asked Little Steps.

"I will," said Grasshopper as he picked up his nephew and sat him on his shoulders. Alejandro carried the Martini-Henry rifle strapped across his chest and over his shoulder.

"Are we gonna eat it?" asked his nephew.

"We're gonna get that hare and eat it real good," said Grasshopper. They followed the trails through the bushes and undergrowth and checked the snares they had set up the day before.

"You catch many hares, Uncle?" asked Little Steps.

"Oh, yes, many," said Grasshopper, looking at Alejandro, who just smirked at his brother's lie.

"Can I shoot one?"

"Maybe," said Grasshopper. "The best part of catching a hare is knowing it can run wild and free."

"I like that," said Little Steps.

Alejandro raised his sight and looked at the valley below. "I'm gonna go check the lassos near the fennel shrubs by the riverbed," said Alejandro.

"Can I come with you, Daddy?" asked Little Steps.

"No, wait right here with your uncle," said Alejandro.

As he approached the riverbank, he noticed the shrubs moving. Grasshopper craned his neck. He put his nephew down and approached his brother.

"You wanna shoot it? Finish it off!" Alejandro handed the rifle to Grasshopper. The hare seemed to have been caught recently. She moved in an effort to escape the snare that trapped one of her hind legs.

"Hell yeah, I'm gonna shoot it," said Grasshopper. He grabbed the Martini-Henry and aimed. The animal stayed still, unaware of what was coming. Her soft pelage glistened. Her humble eyes looked at Grasshopper. Quiet. Ruminating. Grinding its teeth. Her mouth twitched as if she were chewing on something. A stalk of fennel perhaps. His nephew looked at him with his eyes wide open. Grasshopper fixed his eyes on the target and looked at the metal chamber out of the corner of his eye. He held the rifle, his index finger on the trigger. His thumb firmly pressed against the metal chamber. He breathed and read the engraved letters on the chamber: *Reverteris*, it read on one side of the firearm; *In Pulverem* on the other. *In Pulverem Reverteris*, were the words.

"Hmmm. No, we won't kill it," he said as he lowered the rifle and reached down to release the hare's hind leg from the snare.

"Why? You said you kill it and eat it real good!" said Little Steps.

Once released, the hare scampered away like the wind.

"I know I said that, but if I killed it, we wouldn't have a hare to chase anymore," said Grasshopper.

Alejandro smiled. "I'll kill it another day," said Grasshopper, looking at the boy. "Maybe one day you will!"

The End

Acknowledgments

The Dust That Remains emerged from three interrelated short stories into what it is today. My thanks to creative writing Professor Beth Couture for encouraging me to write the novel.

Thanks to philosophy professor and editor Yolanda Estes, editor Corey Ginsberg, fellow author and beta reader Peter Haase, and beta reader Juan Escandon Jr. for their feedback, encouragement, and honesty.

Thanks to the many high school and college students I have met in the classroom and who have read excerpts of my work.

Thank you so much for reading "The Dust That Remains". If you enjoyed this book, I'd really appreciate it if you could leave a brief review on Amazon.

About the Author

Author John D. Conandes (Juan D. Escandon) writes young adult and speculative fiction. He is also a teacher of writing and rhetoric and has taught modern languages at various colleges and universities in the United States. To learn more about John's current projects and interests, visit the author's website at www.johndconandes.com.

Now what?!